PETER DOYLE

PETER DOYLE

❧ A NOVEL ❧

John Vernon

For beno brey,

Best wishes

Binghamton, N.Y.

May, 1991

Jack Vernon

Random House   New York

A small portion of this book was
originally published in *New Myths* magazine.

Excerpts from previously published Emily Dickinson letters are from *The Letters of Emily Dickinson*, edited by Thomas H. Johnson, associate editor Theodora Ward. Copyright © 1958 by the President and Fellows of Harvard College. Copyright 1914, 1924, 1932, 1942 by Martha Dickinson Bianchi. Copyright 1952 by Alfred Leete Hampson. Copyright © 1960 by Mary L. Hampson.

Grateful acknowledgment is made to Harvard University Press and the Trustees of Amherst College for permission to reprint excerpts from *The Poems of Emily Dickinson*, edited by Thomas H. Johnson; Cambridge, Mass. The Belknap Press of Harvard University Press. Copyright 1951, © 1955, 1979, 1983 by the President and Fellows of Harvard College. Reprinted by permission of Harvard University Press and the Trustees of Amherst College.

Library of Congress Cataloging-in-Publication Data
Vernon, John
Peter Doyle/John Vernon.
p.   cm.
ISBN 0-394-58249-7
I. Title
PS3572.E76P4   1991   813'.54—dc20   90-44664

Manufactured in the United States of America
24689753
First Edition

For both of my families; for Elijah and Ruth
and the gift of the past; for Ann; for Charles and Patrick
and the promise of the future.

The shapes arise!
Shapes of factories, arsenals, foundries, markets,
Shapes of the two-threaded tracks of railroads,
Shapes of the sleepers of bridges, vast frameworks, girders, arches

> —Walt Whitman

It would never be Common—more—I said—
Difference—had begun—

> —Emily Dickinson

Go west, young man

> —Horace Greeley

PART
I
ST. HELENA 1821

*T*he Great Man lay dead while the little men watched and mourned and the rats in the walls perked up sniffing. In all of Longwood House, only the billiard table proved strong enough to hold his dead weight, and on it, beneath his sheet, he seemed to have swelled up in death—or with death—though he'd already been gutted and all his inner passageways inspected. Still, he resembled a mountain of a creature, the bolus of his body so enormously fat for such a short man—fat and round as a china pig—that over the sternum there lay a coating of fat an inch and a half thick, and on the abdomen two inches, while the omentum and kidneys were also burdened with fat. Having been loosely sewn up on the pretext of decency, but really to still the shrieking armies inside him, the vast plains with their horses, troops, carriages, and smoke, the hills with corpses raining down their sides or pouring through ditches like grain through chutes, and the voices shouting either *Vive l'Empereur* or *String up the butcher of our husbands and sons*, depending on the year and the place, he seemed at peace. He looked like someone who'd experienced no inner struggle in relinquishing his claim upon immortality. He was a shell. His eyebrows and the edges of his hair were noticeably stiffened with leftover plaster from Dr. Francis Burton's unauthorized taking of a death mask, and his flesh and sheet smelled of eau-de-cologne. On a trestle table against the wall covered with bloodstained sheets of coarse linen sat his heart, liver, and stomach, each in a basin of alcohol. Behind the basin with his stomach stood a silver pepper box and behind the one with his heart a silver canister waiting to be sealed with the silver coin beside it. Doctors and surgeons buzzed about the room. Only they were left now—the others had gone—they and the Great Man's valet-de-chambre and first mameluke, whose tears had dried, who were actually yawning unmercifully, having sat up with the body the previous night to guard it from the rats who, since his death, had made several attempts to get at the flesh. The island of St. Helena, and Longwood House especially, were famous for their rats; a rat once jumped out of the Great Man's hat as he was putting it on.

It was six o'clock on the evening of May 6, just after the firing of the sunset gun. Thirty-six hours before this he'd spoken his last words—"*à la tête de l'armée . . . Joséphine*"—before sinking for the next twelve hours into a clotted sea of pain from which the historian—even the psychohistorian—may avert his inner eye. As the Great Man put it, "Greatness has its beauties, but only in retrospect and in the imagination." He also approved of defining history as a pack of lies agreed upon.

This was the man who claimed to have unscrambled chaos, who never spit, turned his head, or blew his nose, who, when he exposed himself to enemy fire—bullets and grapeshot humming past—said that he was condemned to live because his mother had made a bargain with God at his birth: if God would protect him, he would reestablish the Catholic Church in France. This was the man who nursed on olive oil instead of breast milk, who said that he respected and honored every woman because she reminded him of his mother, and who described making love as an exchange of perspirations. Wishing to discover what the People thought of him, he went for a walk incognito and met an old woman on a hill outside of Tarare, near Lyons, with whom he conversed, raising the subject of Napoleon—just another tyrant, he suggested. "Maybe so," she replied, "but the others were kings of the nobles, but he's a king of the people, and we chose him ourselves." This was the only man ever to father a child born a king—the King of Rome—though he probably didn't. As Chateaubriand put it, Count Adam Adalbert Neipperg got there first and dared lay his eggs in the eagle's nest. But the child was fêted as Napoleon's heir, even grew to resemble him if you squinted closely . . .

When the birth of the King of Rome was announced, Madame Blanchard set out from L'Ecole Militaire in a balloon to carry the news into all the towns and villages of Europe.

This was the man who said before a battle, "Soldiers, I need your lives. Give them to me"—and the soldiers cheered. According to the English nannies who disciplined a generation of children with stories of him, you knew he was coming when you saw three suns in the sky, blood oozing from bread, and rainfalls of gory innards, and then when he came he ate five black sheep a day and all the children he could lay his hands on. This was the man who, upon his triumphant return from Elba, was praised in official proclamations as Emperor of the World, God of Victory, Conqueror of the Nile and Neptune of the Sea, Savior of his Country, Arbiter of Europe, Universal Peacemaker, and Phoenix Risen from the Ashes. But some people said it wasn't him, it was an impostor, the same nasty rumor they'd circulated when he came back from Egypt in 1799. And when General Duroc died in 1813, they said that the coffin really contained Napoleon's body. Informed by her astrologer that he'd escaped from St. Helena, his mother, in Rome, refused to believe that he'd died or that it was her son's body that had been dissected in preparation for burial in a coffin of tin to be hermetically sealed inside three more caskets, one of lead, two of mahogany, which in turn would be lowered into a grave of stone and Roman cement twelve feet down with walls three feet thick. It wasn't him because an impostor had gone to St. Helena in his place, a double, a rifleman named Robeaud or Roubeaud, and the real Napoleon was running a shop selling spectacles in Verona. Or it wasn't him because the body of his majordomo, Cipriani Franceschi, had been substituted for his. Or it wasn't him because he didn't exist. For this was the man who, years later, would be proven not to have existed by two proto- or paleo- psychohistorians, Richard Whateley, the future archbishop of Dublin, in his *Historic Doubts Relative to Napoleon*, and Jean-Baptiste Pérès in his pamphlet, *Comme Quoi Napoléon n'a jamais existé: Grand Erratum source d'un nombre infini d'errata à noter dans l'histoire du XIXème siècle*. After all, this was the man whose friend Talma, the tragedian, had taught him to play the role of Emperor, who practiced whenever he could before mirrors, and who in his last years on St. Helena enjoyed standing around, or squatting on his seesaw, fingers in his waistcoat, lock of hair carefully disturbed, with his battleship of a hat cocked, a nasty scowl on his face, displaying the consummate delusion of the megalomaniac—that he was Napoleon.

Now he lay dead on a billiard table. Vinegar burned in a dish on a chair. A high-collared servant with wide, popping eyes, the kind that scare children, opened the door, looked around, then spit up his sleeve for good luck. Among the doctors there, Arnott was in charge. "No sign of him yet?"

"No, sir."

All eyes were on this servant dressed in green and white livery standing in the doorway; he looked ready to bolt. Having seen an insect buzzing around that unlucky room, a creature resembling a flying ant, he'd somehow conceived that it was headed straight for him, that it would sting his eye and lay eggs in the pupil . . . At the head of the billiard table, Dr. Antommarchi, Napoleon's fellow Corsican, took advantage of this distraction to snip a few locks from his late Emperor's hair and close them up in an empty snuffbox. He slipped it in his pocket approaching Arnott. "If he doesn't arrive soon, he will have defeated the purpose of his coming. The organs will be in such a decomposed state no conclusions can be drawn."

"I've drawn my conclusions."

"So have I, so has everyone here. But our conclusions don't agree."

"Because yours are blinded by politics."

"And yours are dictated by the governor of this island."

The servant slammed the door, a wind caught the edge of the Great Man's sheet, rippling it over his humped-up flesh and releasing an odor of decay mingled with eau-de-cologne, which the flickering vinegar cut into threads and sent spiraling through the room. As if on cue, the chorus of murmuring doctors glanced over at their monument, whose face failed to twitch. In a corner, his valet-de-chambre laid out his clothes on an Empire couch: his silk stockings embroidered in gold with the imperial coronet on the clocks, his knee breeches of white Kenseymere, his diamond buckles and garters with gold buttons, his vest of white velvet embroidered in gold with diamond buttons, his crimson velvet coat with facings of white velvet also embroidered in gold along all the seams, his short crimson cloak lined with white satin with a double clasp of diamonds, his shirt of beautiful cambric to which ruffles of white lace had been added, his cravat of the most exquisite muslin, his collar of superb lace, his bicorne hat with the tricolor cockade. On the floor stood a pair of white velvet boots laced and embroidered with gold. Humming to himself, the valet-de-chambre pinned across the back of the couch the Great Man's cross of the Legion of Honor, his cross of the Iron Crown, and the red ribbon of the Grand Cordon Rouge. He was already planning his book on the Emperor's last days. "A la tête de l'armée . . . Joséphine." What else? "France, mon fils, armée . . ." The mameluke stood by in oriental costume, grinning with approval. Now they could go back to France and be famous.

At last came the sound of a carriage outside. The oil lamps had been lit, but the fireplace hadn't because none of the residents of this former farmhouse in their five and a half years of exile had learned how to prevent it from smoking, and as a consequence the room was cold, since May was the start of the St. Helena winter. Footsteps on the gravel. Dr.

Arnott had stepped into the Emperor's chamber to peer out the window in the gathering darkness, and now returned and nodded to his rival, Antommarchi, now the fun would begin. The door swung open.

"Dr. Kellog?"

"Yes."

He was carrying a satchel. His face swam in darkness. But the British doctors, all seven of them, recognized the uniform of a surgeon of the Royal Navy, one of their own even if he was a Scot.

"Gentlemen, Dr. Robert Kellog."

"Gentlemen."

Antommarchi meanwhile had already snatched the draft of the coroner's report from Arnott's scribe, Dr. Walter Henry, and was waving it in the newcomer's face. Antommarchi himself had lifted the liver, with considerable difficulty, from the cavity of his dead Emperor's body, where he found it adhering to the stomach and diaphragm. Had invited the others to try it also, in order to demonstrate the considerable strength and long-standing nature of the adhesions, which could only be separated finally by a scalpel. Adhesions caused by cancer of the stomach could not have been of such long existence, as that disease had a short course. His conclusion: chronic hepatitis. The liver itself had swelled up and hardened, was distended with blood—he claimed—though cutting into it produced no excessive blood or pus, to Dr. Arnott's satisfaction. Arnott's attention was all to the Great Man's stomach, the nucleus of every self-consuming human, whose internal surface he'd found to be marbled with a scirrhous thickening fast advancing to cancer, especially near the pylorus, where an ulcer had opened a second hole large enough to insert the little finger.

All the British doctors had inserted their fingers; Antommarchi declined, pointing out that the enlarged liver had blocked the opening.

Not enlarged, said Arnott. Slightly larger than normal.

A liver abscess had ruptured into the stomach, Antommarchi said, causing general peritonitis and death.

There is no liver abscess, said Arnott. Show me.

It collapsed after the discharge of its contents.

Its contents?

The red spittle produced by my Emperor. You recall the anchovy sauce sputum.

The spittle you refer to was produced by congested lungs, and remains of little significance, said Arnott.

But Dr. Antommarchi had saved the spittle in a small silver vial, and now produced it, held it up to Dr. Kellog along with the report, as evidence of the British suppression of the true reason his Emperor had died. He had died because the sun on St. Helena, though it seldom appears, nevertheless exercises its influence on the tropical atmosphere in such a way as to produce disorders of the liver in those confined there against their will. The world will know that the British killed Napoleon.

On the contrary, he died of cancer of the stomach, said Dr. Arnott. Of which his father also died. An inherited trait.

Of the two doctors, only Antommarchi had been trained as a pathologist, but trained by whom? By Italian priests, said Arnott. Would an Edinburgh man do for the autopsy, not exactly English—a Scot—and a certified anatomist, a pathologist of repute, one of the most skilled dissectors in all of Europe? He would have to do, he'd been summoned a month ago from Cape Town by the governor of the island, Sir Hudson Lowe, when Napoleon first began his slide toward death, but his ship had arrived a day too late and now the corpse was already sewn up and the liver threatening to decompose, the evidence self-destructing, though there was always the stomach into whose hole doubters could insert their fingers, Dr. Antommarchi.

Dr. Kellog glanced around the room, ignoring both Antommarchi and Arnott. He approached the dead monument on the billiard table. His gesture was sudden, the cries of horror rose all at once before he'd even snatched back the sheet, it seemed, and the assembly of doctors shattered as though struck by a rock, by a piece of darkness zigzagging the room, ducking from boots and flailing canes—it had darted out from the area of the armpit, then leapt to the floor, made it to the wall, and seemed to pour itself along the pieces of tin nailed where wall and floor met, disappearing beneath the couch. "Bloody rats," someone said. Two of the younger surgeons were all for lifting the couch and smoking him out, but Arnott forbade it, then turned back to the billiard table. "Any damage?"

Antommarchi was holding his hands to either side of his face. "Oh, my holy Emperor's body."

Hushed, they inspected the gnawed ribs. It appeared that the rat had only nibbled here and there, then crouched in the armpit for warmth, or to hide.

"We have a plague of rats here."

"I see."

"They imprisoned my Emperor on a rat-infested rock," Antommarchi moaned.

Doctor Kellog retrieved the sheet from the floor then hesitated, studying the corpse. He noted the long postmortem incision with its crude stitches running from the breastbone down to the shrunken genitals, which appeared to be infantile. Covering the lower half of the body, he stood there staring at the rest. Calm returned. The doctors gathered around the table. Kellog touched one of Napoleon's breasts with the back of his fingers. "When did these first appear?"

"This is the first time I have seen him naked," said Arnott.

"You examined him in the dark?"

"Him—or someone."

But Antommarchi, the only doctor allowed by the Great Man to examine him in the light, was thinking, should I tell them? Should I tell them what my Emperor said when he strutted about the room unclothed? See, Doctor, what lovely arms, what smooth white skin without a hair! Breasts plump and rounded—any beauty would be proud of my bosom!

"So you have no idea when the breasts began to grow?" asked Dr. Kellog.

"No."

"The Emperor's pituitary was laggard," said Antommarchi.

"And you consider this a contributing cause of death?"

"Quite the contrary," said Arnott. "It kept him alive. He ate almost nothing for the last month or so. He lived off the excess fat on his body."

"This is more than simply fat. What is his medical history?"

Antommarchi and Arnott looked at each other. "All of it?"

"Summarize."

Silence and the shuffling of feet. Then Antommarchi began meekly. "The Emperor all his life was unable to sweat."

"Yes?"

"It is well known that General Bonaparte suffered from piles," said Arnott.

"And?"

"Skin irritations. Rashes. Dry cough."

"And?"

"Scurvy, seizures, marasmus, diarrhea, headaches, swelling of the legs, as you can see—possible dysentery, obstruction of the pylorus, apoplexy, Malta fever, scabies, dysuria."

"Hepatitis," Dr. Antommarchi added.

"We have come to the conclusion that the cause of death was cancer of the stomach," said Arnott.

"He had a stomach of iron," said Antommarchi.

"Possible paludism," said Arnott.

"Boredom and depression."

"His thyroid turned lethargic."

"He once said to me"—Antommarchi had sidled up to the taller Kellog and was all but tugging at his sleeve—"he said, 'Any type of disease is permitted here except one—hepatitis.' "

"He would cry in his sleep, '*Mon pylore, mon pylore,*' " said Arnott.

"Do you know why he held his hand in his coat?" Antommarchi's face was inches from Kellog's. "His famous posture? Fingers in the waistcoat? He was massaging a painful liver."

Kellog turned away. "Then his liver ailment predated his exile?"

"It was aggravated here, as they knew it would be!"

Dr. Kellog pulled the sheet back up to the Great Man's chin. "You must guard the body more closely," he said. "And the organs?"

"There."

The doctors parted for Kellog, who lifted his satchel and walked toward the trestle table. In the uncertain light, he resembled a jackal, or perhaps a fox, with nostrils pinched, gray lips pursed, eyes—but no one could see the eyes.

He lifted his satchel to the table and turned. "The room must be cleared."

"Impossible," said Arnott.

"Clear the room."

"I cannot leave the body alone."

"Alone? I will be here."

"I have been charged by the governor of the island not to leave the body unguarded for a minute."

"I see. Because of the rats you have so zealously protected it from. Then these two men shall guard it"—he nodded at the valet-de-chambre and the mameluke huddled near the couch—"while I work."

Arnott paused. Antommarchi shrugged. Kellog turned back and opened his satchel. Squatting on the floor beside the couch, the servants grinned mournfully, showing missing teeth. They yawned, shook them-selves, pretended to be crestfallen—another night without sleep—then went back to picking lint off the dead Emperor's clothes, like monkeys picking lice.

The British doctors conferred with Arnott. At last, one by one they left. The final one, Arnott, gestured to the servants, who scraped two chairs across the room, one to the head of the billiard table, the other to the foot, and sat in them. He cautioned each, in broken French and English, to be vigilant and alert, then walked to the door. They were good servants, faithful to their Emperor, they'd been with him for years, they respected authority—then why did he think he heard laughter after shutting the door, why did he think that one of them actually said, from behind the closed door, "Kiss my ass, monsieur!"?

"So . . . He never allowed anyone to shave him?"

"He was shaving himself since we got here. He wouldn't let anyone do it to him."

"Didn't trust them?"

"I should say not. One stroke, monsieur. That's all! Zip zip."

"What about you? Couldn't one of you shave him?"

"Never asked."

"So he didn't trust you, either."

"Ohhh, he trusted *us*. He just didn't trust us with a *razor*." The valet-de-chambre held up both hands in a magnificent shrug, then sipped again from the brandy Dr. Kellog had poured for him. The bottle and three glasses stood on the edge of the billiard table, and the three men sat in a circle beside it around a flickering oil lamp.

Outside, it rained. Wind blew through cracks in the walls of Longwood House, where baby wolf spiders dined on their mothers. The zinc sheets of the roof leaked rain, which ran down rafters and struts to timbers and out across the plaster walls, whose embedded ox hairs sucked moisture inside to feed the green mold in the rooms. When it rained at Longwood House, smells turned meaty and solid, smells of mildew, vinegar, decomposed flesh . . .

The mameluke leaned forward and winked at Dr. Kellog. "You could shave him with a pumice stone, anyway, monsieur."

"You know Constant?" asked the other. "He was valet before us. Then he betrayed the Emperor when he was going to Elba. Constant was teaching him to shave himself, but he did it all wrong. Always shaved down."

"Like the guillotine!" said the mameluke.

Both men burst into laughter. Dr. Kellog poured more brandy.

"So . . . He was good to his servants?"

"Good? He treated us like men. There was something about him. His blood was red just like you and me. The Little Corporal, everyone called him. We'd do anything for him, we would. It wasn't logical. We'd march over a cliff just to make him happy."

"Without breaking step."

"Double time."

"A smile on our faces."

"So you enjoyed working for him?"

"It was a privilege. He was born to be waited on. He might take a bath any time of day. You always had to keep the hot water ready."

"If he liked you he pinched your ear," said the mameluke. "He was always pinching ears."

"He was saying, 'I like you.' "

"One time he ran across the room and saluted me like a madman, then pinched both of my ears hard enough to make me swear like a soldier. 'Well,' he says, '*Monsieur le drôle.*' If he started out the day like that you knew he'd be full of good moods all day. General Bertrand says in his diary the Emperor liked to pinch the tip of the ear of some wag or somebody when he felt his good moods. But it wasn't just the tip! He pinched the whole ear, like this—" He reached for the valet-de-chambre's head.

"*Vache!*"

They pushed at each other, the floor shook, lamps flickered. When the valet-de-chambre landed against the billiard table, the half-full bottle remained upright, but Napoleon's sheet trembled. Carefully, they sat in their chairs again, conscious of the body on the table. The man they were talking of lay there beside them larger than life, beginning to smell.

The mameluke reached up to his own ears. "Sometimes he pinches both ears at once. Sometimes he gives you a friendly slap too."

"You've read the general's diary?"

"*Comment?*"

"You said that General Bertrand describes Napoleon pinching the tip of the ear, in his diary. You've read it?"

The mameluke grinned. "It was open on the table."

"And the Emperor? Did he keep a diary?"

"Everyone else wrote down what he said."

"So he didn't have to?"

"Too busy," said one.

"Too bored," said the other.

Dr. Kellog poured them more brandy. "So . . . Did he ever act strange? Did he exhibit any unusual behavior?"

The two servants looked at each other. "Well . . ."

"There was the smell," said the mameluke.

"Smell?"

"Since the last few years he complained a lot there was smells around his bed. He smelled things everyplace, but especially around his bed. So he wants us to change the bed all the time. To remove it and find another one."

"And did you?"

"We are not maids."

"We pretended to."

"He would turn out the mattress like this and like this, the quilts, the coverlets, turn them over and over in every direction and complain all about the smelling. So, when he was gone we sprinkle everything with rose water. We burn aloes wood."

"He never knew the difference."

"Was he generous? Did he ever give you presents?"

"No," said the valet-de-chambre.

"Working for him was a privilege," said the other.

"This business about presents," said the first. "He never wants anyone to thank him. That's why he was never giving presents. *Comprenez?* He was one of us, in other words, even if he was the Emperor. Anyway, the English gave him nothing here, so how could he be giving out presents? They treated him like a common prisoner here."

"He was generous with his soldiers. He gave them everything they needed. I mean the men on the battlefield. At Marengo he tasted the soup they were giving us and dumped it on the ground. Then he kicks Captain Couthon so hard he has to be carried away. The supply officer, in other words. 'You'd feed them this?' he says. 'And what do *you* eat?' So he switches the menus. We get the officers' food and they get ours."

" 'We'?"

"Comment?"

"You were a soldier? You served in his army?"

The mameluke grinned, sheepish and proud. He stood at his place, glanced over at the Emperor's still face, then looked away. The valet-de-chambre stood also and nodded at his friend. "We still do, monsieur."

"The Grand Army was disbanded six years ago."

"Once a soldier . . ."

"I thought you were servants."

"That's what we told them here." The mameluke had removed his turban, his coat, his flowing red and yellow pantaloons to reveal beneath them the uniform of the Imperial Guard. The valet-de-chambre was also stripping; beneath his high-collared coat appeared the yellow collar of the Guard, the red sash and blue coat, the white pants, everything but the towering bearskin cap. From his pocket he drew a clay pipe and saluted. *"Vive l'Empereur!"*

In the uncertain light, scars had appeared on the mameluke's face. The valet-de-chambre's extended hand lacked two fingers. Each mustached face grinned proudly; the pupils of their widened eyes turned black.

"What makes you think I won't turn you in?"

"What difference would it make? He is dead. We are going back to France to live on our pensions."

Rats watched from corners of the room where the light fell short. The discarded clothes of the two men lay in separate pools on the floor. Dr. Kellog looked from one soldier to the other. "So . . . You were at Marengo?"

"Marengo and almost everything else, including Egypt. Ulm, Austerlitz, Jena, Eylau. We came to Spain late and left early, thank God. Borodino, Moscow, Dresden. We began as line infantry, but he noticed us and made us Grenadiers of the Guard. First of the Guard."

"He picked us out of a line at Jena and promoted us on the spot."

"For what reason?"

"He asked who the bravest men in battle had been. Everyone pointed at someone else, but we pointed at each other."

"After that, he always stopped at a grand review and talked to us. It was a trick of his. He made the men think he could stop at anyone and have him step forward and he would know your name, your town, your father and mother—but it was always me or him."

"He talked to us and pinched our ears."

Dr. Kellog poured more brandy. "So . . . He was smart? A brilliant general?"

The two men laughed. *"Quel question!"*

"He's dead, it doesn't matter, you can tell me the truth. Great generals are often more lucky than smart."

"Ecoutez, monsieur. I saw him one time, this was happening in Jena, he rallied the troops himself. I saw it. He was grabbing the men by the throat and forcing them to turn around and face the enemy."

"One time," said the other, "the Eighth Regiment rebelled. They were refusing to fight unless they were paid and given their promised rations. So he makes them a speech. 'Citizens,' he says, 'I understand your plight.' Immediately rises up a shout, 'We are soldiers, not civilians!' 'Then act like soldiers,' he tells them. And that was that. End of rebellion. The thought of not being his soldiers did it."

"So his men liked him."

"Of course, they couldn't help it."

"Even at the end? Even after Russia?"

"Well. After *Russia?* We won't speak of that. Let's not spoil it. His star was leaving him then."

"His star?"

"His star which was guiding him."

"Why did it leave?"

"It leaves everyone sooner or later. He was one of us, in that respect. But it stayed with the Emperor longer than most."

"And what happened when it left?"

"Then he became just like you or me."

"Was he . . . crude? Was he ever vulgar?"

"Vulgar?" The mameluke broke into laughter. "He was a soldier, monsieur."

"He was the Emperor of the French as well," said Dr. Kellog.

"But he talked like a soldier."

"Was he brave?"

"Mon Dieu! Was he brave? He was brave, he was smart, he was vulgar, he could see in the dark. His right arm was so strong it could poke a finger through your skull. He was the greatest man who ever lived except me, does that satisfy you enough? In all due respect, *Monsieur le docteur*, our job is not to be answering too many questions, it is to guard his corpse from the rats who want to eat it, and your job, if you'll pardon me saying it, is to try finding out how the English managed to kill him at last."

The moist room was cold. Of the smells in that room, the corpse's was winning. They were breathing Napoleon.

"So . . . You were with him in Egypt?"

The two soldiers looked at each other.

"You were there in Egypt? You heard the famous speech?" Dr. Kellog poured more brandy. "He was famous for his speeches before a battle, was he not?"

The mameluke yawned. The valet-de-chambre shrugged, downed his brandy in one gulp, then reached for the bottle himself and poured more. "Yes, monsieur. But his speeches were not like they said they were."

"Oh?"

"Those were famous speeches. He wrote them for books. But in front of his men they were different from that."

"How were they different?"

"Well, in Egypt, monsieur. At the Battle of the Pyramids. You know what he said? What the books say he said?"

"Of course, everyone know. 'Soldiers! Forty centuries look down upon you from the heights of these pyramids . . .'"

"No, no, no. In the first place, the pyramids were a few miles away. We couldn't really see them. It was dark out anyway. You couldn't hear him speaking that much. The wind was blowing the sand something bad, and the horses all started whinnying like crazy because the Turks, they were setting their mares loose to distract our stallions. Well the Emperor, he wasn't the Emperor then of course, but he lines us up, he says something, something, then he tells us at the end to keep a tight ass-hole."

"That's all?"

"He says, 'Bugger the bastards.' Something like that."

" 'Cornhole the illegitimate scum.' "

" 'The heathen scum.' "

"Something like that. You understand the meaning."

"But the best speech he gave was just before we entered Madrid in oh-eight. We were bivouacking at a palace of some archbishop or other, cooking muttons, chickens, rabbits, and such in some huge kettles we found in the convent nearby. We kept the fires going with furniture, mandolins and guitars from the palace, and we sat around, black with dirt and smoke, on gilded chairs covered in damask, with two chairs each, one for our smelly bottoms and one for our muddy boots. Well, monsieur. Everyone lights up torches of straw when the Emperor comes out to speak. He makes it sound like we are defending France by occupy-ing Madrid tomorrow. He says we are fighting for our firesides and not to let the Spanish come and warm themselves beside them. Then he says they are studying the French language right this moment to learn how to welcome their conquerors. They are giving up sex and war to study books, he says, and he makes a funny face. They are locking up their wives because they know we are coming. *Lock up your wives!* he shouts, as though they can hear him. He actually cups his hands to his mouth even though the city is ten miles away. Lock up your women, men of Spain! Your wives, your mothers, your daughters! We all start cheering, we can't help it. And block their delicate ears, men of Spain, he says, so they won't hear your dying squeals. More cheers, but we are laughing too. He is too, the Emperor is laughing right through his teeth while he watches us laughing. Then he says, when we've captured your city, men of Spain, we will then block *your* ears to spare you the cries of love that will come from your mothers! From your daughters! From your wives! He is rolling his eyes and making crazy faces, nasty ones really, but we can't stop laughing and cheering by this time. And new and wondrous cries they will be, he says, to you who never produced them yourselves! By this time we are all frothing at the mouth. If he told us to go disem-bowel ourselves, we would have lined up while he passed out the fish-hooks. The man cast a spell. So you see what a great man he was. He starts making jokes about butter, about piercing their lines like they are butter, and how we can do the same to their women, but it is the way he is saying it, butter, *beurre*, smearing the word, you might say, across his mouth, drawing it out very disgusting so you can't catch your breath, you are howling so much. Then to top it all off he wheels out a giant cake for a surprise, it fills a whole cart, a cake in the shape of the city of Madrid. Children! He called us children in his speeches. Attack! he shouts. So we fall to the cake and tear it apart and are eating the whole thing in a matter of seconds, stuffing our mouths until we are choking. It was very good food for the night before a battle. It filled you with air. Thick and rich cake made from fifty pounds of chocolate and one hundred pounds of butter, I heard. Not a crumb left.

"Then it is almost midnight, I think, and no one can sleep and we are wondering what to do, so we play prisoner's base during the next few hours."

"The Emperor too?"

"Of course the Emperor. His favorite game. When he played prisoner's base he tutoyered us. We were his children." The valet-de-chambre poured himself more brandy, then elbowed his fellow soldier, who had fallen asleep in his chair. At the foot of the mountain of Napoleon's body, he held the brandy to the mameluke's lips as though he'd been wounded in battle. "So you see," he said, "what a great man he was."

Dr. Kellog smiled at the valet-de-chambre. "I find it difficult to believe that the Emperor of the French played prisoner's base on the night before a battle."

"You keep on saying Emperor of the French. Of half the world is more like it, all except the ones that wouldn't listen to reason. Anyway, it's mainly true, monsieur. Certain parts of it are true. Why not play prisoner's base with his men? We made him what he was. How could there be a Napoleon without his monthly income of ten thousand men? If you want to know the truth about the Emperor, listen to us. It's the books that lie."

"A cake in the shape of Madrid. Would you swear on a Bible it's true?"

"Of course. But it wouldn't help you, monsieur."

"Why is that?"

"I'm not a Christian."

"What are you, then? A Mohammedan?"

"I'm nothing. I've been inside churches and cathedrals, I've been to mass a few times, I even received holy communion before a battle, just to be on the safe side. But I never was baptized. My father was the hangman in our city and no one would act as my godfather when I was born, so I'm neither Christian nor Turk nor Jew nor heathen, I'm nothing. So bring on your Bibles." He slapped his knees. Beside him, the mameluke yawned and sat up.

"So . . . The Emperor was powerful. He inspired you with his power?"

"Some say it was divine," said the mameluke. "The fact is, you couldn't kill him, for one thing. They tried killing him with poisoned tobacco in his snuffbox after he came back from Egypt. A marble cutter at Malmaison put it there. They put a bomb in a barrel on a little street in Paris when he went to the opera, and it blew up twenty people but it didn't hurt him. The wounded ones stopped their moans and groans to ask how he was doing."

"Tell him about the petitioner," said the other.

"The petitioner! Of course! It was Paris, monsieur, in 1815, at the beginning of the glorious Hundred Days. Glorious at first. All the regiments are passing in review while the Emperor stands there on the steps of the Tuileries. They shout, 'Vive l'Empereur!' and he just stands there. He doesn't nod, he doesn't smile. He is taking a little snuff. Then half the soldiers break from their ranks and rush up with their petitions, which we take from their hands, we being the Old Guards. He keeps taking his snuff without moving at all. Suddenly one old soldier dripping with filth leaps from the crowd, draws his sword, and rushes right at the Emperor, who doesn't even glance at the man. He doesn't flinch. He keeps on taking his snuff. This man is so quick for someone so old that he gets almost a sword's length away before Picart grabs him by the collar and throws him down and the rest of us jump on him. And the Emperor acts like nothing is happening. He isn't even looking at the man until he's collared, then he tells us, of all things, to let him go. He wants to talk with him. This man still has his sword, you understand. But the Emperor's slightest wishing is law so we let him go and he stands there and talks to the Emperor with his hand on his heart during five or ten minutes and he's waving his arm with his petition, practically shouting. And the Emperor listens carefully, with respect, as he always did to the old soldiers. He was saying he was placed on the list three times for the cross and each time had been disappointed, he was raving about his wife and his pension. He married a whore to pay homage to his Emperor on the anniversary fête of the coronation, he was saying, and his wife was unfaithful, and so on and so on. So the Emperor takes the petition and puts it in his good pocket, just like that."

"His good pocket?"

"His private pocket where he keeps the petitions he intends to grant."

"And did he grant it?"

The mameluke grinned. "No, monsieur. I don't think he did."

"What happened to the man?"

"When the review was finished and the crowds went home and the Emperor went back inside the palace, we cut off his head. At the Emperor's orders."

The two soldiers laughed. Dr. Kellog poured the last of the brandy in their glasses. Raising his glass, the mameluke sniffed at the brandy, then sniffed the air, wrinkling his nose. "Phew!"

"What a glorious leader of men," said the valet-de-chambre. "What a man himself. You see his noble brow." He glanced behind him at Napoleon's corpse. "Vision," he said. "He had vision. He doesn't have it now, but he had it then. It was something about the way he did things. He made everything noble, even freezing and starving to death. Even crawling along the rows of the dead, looking for your missing fingers on the battlefield. Even marching away from the wounded who are grabbing at you and pleading that you should please be taking them with you because as soon as you are gone out of sight the carrion peasants will come and slit their throats and strip them of their clothes. You did it for him and for a cause, because he was keeping the revolution alive, it would have died without him, that's what he said, but mostly you did it for him. The way he looked at you went through your bowels just like a sword. You could be dressed in rags while he wore fur-lined cloaks and velvet caps and black fox furs and all those lovely things, and meanwhile your own feet were wrapped in rags, your fingers and toes were black with frostbite, you were stuffing straw in your sleeves and pants, you were warming your fingers at the nostrils of horses, the officers were pricking you with swords to keep you going, but still you loved the man."

"He had to walk on foot just like you, for one thing," said the mameluke. Both servants had stood to look at the corpse.

"That's right, the poor bastard. This was coming back from Russia, monsieur. It hurt him just as much as us, except for his fur-lined cloak. We didn't have that. We didn't have the velvet cap either. I noticed the bald ones died first. Men died standing up, frozen to the spot before they could drop. The ground was too frozen to bury anyone. A man rushes up to you laughing and staring with his sunken eyes and you know he will die. He's doomed. And the constant harassment of the Cossacks also who were sticking us from their horses like boars. No food, freezing cold . . . Madness. When all the horses died and we ate them all up, even his, then he had to walk too. The great Emperor we loved so much. I saw it myself. He was walking just like us."

"There was always more men. The men were just soldiers. It was him that was important."

"That's right. He set the example. He kept you going, even when you wanted to lie down and curse him for taking us there. I know, I made the whole trip, all the way to Moscow and back. Only ten thousand came back out of four hundred and twenty thousand that went in, and we still loved the crazy bastard, we did. The sharp-eyed devil. The greasy little Corsican. Any more brandy?"

"No. There's no more."

"He invented a wonderful torture," said the mameluke. The two men turned from the corpse and staggered toward a corner of the room, panicking the rats scratching this way and that in the shadows. They removed a piece of tin nailed to where the wall met the floor, and pissed in a rat hole. "Fill a man up with wine. One bottle, two bottles. Then tie off his prick, so he can't piss. I've seen it myself. They turn brown."

"They swell up."

Dr. Kellog stood. "These chairs are in my way," he said. "Take them to that corner and guard the Emperor's uniform. Leave the body to me."

"It stinks," said the mameluke.

"He died like a pig," said the valet-de-chambre.

They dragged their chairs over to the couch and slumped in them. The mameluke yawned, his eyes shut already. "It would have saved many people a lot of trouble," he muttered, "if someone had pinched off his head when he was born."

Within minutes the two men were sound asleep. Outside, the rain continued to fall. Longwood House was quiet, all its residents in bed. Dr. Kellog—though that wasn't his name—reached into his satchel for a small leather case, opened it, and chose the largest scalpel. He lifted the Emperor's sheet and stared down. He noted the finely shaped hands, whose nails appeared to have grown. Napoleon's ears were small and perfectly formed, but his head was large, and his nose of Grecian shape, his lips straight and firm, hair a rich brown. Very fine hair, and thin on the temples, his forehead very high, a noble forehead. His face looked pale, yet seemed to be shining. In death he was beautiful. The breasts, the general feminine shape, contributed to the impression of beauty, though the ugly incision down his middle diminished it. He'd already been cut up once, so this wouldn't hurt, this little bit. The doctor— though he wasn't a doctor—thought of the Great Man's brilliant madness, his magnificent ability to spend the lives of others. No one in the world had held so much power. When he was alive, there was no old age, only glory. One spends more and more lives for less and less glory, for glory is subject to inflation like money, until only one person's glory counts, the man left standing on a plain of endless corpses, the colossal figure alone and transfigured. And where was the root of all that glory?

He cut off the Emperor's thumb.

From his satchel he drew a small silver bottle half filled with alcohol and dropped in the thumb. Then he peeled the sheet down to the Emperor's ankles. He noted once more the shrunken genitals, the seat of power, the source of life, scant to be sure in that epicene body—negligible indeed—but the roots of great things were often modest, were they not? In his satchel he found the other silver bottle.

At nine the next morning Dr. Arnott was summoned to the entrance of Longwood House, where a visitor awaited him. The rain had stopped, but clouds threatened more. Dressed in the uniform of a surgeon of the Royal Navy, this smiling man stood there, short and plump, with bushy eyebrows, hairy ears, a red head, and ruddy nose. He carried a satchel.

"Dr. Arnott?"

"Yes?"

"You haven't begun yet?"

"Begun what?"

"Begun. The opening of the body."

"The autopsy was held two days ago. May I ask who you are and where you come from?"

"Two days ago? My ship arrived in Jamestown two days ago. But your message specified nine o'clock this morning."

"And you are . . ."

"Dr. Robert Kellog, out of Cape Town."

Dr. Arnott glanced out at the blackening sky with a look of profound disgust. He was thinking how useful an ally is discipline, it helps to fight the alarm, the confusion, all that smoke and noise before the light breaks through. "Dr. Kellog? Impossible. I never sent you a message. Who delivered it?"

"Tall man. Sharp nose, pinched nostrils . . . Are you quite all right?"

Arnott had pivoted back into the house. Dr. Kellog lifted his satchel and followed. They almost collided when Arnott turned. "Your ship. It leaves when?"

"Left this morning, bound for London. Storeship from Cape Town. Only passage available on such brief notice, stroke of luck . . ."

Arnott turned and left the man standing there.

". . . devil of a time getting back, I should think."

In the billiard room, Antommarchi and Henry had just sealed the vessels containing the Emperor's heart and stomach. The two servants were piling Napoleon's uniform on a chair beside the corpse in preparation for its final dressing. Dr. Arnott burst in, rushed to the billiard table, pulled back the sheet, and looked down in horror.

PART
II
LONDON 1868

"Will he fall for it?"

"Of course. I know him well. Acts sharp, but he's easily skinned."

" 'Skinned?' Such language! I shouldn't think wearing their clothes obliges us to speak in their—lingo. If I didn't know better I'd suspect you'd become one of these . . . *creatures*, Jo. Like . . . *him.*" He nodded at the oarsman.

"Shhh."

The two men whispered in the back of the skiff, riding high in the water between the pale sky and the paler river. The oarsman, dressed, like them, in a fantail hat, a black smock down to his black knee breeches, laced-up boots, and loose cotton kerchief tied around his neck, the costume of a coalbacker—though he'd really been one, unlike them, you could tell by their womanish hands—this brute stared at the bright slash of river between the two men, at the loops and eddies his oars left in the water, and didn't see anything. He was used to it. He rowed more for show than work, since the river moved in the same direction they did, the tide running down and the river going out, but it never occurred to him to save his strength, he liked the mechanics of it.

To the men in the back of the boat he looked large. Like the huge shadows of ships all around, masts and stacks poked up and drifting past, he seemed to loom over them, his face in the darkness—everything now had grown dark except for the sky and the river beneath it. Jo thought of Stokes. *Will he fall for it?* Just the proper foolish question, just the right twinge of fear. It wasn't just Stokes who'd come tumbling down, if all went as planned. Out of habit he patted his pockets, empty save for the medallion. I could use a pinch of snuff, he thought—more than all the money owed me by connivers, more than Stokes's entire collection, but coalbackers didn't take snuff, couldn't manage, what with all the coal dust on their clumsy fingers. He laughed out loud.

"Goodness. What is it?"

"The thought of these costumes . . ."

"He knows we're disguised?"

"Of course. His idea."

Edmund liked the idea of the costumes; you dressed down to consort with lowlifes. Besides, in this part of town, at night, a gentleman made too obvious a target. Hadn't Napoleon himself donned the costume of a peasant to walk among his people? He thought of the lock of Napoleonic hair, safe in his room back at Lincoln's Inn, then pictured the substitute, inside its medallion in Jo Benton's pocket. Who could tell the difference? If their man fell for that, what wouldn't he fall for? Why, Edmund Angelo Atkinson might become a prince of collectors, and with minimal outlay! It was all the brilliant idea of Jo, who said he'd pulled a switch or two before. What a stroke of luck, Edmund had cried— meeting up with him like that at his own club . . .

As the brute pulled the river past their boat, his oars groaned and snored in their wooden struts. He never turned to note their course. He'd already pulled London Bridge like a wrap over their heads and sloughed it behind them, that was fifteen, twenty minutes ago, didn't turn around to look then either, aimed them perfectly through the middle arch, pitching forward and back like the beam of a well-oiled engine . . .

At last they threaded two enormous ships, emerged in a clearing, and struck the pilings of a wharf. In the fading light, Jo could just make out the gobs of green slime hanging from the pillars. The tide was too low to tie up on the wharf, but their guide found a ladder—his upper half stretched across the bow—and with a swift flick of his clumsy wrists tied their long painter onto it. He climbed up the ladder in the woolly dark. Jo signaled his partner to go on. After you, shipmate. Thank God for a trusty chum.

Between the tiers of ships and the wharf, the exposed river reflected enough leftover sky to light their way through the benches and capstans, the discarded rigging, the stacks of softwood and bales of blue indigo scattered here and there. They climbed another ladder bolted to the side of the six-story warehouse above them, this one more giddy—you landed in stacks of lumber if you fell. The brute above them performed a perfect arabesque and stood on the platform of an open loophole looking impassively down at the two of them. Edmund stopped. "Are you absolutely certain . . . ?"

"Move on," said Jo.

Their guide extended an arm to Edmund. When his turn came, Jo waved off the guide and lunged for the platform. I could be this, he thought, a dockworker, coalwhipper, lighterman, sailor, instead of the two-hundredth illegitimate cousin of a counterfeit emperor on a sinking throne . . .

From the open loophole came the smell of cinnamon. Their guide went ahead with a lantern. Inside, in stacks around the cast-iron stanchions, stood bales of cinnamon sticks wrapped in burlap, cinnamon from China. The sweet smell felt more like a taste, here and there mixed with the fungus of dry rot and something else worse—rat poison, dead rats. At the far end, the cinammon gave way to casks of cheap sugar from Belgium. Here, the sticky floor adhered to their shoes as they walked, vexing Edmund. "Bother the floor."

They passed through doors to a metal bridge crossing Rotherhithe Street, two stories up. Jo barely made out the narrow street below, between the long rows of warehouses, though he felt its cool updraft. You could tumble a man from this bridge. Would he fall for it?

Into another warehouse, this one fragrant with coffee from Turkey. They marched through the smells of an empire: coffee, coriander, sulphur, rum, the stench of hides, licorice, wine. They passed a locked iron cage with crates stacked inside: whiskey. Through a door to a landing, down steps to a cobblestone courtyard, past windows filled with shining brass quadrants and sextants. A figure slumped against a wall beneath an overhang jumped up and knocked. SAMPLES OFFICE. NO ADMITTANCE EXCEPT ON BUSINESS.

Stokes roared with laughter when he saw them. "Is it," said Jo, "the hats or the coats?" He'd removed the close hat with its tail hanging back exactly like a beaver's.

"Never one," said Stokes. "It's the cleanliness. Where's the coal dust? The grime? You wouldn't fool a drunken lumper."

Gas lamps burned on the walls. In this tiny office, Stokes, with pointed nose and face tugged down like a piece of taffy, sat on a stool behind a slant-top desk. Stokes's large moist spongy face looked disorganized, formless at the bottom, so the under lip appeared continuous with the jaw, which quivered wetly with laughter. His lubricated throat sounded under water.

Beside the desk stood a cane litter basket. In corked jars ranged on shelves along the walls sat samples of the world brought to London:

turmeric fingers and divi-divi from the East Indies, sorghum seeds from Australia, black pepper from Singapore, star aniseed from China, Indian hemp, Persian licorice root, clove stems from Zanzibar, Ugandan vanilla beans, North American black haw bark, jalap root from Vera Cruz, tobacco from the West Indies, gentian root from Florida, sugar from Port Natal. In cases on the floor were Japanese refined camphor, Chinese vermillion, Chinese soy, and a burlap bag of Japanese chiles. Empty bird cages hung from the ceiling in clusters. On a deep shelf against the far wall sat a stuffed orangutan, and beside it various large Punch-and-Judy dolls and some fantoccini with lifelike faces painted orange and red. Stokes's factotum with his heavy brow and carved wooden face sat beneath them. A skinny man with the face of a lynx slipped out the door, tinkling the bell. The factotum stood and locked it.

"Now. Do we have a sale? I don't haggle regarding curiosities. Timothy Stokes, sir."

"Charmed," said Edmund.

"I can't say no to a pound or two. A few pounds is nothing to me. You're up to the business, so you must know it's fine times for curiosities, but never the times it used to be. A lock of his hair last come to market back when we had us a king, not a queen. What price did Jo give you?"

"Five hundred pounds."

"You shall have it for four. Anyone else would haggle, I should think. Not Timothy Stokes."

"I'd like to see more, please."

"More what?"

"Curiosities."

"Curiosities various or those kind?"

"Those kind."

"Sacred or secular?"

"Both."

"Follow me. Jo, you come too."

Stokes took a ring of keys from the wall and stepped to a door in the back of the office. In his corduroy waistcoat buttoned to the throat, as long as a groom's, he walked too gravely for a dumpy man, with swollen chest and eminent buttocks on display, aggressively squeamish. He looked like he'd rather be sitting, but in this next, airless room there was nowhere to sit, barely space to stand. The ceiling here was lower too, and gas lamps made the place hot. Dressmaker's dummies stood about blank and erect, one with the uniform of a Russian Cossack. In crates on the floor were artificial arms, feet, hands, and legs sorted by size, along with boxes of wigs sorted by color, a sack of glass eyes, and a crate of skulls. A row of painted skulls sat on a shelf, the red one labeled SKULL OF A ROBBER, the blue one SKULL OF AN ASSASSIN, the green one SKULL OF A BANKRUPT, the yellow one SKULL OF A PEDERAST. Beside them were puppets and gutta-percha heads with long flowing wigs made of grass. A display case held piles of exhibition medals and fans. There were also boxes of bones, fossilized eggs, stuffed birds, the skin of a badger hanging on the wall, and, in open cartons, stacks of birds' wings of every gorgeous color. On shelves were monstrances, jewelry, pewter statues, music boxes, vials, snuffboxes, and jars of bloodworms and brainworms from famous horses. A pair of dueling stuffed mice stood frozen on a table beside a basket of keys, into which Stokes dipped his hand. "Laid on the grave of Saint Peter in Rome," he said, "as the papists fancy. Gives their keys holy powers. Fragment of the true cross in that." He pointed to a monstrance on a shelf. "Which they believe it reproduces itself. Like the loaves and fishes. That's why there's so many. Bonaparte himself when he crowned himself king placed on his own head a crown which contained a piece of the true cross, I heard tell. Made by the Queen Theodolinda."

"Do you have it here?"

"In course not. But of Bonaparte I have a fragment of the rib, a piece of intestine, a vial of spittle, the dueling pistols, and that bit of a lock of hair in your keeping."

"Jo has it."

"In course."

"I should like to see the dueling pistols."

Stokes rummaged in a cabinet and came up with a mahogany case. Inside, the pistols lay on velvet. "Presented to the Count of Forzine by Bonaparte himself. Who was a colonel of the Imperial Guard as he made a count—the Count of Forzine—for attacking a bridge. Versailles workmanship. See for yourself." He handed the case to Edmund.

"How came you by these?"

"Roundabout. The count gave them to his brother, the baron, which passed them on to his son in the family. Well, his son presents them for use as a second to the exiled duke as fights a duel in England in 1855 out to Wimbledon Common, the greatest dueling grounds of that day. But the inspector stops it before they line up and confiscates the weapons and throws the varmits in jail. But the chief clerk at Bow Street's a friend of mine, sir. After the trial, he disposes of the weapons in my direction, for considerations."

"And how does one know they belonged to Napoleon?"

"By the writing on the case. See?" Stokes closed the case and held it up for Edmund to read the engraved inscription: *"Donnée par l'empereur Napoléon au général Hulot."*

"Who was General Hulot?"

"The Count of Forzine, sir."

Edmund looked over at Jo, who was whistling in silence, who shrugged his shoulders, then turned away to examine a pewter reliquary on a shelf.

"That there's Galileo's thumb," said Stokes.

"Oh?"

"As invented the telescope."

"I see." Jo examined closely the cylindrical brass turret on a pedestal surmounted by a stemmed crystal bulb in the shape of an egg, with a blackened, shriveled digit inside. It certainly looked like it could have been a thumb.

"I shall purchase these pistols," said Edmund.

"Five thousands pounds, sir."

"Preposterous!"

"A thousand, then. Say eight hundred and it's yours."

"I am prepared to offer you two hundred pounds on a note and surety of thirty pounds."

"Pieces of paper! You're larking, sir. You was to bring your cash, it was strictly understood."

"I brought as much as I thought it safe to carry in this—district."

Stokes looked over at Jo, still engaged in examining Galileo's thumb, now with a jeweler's glass. "Done," he said. "Pistols is cheap. Locks of hair dear. Right, Jo? We've made us a sale."

"Very good."

"Stand backer, you'll melt it."

Jo turned around. "When did you get this?"

"Monday."

"From whom?"

"I bought it of a man as sells Galileo's thumbs." He turned to Edmund. "Well, sir. You've done famous. Them pistols is yours. I'll send my friend Jo here to fetch back the rest of your money tonight. Thank you, sir." He pocketed Edmund's note of hand and cash. "And the lock of hair? From Bonaparte's own head? Did it strike your fancy? I've heard it said his hair growed two inches after his death. Extraordinary thing."

"Quite. I should like to know what else you have."

"In the line of relics? Sacred and secular? Jo, fetch the list." Jo regarded Stokes with one cocked eyebrow, then stepped to the outer office and returned with a ledger. "Lay it on the table." He dropped it crashing beside the holy keys. Stokes fish-eyed Jo. "Thank you," he said. He licked his thumb and opened the book.

"Item. Wedding at Cana: waterpot used at." He looked up at Edmund.

"Go on."

"You understand, these are in the order as acquired. The ones I sold is the ones crossed out. I won't read those. You stop me, sir, when you're bit with curiosity. Item. Six fingers, hand with. Item. Albertus Magnus, brazen head of. Item. Virgin Mary, milk of. Item. Poet, ashes of."

"Which poet?"

"Dante of Italy. He died in Ravenna I heard it said, but the poets in Florence wanted his remains to bury theirselves. Well, the monks in Ravenna said no to the poets in Florence and hid what was left of him under their wall. But a scholard as knew the history of it smuggled some of his ashes out. In a snuffbox."

"Where is it?"

"Sold."

"There is no line through this entry."

"It's spoken for. My records is slack. Item. Bonaparte, hair of. That's the one you have. Item. Saint Theresa, parts of, various. For the testification of this, sir, we invoke the very Reverend Baring-Gould, if you'll allow me this brief summary, written down here. Died in ecstasy, 1582; honorably buried at Alva; nine months later the coffin brought up and the left arm took, found juicy and oily; arm sent to Lisbon, body enshrined, but slices of flesh cut off it now and then; 1585, body stolen to Avilla; 1586, brought back to Alva; 1616, Father Didacus cuts off the foot, which already has two toes took; 1750, body dug up and inventoried—right foot in Rome, left hand in Lisbon, slice of flesh from the breast in St. Pancras at Rome, left eye, some ribs, bits of flesh and some bones dispersed in the wider Christian world. Head cut off. Parts of neck missing. Pupil of the right eye and eyelashes intact. *Eyelashes*, mind you. Bits of the right hand pulled off. Extraordinary thing is—"

"Enough, Mr. Stokes. Spare us."

"And the lock of hair, sir?" Stokes slammed the book shut. "You've decided about the lock of hair?"

"I don't want it."

"Then give it back. I miss it already."

"Jo," said Edmund. "Give the man his precious lock of hair and let's be off."

"Let's be off and let's fetch the rest of the man's precious money," said Stokes. "Plaguy quick."

"Yes, of course. Jo shall bring it."

"Very well then," said Jo. "We'll go." He held out a gold medallion on a chain. Stokes wrapped the chain around his fingers and regarded the locket.

Edmund and Jo started for the door.

"One moment, gents." They stopped. "One precious moment if you please." He was gazing down into the open medallion and stepped to a gas lamp for a better look. Edmund turned to Jo near the door, who watched Stokes. "Jo, my friend. This is never the lock of hair as you took."

"Of course it is. Don't be silly."

" 'Tisn't." Jo's hand found the latch of the door. Edmund stood erect but tipped to one side. "Bonaparte's hair was reddish-brown and silky. Looks oldish like. This here looks fresh. Looks like doggy hair."

"Very funny."

"It's got fleas, Jo. Where's the lock of hair what I gave you?"

"That's it there."

"No it ain't. See?" Stokes threw the open medallion at Jo. It struck him in the face. Edmund gave a little cry and Jo started for the door, but Stokes's factotum collared and threw him back inside, then knelt over him, jerked at his arms, and tied them with a cord. Edmund huddled back against a table. Jo's brow was bleeding where the medallion had struck.

"Now then. This is a rum business, Jo." Stokes leaned down and retrieved the medallion. A sunburst of hair stuck out behind the cameo silhouette of the Great Man himself. "Here's this hair here." Stokes opened the locket and dumped hair on the table. "And here's yours, Jo." With a clasp knife, he leaned down, seized a clump of Jo's hair, and cut it off. "Note the resemblance? It's shocking similar. I know what you're thinking. Hair's hair. That's true. But hair's a living thing, Jo. Compounded of skin and sort of a dust. I recollect when they opened her grave, Saint Lucy's hair had growed so much it filled the whole coffin. Saint Lucy what plucked her own eyes out." He gathered the hair and held it before Jo's face. "Eat it."

"I—" Stokes jammed the hair into Jo's open mouth. He tried spitting out, but it clung to his tongue and teeth. When he breathed, flecks of it bloomed in his lungs.

"It tickles going down," said Stokes.

Jo coughed and spluttered; wide-eyed Edmund stood stiffly above him and at last spoke up meekly. "I shall fetch the lock of hair."

"I don't want your precious Bonaparte's hair! I'm sick of hair. I wants to be *paid* is what I wants. Now then," said Stokes. "I needs hair for wigs, fingers for pickling, and a foot for a relic as could be Saint Andrew's own, on special order to the Bishop. I'll take what I needs from this friend of ours here," he nodded toward Jo, "unless I'm paid for your Bonaparte's hair. You go back and get the money, sir. Max here will take you. Four hundred pounds, agreed upon price. Plus two for the pistols. No queer paper. Banknotes. Bring it here straightaway. Arter I've shaved off his hair comes the rest."

"Will he fall for it?"

"He was took in. I can tell."

"That business with the hair . . . We never discussed it." Jo sat on the floor picking hairs from his mouth and extruded tongue.

"The hairs of the Bonapartes flows in your veins."

"It's a bit much, really. Ordering me about like that."

"Shall we shave your head, *sir*? Cut off your fingers? I fancied you'd appreciate them touches. More realistic like."

"Realism is for small-minded people."

"That's him all over. You seed his eyes. He was regular done up. You're certain for a fact his money's handy?"

"We'll soon find out. And the—item? You have it?"

"Pickled and salted."

"I've fulfilled my part of the bargain, Stokes."

"Fulfilled when the money come rolling in."

"Let's see it now."

"See it you shall. Have it when you've set me to rights." Stokes reached down to help Jo stand. "It's in the garden," he said. "As you've never seen. I calls it my garden." He pushed aside a table and pulled boxes and crates to the center of the room, then struggled with a tall wooden cabinet whose small drawers of every crazy size—no two the same—all rattled with something sounding like gravel.

Jo helped. "What's in this?"

"Teeth."

Behind the cabinet stood a door in the wall all of three feet high. Stokes bent to unlock it, then crawled in on hands and knees. "Wait there while I strikes my fuzee." Light flared out from the opening, then calmed. "Mind your head." Jo crawled in and stood facing Stokes, whose grin filled with teeth in the flickering light. "My garden."

The floor was empty except for Stokes's lantern. This room resembled a pantry or jam closet, more tidy than the others, regimented really. On tiers of shelves along every wall sat stoppered jars of clear liquid, inside each of which floated, like a flower, a human penis. They stood in columns arranged by size, from the diminutive on top to the monstrous on the bottom. Jo looked around, awestruck and jumpy. It made him feel helpless, this horde of blind and bald amputees, but all he could say was, "Fancy that."

Stokes leaned down to a label on a jar. "Samuel Foote, actor and mimic, died 1777. One of my eldest. Frank Clarence Mangan, poet of Ireland. She died in 1849."

"She?"

"Well, Jo. For the lack of this item a *he* becomes a *she*, I should think. Alexander Hall Medford, American diplomat, died in China of 1847. Sir Martin Archer-Kennedy as fought in the Napoleonic wars and was made a general by Wellington himself. Girolamo Crescentini, the greatest tenor in Italy of recent memory. Ah, here it is. Here is my eldest. Theodore Neuhof, the first and only king of Corsica, what took refuge in England and died here in 1756. Gaoled for debt. Bequeathed her kingdom to her creditors, which if they'd been able to collect, I dare say you wouldn't be here now trying to scrooge out the private parts of a Bonaparte, eh? Leastwise not one as conquered the world. He'd of been a British subject then, and *we* don't go about conquering the world."

"You don't have to. You purchased it."

Stokes's head rolled back on his neck when he laughed. "We purchased it! Very good! Swag shop of the world!"

"And where is—?"

"Right back of you. Allow me to fetch it."

Jo turned; the shelves of the wall behind were empty except for a jeweled silver chest. Stokes lifted it down to the floor beside the lamp, then selected a key from his chain and unlocked it. From a well inside the velvet-lined chest, he lifted a jar. Jo's eyes widened.

"It's—"

"Uncommon handsome."

"Of mammoth proportions."

"In course. He being emperor of the world."

"And how do you know—"

"That it's his? By this receipt, if you please. Signed by the Maggs Brothers of Berkeley Square, as bought it of the Vignali family of Italy. Eighteen thousand pounds they paid. So you see what a bargain . . ."

Jo examined the receipt. "How came you by it?"

"Roundabout. Ask no questions on methods. Mortal tongue won't tell. Here, Jo. Heft it." Jo took the jar. "Have a care."

"This receipt mentions no chest."

"My offertory. Mind the jar."

"Dear me."

"Christ!"

When Jo dropped the jar it burst like a shell, soaking their ankles and releasing all at once a stink of alcohol. Stokes fell to his hands and knees to rummage for its squirming cargo. "Clumsy oaf!"

Jo watched the man scrabbling around on all fours below him like a drunken rat catcher. His stringy gray hair fell down across his face. The chest felt heavy as a rock, but Jo heaved it up with barely a grunt, then brought it down on the back of Stokes's head. He gave a yelp and pitched forward on the floor. "That's for trying to skin me, Timothy." Jo found the clasp knife in the pocket of Stokes's waistcoat. "And this," he said, "is for going too far." He pulled at a tuft of Stokes's hair, sliced it off, and stuffed it in his mouth. Stokes groaned and jerked, showing his eye whites. "And this," said Jo, "is for your nasty profession." In one swift motion, he sliced off the tip of poor Stokes's nose and dropped the bloody thing in the silver chest.

In the next room Jo went straight for the reputed thumb of Galileo. The thumb itself looked black and shrunken, a broken stick. He checked the base of the turret again and this time found the catch underneath, popped open the hidden compartment, looked inside . . . Then he closed it, removed his smock, and wrapped the reliquary with care, as a butcher wraps meat. When he passed through the outer office, one of the fantoccini dropped to the floor; Punch and Judy turned their painted heads, following Jo's hurried footsteps, grinning at his haste, heeding the tinkle of the bell above the door.

Strange to say, the skiff was still there, now beached in the mud below the wharf and the ladder to which its painter still led, ten or fifteen rungs up. It hadn't been touched. Two men could have moved it, couldn't they? Jo leaned down in the moonlight to give it a push, mud sucking at his boots, but it wouldn't budge. Footsteps cratered the mud all around, they'd been here for sure, but must have given up the skiff. Good—on foot, it would take them all night.

Then he spotted the body floating near the shore. Beyond it, the great ships in the river with their forest of masts and stacks appeared tipped by moonlight. He stepped closer. A coalbacker, or someone dressed like a coalbacker in fantail hat and black smock, face down, spread-eagled, at peace. Jo shivered. It had to be Edmund. But if Stokes's man killed him before he got his money, where was the benefit of that? Unless he found out he was carrying more cash than he'd said. That must have been it, the brute had acted on his own, and Stokes wound up stung twice the same night. Jo laughed out loud. Then he huddled in his coat—*shut up*, be careful, he might still be lurking . . .

He waded in the water for a closer look, then wished he hadn't. A fist-sized hole had blasted open the back of Edmund's head, right through the fantail hat. With some effort, clutching his prize to his chest, Jo turned the body over. He noted the smaller hole in the forehead, between the eyes, noted it before even registering with shock the rude face floating in the uncertain light, not Edmund's at all, it belonged to that brute, still expressionless in death. But that's how you died when shot through the head, Jo knew—expressionless. He'd killed two men in duels himself, he knew all about it, you were dead before you could blink, before your brain said, *What?*—

Then he remembered the dueling pistols.

"Hello, Jo."

He turned.

"Thought I'd come back to rescue you."

He recognized the voice—Edmund's—though the figure stepping out from beneath the wharf was hard to make out against the darkened pillars, under the looming warehouse above. Two loaded pistols meant Edmund had one left, but Jo knew those pistols—they were his, not Napoleon's—knew one was dead accurate, the other's trigger stiff, how else win two duels? Stiff triggers made anxious men jerk their shots, so Jo swayed right. Ankle-deep in the water, he swayed right and clutched the reliquary to his chest for double protection, in case Edmund aimed for the heart.

"Still have all your hair, Jo?"

Joseph Bonaparte Benton didn't answer. Why help Edmund in the darkness? He had only one shot. And if Jo swayed right, just a bit right . . .

That's what he'd done when he killed the journalist, it worked then, the bullet merely grazed his ear. But he had to hand it to Edmund. He'd seen right away those pistols were loaded, knew in all likelihood they weren't Napoleon's, how could they be Napoleon's? The *case* was Napoleon's, but the pistols were percussion pistols of a species invented after Napoleon's death. However, those pistols had defended the glorious name of Napoleon. Not Napoleon III, not *his* name, Jo cringed inside at the thought of that.

"Your fingers, Jo? Still got your fingers?"

Jo had challenged the journalist to a duel for saying exactly what he himself thought about the current emperor—that Napoleon III bore not the faintest resemblance to a Bonaparte. But he'd said it in print, he'd insulted the *name*. His accent was faintly foreign, said the journalist. His phlegm was certainly Dutch! The article he'd written raked over old coals. It told how Louis Napoleon before he became Napoleon III had marched on Boulogne in 1840 with a band of fifty tramps and one-eyed soldiers, with a piece of bacon secreted in his hatband for the purpose of enticing an eagle, a vulture really, that's all they could find on short notice, to flap symbolically about his head. The vulture flew off and Louis was arrested. But later on it happened, he became the new emperor. The article described in scandalous detail Napoleon III's doubtful parentage—nephew of the first and true Napoleon, son of Louis, one of the Great Man's brothers, who'd married Hortense, daughter of the Empress Josephine by her first marriage. But Hortense was notoriously unfaithful, it said, a Dutch admiral named Verhuell was known to be her lover, and no one really thought—did they?—that Louis Napoleon was his father's son. Even the famous Victor Hugo, said the article, in exile in England— fancy sending a challenge to *him*—had ridiculed Louis as a fictitious Bonaparte. Hugo's opinions were common knowledge, but this upstart journalist wrote it in a newspaper, wrote all these things down for every- one to see, they were going further than ever before because the Empire was crumbling and everyone knew it. Mexico was lost; Prussia threat- ened. Newspapers had begun to ridicule in print not only the ersatz emperor but the members of the imperial family and the Bonaparte name and all it stood for, someone had to stop it—

"What about your foot, Jo? That item still intact?"

Jo muttered to himself his mother's sacred name, Caroline Bonaparte Delafolie Benton. She'd taken in washing when he was eight years old. Then a Bonaparte returned to the throne in France—he called himself a Bonaparte—and family members from across the world returned to spawn at their origins. Even Americans, he called them his American cousins, he welcomed them into the gay world of the Second Empire, even bastard Bonapartes, they were no worse than him. He welcomed them all. He made Jo's mother a lady-in-waiting! After all, *her* father was Joseph Bonaparte, another of the Great Man's brothers. After Waterloo, Joseph had fled to America and taken a Quaker mistress, who, when she no longer pleased him, he married off to a fellow exile with the preposter- ous name of Charles Delafolie, gave them property too—a house in upstate New York, thousands of acres of timberland—but she brought up the daughter Joseph had seeded as a Bonaparte anyway, proud of the true blood. Her lovely daughter Caroline married an American colonel,

Zebulon Benton, and raised her son equally conscious of his great-uncle's name, raised him as Joseph Bonaparte Benton, then dragged him with her to France when her cousin, though hardly a Bonaparte, assumed the throne and regilded the name.

Ten years later Jo went to trial for killing the journalist who insulted that name, but the Emperor still possessed enough authority to order his acquittal. Jo was released, but had to hide. He couldn't show his face in France anymore, where the tide had turned, where journalists and communists were preparing the public for a world without Napoleon III. So he came to England, to London, with his pistols, he hunted up relics of his famous uncle's power in the city where all commodities found markets, a vial of his spit, a piece of his rib, and now he had the prize, not Galileo's thumb, he knew it wasn't Galileo's, and knew what the turret held in its hidden compartment, powdered with sulphur . . . Stokes hadn't fooled him. And Edmund, this gentleman he'd tried to pigeon, Edmund who'd turned out to be smarter than he'd thought, wasn't quite smart enough, was he?—because, of those two dueling pistols, he'd already used the good one, he'd fired it and now the bad one was left, all Jo had to do was sway just a bit, just an inch right . . .

"What's that you've got, Jo? More curiosities?"

Jo leaned right in the water, just a hair.

Then something wonderful happened.

Edmund stood in front of the pillars half in moonlight, half out, and something half dropped, half slithered from the wharf above him onto his shoulders. Jo registered the hanging shape of it an instant before it fell with a sound like hissing or laughter, hard to tell which, causing Edmund to drop the pistol. A ripping sound, a soft crack, a thud, and Edmund lay sprawled in the mud with that grinning shape, knee high, already scrabbling toward Jo, releasing a gleam of moonlight now and then from the folds of its coat and slobbering something barely audible from where Jo stood, something like *Wantzit. Wonzit? Wants it*, most likely . . . It was *fast* for something so small and shapeless. From the moment it landed on Edmund's shoulders and smeared itself over him like a leech or crab, Jo had stopped leaning and begun backing up, and now found himself up to his thighs in the river, now fell backward and panicked and tried to swim and hang onto his prize simultaneously. He flailed around knowing that thing—what *was* it?—was coming toward *him*, so he'd better start moving. He'd learned to swim as a boy in Lake Ontario. Splashing wildly at first, catching gulps of air half filled with stinking water, he sputtered and coughed and adjusted his crawl to a side stroke, then made for the big ships anchored in the Thames.

Jo swam the filthy water of the river. All around him the little fishes thronged as at the morning toast that floats along. One great ship, the *Narragansett*, loomed over him. Climbing up the slimy chain, still clinging to his reliquary, searching the water below him for shadows, Jo thought this a perfect time to go home.

The Christians of Saint Thomas in southern India claim the apostle Thomas, who placed his finger into the nail holes in Christ's hands, and his hand into the wound in his side, as their founder. Legend has it that he suffered martyrdom in India, though the Indian king Gundophar of the Syriac *Acta Thomae* is almost certainly the Parthian Gondophares, and the most ancient traditions make Thomas the evangelist of Parthia. His bones were claimed by the city of Edessa.

John's gospel translates the Aramaic name Thomas by the Greek equivalent, Didymus, or "twin," and the *Acta Thomae* claims that he was Judas Thomas, the twin brother of Jesus. Therefore, his bones were highly prized, and of those bones, the hand and the finger especially singled out for adoration. Blessed are they that have not seen and yet have believed, but blessed also are they that touch the hand that learned to believe by touching the hand. Thomas's hand made its way, through its human agents, to the basilica of Mount Sion, in Jerusalem, where it fell into Persian hands when they captured that city in 615. From Persia it was translated to Alexandria, where Egyptians of the Coptic Church claimed it as their own, and guarded it from the persecutions of the Muslims. During the ninth century, Byzantine merchants learned that the Caliph of Egypt planned to destroy it, and took it off in a basket covered with herbs and pork, shouting *"Hanzir! Hanzir!"*—Pork! Pork!—to ward off Muslims. They brought it to Constantinople, where goldsmiths fashioned a bejeweled golden hand and mounted it with one finger pointing up on a brass turret with a hidden compartment in its pedestal, into which the actual bones, now fragmented and reduced by attrition, were placed.

Relics change their residence of their own free will, which is nothing more than the will of the actual saint, whose outward sign is a fragrant odor, the odor of sanctity. Thus it was that during the Fourth Crusade, in 1204, tens of thousands of relics moved themselves to western Europe, especially Venice, when the French Crusaders who'd sold their services to the Venetians broke into the churches of Constantinople, got drunk on communion wine, sang lewd songs, murdered whoever stood in their way, and led mules to the altars to load up their booty in a massive and collective act of *furta sacra.* They stole crosses, gold plate, priest's vestments, relics and reliquaries, and sold them to churches and noble families from Italy to England.

A French duchess purchased the hand of Saint Thomas for her private collection. Price, sixteen hundred livres. In Paris, selected nonbelievers were allowed to touch it and learn to believe. But by the eighteenth century, in the recrudescence of reason which struck even the nobility of France, the bejeweled golden glove and its ancient bones had become an object of bemused embarrassment to their present owner, an Encyclopedist and friend of d'Alembert. He learned of the exhumation of the great Galileo's body in Florence, learned that several fingers and a vertebra had been removed and preserved when the body was transferred to the church of Santa Croce. He proposed a witty bargain—Saint Thomas's relics for those of Galileo—and didn't blink when the bones of the saint gave off a fragrant smell upon their removal. The hand of Saint Thomas made its way to Italy, where it chose its final resting place, the church of Santa Croce in Gerusalemme, in Rome, and Galileo's thumb and vertebra were installed in its place in the glove's brass turret.

The mania for reason soured. During the French Revolution, while revolutionaires were plundering the body of Mary Magdalene in Vézelay, scattering the bones of Saint Martial in Limoges, and trashing the fragments of the true cross and the tip of the spear that pierced Christ's side at Sainte Chapelle, in Paris, the once wealthy owner of Galileo's thumb was forced to remove the golden hand from the turret and pry off the jewels and melt down the gold. But the turret he saved—for sentimental reasons—and Galileo's thumb he placed in a crystal bulb on a stem he'd purchased in Italy in better days. This bulb and stem had been represented by a dealer in Padua as an early attempt by Galileo himself to invent the thermometer. He mounted them on the brass turret which still held the vertebra, and when, stripped of his estate, he emigrated to England, this was the only family treasure he chose to take with him.

Its history in England becomes murky. Entrusted on his deathbed to his son, who returned to France in the heyday of Napoleon, it nevertheless remained in London in the care of the Conservator of the Royal College of Surgeons. The pathological specimens on the shelves inside the Hunterian Museum of the Royal College—the internal workings of George III and various Lord Liverpools—looked positively antiseptic beside this antique gewgaw, said an article torn from an illustrated magazine Jo had found in an antiquarian's possession. But just how the final exchange had been effected, how Napoleon's thumb and most private part had been substituted for Galileo's thumb and vertebra—which found their way back to Florence—Jo wasn't certain, his researches had gaps, his sources grew mum. They declined to name names. Something about a brotherhood of shady antiquarians who had pieced together an underground network of conduits and drains, a two-way sewer of bodily dregs and oddments which stretched across Europe and linked, among others, England and Italy. The Vignali family in Rome was part of it, Jo learned that much. Also, a London artisan who manufactured antiques, who could imitate perfectly the damascening on Turkish daggers; he'd planned an inscription on the reliquary's brass turret, had begun it actually, the rough scratches grew visible under a jeweler's glass, *Leipsana ne spernas Digiti quo dextera coeli*, Jo had spotted them in Stokes's office. Stokes had done his job all right, he'd ferreted out the most intimate and the most highly prized of Napoleonic relics, but he'd decided to keep it for himself, or hold it until the market value soared. He hadn't counted on Jo's research, didn't realize Jo had a sharp eye out for precisely that brass turret and that crystal bulb which had once contained Galileo's thumb. Jo had also possessed ample foreknowledge of the modest dimensions of Napoleon's private parts, that was his touchstone. They'd been described to him in an alley in Paris by a small young man with a limp, a thin, pinched face, cold eyes, dressed in black, wearing white gloves and sporting a cane, as resembling a shriveled worm, and at first Jo had been mortified, he'd almost struck the man, they might have wound up dueling. But later, the offending newspaper article also mentioned this curious relic, calling it *"une pièce anatomique parfaitement identifiable dont il est impossible de préciser la nature sans offenser la décence,"* and went on in its climactic series of scandalous puns to berate pocket empires, pygmy Bonapartes, and their illustrious if petite progenitor, and to wonder how it ever could have happened—how the impotent and the sterile could have managed to pass on to the illegitimate and the incompetent all those family traits. The article also mentioned in passing a suppressed report by a Scottish doctor, a certain Robert Kellog, present at Napoleon's burial, who described in anatomical detail the mysterious and bizarre mutilation of the Great Man's body. Jo had located this report at the Naval Academy in Portsmouth, then one thing led to another, he'd been directed to Timothy Stokes, dealer in curiosities, but Stokes couldn't fool Jo, no, Jo had done his homework . . .

"You want to reassemble his body?" asked Stokes.

"Precisely," said Jo. But he lied. What he wanted was to spare the Bonaparte name any further embarrassment. He'd already disposed of the alleged vial of Napoleon's spittle—it was dry anyway—and the slice of intestine and the two pieces of rib. He'd kept the lock of hair, however, that was innocuous. The real lock of hair, not the one back in Edmund's room . . . But as for the reliquary with its crystal bulb, now that he possessed it at last, now that he was safely stowed away in the hold of a ship bound for America, listening to the hum and throb of the engines and the water gurgling in and out of the scuppers, he thought the easiest thing would be to toss it in the ocean in the middle of the night.

But he couldn't.

For one thing, he'd grown attached to it. He could achieve the same goal of protecting the sacred name of the Bonapartes if no one else ever owned it, if he kept it to himself. No one need know of it. It possessed a certain *aesthetic* sting anyway, a perverse antique charm, he'd gone through so much just to lay hands on it, two men had died, an empire was crumbling. In the faint light of a single porthole down in that hold, he often unwrapped and admired its workmanship. Above the tapered brass turret the glass bulb was really two hemispheres, one on top of the other, joined by a band of finely worked pewter stamped or etched with delicate floral designs. Inside it, the mounting for Napoleon's blackened thumb was a trefoiled silver plant with spiky tips, one bent over like a dog's ear. Now and then he sprang the catch of the hidden compartment—it opened underneath, from the base—and shook out its contents. Despite its size, it was *his*—not just a reminder or memento, not a copy or picture, not even a representation of the Great Man's power, but *him*, a part of him, *his* flesh and blood, as though he still lived. How could Jo part with it? At times it even seemed to be trying to speak . . .

Besides, there was George. The *Narragansett*, an ironclad, screw-driven steamship rigged for sail, was carrying six passengers, a crew of fourteen, and a general cargo in bales, hogsheads, crates, and stacks, of silks, of woolen and cotton goods, of linen, glass, china, dyes, road rails, pig lead, and cheap tin trays for the common people of America. The crew and passengers in their deck cabins above had little occasion to go below to where Jo lay hidden in the forepeak near the ice house, the only part of the hold with some room—two cows were here too, as well as empty barrels smelling of fish, piles of rope and chains, and rusty chunks of metal—except George, the cook's man. He rummaged the walk-in ice house daily for the meat and produce the ship's cook made stews of, all that food that Jo would gladly have eaten raw after his fourth day on biscuits, but the ice house was locked and George had the key. Jo had located some biscuits in a barrel. And water—apparently the water was stored in the ice house too, or maybe on deck, Jo hadn't found any down in that hold. Several times a day he tried the lock on the ice house, and when there was light enough he wandered the labyrinthine hold searching for anything edible or potable. He craved water above all, but settled for the cows' milk he managed to eke sparingly from their teats. As a boy in upstate New York, Jo had milked a cow or two, but the splendid life at court in Paris had erased that rude knowledge from his softened hands.

The sailor who turned out to be George descended to the forepeak once or twice a day. He came down for food, to expertly milk the cows, and to shovel their waste into a bucket and spread fresh straw. Jo had found a comfortable niche behind the bales of straw, he might have made the whole trip without George's help, but on the fifth day, in a rage of thirst and hunger, he couldn't stop himself from reaching for the figure bent over a new bale of straw and pressing to the man's neck the clasp knife he'd taken from Stokes. "Get me some water," he said. "And get me some decent food. If you don't, I'll find you wherever you are and slit your throat and drink all your blood."

Jo was a little delirious by then. He was feverish actually, had spent half that morning talking to his reliquary. Anyone else might have broken his feathery grip in an instant and knocked him to the floor, but George was sly, fainthearted as well. He wanted to see what he could get out of this, and thought it best to allow his limbs to tremble and his breath to come short while feverish Jo, whose mere touch burned, told him what to do.

George brought Jo slices of mutton, ham, and bread, and a jar of water, which he gulped down all at once.

George was a short, monkey-faced individual with small features and eager eyes. He weaseled a promise out of Jo to pay him in New York if he finished the voyage undetected, and he accepted Jo's abuse—even cultivated it—when the food was slow in coming. But the more food he brought the less Jo could eat. Jo was burning up with fever. Two days later, descending the steps into the hold, George heard mumbling. He went quiet as a fish and tried to listen. Down there lying on a bale of straw, Jo talked to something he held in his hands, a statue it looked like. The words came in a parched, hoarse whisper, George barely heard them, nothing was clear except a tone of resentment laced with pleading.

Quietly, George reascended the steps.

When he was gone, Jo opened his eyes. Napoleon's thumb bent and stretched itself—Jo could almost feel its arthritic, stiff joints—then struck a Napoleonic pose. It floated there in its reliquary above him. The hidden compartment was visible also, and the thing inside also bent and stretched. Their hoarse voices squeaked, metallic and thin. The thumb did a pirouette.

Dance, Thumbkin, dance.

Go away, said the thumb.

Thumbkin, he can dance alone.

You worm! I had everything but an heir thanks to you. I could get the best out of mediocre men, but from you I got nothing. I liked my bed as well as anyone else. I enjoyed the company of women, provided they were women of charm; the women of virtue I left to their patriotic duty of raising families for France. And they did! Endless families, batteries of families, entire infantries . . .

I *gave* you a son.

You tricked me into thinking you gave me a son.

He died like all your batteries of families.

But they weren't my sons!

You made peasants generals. Popes bowed before you. Why couldn't you make a few sons?

Why couldn't *you?*

Your abuse wore me out. You loved touching yourself.

I elevated those I touched.

Except me.

Except worms.

Dry up.

I am dried up. I'm thirsty as hell.

Use your magic rod! Command the waters to rise! Losing an empire feels like being thirsty, but you think the solution is just finding water. I've got news, Thumbkin. The well's gone dry.

I'm burning up! I'm dying of thirst!

Go milk a carcass.

I didn't need you, I didn't need anything. The rules I followed were the ones I made up. Who needs rules anyway? No rules, no religion, no imaginary terrors, no fear of the future . . .

No stomach, no heart . . .

I was forever!

Then what happened?

My hemorrhoids got worse.

His hemorrhoids got worse! The laws of nature wore themselves out because his hemorrhoids got worse! He grew fat, he lost a battle, it rained a lot, the rivers froze over. Nothing worked anymore because his hemorrhoids got worse! We found ourselves headed straight for an abyss . . .

An abbess . . .

An absence . . .

They drifted off into muffled squeaks that Jo could barely follow. An *abscess* . . . An *abuse* . . . Meanwhile, around him, matter in its different skins continued rubbing against itself. Always, Jo was dimly aware of the ocean's perpetual scraping past, of the sound of the wind, of the hammer and thrum of the distant engines turning the screw that ground up the water.

The crossing took ten days. As they were entering New York Harbor, George told the cook he had to see to the cows. He crept down the steps and tiptoed toward Jo, still prostrate upon the remaining bales of straw, still clinging to his prize. A white crust had formed around his lips, and his pale, clammy face was drawn. He'd lost weight, he looked even younger than his likely age, which was what?—twenty-one, twenty-two, George guessed. His fish-eyes bulged darkly beneath their closed lids. He was beautiful, really. The growth of beard on his face was scant, though he'd been down here without shaving for ten days. Beneath it, the lower part of his face showed pockmarks George found weirdly attractive. His small nose flared as he breathed. His thin black hair, parted in the middle, appeared to be wet. That was the sweating of course, from what George knew as ship's fever. His forehead felt a little cooler today. His breathing sounded easier too, deeper and more rhythmic, and he even stirred and smacked his dry lips, so George held his breath and stood there quite rigid. But Jo didn't wake, not even when George leaned down and loosened his fingers from that strange statuette with its egg-shaped glass bulb and some black thing inside, a dead plant or stick. It had to be valuable, George was no dunce. Otherwise why would he grip it so tightly, even lying there unconscious? George could have ended it simply right then. He could have smashed Jo's head with the base of that thing, it turned out to be dreadful heavy, but George was too timid for bloody misdeeds. Sly, but timid. Really, he wanted to kiss the man, but he smiled to himself at how clever he'd been. They'd find him in the hold when they unloaded cargo tomorrow or the next day, unless he woke up first. George tucked the whatsit under his coat and reascended the steps.

. . .

George tapped the pebble in his fingers on the half-opened window of a shingled lean-to tacked to the back of a Five Points tenement just off Cow Bay, on Manhattan Island. "Pete. Peter Doyle."

"Who's that?"

"It's George Hix."

"Georgie! Come in. How was the crossing?"

"Famous, Pete. Can't come in. Here, take this."

"Georgie, how are you?"

"Swell, Pete. Right now I'm ashore without leave. If they catch me I'm docked. Take this thing, quick. I got to get back."

"What is it?"

"Some thingamabob. Keep it for me."

"What is it?"

"Just take it."

"Is it hot?"

"So long, Pete. I'm off."

"Come see me tomorrow."

"Sure thing. So long."

Then George made the error of returning to his ship. The next day a garbage scow found him floating in the harbor.

PART

❧ III ❧

NEW YORK CITY 1869–70

Chapter

❧ I ❧

Amherst, Mass. December 1, 1869

Mr. Whitman,

I never read your Book before, having been told it is disgraceful. But when R W Emerson called it the Book of the Age, I blushed for my Ignorance and purchased a Copy—keep it in the Piano Bench where it won't bite Father. Mr. Higginson says your chiefest Error was not that you wrote your Book but that you neglected to burn it afterward—but I say since the world is Hollow, and Dollie's stuffed with Sawdust, we had better not so readily expose our Feelings.

I thought of your book till the Moon grew large and I broke several Dishes. I must wear thick Gloves.

In your Book, you shower me with all your Selves—I feel rather drowned—

What do you mean by the love of Comrades? Your mother . . . is she living? Have you ever loved a woman?

Don't be afraid of my questionings—they never harmed a Soul, and they make my dog smile. When I first wrote this the Leaves were falling, soon there will be falling snows. It may seem a Presumption that I address you at all, but I can assure you I've done it for Seasons. You write, the human body is Sacred. I do not care for the Body myself, but I love the timid Soul, the shrinking tiny Soul—it hides, it is afraid—I think we grow smaller, like the Mayfly—this insect life the portal to another. My size feels Small. Are you quite

*large? If you contain multitudes, do they follow in the Dark? You
show symptoms—I'm not here—*

*I presume you are loving your Mother, visiting the Poor and
afflicted, and reaping whole fields of Blessings. Save me a little Sheaf
of them.*

*I inclose my name because, so stuffed with God as you are, you
may forgive me by your own Hand.*

*Confidingly,
Emily Dickinson*

Walt heaved a sigh and folded up the letter, nearly illegible from
countless foldings and unfoldings. He had it by heart now anyway, and
recited it—*I never read your Book before*—while the troubled world slid
past, while the ferry wheels slapped cold, gray water, steam whistles
honked, and gulls flew above in slow wheeling circles.

Dear Miss Dickinson—or is it Mrs? Let me warn you somewhat against
myself—& yourself also. You must not construct such an unauthorized
& imaginary ideal figure & call it W.W. and so invest your loving nature
in it . . .

But her nature was hardly loving. Judging from that letter, it was full
of spleen. Sure, larval hints of love here and there infested the words,
but she also seemed to be laughing at him, it was all just a tease, a suck
and a sell, it could have been a joke. But the postmark looked real. Pete
didn't write it, his jokes were cruder. Whoever she was, she'd fixed Walt
slick, hadn't she? Dear Miss Dickinson—the exposé of personality you
essayed . . . All that vituperative cat squawling bothered me up something foolish. You cut a chip off that kind of timber and you can't expect . . . I doubt if you've gripped the question by the nuts.

The man you address, W.W., is the bedbuggiest individual you ever
seen, so be careful—his slime is catchy. He puffs himself up too much
and then unbosoms it all over the public.

He's quite levelistical.

Yet he is personally dear to thousands as such who love him but can
make neither heads nor tails of his book. There's a prejudice at large
against Walt Whitman. It is believed he ain't ashamed of his reproductive
organs. Dear Miss Dickinson—if you are so small, I suspect I am old
enough to be your father. Are you precocious or just dimwitted? Your
good friend, Walt.

"What's that, Walt?" The shout came from the wheelhouse above, barely audible over the roar of steam and water.

"Letter from the public."

"What?"

"Letter from the public!"

"Someone read your book?"

"Ain't the first."

"Read me it!"

"No."

"I mean the letter."

"I know damn well what you mean. It's a gushing letter, Jack. You don't want to hear it."

"Is it dirty?"

"Yes."

"Well, come up here and read it to me."

"No!"

Walt stood and lumbered to the railing, yanking his slouch hat down in the wind. In that cold December air, he was the only passenger foolish enough to ride outside. Clutching a package beneath one arm, he leaned on the railing and watched the river. In the wheelhouse above, Jack pulled the door shut.

The whistle blew.

Just yesterday had come the second letter. This one memorized more easily.

> *Did I displease you, Mr. Whitman?*
> *But won't you tell me how?*
>
> > *Yours,*
> > *E. Dickinson*

Yes, Miss Dickinson, you displeased every one of us. Leave us multitudes alone. Letters from strangers ain't half of it, Miss Emily. I got troubles of my own. Meet my friend, Pete . . .

Across the river in Brooklyn, the City of Churches, foundry chimneys sent up fire. Warehouses lining the water were moving, everything circled Manhattan, it seemed, even the Brooklyn shore, as well as ships at anchor and ships in motion, hay barges, steam tugs and lighters, the return ferry spewing out coal smoke, that ferry screw-driven, this one a side-wheeler, soon to be extinct. Ahead, beneath church spires, Manhattan showed clefts of streets resembling the spaces between planted rows. In that garden of marble, wood, and brick, down one of those streets, up two alleys, Peter Doyle lay wrapped in a smelly blanket. There were letters from strangers, that was enough in itself to bother up any man prone to the buzzing and humming in his ears. But there was also Pete. Just two days ago Walt had spotted Pete handing a young girl into her carriage. He seemed to know her well, he lingered on her fingers. Hat cocked forward, he was slinging the charm, Walt could tell, he'd once been its object. Pete might live in a sty, but since moving up from Washington he'd made the transition from Bowery B'hoy to Broadway Dandy in little more than a year. His southern twang had all but fled. He hadn't raised a mustache, that spoiled the picture a touch; but he squeezed his feet now into astonishingly small shoes of patent leather, he wore boiled shirts and broadcloth instead of canvas pants with suspenders hung over coarse undershirts. He sported a cane. He swaggered when he walked. He bowed low over the fingers of that girl at the door to her carriage, a pretty young thing—couldn't have been more than fifteen—and the sight of it pushed clean into Walt's vitals. It wasn't the Pete he knew anymore but some young pantalooned coxcomb, a stranger, not the Pete he loved, so he turned away in pain after staring half a minute—this was outside Delmonico's—and fled up Broadway to the refuge of the crowds.

Pete, you're a son to me!

Stop jawing at me, Walt—you're leaning too close.

Walt clutched his awkward package to his ribs, leaned on the railing, and watched the Manhattan landing approach. Who was she, Pete? Men and women were leaving the cabins and crowding forward, he smelled them and felt their breath on his neck, then relaxed a little as they pressed up against him. "Walt!" someone shouted. Majestically he turned, felt himself smiling—as if in benediction—but couldn't find the voice. He leaned back against the railing so the crowd could rub itself across his vision. When the gates opened up he'd let them spill forward, then slowly stroll behind, absorbing their bustle. It gave him his strength. With his vacillating health, he needed all the infusions of life stuff he could manage, needed the name shouted out, the swift flash of eyes in the crowd, the come-hither posture, the nudge in his ribs, the secret unknown hand on his thigh . . .

He could toss the heavy package in the water and spare Pete the rebuff, spare himself the aggravation.

A pale young man in the middle of the crowd looked around nervously. *Be not afraid!* Walt wished he could cheer the poor fellow up and strengthen him with his animal magnetism, but too late, they landed, the gates opened up and the crowd poured ahead, first the horse carts and handcarts then the multitude padded in winter clothing, each person with his own ghostly breath on a string. As they spread out, the men began to spit—they'd been holding it in—and soon the yellow lines of tobacco juice flew everywhere. You couldn't look down—Walt never did—no way to avoid the noxious stuff. Why don't the ground itself sicken beneath it?

He strode forward slowly, smiling expectantly, maybe someone he knew was hanging around. Some dockworker, ticket taker . . . You could almost feel you were Christ sometimes if it weren't for annoying smart-aleck letters and the betrayal of friends you thought loved you. How grand it would be to lift that girl selling hot boiled sweet corn—it smelled so good!—up onto your cloud and allow her to linger. She'd seen Walt disembarking often enough to know who he was by now. Walt Whitman, a cosmos. Liberal and lusty as nature. He could elevate her with a powerful embrace if it weren't for the faintness and trembling he experienced, somehow tied in with those red lines running up his arm to his chest. It had come from repeatedly bending down to kiss the white faces of dying men in hospitals during the war, Walt was certain—but how could he have stopped himself? One kiss in '62 lasted thirty seconds and the boy died during it, Walt felt his breath go. Sometime during those war years, absorbing all the effluvia of dysentery and gangrene, all the noxious vapors of disease, he'd lost his health and strength, his system had been penetrated by a deadly virus, or maybe the malaria, which crawled straight into his heart like a worm. Now he felt merely the shell of his strength. It came back in wishes, in powerful projections, in hallos and embraces so surprisingly large he felt himself double in size, then deflate all at once while whatever it was—that burst he'd just felt— evaporated in the air.

On the landing behind the corn girl stood boys selling papers—the *World*, the *Tribune*. Up ahead a horsecar pulled out with a noise that crept up your legs to your molars, that heavy iron rumble of wheels in the tracks. Two boys ran by with hay from the hay barge they'd slept in last night still clinging to their coats. Walt lumbered forward to the Broadway coach.

"Duffy!"

"Hey, Walt."

"You're driving this line?"

The hard part was getting up—one foot on the shaft, the next on the footboard—but Duffy helped with a strong swift pull that gave Walt the sudden sweats.

Then he was up there, next to the driver, his favorite spot in creation, and the stage pulled forward up Fulton Street. As the fares boarded, Walt checked back through the hole in the roof to make sure they paid.

"That time they reported me," Duffy was saying, "I had to go drive the Third Avenue horsecars."

"That's hell on horses."

"Lost nine horses in one day last summer, Walt. Long routes on the rush—the line don't show no mercy to cattle."

"Frank McKinney still drive that route?"

"All new drivers, every one. Staging too dull. Frank died of the hacking cough he had."

"Such a young man."

"Old. Retired."

Walt felt his face form a querulous *Oh*, an old man's confusion. He looked around puzzled. I'm only fifty! Always bodily sweet and fresh, eat the right foods, dress plainly and simply. Leave my window open at night . . .

He couldn't quite remember Frank McKinney but tried to prevent all his friends from the past, young men also, from turning into names like him and running out through the same hole in his brain. Fred Kelly, Charley McLaughlin, Balky Bill . . . When you die, just your name is left.

Then he thought of Pete handing that girl into her carriage. After all the flowers he'd sent him! The tender notes with kisses in the pages . . .

"What's that you got, Walt?"

Walt gripped his package. "Present for Pete."

"Pair of boots?"

"Sure. With the muck worms still on them." Walt laughed out loud. "I'm *returning* a present."

"Oh-oh."

The stage made the turn at Broadway and squeezed into traffic. Votaries of fashion hooped up and down past St. Paul's Chapel. The carriages on Broadway, the stages, carts, the hotel and private coaches, the green and yellow mail truck pulled by horses, the large vans with lanterns still hung beneath their rear axles, the flat-bed drays piled high with casks,

all inched forward down below Walt exclusively for his personal amusement. Druggists, grocers, shoemakers, tailors—printers at their cases in
a window—rooms filled with goods at wholesale, so much broadcloth
and silk, so many boxes of ribbands, countless shelves of chisels, locks,
saws, screws, knives, brass knobs, hinges. Five thousand dollars worth of
goods on one person walking down Broadway! Plumes, fringes, scarfs,
cloaks, gold watches and chains, curls, whiskers, glitter and gloss, bows
and smiles, spit and brass, glass and marble. It gave Walt such joy he
simply observed it for the five-hundredth time and wondered if it wasn't
all flashes and specks. When the traffic stopped he leaned back and
smiled. The fine curls on that woman on the sidewalk took eighteen
hours in papers to produce, and her bedroom at home was a scene of
disorder even now, teacups half full, brushes and combs strewn across
the sheets . . .

Past City Hall.

The splendid buildings, the endless panorama, spread out and crum-
bled at the edges east and west. A pig scurried down Reade Street
through garbage and earthenware jars full of coal ashes. Children
pitched pennies on a brownstone's steps. Up here, the farther east and
west from Broadway you went, the more entire buildings you found shut
off from the sun both winter and summer. No wonder gangs like the
Swamp Angels—wastrels and laggards who enjoyed mashing duffers and
chumps—preferred living in sewers, where they also stored booty. One
tenement called the Dirty Spoon had caught fire six times that winter,
but refused to burn when the dirt on the walls proved too thick. Whole
families lived in rat-infested cellars and came out for light only at midday.
Cholera epidemics spread through air shafts, alleys, lead pipes, through
holes in rotten floorboards in closets and stairways. In the hallways,
bacteria bred in explosions on handles of pumps above communal wall
sinks.

"So long!" Walt stepped down at Worth Street. He felt stronger now,
but Duffy still helped him. Walt seemed to tip and pitch when he moved,
anybody might be afraid he'd spill. Worth Street to the east began the
Sixth Ward and Five Points, but Walt turned west. One night last
summer, in a doorway here on Worth Street, Walt had told Pete about
the heavenly bodies, the stars—something deep—and found him in the
middle of it fast asleep with his head on Walt's shoulder like a chunk of
wood.

A boy walked by carrying a pail of beer. Walt clutched the package
to his chest. On the sidewalk, what with the boxes and old barrels amid
rusty chunks of iron and the rubble of brick, you couldn't exactly stroll,

more like pick your way and shuffle. He felt himself entering a darkness. Down one alley that put out the sun—hardly any sky there—all you could see were rotten back porches. And an Indian stood in the middle of this alley! Or a person dressed in full Indian costume, sash, beads, feathers, mocassins. Small, less than five feet tall, hardly ninety pounds, he held something out, thrust it right in Walt's face. Walt had no choice but to take it. "What's this?"

"A million-dollar bill."

The small man with a large white nose smiled at Walt in his Indian headdress. He sported a handlebar mustache. The million-dollar bill on heavy rag paper held moonlit landscapes in exquisite detail, fine printing, all those numbers, and right in the middle a miniature portrait of the grinning man himself in his mustache and high white collar . . .

Walt dropped the bill and scurried up the alley gripping the package tight to his chest . . .

In Cow Bay—an alley off an alley—Peter Doyle blew on his fingers and reached in the box for another shirt collar. Paper collars. He could burn them all if he ran out of charcoal, the charcoal which smoldered in tin pails below him at the foot of his cot, beside the bedpan—another tin pail—half sticking out. It stunk, but Pete smiled when the collar stayed put. He did a little break-down jig on the dirt floor in the only space there not piled high with his junk.

Pigeon feet landed on the corrugated roof, or maybe garbage. It seemed to trickle down like peelings. The disadvantage of this lean-to of course was the tenement house and its windows up above. And why even empty the bedpan? When the breeze was right, the foul smell wafting from the row of closets outside crawled into bed with you anyway. No matter how deeply you burrowed down into your muddy old blankets, it was always there.

But Pete didn't mind. He whistled "Dixie." He tied his red tie and pulled on his jacket, the single-breasted worsted he saved for less ceremonious occasions. After the meeting he could return and change to the clawhammer tailcoat of fine gray linen, the trousers of broadcloth, the white lawn tie . . .

He always emerged from his hovel first rate, sharp, up to the scratch. He left the dirt behind. He owned clothes for every occasion, for every hour of the day and day of the week, and by careful sorting and strict segregation they stayed clean and trim, the garbage never touched them. To see Pete strolling down Broadway you'd never guess what kind of wretched cocoon he'd just emerged from. He'd lived here since moving up north from Washington, one home was just as good as another, the place where you slept didn't say what you were. Pete knew what he was—Walt had told him—the product of our complete break with Europe. It took two generations, said Walt, to erase the social memory. And if you broke with Europe, England above all, you could be anything you wanted once you stepped out that door—a bum, a dandy, a financier. A stage driver, lady's man, cowboy, congressman.

He pulled a towel down from a nail and stepped out onto frozen mud. If the air here was colder than inside he could barely tell. Hope the pump ain't frozen. Everything's gray. Ragpicker's sacks propped against walls made Pete think of dead Confederate soldiers, except the sacks looked fatter. He removed his coat, laid it smartly across a high burlap bag, and pumped with a fury to get a good stream. He stuck his head under, blowing all the while with pursed lips just as hard as he could. And the cold water came, it wouldn't stop pouring. Eyes closed, Pete heard the handle squeaking madly just before his flailing arms struck a belly. "Who's that?"

"All gussied up, son? Hands clean? Inspection." Walt pumped as hard as a man chopping wood. Pete shook his head, looking at Walt, then thrust his hands beneath the cold stream. "You wash too much, Pete." Walt kept on pumping.

"Don't rupture yourself from overexertion."

"God knows, I'm not opposed to clean hands, but clean hands *can* be disgraceful too." Walt pumped harder. "You're getting too damn uncommon decent, son. You like your nice white hands too much. Let me shake some of my dust off on you. Are you that sore on dirt? Dirt's the cleanest thing there is. Children that eat it grow big and strong. Those are first-rate fancies you're wearing there, Pete. Nice tie. Has a grandmotherly tinge."

"Walt, don't whip yourself up so." Pete began drying his hair and hands on his greasy towel while Walt still pumped. At last he stopped and they walked to the lean-to, Pete up ahead on his pert little feet.

"Stepping out, son?"

"No."

"So you dressed up this way as you knew I was coming."

"Stop heaving yourself at me, Walt. I never knew you was coming."

Inside, Walt's head nearly touched the tin ceiling. "Here's Pete in a heap of nothings and somethings. You ought to push that shit pot under the bed, it stinks to the devil. Here's Pete in his sty as clean as a whistle. Someone *else* is coming. All I can figure."

"Shut your fly trap, Walt. Ain't nobody coming."

"Oh Pete." Walt sat heavily on Pete's cot—it sagged beneath his weight. "You used to tell me everything. All your cares and hopes. What happened? I wish you'd think of me more." Walt looked around at Pete's appalling junk as though seeing it for the first time, amazed. Pete rummaged in a pile of it by the door. Then he turned and glanced down at Walt, who smiled sweetly and—he couldn't help it—batted his eyelashes. "Duffy asked for you, Pete. He's back on the Broadway stage."

"I heard."

"Pete. Dear son. I think about you every day. I even miss your growling and complaining. First you'd complain, then you'd put your arm around my neck to make it all right again. Who would have thought I'd wind up like this? I mean my general caving in."

Pete dipped his fingers into a can of macassar oil and rubbed it in his hair. He stood by the single window, where a fragment of mirror hung. Walt's whine sunk deeper into his throat. "Who would have thought you'd wind up so healthy and me so sick, Pete? Come back to Washington City. I could get us a good room or two in some quiet place. You could take care of me and root out my sickness and make me stronger and healthier than ever—I know you could! I could go on at the Attorney General's office and you could work on the trains. We'd send your mother enough to keep the pot a-boiling at home."

"How much?"

"What's that?"

"How much would we send my mother?"

"Name a sum."

"Twenty-five pieces of gold a week."

Walt jumped to his feet, hefting his package. "Very funny, son. You think I'm a fool."

"Oh Walt, settle down. I was just teasing."

"Don't try my patience, son. I'll get square with you if you make fun of me. When she comes, your sweetheart, tell her Walt Whitman was here." Under the low ceiling, Walt towered over Pete. His voice rose and trembled, and he staggered a little. "Tell her Walt Whitman had been to Manhattan for a long walk and at the end of the walk he'd come to this hovel and found you all diked out in your finest fancies and asked for some friendship and been refused. Tell her that!"

"My sweetheart? Are you touched?"

Walt lumbered to the door and half tore open the package. "And give her this!" He heaved it across the room where it struck a post with a clunk, shaking dirt down from the corrugated roof, then dropped to the earthen floor.

Pete looked down at the ugly thing, stunned. With a rag he brushed dirt from his shoulders and head. Walt had left the door wide open, and the light, such as it was, caught on the floor that familiar crystal bulb, that tapered brass turret, that silver mounting with its funny spiked tips. He remembered it at once, his loving gift to Walt of a year ago now. When friends return gifts is it finally over? Pete hoped so, then regretted the hope. Walt was such a father to him, he missed him already. He could have struck *me* with that thing—was he aiming? And look, he broke it, a plate or something cracked open on the bottom. Pete knelt before it. And what's *this* dingus that fell out . . . ?

An hour later, after aimless wandering, Walt entered the Fowler and Wells Phrenological Museum on Broadway to have his head read. The dollar charge for a reading—down from years ago—usually proved worthwhile for the peace of mind it gave. He loved to sit there amid all those busts, death masks, and plaster skulls—Washington, E. A. Poe, John Wesley Powell, Napoleon Bonaparte, famous Indian chiefs, African cannibals, wives of great leaders, geniuses, dwarves, lions, hyenas—and listen to the familiar litany of his own robust qualities. They liked Walt's head here because it was large. When they read it he sat right in the window, a living advertisement.

Charts on the walls showed the circumference of the heads of various presidents, rows of chins and noses, fetal heads in successive stages of growth, and the names, numbers, and locations of all the mental organs, each illustrated on the profile of a head by appropriate pictures: Memory by a clock and book, Agreeableness by a smiling child, Combativeness by two boxing boys, Veneration by a kneeling woman . . . Just staring at it made Walt's brain light up, made gas jets turn on in room after room of his head so that certain areas seemed to grow and throb. For such an important reading, Lorenzo Fowler himself did the honors. His fingers were soft. Of course, he'd grown old in the twenty years since Walt's first reading, as the world had grown old. He had horrible dandruff, he shuffled and stumbled. His wall charts had yellowed as well, the busts and plaster death masks had cracked, nothing been dusted in dozens of years, and the rug in the reading room had long ago worn clean through to the floor in a semicircle around the chair.

But Lorenzo relaxed Walt. Just his voice, the feel of his fingers, the

reassuring list of character traits that reminded Walt he was indeed Walt
Whitman. He looked Walt over, noting his bone structure. "You were
blessed by nature with a good constitution and power to live to a ripe
old age."

"Nothing wrong with me?"

"You were not—like many—prematurely developed. Did not get ripe
like a hothouse plant. You can last long and grow better as you grow
older, sir, if you obey the laws of health."

A secretary sitting at a desk nearby took down all the phrenologist
said. From his pocket, Lorenzo drew a tape and measured Walt's head.
"Twenty-three and one half inches," he said. "A magnificent circumference." Then, with one hand on Walt's forehead and the other on his
basilar portion, he felt with the balls of his fingers, pressing the skin
gently but firmly enough to move it over the bone in little circles. He
plowed deeply through Walt's long white hair, then leaned forward,
cocked his head, probed, listened, and moistened his lips. "You are one
of the most friendly men in the world," he said, "and your happiness is
greatly dependent on your social relations."

Amen, thought Walt.

"You are familiar and open in your intercourse with others but you
do not by so doing lose your dignity. You are no hypocrite but are plain
spoken and are what you *appear* to be at all times. In fact, you are most
too open at times and have not always enough restraint in speech, sir.
You can adapt yourself to time, place, and company, but you do not try
to act another character." Lorenzo's fingers probed deeper and lower. He
felt along the middle lines of the head toward the base of the skull on
the back of Walt's neck, then below the occipital process, behind the
bottom of the ears, for the organ of Amativeness. Ah, there it was—Walt
felt it too—you couldn't miss it, it throbbed with such life! "That jug's
full," said Lorenzo. "Six or seven."

"*Seven*, sir?" The secretary looked up.

"I've seldom seen such a tendency toward connubial love and friendship, combined with such a strong inclination—bless my buttons!—
toward the pleasures of Voluptuousness and Alimentiveness, and a
certain reckless swing of animal will too," said Lorenzo.

Walt smiled to himself and relaxed beneath the fingers.

"Philoprogenitiveness, six. Adhesiveness, six. Inhabitiveness, six.
Concentrativeness, six. Combativeness, six . . ."

What about Acquisitiveness?

"Acquisitiveness low, about three or four . . ."

Walt nearly fell asleep beneath the fingers. He was back in Huntington, driving snakes from the springhouse, swimming naked in the surf off Paumanock. His mother stood talking with a squaw at the door . . .

Dear Miss Dickinson—

"Lorenzo, some stationery. Could I trouble you for a lap desk?" Walt felt imperious making such requests, but knew Lorenzo wouldn't mind. He'd chalk it up to Walt's reckless animal will.

"At your service."

> *Fowler and Wells*
> *308 Broadway*
> *New York*
> *23 Dec., 1869*
>
> **Dear Miss Dickinson,**
> *You will think yourself neglected or ignored by your unknown friend—but twenty times in the last month I have promised myself to write you.*
>
> *I live for these two months in the house of my mother, but work the rest of the year in Washington—Write this from the office of my medical advisers. Life rather sluggish here. My health is good but nibbled at the edges by the betrayal of friends and comrades. But your letter brought a ray of sunshine.*
>
> *I am very soon going to bring out a new edition of my Leaves, and will send you one.*
>
> *And now, my dear Miss Dickinson (or is it Mrs.?) I send you my barbaric yawp, & hope you will not think hard of me for not writing before.*
>
> *Walt Whitman*

Walt folded the letter and handed it to Lorenzo's secretary. "Would you . . . ?" She nodded. Out the large plate glass window before him the traffic passed in an unending stream. He blinked—there was Pete, strolling down Broadway with a grin and a swagger. It went straight to his heart. He was carrying something. Pete!

For the finishing touch, Lorenzo had pulled out his craniometer and held the thing up with trembling hands. It resembled a skullcap made of armadillo hide. But Walt heaved to his feet quick as lightning and pulled out his dollar—"Hold my chart, Lorenzo"—then brushed past the old man and scrambled to the door to catch sight of Pete before he disappeared in the Broadway crowd. Oh, the pain of it—Walt's heart swelled up. He had to ask the dear boy's forgiveness. But where was he off to? And why the smile on his face?

Chapter

❦ 2 ❦

The smile on Pete's face sprang from his plans to start a new life and become a new man. He skipped down Broadway in and out of the crowds around bustles of upholstered cloth and straw, jumped into the street and back on the sidewalk dodging carriages and stages, snatched his dainty feet in a jiffy away from the copious golden jets of descending tobacco juice. At the corner of Duane Street, a knife grinder grinned because Pete was grinning. A grin was not your personal possession, it skewered flocks of people at once—ran through a crowd on the street like a fracture. It was money, it flowed from one person to another, but first you had to have it. Bowler hat cocked forward, Pete with his free hand reached deep in his pocket for that five-dollar yellowback, soft as cloth. That grin. To start a new life cost five dollars on deposit, the rest payable at delivery. Ralph said he could work off the rest. Work doing what? Anything, everything. He could dress as a servant for dinner tonight and keep the water flowing. He could help Josie with the preparations. Stick around Pete, Pete the Great—you'll be useful. Pete wanted nothing more than to be useful. He liked Ralph Meeker; had told him frankly what a fine writer he thought he was. Ralph's father also wrote for the *Tribune*, America's newspaper, and Pete had once sold *Tribune*s on the street, then later worked briefly for the paper as a bellboy. So when he spotted that article three weeks ago, "A Western Colony," written by a Meeker, he'd naturally gone to Ralph to inquire, and found to his interest that Ralph's father wrote it and the whole Meeker family was in on the enterprise, with the backing of the *Tribune*'s editor, Horace Greeley.

Pete knew a main chance when he smelled it.

Besides, there was Walt, always pawing. He was grand, sure, but he could be a pest—had a lot of queerities and transcendental mummeries. He'd given Pete money so often that Pete finally had to tell him to keep it—he wanted Walt's friendship, not his money. Walt could be wonderful, of course, full of unction, he could stir you up clarion-like. When he wasn't tied down fast to his infirmities, what a good time it was just to walk down the street beside him, arm in arm. He knew all the men driving horses, every one. Hey Walt! Tough men in drays shouted at him to get his attention and make him shout back. When he smiled, you knew it—people stopped to watch as though some exotic Barnum animal had got loose. If you listened careful, you could hear the whispers too. Who's that? Walt Whitman. Who? Walt Whitman.

But you had to stay everlasting close with him, he was never satisfied with just a few words. If you rubbed his fur wrong what a rage he got into, but never as bad as today, he never threw things before. Pete had left Washington so Walt couldn't press him, but wouldn't you know, he followed him here. And that "sweetheart" business—he thought Pete had a sweetheart! Of course he was thinking of Josie Meeker. Pete knew Walt had spotted him with the Meeker family practicing his ministrations in a rented carriage—he'd seen Walt lurking outside Delmonico's. He knew when Walt followed him, he was doing it now. Let him follow. Let him think a fourteen-year-old child was his sweetheart. Pete could have told him who she was—the daughter of his prospective employer— but why bother? Walt never listened. Good riddance, Walt. She's a child, a sapling, uncommon pretty, sure, but a sweetheart?

Pete hefted his package under one arm and crossed Broadway down toward City Hall Park.

Two years ago he'd woken up one morning and realized he no longer talked like a Southerner. He'd lost his accent by rubbing up against countless Yankees as a conductor on the horsecars in Washington City. Later he became a driver, up front. It never got as cold in Washington as New York. After losing his accent he saw new meanings everywhere, and pictured his trek north as a steady climb upward, from South Carolina to Washington to Manhattan Island. If the Yankees won the war, they must know a thing or two; Pete could guess where his bread would be buttered. Besides, there was trouble back in South Carolina. He'd stopped a man from beating his wife—stopped him cold. But he didn't care to think about that. He only thought of it from far away, the farther the better. That way, the quick loud words went silent, the blows turned soft, the bearded face down below on the floor grew small, small as a prayer etched on a pinhead . . . With effort you could lose a memory that meticulous, but the effort meant going far away, first north and now, who knows, maybe west—west with the settlers.

At first in New York Pete had driven the horsecars. But he'd lost that job after being reported for allowing friends to ride free. Then he kicked around, did this and that. He worked on the docks loading cargo a while. He sold *Tribune*s and met Ralph Meeker, who got him temporary work as a copyboy, a job that brought him into daily contact with the great Horace Greeley.

Then he'd seen that article, gone to Ralph about it, and found that Nathan Meeker was Ralph's father, by golly. He was the one who proposed to unite with the proper persons in establishing a colony in Colorado Territory.

That's me, thought Pete. I'm a proper person.

It was spread out there on page eleven of the *Tribune* and described in sober prose a country well watered with streams and springs, with rich soil, temperate climate, healthy grass, pine groves, and snow-capped mountains in the distance. That wasn't the West Pete had read about, the place with savages, grizzlies, wolves, and barren deserts. During the war, the West was where deserters fled to, along with claim jumpers, gamblers, bounty hunters, bushwhackers, and assorted crazies escaping the law. The possibility that others might go there to escape not the law but overbearing poets and memories that crawled up from South Carolina had never occurred to Pete before. This man, Ralph's father, proposed to build a village on a railroad line modeled upon New England villages, with a church, a town hall, schoolhouse, village green, library, and horsecars. And he said he wanted temperance men. That was Pete too, he didn't drink—not much. He wanted folks with money as well. Here Pete felt on shakier ground. Among as many as fifty people, said the article, ten should have ten to twenty-five thousand dollars each, while others might have two hundred to a thousand or upward. "After a time poorer people may be received and have a chance." Amen. But five dollars got your foot in the door, hundreds had sent their five dollars in—more would bring them today to the meeting—Pete knew that from talking with Ralph. Today they would meet for the first time and organize. Pete thought he'd see what the organizers looked like, find out how the cat jumps. He could make himself handy and see what came of it. Someone had to pass out the paper and pencils. Someone had to count votes, take minutes, lug the money around, print circulars, run errands, and later on purchase the train tickets and shovels and seed and lumber and nails and kerosene. They needed sharp young people as much as rich old ones, didn't they? Think of Julius, who'd gone west on the train, saved a young child kidnapped by an Indian drunk on firewater, and bought a farm with his reward. At the end of the story he went back to New York and told all the newsboys to leave the city streets and go out west if they wanted to be rich. Pete still had the dog-eared book somewhere in his junk. *Julius; or, the Street Boy Out West.* It was kid's stuff but it stuck; they needed someone like Julius, didn't they? Someone with the knack of being in the right place at the right time. Sure, said Ralph. Come along and see what you can do—see if you like it. Come to the *Tribune* office beforehand and make yourself handy—help us get launched. Have you ever been a footman? Greeley needs a footman for the dinner afterwards. He doesn't keep servants as a practice, just special occasions.

Pete thought he'd give it a try.

He cut through City Hall Park in front of the courthouse toward Park Row and Printing House Square. Crossing Park Row was a nation of trouble—five sets of horsetracks, and stages, hansoms, trucks, and coaches slicing every which way through the milling people. He thought of Walt back there, lumbering precariously through this mess to follow, but resisted the impulse to turn back and take his arm. Walt could manage. Pete was a new man! By golly, he could have sweethearts if he wanted. And he could give gifts to pretty young girls and stoke up Walt's jealousy, just for spite if he cared to . . .

A man in a plug hat guessed people's weights on the sidewalk outside the *Tribune* building. Someone else leaned down to peer through a telescope for a penny's worth of daylight moon. Pete shot through the crowds and went in. He took the marble steps to the third floor slow, as the bundle in his arms weighed ten or twelve pounds. EDITORIAL ROOMS: RING THE BELL. But the door was open, folks swarmed in and out, and there was Josie—she smiled! Her brother jumped up from a couch and thrust a wooden box at Pete. "Pete the Great! Take this."

"What is it?"

"Ledger, paper slips, cash receipts, pens—you name it. A gavel. For the meeting."

Pete handed his package to Josie, who raised her eyes and tipped her head. She often appeared to slant when she stood. It was how she was growing up, Pete knew—at an angle to everyone else. If no one deserved that milky skin, those sharp eyes and nose, and the oversized lips that offset the rest, as though they'd been borrowed from someone else—

from Walt, let's say—then she'd live on a tangent. She'd be *strangely* beautiful. Her limbs reminded Pete of a crane's.

"What's this?" she asked.

"Christmas present for my sweetheart."

She blushed and stuck out her tongue. Ralph nodded at the knot of people in the office. "We'll go soon as Dad and Horace are set."

"It's *heavy*," said Josie. "What is it?"

"You'll see."

The couch in that office was piled high with books and newspapers save for a small worn spot at one end. Two busted cane-bottomed chairs stood beside it. A bookcase stuffed with directories and almanacs sat beneath an engraving on the wall, "The Landing of the Pilgrim Fathers," hardly visible beneath a layer of dust and fly excrement. Suspended on a heavy string hung from block and tackle over Horace Greeley's desk was a pair of scissors, and beside them dangled a bellpull for summoning copyboys. Uncle Horace himself—homely, spindly, large-headed, round-eyed—made the most noise of the men in that room. His voice squeaked like pulleys raising crates of air. They were waiting for his punch line. "I never said all dimmycrats are saloon keepers; I only said that all saloon keepers are dimmycrats!"

The laughter struck like a fish breaking water, and whiskered men stirred and shuffled, bankers, railroad men, prospective investors, colonists. One waxed his mustache with two deft strokes. Seated at his desk—all the rest were standing—Greeley swung around to check his clock. His long white hair looked powdered, and his colorless face, swinging back like an owl's, was chased with a thousand hairline cracks. His whiskers seemed stuffed in his collar. From the top of a layer of books, papers, clippings, and letters spread across his desk, he grabbed his hat—his famous wide-brimmed, fuzzy white hat—and jumped to his feet. "Gentlemen—go west!"

"Haa haaa."

"What chin music."

They parted for him while he skirted the desk, arms flying—"Nate!" He'd surrounded his profusion of shirt collar with the immense black silk handkerchief he preferred to a necktie, and now pulled on the duster he wore through the winter—he knew it made a spectacle, oversized and white—and headed for the stairs. "Where's Nathan Meeker?"

"Right here."

It struck Greeley that his protégé, standing by the door, dressed in a sober black clawhammer frock coat, resembled a species of dignified undertaker. He needed more spunk, this wasn't a wake they were off to, but a birth! Horace took his arm. "Our friends have bottom, and the bottom won't drop. Let the heathen rage," he said. "Irrigation is the key to prosperity in the West. I'll say as much by way of introducing you. I wager they'll be a cooperative bunch."

"Some of these here look like sharps," said Meeker.

"In the absence of other testimony, I judge righteous judgment—not from appearances."

"Well. Long ago, I learned how much cooperation people would bear."

"They'll bear as much as you can pile on if it means a new life in a new world."

Nathan Meeker lowered his head and spoke with conviction. "It does."

When they left, Pete was the last out the door and down the steps, waddling with that heavy wooden box. On the street a carriage waited with Josie, Ralph, and Nathan inside. He heaved the box up; the coachman strapped it down. Then Josie extended her hand to Pete as he stepped in, and instinctively he swiveled his head to search the busy sidewalk. There he was—Walt—in a crowd around an apple cart, with as mournful an expression hanging from his face as Pete had ever seen. Poor old horse. Pete's heart went out to him. Had he noticed Josie's package? He ducked behind two women out of sight.

Pete sat down across from Josie.

Up Park Row to the Bowery went the carriage. Josie's present lay across her lap under the blanket that covered her legs. She bit her lip, smiling; Pete smiled back; then she closed her eyes.

She knew he was watching her, that's why she'd closed them—to think undistracted. But what shall I think of? Skating. Falling from a great height. Let's try Colorado Territory, as described by father. The valley with the strange reddish monumental rocks shooting up like sculptures or temples; the river emerging from a gateway in the mountains; the peaks with eagle nests on their very summits . . . And the savage Indians, who once had come down from the mountains regularly to hunt buffaloes on the plains, but now came to get their free blankets and flour from the government, came riding on their horses with faces all vermilion paint, Daddy said, and babies strapped in cradles on their backs, and you could hardly tell the women from the men, they both had such long black hair and no beards. When Josie grew older she could teach them in a school. She'd calculated that would be in almost fourteen hundred days, when she turned eighteen.

Then she opened her eyes and looked out the carriage window at a dead pigeon frozen on the sidewalk by a horse trough. She smiled to herself. I wonder if I shan't die on such a day as this? In her mind, she carefully formulated the words describing the scene of the tragic hour. One o'clock in the afternoon, the pigeon frozen by the horse trough, and the sparrow shivering with ice in his mouth . . .

Pete was funny. His jaw dropped that time she'd told him she had seventeen thousand more days to live. In other words, Peter, a lifetime. Say I live to sixty, that's forty-six times three sixty-five. Seventeen thousand, more or less. What if you lived to seventy? he asked. It was obvious to Josie he'd never thought of such things. She and her sister used to calculate their future regularly; in two thousand days I'll be married, said Roz. They tried to imagine what they'd look like then, gazed in the looking glass and pictured some future Josie or Roz looking back, or failing that, carved this picture of themselves gazing and yearning toward the future into their very brains for grown-up Josie and Roz to remember thousands of days in the future. Now Roz *was* grown up, in Philadelphia—unmarried—and did she remember? They never heard from Roz. She'd almost drowned when Josie was five, and claimed she'd had water on the brain ever since.

Josie shifted the bundle in her lap. A present from Pete! Boots. A silver spade to break ground in Colorado Territory. A candelabra maybe. Cuckoo clock or musical instrument, oboe or trumpet.

I could have figured wrong. She coughed. Let's say seventeen *hundred* days. I could die of consumption before I'm twenty-six, just like John Keats. She coughed again and her father swiveled his head to regard her, with concern. My goodness, she thought, it hardly takes any effort at all to make yourself cough, it feels so—so *natural*—feels suited to my woolly lungs.

They passed Grand Street, where the Christmas shops and sidewalk vendors clustered and the swarming crowds slowed horses to a crawl. In windows lit up by gas jets were rows of umbrella-shaped windmills whose revolutions set two black men to ferociously saw a fallen log, or a lord and a lady facing each other to sink into a paroxysm of bows. Dolls sat in rows on shelves in those windows, and chameleon tops made in Paris spun on the floor for as long as ten minutes, Ralph Meeker had timed them. He'd shopped on Grand Street just that morning, poked his finger into bushels of bonbons heaped in carts on the sidewalk. Of course, he couldn't eat bonbons, only Graham bread and apples, at least as long as his father was nigh. No grease, meat, alcohol, tea, coffee, butter, or salt. Boiled vegetables, whole fruit, and bread, and external and internal applications of water. And be *cheerful* at meals. At night, leave your bedroom windows open, even winters. Chew that stale bread over and over, the exercise does you considerable good, Ralph. He'd noticed his father chewing today, but it wasn't Graham bread—he was back on tobacco. And Ralph knew what a caving-in that meant, what chastisements his father would silently heap upon his own head for his weakness. No doubt he was nervous about the meeting today. Too much to attend to, too many details. Strangers had sent him their money on trust. To *found* a colony—what an awesome responsibility! To make the desert bloom . . . Someday it might be a thriving city, thought Ralph—a whole empire, who knows—and his father be thought of as Romulus and Remus, or maybe Aeneas, or at least William Penn.

But Nathan wasn't thinking of his awesome responsibilities. Across from Ralph, staring out at Grand Street, he was fighting the pain in his face. He had the ague in his jaw again. Maybe it was the tobacco this time, but it seemed to come every winter regardless, making the jaw inflamed and swollen and throwing the whole face into a fever. Trailing in its wake would come the indigestion, the first rumblings of which he began to feel now in the pit of his stomach. Soon the cholic would begin shooting through his bowels—and he had to make a speech within minutes.

Of course, the ague gave him good color. In his collar and tie and modest frock coat, he knew he looked handsome. Distinguished and responsible. That would quiet the doubts of those who recalled he'd once belonged to a Fourierite colony that had failed miserably, though he didn't organize *that* one. From his experience at Trumbull Phalanx, twenty or more years ago now—when Ohio was still thought of as the West—Nathan had learned that two things were absolutely necessary for a colony to succeed: money on the table and a healthy climate. In Ohio, the low ground and swampy conditions meant everyone had the ague half the time. The doctors dosed with quinine wholesale, but still the noxious vapors spread. Most of the organizers, who'd bought the land on credit, fled at the first signs of illness, leaving latecomers like Nathan to scrape their meager savings together just to make the annual interest payments. He'd lasted six years; Ralph was born there. Two years after he quit he went back and found the place cleared out, the shanties torn down and carted off for materials, no tannery, wagon shop, smithy, or sawmill, just the stone foundation of the boardinghouse left.

With a lesson like that to go by, Nathan knew what he was about this time. So did Horace Greeley. No ague in the Colorado Territory because it was dry, but of course you needed water for crops. Therefore, locate next to a river and irrigate. Horace was all for it. Buy up all the land around beforehand so you have room to grow and the shameless land-gougers can't thrive. Joint stock and labor according to the Fourier system, in which the profits of their products go to the producers instead of being made pawns of speculation and traffic. Let the nonproducers rot; locate your colony far enough away from middlemen and financiers so *they* couldn't get their fingers in the pie. The capital stock to be upwards of a million dollars, made up of real estate, movable property, monies, or equivalents, divided into shares and controlled by a board of directors, Nathan Meeker president. Horace had such faith in the concept he'd already loaned Nathan fifteen hundred dollars. All they needed were more men of conviction, people who shared the values Nathan and Horace shared—temperance, the Graham table, the Fourier system, and no tobacco, not even a spittoon.

Nathan looked across at Pete in his cocked hat; maybe Pete could hold his tobacco a while, so Horace wouldn't see it, then dole it out gradually, a little less each time. He could chew newspaper, he'd done that before.

The response to the call in the *Tribune* had been nothing short of overwhelming. Over a thousand letters received—half sent money too, while others averred as they had plenty of it. Who knows, they might even reach Charles Fourier's magic number: 1,620 souls. That's when the laws of social harmony tripped in, when the geometrical calculus of passionate attraction reconciled and placed in peaceful order the appetites and conflicting interests of all. They could even try some of Fourier's more innovative ideas, such as dignifying work by placing it within colonnaded tabernacles surrounded by orchards and fountains.

But no free love. No amorous and gastronomical orgies. And Nathan seriously doubted Fourier's assertion that humans would grow seven feet tall and develop a sort of tail, the archi-arm. Or that Constantinople would become the capital of the world once the Phalanx system was universally applied. He'd thought years ago maybe Association *would* sweep the world, but then Trumbull Phalanx failed, and one by one all the others—Brook Farm, New Harmony, the Icarian colonies. So practical-minded Nathan Meeker had lowered his sights; for the last twenty years he'd owned a store in Illinois. But then he'd become Agricultural Editor of the *Tribune* under Horace Greeley, he'd moved to New York, reported on innovative agrarian ideas, and gradually, lighting each other up, he and Uncle Horace—both in their sixties now—had rewarmed the dreams of their youth, tempered now with wisdom and experience. They agreed that sober, industrious men like Nathan Meeker had to weed out Fourier's more locofoco ideas in order to reap the benefits of Fourieristic association. In a right-thinking community there would be no idlers, hangers-on, groaners, militia, tax collectors, or divorcées. The rich and the poor, the smart and the stupid, the handsome and the ugly, would all live in harmony. But you needed some practical notions too—good fencing, irrigation—in order to properly seize the dream. Seize the dream and plant it—Nathan made a fist.

Then a colicky dart shot through his stomach.

But the light was in his eyes now. Ralph could see it across from his father. Pete would have seen it as well if he hadn't been casting sheep's eyes at Josie, who had curled against her father to borrow some of his heat.

People seemed to be expecting them. On the sidewalk, men and women gave way, and the lingering crowds on the steps to Cooper Institute followed behind. First came Nathan, with a long steady stride, eyes fixed dead ahead; then Josie, whose high legs gathered in considerable yardage and whose skinny arms carried with ease Pete's mysterious gift; then Ralph, short of breath, scrambling to keep up; and lastly Pete with his wooden box, the box without which the meeting couldn't happen. He had to crane his neck around it to keep from tumbling down the steps inside.

The long marble and wood Great Hall in the basement of Cooper Institute contained enough people, it seemed to Pete, to spawn half a dozen colonies. "Make way, mind the box." They sat on chairs, stood against the pillars, and filled the entryways and steps leading down, men, women, and children, but the majority men, mostly strangers to each other, faithful readers of Greeley's *Tribune*, fully prepared to board up their hardware stores, sell their farms, pack up their calipers and trowels, their surgical instruments, law books, sewing machines, rifles, scales, meat cleavers, baseball bats, curling papers and bird cages, and board a train for God knows what greener pastures in the great West. They were going to do it rationally this time—no wagon trains, no tent cities, no saloons and whiskey tents selling forty-rod whiskey at twenty-five cents a glass—no flour at fifteen dollars the bushel and water at a dime a bucket. You planted a town in a gridiron pattern next to the train depot, with the north-south streets named after trees and the cross streets numbered. Water flowed down irrigation ditches into everyone's fields. At the center of it all was the bandstand where Germans gave concerts on Sundays. The folks in Cooper Institute moved their feet restlessly, as though itching to be off already; some had come from as far away as Kentucky. They looked around at each other buzzing and frowning—a few introduced themselves and shook hands—with a thin scowl of country skepticism coating for good measure faces that entertained openly the possibility of creating a New York, a Philadelphia, a Boston, or a Baltimore in the wilderness—eventually. They were ready to be galvanized.

In that unheated room they gave off enough warmth that Pete had to remove his coat once he'd thumped down his box on a table up on stage. Horace Greeley had already removed his; but Nathan Meeker kept his on to maintain his dignity.

Right away Pete smelled the various shades of sweat, leather, powder, and soap given off by the seven or eight hundred people there. He could see that some, unsure of what to wear, had overdressed in fancy frock coats and silk vests, whereas others wore their bib overalls, jerkins, and plaid shirts with wool underwear peeking out.

Just my type, he thought.

But he sat next to Josie up on stage anyway, and resolved to keep his mind open. If you let yourself become a kind of conductor you could pass along the electricity, and it didn't much matter what generated it. He reached for Josie's hand—it was hot.

"Gentlemen!" Horace Greeley was rapping the gavel like someone already nailing together his castle in the desert. "Gentlemen! To my left, Mr. Nathan Meeker, originator of the idea that has brought us together. To my right, General Palmer of the Kansas Pacific Railroad. Mr. Phineas T. Barnum." A cheer rose up. "Mr. Oliver Ames, president of the Union Pacific Railroad. Mr. Jo Benton, his associate. Mr. Albert Brisbane of the *Tribune.* Mr. Joseph Young, from faraway Salt Lake City." This set the crowd to buzzing—Brigham Young's son! "Members of Mr. Meeker's family and entourage." That meant him too, Pete realized. He shifted in his seat, gave a slight nod—suddenly they all seemed to be watching *him*—and stole a peek at P. T. Barnum, who looked fat and genial enough. He released Josie's hand, in case someone noticed.

Next to Barnum, Joseph Bonaparte Delafolie Benton surveyed the crowd, gauged the level of anticipation, and judged it to be just about right. The colors red and gray prevailed; everyone looked ready to gobble. He adjusted his cravat, sighed through his nose. This might be *fun* if he kept alert . . .

"Gentlemen. This is a meeting of persons who propose emigrating to a colony to the west. I've been there. I've seen the border ruffians, the savage Indians, and the land sharks and idlers squatting on their quarter sections in cabins that would make fair hog pens, living hand to mouth, with hardly an acre of prairie broken. I've seen the bad, but I've seen the good too. The Indians don't bother settlers much now." Speaking, Greeley waved his arms and swayed backward and forward, as though it were anatomically impossible to stand erect and talk, both. The tufts of hair on either side of his chin had crawled out like a form of corrosion. He stood behind the box Pete had carried in and had to shout a bit since his weak and husky voice didn't carry too far in that big hall. The colonists sat very still to listen. "The railroad has changed everything out west. Eight months ago on a lonely alkalied plain in Utah the golden spike was drove and the great national road completed." A faint cheer. "New York is filled with people. So is Boston. There are thousands who want to come hither never thinking that the cost of living will eat up their earnings. I dislike to see men in advanced life working for salaries in places where they're ordered about by boys. I believe that there ought to be not only one but a thousand colonies. The earth, air, waters, and sunshine were divinely intended for the sustenance and enjoyment of the whole human family. But the present *fact* is, most people are landless. Well, now's your chance, boys!" Another cheer, this one louder. "Providence is not bankrupt. The time is to come when every foot of the desert will bloom. It only needs water, and this can be had by systematic irrigation, and the great plains and the mountains too will be covered with a great, industrious, independent people." More cheers, but Greeley didn't smile—he more or less grimaced. He'd done this before, given rousing speeches—it still felt good—but he was just bearing witness here. "Now then. The first thing to do is organize. One man cannot do the work of a hundred. Mr. Meeker will tell you what we propose."

The crowd huzzahed, then sobered up when they saw Nathan Meeker. Tall and erect, he stood there like a judge. They waited while he waited, looking solemn and handsome, before the faint smile on his lips opened up and words came marching out. "About one thousand letters have been received, which are filed away." He tapped the box. His deep voice carried with ease in that hall. "The writers represent all pursuits and all professions, and their aggregate wealth exceeds one million five hundred thousand dollars." This set the crowd to buzzing again; Pete scanned the audience. These people? That rich?

Jo Benton perked up too. Smiling, he nudged Oliver Ames, impassive in the seat beside him. He looked out at the crowd. American industry, thought Jo. American wealth in *those* gnarled hands, so clumsy and rude. When fools like Greeley and Meeker thought they were farmers— and the farmers bought it—it showed you what farmers' shrewdness amounted to. It didn't take much to pry such men from their cash. Just encourage the delusion of growing bigger turnips somewhere else, far away.

"Mr. Barnum plans to invest in our colony. So does Mr. Greeley. As soon as we propose a location, money should be ready to buy all the land the members want in a solid block. We should have enough land to sell lots for establishing schools, a library, a town hall and park, and it may be possible for some to have as much as 160 acres nearby. Irrigation will be necessary. There will be privations, at first. You will agree that the leading object is to have schools, churches, and good society; and those who are idle, immoral, intemperate, or inefficient need not apply, for they will not be received. Nor would they feel at home." He paused for a wave of polite applause. "A man with a family will require five hundred dollars, and even then there will be privations, as I said." Meeker glanced down at the squirming multitude, suddenly at a loss for words. Their faces went puzzled but still looked eager. One grizzled man toward the front sucked a lemon. A thought haunted Nathan—what if they could see the birthmark on his side? Larger than a watermelon and blue as ink, it wasn't visible through his clothes, he knew that, but if people *could* see it, what would they think of him?

At last someone shouted, "Where is this place?"

Nathan didn't answer. He continued to stand there looking serious and thoughtful till Greeley jumped up. "Mr. Meeker does not wish to give the locality of the place for fear that speculators will flock in and buy up all the desirable land. That's the way things are done nowadays."

"We have several locations in mind," Meeker said at last. "All healthy, well wooded, with water close by, and a varied and rich soil suited for grass. Coal and other minerals nearby. Fruit trees, pine trees, natural resources, beautiful scenery. I propose we establish a Locating Committee to choose the best of these."

"Seconded," said Greeley.

Ralph Meeker leaned across Josie to Pete and tugged at his sleeve. "You'll be wanted as recording secretary," he said.

To thunderous *ayes* in that cavernous hall, the colonists elected a Locating Committee; then they backed up and elected officers for their colony: Nathan Meeker, President; General Robert A. Cameron, Vice-President; Horace Greeley, Treasurer. They elected an Executive Committee; they resolved that each member present pay five dollars for current expenses. Those who'd already sent their money in had been duly recorded, the rest would be now. Questions?

"What about the redskins?"

"I think it is an answer," said Meeker, "that I propose to take my own family."

"Is there grizzlies and wolves?"

"None to speak of."

"Mr. Greeley, do you propose settling in this colony?"

Greeley stood up again; Meeker sat down. "I have my newspaper to mind and feed in New York. I'll be your distant champion, men, in more ways than one. You speak of the Indians. In Colorado, they are friendly and tame. The grizzlies and wolves have been driven up the mountains, they won't bother you none unless you go trekking there, then take your torches—that's the way it's done. I've seen this country, boys—it's sweeter than honey. The air's blue and clear and smells magnificent sweet. It don't snow much winters at all. Don't rain to speak of either, but if you have water at your command, rain is a superfluity. It's a new age, boys. You've got your passage to China—the railroad. You've got industrial progress everywhere. It's the railroad that brings it. Never mind about the grizzlies; the steam engines scared off the varmits. We've succeeded in bending the powers of Nature to serve the general purposes of human life. Ain't that the damndest thing you ever heard of?" They were cheering again, they'd begun moving forward. "Hail to the age of steam, I say! We're the youngest of peoples, but we're teaching the world how to march forward. We've built the longest ribbon of iron ever built by man. Mr. Ames, take a bow. Mr. Oliver Ames of the Union Pacific Railroad."

Oliver Ames stood up and displayed a face of slab wood. The crowd cheered him, pressing forward. Greeley shook his hand, then disappeared into the swarming multitude, wiping his own hand on his pants. His praise of the transcontinental railroad was for the idea of it, the patriotic purpose. As for the Union Pacific company itself, he was a journalist, he had his ear to the ground. He knew the den of thieves who'd built the UP had picked the government's pockets, and the scandal would boil over sooner or later. He'd break the news himself in the *Tribune*—but first let this colony put down its roots. Let it buy railroad land if it had to, he could lean on Oliver for a decent price. He could weasel bargain rates for the trip west too if he buttered up Oliver and his assistant enough.

At the table, Pete was besieged by prospective colonists, all wanting their names recorded. With the tip of his tongue caught between his teeth, he wrote them down till his hand grew numb. He wrote down his own name too, but kept his five dollars buried in his pocket, because these people were wealthy when you added them up—Pete saw that now—so why spend his own cash? Each man peeled off his five from a roll of lifetime savings. If you didn't chew or drink, see how much you could save! "Thank God for Horace Greeley," he heard someone say. Someone else said, "It's a beehive of Fourierites." But they handed in their five dollars anyway. They were all excited, it was in the air, Pete felt it too. It's a new age, boys! "Name?"

"George Adams."

"Five dollars, please. Name?"

"Minor Hedges."

"Five dollars, please . . ."

Oliver Ames contined shaking hands and receiving the adulation of colonists. On the bench alone behind him, Jo Benton regarded the hayseed multitude and thought, Oh yes, this would be easy . . .

Chapter

3

When Jo woke up on that ship a year ago minus his reliquary, he discovered the hands on the ends of his arms throttling the neck of a man named George. It came back to him six months later, after his first taste of opium in a house on Greene Street: throttling George had been like grasping in opium dreams the snowy neck of his sainted mother. But how George landed in the river Jo could barely recall. The next thing he knew he'd come to in a hospital bed with no money to pay for it—and where was George now? Worse, where was his reliquary? He thought at first the doctors had taken it, and demanded its return. In reply, the nurses dosed him with carbolic acid and the doctors reminded him this was a pay ward—but Jo had neither identification nor money.

He had connections, though. His signature was good at any bank with links to the Bank of Maryland, whose founder and first president had fathered Jo's Aunt Betsey. With her money he paid his hospital bill and boarded a train to Baltimore to stay with her. He couldn't very well return to France now that the Empire was crumbling, couldn't return to England either after what he'd done to Stokes. Aunt Betsey found him work in the one American company modeled on sound French principles, the Union Pacific Railroad. Its holding company, Crédit Mobilier of America, had in fact been named after Crédit Mobilier de France, with which one of the Union Pacific founders had been impressed on a trip abroad. It was Aunt Betsey's notion that Jo's handlebar mustache and Imperial chin tuft à la Louis-Napoleon, his French lace and gold-headed walking stick, would lend an exotic flavor to the selling of railroad bonds in skeptical, tobacco-chewing America.

Betsey was Elizabeth Patterson Bonaparte, eighty-four-year-old matriarch of all American Bonapartes, bastards and otherwise, Jo included. In Baltimore, Jo periodically endured a ritual retracing of Betsey's link with the Bonapartes, usually late in the evening when the moisture in his aunt's rheumy eyes, and the spittle surrounding her slurred words, took on the soft glow of gaslights reflected in snifters of brandy. He'd heard the same account from his mother. It began in 1803. Eighteen-year-old Jerome, Napoleon's youngest brother, had escaped from a French man-of-war about to be captured by the British off the coast of Virginia, and Betsey met him at a ball in Baltimore when her long chain snagged itself in the layers of gold lace on his splendid uniform. They married; she grew pregnant. But Napoleon wouldn't allow her in Europe. He had other plans for Jerome—made him King of Westphalia, where he bathed in red wine every evening, gave him a queen, a real one, and annulled this marriage to the upstart American, who nonetheless gave birth to Napoleon's nephew at the age of twenty-two, and spent the next seventy-two years of her life in a battle to legitimize him. They tried to buy her off by offering to make her the Princess of Smackalden, but she refused. Thirty years later they offered her son Bo the dukedom of Sartène, offered *his* son Jerome the same title twenty years after that, but both preferred to be known as Mr. Bonaparte, thank you.

Meanwhile, the Hundred Days came and went; Napoleon died on St. Helena. And more Bonapartes came to America, gaggles of Bonapartes, led first by Joseph, the eldest brother of Napoleon, whose estate at Point Breeze outside of Philadelphia was the richest in America, and whose mistress in upstate New York gave birth to Jo's mother. Three sons of Lucien Bonaparte—another brother of the Great Man—also crossed the Atlantic, all of them rakes; one ran through his fortune, then reformed and became an ornithologist of note, author of *History of Birds in the United States*, namesake of the Bonaparte sandpiper. There were also the Murats, sons of Caroline Bonaparte Murat, Napoleon's sister, one of whom, Achille, the crown prince of Naples, became postmaster of Talahassee, Florida.

Most returned to France during the Second Empire, dragging their American children along, including Jo's mother. In Paris, Betsey's pursuit of legitimacy for Bo was blocked by her former husband's legitimate son, Prince Napoleon—Plon-Plon to the French, a good copy of the emperor dipped in German grease, they said—who drove mother and son back to Baltimore. However, Bo's son Jerome stayed on at court; he fought in the Crimean War, he became a hero, he fired up Plon-Plon's undying jealousy, and who knows, by some weird twist of forking events—if Plon-Plon died, say, and so did Lulu, Napoleon III's only son, and if the courts reconsidered, well then, American-born Jerome might very well become Emperor of the French! Yes, the Second Empire was sinking, Betsey knew, and the Republicans were foaming at the mouth, but sooner or later they'd want another Napoleon, they always did. And if not Jerome, then maybe Charles Joseph, Bo's second son, who was studying right now at Harvard.

And if not Charles Joseph, what about me? asked Jo, smirking. He knew the answer.

Your mother was a *bastard*, Betsey said.

His mother was still at court in Paris. What would happen to her? He counted on Jerome to protect her, to spirit her out of France when the crash came, he told Betsey—had her insist upon it when she wrote to her grandson. They needed each other, Aunt Betsey and Jo. He was another Bonaparte, and she was the link to his mother's protector. So Baltimore became his second American home. When he wasn't in New York puffing railroad bonds, he was in Baltimore, pacing Aunt Betsey's drawing room, railing against the interests of nobles and priests imbued with the Gothic prejudices of the Middle Ages, and declaring himself free of all such inhibitions. What he meant was, he was a new man—a financier. He combined the Napoleonic ideal of the self-made man with the American love of money—what a marriage! But he had to admit the American side had gained the upper hand. Why, he'd been so busy lining his pockets he'd nearly forgotten the reliquary for which he'd maimed one man and murdered another.

What a shock, then, to see it in the parlor of Horace Greeley's townhouse.

They'd gathered there for dinner after the meeting at Cooper Institute, the investors and officers, businessmen and parasites, and Jo was singing the praises of Rawlins, Wyoming Territory, the ideal location, he announced, for Nathan Meeker's colony. He described the trees of Rawlins, the birds, grass, water, rich soil, warmth in the winter, mildness in the summer, the very features he knew it appallingly lacked. He'd been told by those who'd been there that settlers in that alkaline landscape smeared canned tomatoes over their mouths to cut the taste of the dust, but he didn't mention that. His job was to sell. "When the avalanche starts, boys"—his eyes ranged around the room—"you want to climb a hill and put your money on the avalanche!"

"Then jump like hell to get out of the way." Greeley's squeaky voice raked Jo's spine, but he didn't flinch. Greeley in his reach-me-down suit was a clown, Jo knew, but a dangerous one. He laughed with the rest.

Then he felt a blushing warmth at his elbow—that lovely maid who'd answered the door, with limbs of a stork, offering canapés. He caught her eye and smiled. The plate she extended held squares of toasted Graham bread smeared with caviar, slices of apple, and cheese. Only cracked-wheat prophets knew how to thoroughly ruin good caviar. But Jo took one anyway. "You're a Grahamite, Mr. Greeley?"

"I keep a Graham table."

"I've always thought the Grahamites would be first-rate hands out west," said Jo. "They could clear new land and live off the browse." Even Greeley laughed at that one, he had no choice. Then the cluster of men around Jo stirred; a smell of ocean filled the room. A butler carried in oysters on the half shell, large as baby kittens, laid in a bed of crushed ice on a pedestal tray, and set it on the side table.

That's when Jo saw it, next to the oysters. Immediately, he returned to singing the praises of Rawlins. He was good at not wavering, at speaking without a stammer, at keeping his gaze fixed hard and his trigger finger steady. He sipped a glass of water; no wine at Greeley's. He *felt* the presence of the reliquary, no need to stare. Brigham Young's son had cornered Greeley, and Jo felt the need to watch them too. He knew Joseph Young was here to boost Utah Territory for Meeker's colony. Everyone here was either selling or buying. He could break in and nonchalantly mention that curiosity beside the oysters. What an interesting piece, Mr. Greeley. Silver? Looks old. My Aunt Betsey might fancy it. Interested in selling?

Then again, why buy it? It was Jo's by right of prior theft. He could simply return in the dead of night. The curious thing, Jo knew, was how much the financier in him was aroused along with the Bonaparte. But, then, the two were inseparable. It had to be worth something—didn't it?—if he wanted it so much, and no one would want it if it weren't Napoleon's. Not that anyone here knew what it was. Greeley had probably obtained it from Barnum, in whose hands most what-is-it's wound up. He sneaked a peek. Of all things, someone had pried off the top half of the crystal sphere and rested a stemless rose on the bottom half, what a desecration! The thing now resembled an ornate eggcup upon a stem, though the rose meant they'd taken it for a vase of sorts. Had they looked in the base? The rose floated softly on Napoleon's frail black left thumb . . .

"Jaspar," said the maid, "we need a pot for the shells."

"Yes, ma'am." For some reason, the butler winked at Jo. It made him cringe. Jaspar? Outside, dressed in preposterous green livery, Jaspar had been Samson, the groom. For a famous newspaper editor with a town-house near Gramercy Park, Greeley did things on the cheap, no doubt about it. Imagine a groom doubling as a butler. Or a *maid* answering the door! It angered Jo, as little things will to those in the grip of large wants. Still, some distractions could be almost—agreeable! That maid, for in-stance. Uncommonly handsome, in a queer sort of way. She couldn't have been more than fourteen years old. It struck Jo that he'd seen them both somewhere before.

In the kitchen, Pete, bending over to search in a cupboard for a pot, reached back, threw up his tails, and cut a rampageous fart. Josie waved her hands in gulps of laughter. "I could have done that out there," he said, "and gone undetected. I swear them oysters are on the turn."

"I'll tell Ralph and father."

"Too late. They got the first licks."

"Then you'll just have to carry them out feet first." Josie made a curtsy in her pretty maid's uniform. The high neck made her look tall. "With-out my help. *Jaspar.*"

"Unless they're swole up."

Pete yanked a tureen from the cupboard and left through the pantry. At the iron stove, Josie stirred the gumbo filé concocted by her mother earlier in the day. Fry six cut-up chickens, boil them to rags, add two hundred oysters, then after ten minutes sprinkle in one hundred spoon-fuls of powdered sassafras leaves. Just the thought of it had turned Arvilla Meeker's stomach—it was Horace Greeley's recipe, cooked on his or-ders—so she'd left hours ago and returned to MacDougal Street, where the Meekers kept their apartment.

Pete returned, pinching his nose. "Test it on the goat."

"He'll sicken and die."

"Goats can eat anything." Pete dipped a ladle into the stew and opened the back door. "Gracious!"

"That his name?"

"Gracious, some grub!"

"Oh, Pete. Shut the door, it's cold."

"Look, here he comes."

Josie tiptoed over and peered around Pete into the dark yard behind the townhouse, resting her hand on the small of his back.

"We got soggy toast, blanket cakes, and *café au delay.* Your choice of wine at five dollars the bottle all mixed together in the same cellar." Pete, with a white towel slung on his arm, crouched down to hold out the ladle for the goat, but it pushed right past him into the kitchen.

Josie squealed and clapped her hands. "Shoo!"

Pete chased the creature around the room, trailing gumbo filé, while Josie laughed and coughed. The shaggy hair depending from its belly dragged buttons of dry mud across the floor; one eye was milky. It crashed into a table before running out the door. "Mr. Greeley told me it likes fried turnips, boiled potatoes, and cabbage mixed."

"I wish it was mine," said Josie. She was out of breath, though Pete had done the chasing. "Mother tried to make me eat the mince pie she cooked up yesterday—pugh!—I threw it in the fire. I could have used a goat. Her griddle cakes taste like flannel."

"It's the lard."

"It's the flour. Father don't keep lard in the house."

Pete returned the ladle to the stew pot and stirred it once, peering in. "Lots of dogs and cats disappear in New York that folks suppose they committed suicide, but I don't agree. In my own Fifth *Avenoo manshun*"—he did a little jig on the kitchen floor—"I won't allow *my* cook to lay such hash on the table. You never know what might stuff a sausage these days, Josie. Them swells don't care, do they?"

"They'll drown it with whiskey."

"Not at Horace Greeley's. Everything but a tipple." He looked over at her dropping stemless roses into the wine glasses lined up on the table. For a set dinner you needed wine glasses at least, even lacking the wine. Josie aimed each rose, pointing exquisite fingers that splayed out as it blew from her hand.

"I mean after," she said. "They'll leave here and laugh at Pa and Horace behind their backs and soon as they step out the door stuff huge wads of tobacco in their mouths, then search out a saloon. I know these railroad men. They got no more sense than a horse."

"Not Joseph Young."

"He don't need tobacco and liquor with a hundred wives. What time's it now?"

"Wants five minutes to eight."

"You'd best ring the bell. I'll set out the rice. Take these out there first." For such a spindly child, Josie gave orders like a regular man. She talked western, Pete thought—Illinois talk—even though she'd lived here two years now.

He bowed low and scooped up the wine glasses, as many as he could gather all clinking together, then left through the pantry.

Josie wished she could hear him saying it. "Gentlemen, dinner." Or,

"Dinner is served." If he knew she was listening he'd break up laughing, he'd muff it somehow, that's what she thought. But Pete could compose himself perfectly when he needed. He walked through that door shaking with laughter and emerged on the other side sober as a nun. Setting out the wine glasses, each with its rose, he hummed to himself above the long cherry table set for eleven, with extra room on one side for Barnum. He turned down the gas jets, walked to the door, and cleared his throat. "Dinner." Neither too servile nor sonorous, merely a statement of fact. He gave it some snap to cut through the talk. Take it or leave it, gentlemen; I'll serve you but I won't butter your bread.

Across the room, Greeley looked up and smiled his approval. He'd been talking with some greasy foreigner about Pete's reliquary. Or Josie's reliquary; it was hers now. What *is* it? she'd squealed in the kitchen unwrapping it, hours ago.

Some thingamabob.

I know, she said. With a knife, she'd pried off the top of the crystal bulb where a band of pewter joined the two halves. Pete reached to stop her, then let it go. A smell like rotten leaves came out.

Then she dropped the rose in, stepped back to admire it, and carried it out to the side table in the drawing room. And there she did something that crawled up Pete's neck. He loved it and hated it—didn't know which. She wrapped her arms around him and kissed him on the cheek. The warmth of it glowed even now, in the dining room. She was just a child. Arms stiff by his sides, he stood there like a tree. And why did that picture rise up just then with his cheek still ringing, that bearded face on the floor below, way down below? For five years he'd tried to smother the memory. Back in South Carolina, where revenge was always death, he'd stopped a man from beating his wife, stopped him cold . . .

They served the dinner with well-oiled efficiency, Pete and Josie—or Jaspar and Marie—though Josie said he had ice boats on his feet. First the Little Neck clams, then the split pea soup, then Greeley's specialty, the gumbo filé, and vegetables each in their little dishes—cold boiled carrots and cold asparagus with a French dressing and sliced tomatoes with sugar burnt in malt vinegar. Between the main course and the Camembert cheese they talked in the kitchen about going west. Pete put some wood in the cast-iron cookstove. Josie said she wished she wasn't a girl; she wanted to be a boy, a cowboy. She revealed to Pete that her sister wore trousers—Roz, in Philadelphia, the nurse. Fanny Wright, Lucy Stone, and Dr. Mary Walker recommended it. Josie would do the same, she declared—no corsets, cramped shoes, and crinolines for her. Trousers and coats and freedom of movement and stay healthy, and the public be damned! Who cares what people thought? "What a monstrous falsehood society is!" She stamped her foot.

" 'Less you need something from it," said Pete. He sat down in a chair facing Josie. "Then you learn who to smile at."

"Not me. I won't smile. I won't give them the pleasure. I'll do it for Father, no one else. It's all because he's bent on reforming society that he must entertain such people as those out there. They're fools and ruffians. They don't see with my eyes. They can't see what I see."

"What do you see?"

"Low, mean, vulgar, debasing, narrow, contemptible, wretched, distasteful dogs dressed like humbugs and parading around like they owned the world."

"They do."

"Everything they do is unnatural and forced. They should—relieve themselves on trees like the dogs do."

Pete grinned and blushed. "That's natural."

"Peter, there's something you should know about me. I ought to be shot." Josie leaned forward, hands on her knees; her pale cheeks each displayed a circle of red the size of a dollar coin.

"How come?"

"Because I eat up folks. I'm surprised they haven't found it out yet. I did it slyly at first, but now it's out I'll tell you all about it." She moved closer, raised her eyes, and lowered her voice, inches away; her breath smelled sweet. She wasn't smiling anymore, and Pete felt his own grin like a bit in his teeth. "Very handsome children I entice into secluded places, cut their throats, and eat them up with pepper and vinegar."

"No salt?"

"And no young man is safe in my clutches. I ought to be shot. If I catch him alone—a young man like you—I commit horrible rape upon him, then sprinkle a little salt and swallow him whole."

"That's a way to go."

"The *least* I do's make a horrid, devilish face and make his heart burst and leave him for dead."

Pete clutched his chest and dropped to the floor with a thud; his legs twitched.

"Oh Pete!" She stood laughing. "I also shoot valuable dogs, hamstring horses and cattle, mutilate works of art, and drive sheep into meeting houses during service."

"Then we're a pair. I dumped arsenic in the gumbo filé."

"To cure the bad oysters?"

"No. To break up the rat's bones and guts you put in . . ."

They talked about fighting injuns in the great wide West. They talked about what they would do with the gold they found there. Josie would start a school and teach everyone, injuns included, how to be a genius. What a wretched thing it is to be common! And what a great woman I should make, she said, if I were a genius. I could make *use* of the bright thoughts and feelings that run through my brain half the day . . .

She tried a little cough.

When he came back from serving the Turkish coffee, Pete told Josie that the foreign gentleman, the one with the chin tuft, was giving a dose to her father, it looked like. Trying to melt him. "He's a foxy man. He's buttering up your pa an inch thick."

"Pa can't be sold."

"Any man would tumble if a brick chimney fell on him."

"Not Pa. What's he saying?"

"I couldn't hear much. Some river he claims is three-fourths of a mile wide and three-fourths of an inch deep, and the water is beautiful. They built a bridge over it. He's puffing the railroad. Don't some folks make you tired? He thinks he's still cutting up the pig. Makes me want to tell him, 'Smash your baggage, sir?' "

"Who is he?"

"I don't know. Too greasy for me. Looks Frenchified."

When the books first opened for subscriptions to stock of the Union Pacific Railroad, few shares sold except to members of the board themselves. Only fools and visionaries thought a railroad line could be laid across the Rocky Mountains, and everyone agreed it would prove more or less worthless if by miracle it did get built, since nobody lived out there anyway but redskins and gold seekers. If you wanted to get to California, you took the Pacific Mail—a steamship left you on one side of the Isthmus of Panama, the Pacific Mail chugged you across, and a new steamship completed the trip on the other side. Pacific Mail stock was gold.

But Congress granted a charter for the Union Pacific Railroad anyway, and for the Central Pacific too. They would lay track from either side—from Iowa and from California—and where they'd meet God knew; let the two companies sort it out. For incentives, Congress gave them land along the line: ten alternate sections on each side of every mile, or about 12,800 acres a mile. The railroads got the odd-numbered sections, and the U.S. government kept the evens. In addition, Congress provided subsidies for every twenty miles of track laid; the company could issue bonds for $24,000 per mile on the plains, $48,000 on the plateau, and $96,000 in the mountains, interest paid by the government for the first year and guaranteed thereafter for nineteen more years.

In other words, Congress provided the gravy train, and the hungry lined up, from board members of the Union Pacific, who distributed stocks to members of Congress in gratitude, to government inspectors who had to be bribed as a matter of course to certify each twenty-mile section of the line so the company could collect its subsidy, to suppliers who overcharged and land jobbers who got there first and bought up the surrounding land on spec, to financial agents who watered stocks, charged heavy commissions, or didn't even bother with commissions, just pocketed whatever loose change was lying around. In their race to lay more track and collect more subsidies, both the Central Pacific, building from the West, and the Union Pacific, building from the East, left a wake of half-abandoned towns made from tents and portable buildings purchased in Chicago or San Francisco for three hundred dollars and put together with a screwdriver. Deadfall whiskey ranches in giant tents followed the crews across the desert like tipsy clipper ships, and in them the workers who laid the track could drink and gamble and whore it up, then go outside and shoot their best friends and get hanged by vigilantes.

Jo had never been west. To him, sections of track were numbers in a book, and a locomotive was rolling stock, so many dollars to write off as capital. The material pig iron, the timber, dust and smoke, the grading crews, the bubbling engines, were the abstract part to Jo, as opposed to, say, the sale of first-mortgage bonds and land-grant bonds at eighty-five and fifty-five percent respectively to raise more capital. Jo had looked at the company's books—they were real. You stood on a real floor, leaned against an actual table whose upward pressure resisted your outspread hands . . . Still, he couldn't quite tell whether before his employment the books had been cooked or underdone. People wrote checks for thousands of dollars to pay notes, then neglected to reclaim the notes or even record their dates or possessors. One banker had apparently been over-paid $250,000, while several banking houses held certificates for bonds that couldn't possibly be delivered as promised. Meanwhile, the holding company created by the UP board of directors—Crédit Mobilier of America—made the whole enterprise sound more legitimate while helping folks to forget that the founders of both companies had been shovel manufacturers. Examining the books, Jo saw right away that Crédit Mobilier had been invented so the high rollers at the Union Pacific could engage in contracts with themselves. All but one member of the executive committee of the Crédit Mobilier and all seven of their trustees sat on the Union Pacific board. In fact, it was never clear which company any given employee worked for. Did Jo answer to Crédit Mobilier or the Union Pacific? He wasn't certain. But it didn't much matter. He worked on commission and pocketed the expenses he charged off on the UP books, accumulating money the way hawkers spin sugar out of air at village fairs. In addition to beating the pavement selling bonds, to composing pamphlets, advertisements, and prospectuses containing stunning rhetorical flourishes—lavish words in praise of a western landscape he'd never seen—if he needed cash he could borrow, say, $400,000 for the company and pocket five or ten for himself. You could always take a shovelful from here to fill a bucket over there as long as you kept the stuff moving. And if nothing else worked, the board declared dividends; after all, its members owned most of the stock. When one of the company's engineers wrote back to New York that pretty soon there would be no more West, Jo recognized his error immediately. There never *had* been a West, only figures in a book. The actual wilderness existed inside those greenhouses the company threw up all over the East, those glass houses with their steam heat that could bring shares in the Union Pacific prematurely to bloom in great bloody garlands of dividends. What alchemy! All it took was pen and paper, plus some well-steamed soil . . .

Of course, the whole thing would blow up sooner or later, but that was really the only objection.

When the golden spike was driven that summer, on May 10, 1869, Jo heard the bells peal at Trinity Church. It was a grand time for selling bonds, for cooking the books, for borrowing on a promise. On top of all that, he could now turn to land jobbing. Sure, there existed an army of creditors clamoring to bring the company to protest, but they couldn't, not yet. Boss Tweed's son had tried to impound the books on behalf of the financier James Fisk, whose claim against the Union Pacific had reached the courts; with five brawny deputies he'd sledgehammered open the safe at the UP office that summer, but Jo had already spirited the books out to the offices of the New Jersey Central across the river. What could anyone do, really, now the line was completed? It was like laying track—stay ahead of the engines. Once the last spike was driven, full steam ahead, watch out for the cowcatchers! The company now enjoyed the leisure of observing those powerful black locomotives, water buffaloes from hell, racing back and forth in front of the chairs and benches it had set up on its odd-numbered sections marked out with ribboned stakes beside the tracks. We sold the railroad, now we'll sell the land. New York to San Francisco in five days, imagine—the greatest event since Adam and Eve! Through a paradise of capacious and un-equaled forests, over mountains stuffed with gold and silver, past grazing plains and fields of wheat . . .

"What about the climate?"

"Of singular salubrity. The climate of Wyoming is much like that of central New York State, without its dampness and chill."

"You've been there, Mr. Benton?"

"Of course. I intend to settle in the area."

But Nathan Meeker felt suspicious. He'd been there himself, or near the place—they'd had to turn back because of a blizzard. All that timber Benton mentioned—Nathan hadn't seen it. Possibly the snow was too thick.

Besides, his heart was set on Colorado Territory, not Wyoming or Utah. Seated at one side of him, Jo Benton puffed Rawlins, while at the other Joseph Young praised the physical as well as the moral advantages of the area adjoining the about-to-be-completed Utah Central between Ogden and Salt Lake City. But Nathan had traipsed all across Colorado just last year, and liked it. He'd found the reserves of coal in Denver inexhaustible, the weekly edition of Greeley's *Tribune* in good supply, the Indians—poor children of nature—passive and docile, the gardens of settlers teeming, trade with Mexico booming, the rivers full, the cli-mate . . . salubrious. He said as much. Joseph Young shook his head. "Come out and take a look."

"Take me with you," Jo shot in. "With your Locating Committee. I may be able to assist your efforts. I could act as adviser—financial adviser. I represent—not only the Union Pacific. My connections are widespread. You need someone like me."

"At whose expense?"

Jo was improvising, of course. If Meeker's heart was set on Colorado, his own loyalties could serve to accommodate him. Commissions were commissions no matter their origin, and land spec was who got there first, not what company. "My own."

"Very well. I'll present it to the committee."

"In what light?"

"As a land agent to accompany us."

"And financial adviser. At no expense to you, emphasize that."

"Eleemosynary, Mr. Benton?" Nathan spoke with a mouthful of food while gazing down his handsome nose at his prospective financial ad-viser, and Jo wished he had a drink. A cigar at least, or a chew of tobacco. "Let me give you my own small piece of advice, since I'm older than you.

Nothing is free in this country. I learned that the hard way. You will too."

Jo sat there, humble and sweet as could be.

Pete served the coffee in china cups whose handles proved too small for any fingers but his. Ralph Meeker asked P. T. Barnum if he'd ever been out west. "Once," he answered. "Train got caught in a blizzard. Nothing moved for a day. Man had a photograph of a chicken and we all lived off that for twenty-four hours."

This set off a spate of blizzard stories. Nathan Meeker, who'd eaten heartily at dinner—his cholic had left him right after the meeting— glanced at Jo and told of the snow that had turned back his train in Wyoming just last year. The train slammed into a snow bank, throwing everyone out of their seats. "First time my poetry served me a good turn," he said. "The upper story of my tall plug hat was filled with bunches of my poetry; that's where I kept it then."

"Close to the soil it grew from," said Greeley.

"Yes, well. When the train ran into that bank, my hat saved my head from splitting open. The poetry cushioned the blow—and that's the most good it's ever done me."

When the company at last filtered out through the parlor, Jo pulled Greeley aside once again. "A beautiful piece, this," he said.

"You like that thing, do you?"

"Family heirloom, Mr. Greeley?"

"Never saw it before. Some doodad Mary picked up, most likely."

"Marvelous workmanship."

"Ugly as sin. I'd pitch it out the window for the goat if it looked half digestible. Looks like some kind of spittoon for girls and infant babies. Take it with you, I don't want it."

"But your wife?"

"Let her fuss. I don't believe she'll notice. She's seldom here."

Jo hefted the reliquary, calm and polite. It took such masterful control to get the things you wanted that even when they fell in your lap you couldn't gloat. The thing felt heavy—he tried not to smile. "Oh, I couldn't. Are you absolutely sure?"

"Suit yourself."

"Do you really mean it?"

Greeley squinted at Jo with a look of utter distaste. "Mister, do me a favor. You want that damn thing so bad, stop shamming. Just get it out of my house."

Chapter

4

Jo so loved the weight nestled in his arms that he sent his man ahead with the phaeton and walked the five blocks from Greeley's house to his rooms at the Fifth Avenue Hotel on the corner of Twenty-third, blessing along the way the streetwalkers in their flounces, jabots, and capes, the shoeshine boys curled in unlit doorways, also sexually available, he knew—those who reached for his trousers received on the wrist a sharp blow of his cane. Half of them carried knives in their kits. Up and down Fifth Avenue, the citizens pulling out their dollar watches under gaslights looked perfectly ridiculous to Jo, the men dressed like cylinders in their swallow-tailed coats tipping back and forth in the squares of light, but he blessed them too, what the hell—like everything else on this sorry island, they were here for a purpose. They propped you up. First came you, then the rest of the world, which was something you walked on . . .

In the damp cold Jo cradled his prize with both arms and grew warmer around it. It was like finding part of your own missing body.

Therefore, his rage in his rooms when he discovered the hidden compartment in the base of the turret to be empty was understandable. The lack of half the crystal sphere on top had already irked him, had worked away inside his satisfaction like a pebble in a shoe; but what could you expect? When things passed through hands they eroded. The solution was, take them out of circulation. Once in his bedroom he'd planned to lock the reliquary in his personal safe, the one beside the bed, so he had mounted the hotel steps with dignified calm, forgoing the elevator, and resisted the temptation to flirt with the pretty women at their late supper in the second-floor dining room. What a virtuous night! He wanted to spend it alone with his legacy.

But it wasn't there; just a few grains of sulphur trickled out in the gaslight. The thing grew cold and ugly in his hands, its penetralia empty, and with a horrid shout he threw it at the wall, where it cracked the plaster and slammed to the floor.

Jo's fourth-floor suite at fifteen dollars a day contained two bedrooms and a parlor. The back bedroom he used to smoke opium so the smell wouldn't drift out into the hallway. There he cooked up his last small piece and smoked himself into a stupor, groping through folds of his brain for a corner to curl up in, away from his mother.

The next day he returned to Greeley's house. No groom took his horses and no maid answered the ring. Greeley himself, white as a moth, pulled the door open and stood in the hallway regarding the bundle under Jo's arm. Glad you come back, he said, that thing wasn't ours to give out, I learned.

Whose was it?

Half an hour later at the Meeker house on MacDougal Street, Jo delivered the reliquary safely into Josie Meeker's arms. She squealed when she spotted it. In the midst of his vexation, what a pleasant surprise this was, finding last night's lovely maid joined up by blood to his prospective client! So young, and so grateful. Was her father home? No. She offered him tea; with deliberate care he removed his gloves, set his cane and hat with the gloves laid inside on a table in the hallway—no maid here—and followed her into the front parlor.

How sweet.

The armchair and couch were hung with thousands of little tassels; someone's delicate hands had done all that, had knitted and fastened each separate tassel to the upholstered cover, the same hands, perhaps, that played the ornately carved organ standing massively against the wall across the room. Josie left to fetch the tea. The rugs appeared new. The room felt plenty warm, thanks to the fireplace Jo thawed his toes at. And they'd leave all this for a sod house out west?

Carrying in the tea she looked delicate as a bundle of pencils, but sitting down on the couch seemed to wire her back together. She stared right at Jo without smiling. Gently, he began; he expressed his regret at taking her—vase. Had no idea it was hers, nor did Greeley. Curious thing, have you had it very long? A memento?

"It was given me just last night."

"And you—inspected it closely? You opened it up?"

"Pried the top off."

"I see. That's all?"

"Yup."

"And who gave it to you, if you don't mind my asking?"

"Pete."

"Pete?"

"Peter Doyle."

Jo sipped his tea. "And this Peter Doyle, now where might one find him? I'm interested in the origins of that bewitching curiosity you call a—vase. It could be quite old. You may have a prize there. Have you looked it over carefully?"

"Hardly touched it."

"What's he look like? Peter Doyle."

"Butler last night."

"Oh. That one. And he lives where?"

"I haven't a notion."

"You met him through—"

"Ralph."

"Ralph?"

"Ralph Meeker, my brother, who works for Mr. Greeley—and you can find *him* at the *Tribune*, I suspect."

"I see. Let me explain. This workmanship . . ."

Jo slid closer on the couch to show Josie the intricate pewter work, the trefoiled stamping on the pewter band, the delicate silver leaves inside the cup. "And here, this inscription. Run your fingers across the damascening, don't be shy. Close your eyes, Miss Meeker. Pretend you are blind. *Leipsana ne spernas digiti quo dextera coeli . . .*"

"What's it mean?"

"Do not spurn these lovely fingers . . ."

Ralph was no help. He knew Pete lived somewhere in the Sixth Ward, but where he couldn't say. Nor was he acquainted with any close friends of Pete, or places he went.

So Jo had arrived at a dead end for now. But he knew what he could do. He could visit Nathan Meeker, and if Nathan wasn't there find out from Josie if she'd seen Pete again. He could follow her when she went out if he had to, or meet her on the street by surprising coincidence, that was more pleasant . . . Once Nathan informed Jo the Locating Committee had decided to let him come along out west—in return for favorable rates on the Union Pacific, of course—his excuses for showing up on

MacDougal Street multiplied, even if, he couldn't help noticing, the more he came to call the more Josie seemed unaccountably absent.

She kept the reliquary on the side table.

A week passed. The three members of the Locating Committee plus Jo would leave soon, and still no trace of this Peter Doyle. Jo used the time to explore arrangements on the sly with his employer's greatest rival, the Kansas Pacific Railroad, which owned not only the Denver Pacific but most of the other lines in Colorado too, and so owned the railroad land there as well. The KP could use another agent, it turned out, especially one so well connected. No one need know of it, of course. Not the Union Pacific, certainly, nor Nathan Meeker either.

Meanwhile, Jo wandered through the Sixth Ward and Five Points, hung around the docks on South Street, dropped in on the dance halls and stag shows and brothels, looking for signs of Peter Doyle. Jo had connections in this part of the city. He knew which cigar stores downtown merely sold cigars and which had private rooms where the pretty young girls who charged the outrageous price of five dollars each for cigars at the counter made up for it by serving liquid refreshment and other pleasures in the back. He knew the saloons that held dogfights, those that held cockfights, and the ones that staged rat-killing contests, butting contests between billy goats, and boxing matches featuring bare-breasted women.

On the East River docks he strode past the piers and rail lines, horse-cars, hay wagons, handcarts and red and yellow drays loaded up with barrels, past workers sorting timbers for the caisson of the new bridge to Brooklyn—a pipe dream, Jo thought—past sailors carrying carpetbags and crowds of merchants and knots of dockworkers loading grain into bags from floating elevators and trying to shout above the metallic scream of winches and cranes and the roar of grain coming through the chutes—flap of flags on the masts, blasts of whistles and horns—a material clatter Jo ignored with perfect aplomb. When he swung his gold-headed cane and adjusted the stride of his boots with the punctilio of a thoroughbred, men and boys who would saw off your head for fun cleared a path. Beyond the commercial piers in the mudflats, old men warmed their hands at burning pans of horsechips propped up on tripods made from scrap and driftwood. Boys sold the horsechips for four cents a pail. Clouds in the late afternoon sky glowed a dull red. Jo picked his way across piles of rubble, through discarded cans, rags, bones, and cinders beneath the wheeling gulls. Under the pier at the Jackson Street dump a gang of men in identical bowlers, vests, and black frock coats crouched on pails passing growlers of beer. Around them stood heaps of tin cans and stacks of copper bottoms stolen from wash boilers.

Jo selected two by name and ignored the rest. Crouched beneath the pier, he gave them Pete's description: pug nose turned up, no facial hair, blue eyes, quite small, cocky and quick-tongued, favors a bowler hat cocked forward, black curly hair, dainty hands and feet . . .

Jeepers. Sounds like a Nancy.

Lives in Five Points. Name's Peter Doyle.

Whereabouts?

You tell me. Find him and you shall have—Jo reached in his pocket— the rest of this. He pulled out the neatly scissored half of a hundred-dollar greenback.

Their eyes didn't widen but they threw back their heads and peered out at Jo from half-closed lids. Shake, pal. We're with you.

Out on the mudflats screaming gulls dived for offal washed down through crevices in the dump.

Jan 7, 1870

Mr. Whitman,

We who arrange the Arabian Nights for their Spectacle escape the stale Sagacity of supposing them Sham.

We miss your vivid Face.

Each day in the desert we count our Tents.

We await the Book you send twice triumphant—once for itself and once for Him who sends it.

Mother was stricken Tuesday. I thought you would Care. Is your mother well? You speak of the betrayal of friends and comrades. I never heard anyone speak of the betrayal of friends and comrades before.

How do most people live without any thoughts. Tell me, Mr. Whitman. There are many people in the World, you must have noticed a few in the Street. How do they live. How do they find the strength to put on their Clothes in the morning. I cannot say myself myself.

We are both women.

I will be patient and never reject your words. You might think me ostensible. Fold your big hands. So few that live—have Life. Perhaps Death—gave me awe for Friends—

'Tis not that Dying hurts us so—
'Tis Living—hurts us more—
But Dying—is a different way—
A Kind behind the Door—

The Southern Custom—of the Bird—
That ere the Frosts are due—
Accepts a better Latitude—
We—are the Birds—that stay.

*Is this—Sir—what you asked me to tell you? I should like to see you
before you become Improbable, but I do not cross my Father's
ground to any House or Town. See for yourself—send me your
Resemblance—I am harmless as an inchworm. You might be required to crawl on all fours to measure my gait. Should you, before
this reaches you, experience Immortality, who would inform me of
the exchange?*

Your scholar—
Miss Emily

Brooklyn/107 north Portland av/Jan 16, 1870

Dear Miss Dickinson,
*Your letters have been received. I will say that I accept your appreci-
ation and thoughts. Those tender verses of such a personal nature
touched me deeply. I too am one of "the birds that stay."*

*I frankly send you my best wishes—& hope we shall one day
meet—& wish to hear from you always. Often when I'm low I take
out your letters and verses and am sure I feel uplifted.*

*As you must know, the best established magazines & literary
eminencies quite ignore my poetry. I have my small minority of
approval and discipleship, but the great majority result continues to
bring sneers, contempt & official coolness—though my book flourishes in foreign lands at a great rate. As for the betrayal of friends
& comrades, you must not think me always open to the imputation
of a complaining spirit. I am more than satisfied with my case,
despite the bad spells in my head. My dear mother is living & well.
I eat very moderately, but with quite a relish. Salmon, Graham
bread, coffee, &c for breakfast this morning. I have just eat my
dinner—beef steak & potatoes, with pumpkin pie & a cup of tea.*

I send as I think you requested it my photograph with all its shaggy, dappled, and rough-skinned character. You will see that the spot at the left side of the hair, near the temple, is a white blur & does not belong in the picture. Of course no one could smooth & prettify my countenance.

I must tell you Miss Dickinson that I experience Immortality every day. That has never prevented my bad spells and fall backs, however. At present my head cannot stand any thing. A vague impressiveness, a thought, not without solemnity and sadness—which you must understand without my writing it—comes over me like a cloud this cold day. & with that, & once again my best regard, I close.

Walt Whitman

That struck the right note. You couldn't always say how bitter you felt since the reputation of a whiner hung close. Best just to hint at disasters. Either way, it didn't help much, the world looked black either way. Walking to the ferry, Walt posted the letter, but even at the post office—flag still at half staff for Stanton's death—the doughfaced Brooklynites, pygmies they seemed, shied away from his mournful presence. He could sweep them aside with one powerful swing of his arm if he wanted, if he didn't feel so bad—all the spies, blowers, electioneers, body snatchers, bawlers, bribers, compromisers, runaways, lobbyers, sponges, ruined sports, expelled gamblers, duelists, carriers of concealed weapons, blind men, deaf women, pimpled rakes gaudy with gold chains made from the people's money and harlots' earnings all twisted together—crawling, serpentine human vermin and freedom sellers—

Let him who is without my poems be assassinated!

He was going to see Pete, to give him one last chance. He'd seen many defections, young fellows who took to him strong, then as they got older receded, sometimes came to disavow him entirely. But Pete? Surely Pete had better stuff in him. If he didn't, so be it. Walt's heart could take it even if his head ached terribly. Every so often, for fifteen- and twenty-minute stretches, some trapdoor hooked up wrong in his head unlatched by surprise and all the contents dropped out. Suppose a string of beads broke and went scattering every which way, but then on your hands and knees retrieving them you couldn't remember what all they were for or how the beads pertained to the string in the first place. When it happened like this, Walt had to stop and stand there to let his mind slowly fill back up while people skirted his rooted bulk as they would any inconvenient obstacle.

The crowds waiting to board the ferry were packed together tighter than usual because half of the huge pier at the landing had been dismantled to clear a site for the new bridge's tower. A bridge from Brooklyn to Manhattan! Walt felt certain he'd never live to see it, as they talked of finishing not in years but decades. Beyond the board fence hastily nailed together, an enormous steam crane on a barge chuffed and squealed, pulling out old piles. One dangled now from a chain, thick as a tree trunk above the water line, but eaten to a skinny pole by sea worms below it. At last the gates to the ferry opened and the crowd surged in. Walt sat in the cabin with the multitude, feeling the engines with his feet through the floorboards. Someone on the bench behind him sneezed. Crowds of men and women attired in the usual costumes—what a parcel of idiots they were. Men and women crowding fast around—go fuck yourselves. You are more curious to me than you suppose, but your incessant caterwauling makes me sick. Goody-goody men and women shouldn't air their ignorance in public so loud. The ragtag and bobtail, the dreadful stupid, the gussied-up scurf heads . . . I see you face to face. Closer yet I approach you. I considered long and seriously of you before you were born, and concluded the batter got spoiled in the pot. Others will enter the gates of this ferry and stink it up too. Others will lay their arms on my neck . . .

What is it, then, between us? Nothing.

Walt sat there glumly on the bench.

His poems were nothing. Homer, Shakespeare, all the poets, all the philosophers, were nothing. Hopes, fears, desires, sentiments, lofty notions—nothing. The ferry could sink and everyone drown, what did he care? Except, where would Walt Whitman come in on that deal? The idea scared him . . . Still, it was right. Ain't it right, Pete? The sooner we kick everything pot and kettle overboard, the better. Right?

It did make him feel better.

As for Walt Whitman, there were plenty of him. Walt met new Walt Whitmans every day. He didn't know which Walt Whitman he was—the ennuyé, the drunkard, the onanist, the sacred idiot, the beautiful gigantic swimmer . . . Look in my face, look under your bootsoles. I turn the bridegroom out of the bed and stay with the bride myself. My lovers suffocate me! They give me the trembles. I hate them root and branch. But sometimes I enjoy hating them.

When the crowds surged forward on the Manhattan side, Walt shoved ahead. Then the Broadway stage, the heave up, the driver—Pensey Bell, an old railroad man. Had been in a smash once, never said much. The hubbub, the cart wheels on the pavement . . .

He could write Greeley at the *Tribune* and suggest they run another personal. Horace would do it; times were slack for news. After an absence of some weeks, Walt Whitman, the poet, is just returning to Manhattan, on leave of absence from his employment in the Capitol at the Department of Justice. Beside visiting his mother at Brooklyn, and recuperating down Long Island, he has spent quite a while "loafing at his ease" in New York. It is understood by his friends that Mr. Whitman is now principally engaged on a poem, or a series of poems, intended to touch the religious and spiritual wants of humanity.

Greeley would run that. He'd run others before, all composed by Walt; even printed one of Walt's anonymous reviews of the *Leaves*.

He has also, we hear, readied for publication a new edition of *Leaves of Grass*; and his characteristic habit of abandoning himself to the life and scenes of New York while riding the Broadway stage is not for pleasure alone—so we have heard—but to lend the final touches of color to this new edition of his poetry.

To this nauseating drivel about armpit odors . . .

Pete should be home. It was early yet. On cold days like today he let his late-morning sleep melt right into his early-afternoon nap. It wasn't so much that he spreed it all night as he liked to sleep—Walt had never seen such hibernation in a person. He climbed down from the stage just past Fowler and Wells.

Up Worth Street to a nameless alley. One tenement here built at a crazy angle to the rest made the alley zigzag and narrow to a squeeze. Cow Bay seemed a spacious square by comparison, but to get to Pete's lean-to you had to circle around behind, through more alleys, back to the shit holes.

Pete's door was locked. Walt knocked till his knuckles grew red. He kicked with his foot. "Pete! You, Pete!"

At last, wrapped in a blanket, Pete unlatched the door and stood there blank and hangdog, looking down. One whole side of his face appeared flat.

"Here's Pete in his tipi. It's bitter cold here."

"Walt? Come on in . . ."

"Ought to light your charcoal."

Inside, Pete sat on his bed huddled forward. "Where you been, Walt?" He stared at the floor.

"Washington City."

"You get my letters?"

"Letters? What gush. You never sent letters. I wrote you buckets, but you never wrote me."

"I've been done up, Walt."

"You're healthy as a clam."

"My foot was all swole."

"Let me see."

"It got better. I went to the steam doctor."

"I'm not remarkably well myself. I've been in a bad case. A general sinking of the physical fluids."

Walt and Pete sat there on the cot. Pete's breath stank; it made Walt feel positively healthy, almost. He thought of the woman who in fifty years of marriage had never told her husband his breath was bad because she assumed all men smelled like that. "This place is a cesspool."

"You always say that."

"Ain't it a curious retrograding transmogrification that a whale should turn into a fish," said Walt, "and a Pete into a slug? I always say cold weather was intended for—sleepy men. They sit by their fires and whittle sticks. Suck their thumbs till July. Give them shortcakes and butter, warm blankets to lay across their knees, and they go straight to bed."

"That's me, all right. Where's the shortcakes, Walt?" Pete exhaled a powerful yawn. "I'm hungry."

"Let's go to Shakespeare's and get us some oysters. My treat, Pete."

"That's what done me up. Winter oysters on the turn."

"You really were sick?"

"Most am still. I feel a little better."

The possibility that Pete had actually been ill instead of parading all over town with that girl in her carriage lifted Walt's spirits. He felt sorry for Pete—poor sick boy—but couldn't help the faint smile pulling at his face. After all, he said he was better; the worst was over. On an impulse, Walt snatched Pete's hat from a pile of junk beside the cot and balanced it on his own head. "How's that look?" It sat there on his sea of white hair, much too small. He cocked it forward and smiled sweetly. Pete forced a grin like someone opening a tin can. "Pete. What distrust there is between people these days. Nowhere do I find open hearts."

"What brought this on?"

"I think about you every little minute."

"I think about you too, Walt. Ain't we in it together?"

"It's just—" Walt stood and faced Pete. In that thimble of a hat he looked perfectly ridiculous; Pete couldn't help laughing as he watched. "I stand before you self-condemned. I'll endeavor to do better, Pete darling—endeavor most decidedly to govern my temper. My damnable pride and habit of petulance." By now Pete had doubled up on the cot laughing to lick creation, couldn't stop if he wanted. Walt shrugged; what bracing cold air! "Pete. Darling boy."

Folded up on the cot in semifetal retreat, Pete pulled the blankets up to his chin. "How come you weren't here to nurse me, Walt?"

"I was in Washington City. Oh, Pete. If I'd known . . .'"

"Get me some water."

Walt sprang up and found Pete's tin cup at the foot of the cot. He rushed outside to the pump but it took so dreadful long for the water to rise!

Inside, Pete's eyes had closed. Walt held the cup of water to his lips. He felt Pete's forehead. "Poor boy. Feverish." He tipped the cup, but the lips stayed closed. Water ran down his neck to his chin and soaked in the cot, then his whole body shook. He burst into laughter, sat up and stuck out his tongue.

"Blahhh."

Walt laughed too. "Pete! You got the shakes. Hold him down, boys!" He tackled Pete, who went limp as a sack. His head dangled back and his tongue hung out.

"Bury me at Sharpsburg."

"*Antietam*, you Johnny Reb traitor. You low-down rebels don't know enough to call the battles you lost by their proper names."

"I didn't lose that one. I was home in bed."

"You were home in bed the whole war."

"Not very likely, Walt."

"Cavorting with some soldier's jimblecute he left behind, eh Pete?"

"Sech lies I never heard!"

Walt squeezed tighter. "What's this?"

"Some dingus."

Around Pete's neck hung a leather thong and pouch. Walt sat up and poked it with his finger. "What's inside of it?"

"Good luck charm."

"Some kind of rock?"

"Just some dingbat." Pete opened the pouch and shook its contents out on his lap. Seated beside him, Walt watched with interest. Hands on his knees. He felt giddy prying, and smiled to himself. To know everything about Pete! Just about every last detail . . . Black and shriveled up, the thing lying there looked like an old stick or rabbit's foot. Petrified wood? Walt picked it up.

He threw the thing down and jumped to his feet.

"Take it easy, Walt. You'll fall on yourself."

But Walt wasn't listening. That thing in his hand had taken a shape when he looked closer and it scared him half to death. Of course, it couldn't be . . . But he felt contaminated. He wanted to gag. He let himself stagger, but only half conscious of the dramatic effect—almost tipped over—then slumped back to the cot next to Pete, who'd closed it back up in his pouch by then. It was some kind of larva with blackness inside . . .

It ruined their reconciliation for Walt. He had Pete back, yes, and Pete acted glad, but Walt couldn't focus on anything much now. His confusions and dizziness came back full force. On the street Pete had to take his arm. They found a saloon on Pearl Street and stuffed themselves full with pickled eggs, salt herring, baked beans, crackers, cheddar cheese, bread, and other good things all laid out on a table in back—or Pete did. Walt wasn't hungry. He felt as though something had kicked him in the head, and had to stop now and then to lean against a building. He was mumbling to himself, he knew, moving his lips like a much older man. Shaded ledges and rests, firm masculine coulter . . . Root of washed sweet flag, timorous pond snipe, nest of guarded duplicate eggs . . .

Chapter

5

Pete didn't mind helping Walt around town as he felt stronger now after days of diarrhea, swelling, fever, stomach cramps, and, when the cramps subsided, the deadest sleep he'd experienced in years. He felt just about quit of it now, and the extra sleep had helped pool his vigor. Sometime back in that feverish blank he'd wondered if the others had caught it too, but his rag of a body was too weak to drag up to Josie's and check on her.

Wrapped in his blankets those first few days, he thought he might die. But the same Irish peasant/Confederate stock that gave him his out-look—don't let death get the first lick in—boosted him on and cured him in time. The steam doctor helped too; at Dr. R. T. Trall's, he'd been packaged in wet sheets and propped up in a steam bath, even allowed to fall asleep. It siphoned his sweat pores and shrunk up his limbs until, when he woke up, he felt he might fit in a chestnut burr.

Now he supported half of Walt's weight as they stumbled uptown. Pete knew just what had staggered Walt: the good luck charm he'd found in that reliquary. Sure, it was ugly. He knew what it looked like too, he'd examined it. Walt was so touchy anything might bother him. Pete fingered the pouch. It was just a harmless petrified pisser, probably off some Egyptian mummy, it cured him of his sickness—who knows, it might have. It was most likely nothing. Half the monkey's paws and rabbit's feet in the shops downtown were fake; they came off dead cats. This one might be a tree root or some twisted up calf's ear; it had a shriveled leathery feel, stringy and hard, but heavy for its size, like a stone. You could throw it at someone and knock off his hat.

Pete liked the thing. It made him feel good.

What to do about Walt he had no idea, so he just let him mumble. Walt was all right but he'd lost all his stamina. He'd lost the strength to support his needs without losing the needs. It was like being hungry but too weak to chew. He didn't want what he wanted. Pete knew he couldn't tell Walt his plans, not in this state. The news might kill him. I'm leaving to start a new life, Walt, so long old chum . . . Sure. He could shoot him at point blank too.

Besides, it was good to be back with Walt. He liked the weight of his friend on his shoulder. Nothing wrong with a friendly kiss either—it reassured Walt—besides, he knew the rules. A year or so ago when Walt clapped his hand down on Pete's inner thigh, Pete kicked him in the shins—that was too close for comfort. He put an end to *that* right away. Except he'd had to endure the spectacle of Walt on his knees begging forgiveness. So he kissed Walt once in a while, even let him press against him if it made him feel happy . . . How could he tell a man like that he was leaving to join a colony out west?

Not only that—if he told Walt about the colony, he'd want to come himself and spoil all the fun. Walt was too weak to be traipsing out west. What would Josie think? It was out of the question. It took hard work to build up a colony, you couldn't be scribbling poems all the time.

"Pete, you won't ever leave me, will you?"

They were walking up Broadway with Walt on Pete's shoulder. Never you mind, Walt, don't even bring it up. Here's a nice carriage. Chill in the air . . .

"You won't, will you Pete?"

Horseshit, I knew it, just when you think he's slow as cold molasses he's jumped on ahead! Won't leave you? Me? At least the sun had started to set, it was hard to see Pete's rising color. Walt had turned his head—to hide a tear?—and wouldn't notice Pete nervously fingering the pouch around his neck. The man was uncanny—he saw into your soul. "Course not, Walt."

"Good. That assures me. I'm prepared. Are you?"

"For what?"

"For the worst. The dreadful end."

Pete looked up at Walt, who was staring into the distance ahead. "Sure I'm prepared."

"I've rewritten my will. What little I have to leave I left mainly to Ed—poor man. He's lame, he'll need it."

"That's fine, Walt."

"I left you two hundred dollars and my gold watch, Pete. If I recover—I don't say I shall—but if I do, it will be much better for us to spend the money together. I think I'll pull through. Don't be alarmed yet. I tell you *honest*, Pete, my heart is black and lonesome, utterly. But I think it will pass over. I honestly think I shall yet come around . . ."

"Sure thing, Walt."

"Long as you don't leave me. I couldn't—I'd never survive that, Pete."

As they walked up Broadway Pete said nothing, but felt shrunk up and dipped in hot guilt. He tried a whistle. He knows what you're thinking, be careful. Of course he couldn't help it, the poor man. The gaffer. Old dog. He was scared and helpless, but don't cross him either—he could rage and storm too. And he wasn't that old! He was sick, though, he needed someone to nurse him. If he went on like this he'd need a wheelchair soon, and who would push it if Pete went out west?

A man approached them, lighting the gas lamps; Walt had to stand there while he trudged by. But then he gathered in all his scattered armies, his strength, wit, memories, wisdom; Pete felt him slowly filling like a tank. He walked stronger when they started again. "Pete. Let's go get our picture taken."

"Great idea, Walt."

"I want a tintype of us. Just the two of us together. You and me, Pete."

"Sounds like fun." Clearly, he was better now the grief was off his heart. He'd perked up. Almost could walk by himself.

How could Pete leave him? Ever?

They caught a stage up Broadway to Barnum's new museum on Fourteenth Street, open all day and evening, and sat for a tintype there at the booth of Alden's Premium Pictures. This was P. T. Barnum's third museum in New York, each of the others having burnt down. Horace Greeley had advised Barnum back during the war to think of that first fire as a notice to quit and go fishing, but Barnum couldn't erase from his mind the two bubbling white whales in his basement tank cooked by the heat until they burst. He wanted to atone; he knew half of New York had grown up on his horrible brass band always tooting away on the balcony, on the white arctic bear, the huge quartz crystal, the pictures of the fat woman, the stuffed monkey riding the stuffed yellow dog, the what-is-it, the albino children, the Feejee mermaid—not to mention General Tom Thumb—so he sent agents out to Europe and Asia collecting a whole new generation of exhibits, opened a refurbished museum in 1866, and watched it also burn down two years later. When the tigers and wolves caught fire in their cages, their howls and screams furnished the topic of sermons for preachers up and down Manhattan for the next six months.

For this third museum, recently opened, his European agents, especially those in London, had tracked down curiosities if not fireproof, at least dead and portable, items small enough to defenestrate in case of emergency—rocks and gems, mechanical figures, hand-carved puppets, shrunken heads, relics, fetal freaks in sulphur. They even had a leg bone of the ass on which Jesus rode into Jerusalem. Pete and Walt wandered the place while their tintype was being prepared, Walt all expansive now—greeting folks and smiling. People knew who he was, or some did.

Who's that?

Walt Whitman.

Who?

Walt Whitman . . .

In a room on the second floor a Punch-and-Judy show was about to begin. Walt wanted something awful to see it, but now it was Pete who'd gone into a sulk, who dragged and held back, hands stuffed in pockets, hung head shaking no. Walt took his arm and ushered him in.

Pete slouched down on a bench with a shrug. He thought of Josie; her kiss gnawed his cheek. He could stay east with Walt, maybe he should— but he didn't have to like it. He'd let him know, not in so many words, but with icy silence, what a sacrifice he'd made. Only trouble was, Walt wouldn't notice. He'd go right on beaming idiotic good will, waving, shouting halfway across the room. You'd think *he* was the show.

"Ladies and gents. I am now going to exhibit a preformance worthy of your notice and far superior to anything you ever seed before."

Pete wouldn't look. Let Walt lap it up. A wave of laughter passed through the room, but Pete studied the stains on his patent leather shoes. "I only merely place this happaratus up to inform you what I'm about to preform—providing as we meets with sufficient encouragement. It's a pretty play, gents, so empty your pockets. It will surpass anything you never witnessed before in the annuals of history. Mr. Punch has one of the beautifullest wifes you ever come acrost—name of Judy—and he'll speak to you in the unknown tongue that's knowed to nobody but us swatchel omis. We can speak in ventrilocution, or biloquism as it's knowed to scholards, and another thing we do is the engastrimyth, which is *bon parlare* for talking through the stomach. Begging your pardon for being so grammatical. My show were a big hit in London, gents." Scattered *boos* here. A man shouted, "Brits go home!" but others shushed him up. Pete decided to steal a peek; dressed like an ersatz Italian clown, with a dunce cap, ruffles around his neck, and stripes down his waistcoat bursting at the buttons, the swatchel omni scowled at the heckler. His face looked too fluid for Pete's taste—moist and spongy—and his pointed nose pointed down, for crying out loud. Beside him was the tall puppet theater ringed with a curtain. FANTASINA, read the arch across the top, and PLAYED BEFORE ROYALTY under the stage.

"No bono alley tooti sweety, monsieur. I ain't British m'self, I'm Italian. Now cough up your pennies and nickels, boys, or the show won't go on. Feel in your pockets but no feela too deepa. We know what them holes is for, lads." A boy—or dwarf—all of three feet high wearing a devil's mask squeezed between knees and the backs of benches holding a stocking cap in his chubby little fists. Strange ugly hands, Pete noticed, all scarred and cratered. He hobbled from one person to the next, stood before you until you contributed; Walt threw a quarter in for the two of them. From the front of the room came a rusty squawk.

"Rooty-toot-to-to-too-to-it!"

"Now, Mr. Punch, I 'ope you're ready."

"Shan't be a minute."

"Tumble up, tumble up."

"I'm putting on my boots!" On his tiptoes, the proprietor peered into the stage with his back to the audience, then bent down and slipped under the curtain. Punch's nasal buzz rose in volume when he popped up on stage, while now the proprietor sounded muffled and distant.

"Well, Mr. Punch, 'ow de do?"

" 'Ow de do?"

"I'm pretty well, Mr. Punch, thank you."

"Where's Toby? Where's my dog Toby?"

A live dog jumped up on stage and sat there in profile. The ruffles around his neck weren't sufficient to hide the mange running down his back. He sat there nonplussed while Punch danced around him, Punch whose neck seemed to stretch out at will when he wanted to leer at someone in the audience. Pete felt the puppet had singled him out, and shrunk in his seat, but couldn't stop watching. One of the puppet's eyes swiveled in its socket large as a boiled calf's eye, and his nose and chin nearly touched. His painted grin looked lascivious. With his back to the dog—grinning at Pete!—he tickled Toby's chin with the hump on his shoulders, a sort of upholstered saddle horn. Then he wheeled around and the dog bit his nose.

"Ow-wow-wow! My nose! My beautiful nose! Get away, you nasty dog! Ow-wow-wow! Judy! Judy!" For all the noise, Punch's squirming hopping form seemed strangely constricted. Pete figured too much of a ruckus might confuse the dog. Sure enough, when Toby finally let go and hopped down below, Punch caromed around the stage like a bullet shot inside a safe, and from excess of pain, or maybe exuberance—Pete wasn't sure—slammed his own head on the side of the proceedings with a noise of wood on wood. Children screamed laughter.

Pete assumed the puppet was knocking his brains back into place. He'd never seen a puppet show before, but he knew the feeling and envied the talent to whack your own head against a wall, not from suicidal impulses but from so much inspired irritation that you couldn't help enjoy it. He felt like trying it himself . . .

"Judy! Judy! My nose, my poor nose! Here she comes, bless her poor heart. Judy, my darling! My duck of several diamonds!"

"Well, Mr. Punch, what do you want?"

"Ain't she a beauty? There's a nose for you! Give us a kiss, Judy. Toby bit my poor nose."

"What do you want, I say?"

"Come on, now. Kissy, kissy, kissy. Kiss my poor nose."

"Oh, Mr. Punch. Wait just a minute." With a foghorn blast, Judy blew her own nose on her apron, then embraced her husband.

"Kissy, kissy, kissy. Play up." Punch hugged his wife and danced around the stage with his arm on her back, hiking up her skirts. The boys in the audience roared and howled. When her bare bottom was fully exposed to the audience, poking out over the stage, Punch with his head butted her nose and Judy farted. "Judy, Judy, Judy!"

She slapped him. He struck her. All the children laughed.

"Now, Judy. Where's the baby? Let's see the baby."

Judy jumped below and shouted up, "I can't find the baby! I can't find the baby!"

Punch raced around the stage to these words.

"Oh yes, here it is, Mr. Punch! It's stuck in the coal cellar between a slice of bread and jam." Judy jumped up with the baby in her arms, a little rag doll with a wooden head, three protruding teeth, and a beak nose stuck on.

"Oh, here's the baby! Give us the baby! It knows its papa, Judy."

"I should hope it would, Mr. Punch. Now give it back." Judy took the baby and Punch snatched it back. To a chorus of rising squeals, they tossed the baby back and forth between them, but much to its credit it didn't cry out. Its smile persisted. Then Judy turned to the audience. "I'll go and make a nice cup of tea. But if Mr. Punch hurts the baby, you'll call me up at once, won't you?"

"Yeesss!"

She went down. Punch nursed the child in his arms. "What a pretty baby! It's got its father's nose. Hush-a-bye, bye." Punch sat the baby against the side of the stage, then from the other side rushed at it clapping his hands. "Catchee! Catchee! Catchee!"

He did this three times. Then he picked up the child.

"Mam-ma-a-a-a!"

"Go to sleep. Poor thing. It has got the stomachache."

"Mam-ma-a-a-a!"

An obscene gurgling sound came from the stage, and Punch dropped the baby to squealing laughter, displaying a brown stain down his shirt front. He picked it up again. "Naughty baby!"

"Waaaaa!"

"Nasty child! Judy! Oh Judy!" He set the child down against the side of the stage, but its cry grew louder. Punch held his ears. "Go to sleep, little baby! Judy, oh Judy!" Punch picked the baby up and looked ready to hug and kiss it, but it clamped onto his nose with its teeth and hung there while he jumped around the stage. "Oh my nose! My beautiful nose!" He pulled the child off and threw it to the floor.

"Waaaaa!"

Lifting the baby up by its feet, Punch struck its head against the side of the stage. "There! There! There!" He struck it repeatedly; at last it stopped crying. He held the limp child by its feet for a moment, then threw it out into the audience.

For all that jumping about up on the stage, the folks in the audience had grown pretty silent, even the children—especially the children—and Pete felt himself squirming in his seat. A real grinning and sweating face appeared behind Punch on the stage. "Ladies and gents—you didn't call Judy!"

"Judy," said a child. Then the rest joined in. "Judy! Judy!" The face disappeared and Judy popped up.

"Where's the baby, Mr. Punch?"

"I don't know."

"He threw it!" said a girl.

"He's thrown it, you say?"

"*Yeesss!*"

"Well, I never! Mr. Punch, did you throw the baby out the window?"

"I didn't do it!"

"Oh, yes you did!"

"Oh, no I didn't!"

By the time Judy left and came back with a stick, the children were shouting and screaming again.

"Now, Judy dear. Don't be cross. You shall have another baby soon. There's plenty more where that one came from."

"Oh, you cruel horrible wretch, to throw the pretty baby out the window!" Judy hit Punch on the head with the stick. "That's a good 'un." Punch snatched the stick and hit her back. "That's a better."

Judy: "That's a topper."

Punch: "That's a whopper."

Then Punch walloped her repeatedly with the stick, to the deafening shouts of the children. They got it this time, they were cheering him on. He laid Judy's body out on the floor and counted to three, approaching it and backtreading on one and two. His nasal squawk lengthened each word; everyone joined him. "One! Two! Three!" On three he dealt her limp form a string of vicious blows with the stick, how she jerked and twitched! Whack! Whack! Whack!

Then he did it again. "One! Two! Three!"

At last Mr. Punch propped Judy up against the side of the stage, rushed at her with the stick and impaled her upon it. "She's dead, the old witch!" He lifted her lifeless body overhead on the end of his stick and paraded it around the stage to the raucous cheers of the little boys and girls before tossing it down below with a thump and leering back out at the audience, triumphant, stretching his neck and rolling his eye while turning his head this way and that, and buzzing and squawking, "Rooty-toot-toot!"

It was too much for Pete, who jumped up from his seat. Walt had to reach up and pull him back down. "Take it easy, son. Enjoy the show."

But Walt didn't know all that Pete knew about wife beaters, and the man he'd stopped cold . . .

Pete sat down while needles clouded his brain. It was just a puppet show. For a while he closed his eyes; the noise was pure noise, meaningless. By the time he was able to watch again, some new creature was up there on stage with Punch—a large scowling figure with hand in his waistcoat and bicorne hat turned to the side gazing out at the audience with the face of Napoleon. But this dead man's face looked alive. Each time it rose up behind the trembling Punch, the audience screamed, and each time Punch turned, it ducked down again. At last it came up with a gallows; Punch faced it. "Bonny!"

"Bon joor." Pete swore the face moved when it spoke. Its expression seemed fixed in a perpetual howl, deep ruts running down cheeks to its chin, but it looked perfectly capable of twitching. The eyes scanned the room like actual eyes. "You are charged with the breaking of the laws of your country."

"I never touched them!"

"You committed many cruel murders."

"That's no reason you should murder me!"

"Mr. Punch, you will suffer."

"I don't want my supper."

"You will hang by your neck till you're dead! dead! dead!"

"What, three times?"

"Who has a pissen pair of pants?"

"Punch hung," came a voice from below.

"Who will piss when he cannot whistle?"

"Punch hung!"

"Come, Mr. Punch, put your head in the center of the rope." Punch stretched his neck underneath the noose.

"Here?"

"No, higher up." He stretched out his neck above the noose.

"Here?"

"No, lower down."

"Please, Mr. Bonny, please show me the way. I never was hung before and I don't know how. Show me the way and I'll be extremely obliged to you, sir, and return you sincere and humble thanks."

"Oh, all right." Bonny looked at Punch, then turned to the audience, scanning them—scowling—and turned back to Punch. Pete saw it coming right off, of course. He had to hand it to Punch, he knew his diplomacy. When he wasn't screaming nonsense he could be downright cunning.

"Now, Mr. Punch, do you see my head?"

"Yes."

"And do you see this loop?"

"Yes."

"When you puts your head in this way, like so, you must look at the ladies and gents out there and tell them: Good-bye, fare you well."

Punch pulled the rope; Bonny's eyes popped. Slowly, a long pink actual tongue slithered out from a corner of his mouth. "Good-bye, fare you well," said Punch. He raced around the stage slamming his head on the sides and the floor. "Rooty-toot-to-to-too-to-it!" He caromed from the side to the top to the floor to the side, then pulled up short at the hanged man and regarded him. "Here's a man tumbled into a ditch and hung up to dry." He swung Bonny's body back and forth. "Oee! Oee!" Finally, he opened the rope and Bonny dropped out with a thud down below.

Pete looked around at the squealing children, the grinning adults. He stole a glance at Walt, whose jolly face all flushed and smiling looked beautiful. The softness of flesh seemed all the more strange after staring at puppets.

Up on stage the Devil himself had risen up behind Punch, and the fun was repeating itself as before. The Devil rose up, the audience screamed, Punch turned around and he ducked—the screams stopped . . .

At last they faced each other. "Good, kind Mr. Devil. I never did you any harm, but all the good in my power. There, don't come closer. How do you do, sir?" It was clear this Devil was on second shift—he was Bonny wearing a Devil's mask, right down to the hand in his waistcoat.

Then Pete realized where he'd seen him before—collecting money when the show began.

The Devil struck Punch a hard blow with his stick. "Oh, my head! What's that for? Pray, Mr. Devil, let us be friends." The Devil crowned him again. "Stop, stop. You must be one very stupid Devil not to know your best friend when you meet him." He struck Punch again. "Very well! That hurt! We'll see who's the best man—Punch or the Devil."

Then a terrible combat ensued with whistles and buzzes, thumps of a drum from below, whirling puppet arms like bolas, and Punch jumping every which way on the stage while the flat-footed Devil with his animal fists, Pete recognized them now, and his slow human legs all twisted and tangled trying to turn stumbled about, and Punch landed blow after blow on his head, it looked like it hurt—no wooden sound either. It sounded like a club striking very hard bone. At last, the Devil keeled over on stage to the wild cheers of all. They were standing up now, even Pete and Walt. "Hurrah!" Punch was shouting. "Hurrah! Hurrah! The Devil is dead! Now we all can do what we like!" Curtain.

Do what we like? Is that so, thought Pete. He felt wrung out dry. On stage, beneath the curtain, the Devil's head hung over the platform upside down, and Pete noticed something dripping, it seemed, leaking out from under the mask. You'd almost think it was blood . . .

He shook his head and turned away. Walt beamed like a saint. "Uncommon funny. Clears out the sinal passages, Pete."

"Like to split my sides."

"That's the true British poetry. Tip top."

"Worth the money."

Arm in arm, he and Walt filed out with the rest, Walt slow and clumsy from sitting so long. His legs were like tree trunks; he leaned his sweating body on Pete's tiny shoulder.

"Interest you gents in a curiosity?"

The proprietor of the show with that moist face and funny pointed nose stood in the corridor in his striped waistcoat, having discarded the ruffles and cap. Behind him, hands in their pockets, looking at the floor, stood some men from the audience he'd managed to corner. "Twenty-five cents. Dreadful amazing. The genuine"—he lowered his voice— "intimate tool of his manhood—the largest which has ever been knowed—the prodigical instrument of that monster himself—Napoleon Bonaparte—as is a secret, gents. You'll be sweared to keep it—"

Walt turned to Pete with eyebrows raised. He reached in his pocket and paid the two quarters, not quite sure what for. With three other men, they followed this shuffling figure down the hallway, watched him up ahead wagging his prominent buttocks with perverse fascination in spite of themselves—then averted their eyes.

Down another corridor, darkly lit. He unlocked a door. This dim room with gas jets turned down looked positively lived in. A screen cut most of it from view, but Pete spotted half a made-up cot back there. In front of the screen, by itself on the floor, sat a jeweled silver chest. With a key from his chain, the swatchel omi unlocked it, opened the lid, and lifted a jar from a velvet-lined well.

Walt staggered back, visibly disturbed. Some demon must have been following him around, he felt haunted by ungodly visions.

Pete felt himself pulled toward the jar along with the other murmuring men. They gathered around it. "There it is, gents. Near as a toucher. Napoleon Bonaparte's own. Feast your eyeballs. Surgically uprooted at the time of his death by a unknown process which is a secret. When he stood there at Waterloo, lads, this is what hung between his legs. When the lovely Josephine approached the imperial bedchamber . . ."

Walt turned to leave with his hand to his mouth. Pete continued to gawk at the thing. It was fascinating, ugly. Of course it was large—it had belonged to the Emperor of the French. Such a big thing on so small a man. Dwarves and hunchbacks had big ones too. Pete's good luck charm was puny by comparison, all shriveled up.

He fingered the pouch around his neck, almost hypnotized.

"Son, let's go. Let's get our pictures." Walt was so touchy. Look at him stumbling out the door wringing his hands, lost and confused. Pete had to scramble to catch up before he tipped over. For all his big heart and his manly talk, some things bothered him up so much you'd think he was a child. Pete took his arm. Walt lumbered down the hallway. Should you pity or love a poor elephant like this? It was just some folks' luck to get stuck with the job of propping up the lame when the lame proved so heavy. Pete had his own life to live, his own plans. Helping gloomy Walt down the corridor, he thought of Colorado.

Can't we all do what we like?

Chapter

6

After they'd left and he'd counted the money, Stokes could relax. He sat behind the screen in his room cooking up his ale and beaten egg at one burner of the gas plate and warming the goose grease for Bonny's plaster at the other. He'd removed his nose—it attached by a hook—revealing underneath the real nose with its suppurating wound which had never quite closed. Across from him, Bonny sat in his little chair propped up on pillows leaning his head back, eyes closed.

"Don't be so lemoncholy."

"Hurts."

"In course it hurts. You was made to hurt. Here, this here will soften your morals." Stokes smeared a cloth with the goose grease and, leaning forward, laid it gently across Bonny's head.

"Hot!" The little man jumped up. "Hot!"

"Don't go into such asterisks. It won't do you no good unless it's quite hot."

"Quite hot enough! Too hot!" He pulled the plaster off, threw it to the floor and sat back down, glaring at Stokes. Stokes, for his part, averted his eyes—nothing *he* could do—and pretended to feel entirely disgusted. Maybe tincture of benzoin . . . But Bonny's fat head always hurt. It hardly mattered how savagely Mr. Punch coshed him with the stick, it was bound to hurt anyway, it hurt when he slept—it was made to hurt. Being clubbed on the head three performances a day—four on Saturdays—only shivered the pain, repositioned it a bit.

"Took in twelve dollars."

"Famous."

"Plus two more arterwards, in the viewing."

"Simpletons."

"Which is pretty good proof there's fields to mow here. Money's in surplus. We can get us a bit."

"Find what we have to find then go home."

Laid out on the cot were Stokes's Punch and Judy; in a basket on the floor Toby slept curled up. Stokes poured his yard of flannel in a mug, leaned back, and took the first sip. "You didn't spot him?"

"Not me."

"You must spread the word out more. Broadcast it about. When he hears what we're showing he'll come straight around."

Bonny rubbed his scalp with his fist and blinked. He shook his head once, wagged it this way and that to slosh the pain around. It made him feel better. "Going time."

"I should think."

The small man, Stokes's own creature, pulled on his greatcoat and bicorne hat hitched to the coat by a cord—he lost things easily—and walked to the door, bursting into totters and lurches every few steps. He seemed to need oiling. Stokes heard him mumbling to himself already, *I wants it, I wants it*, working up steam for the nightly search. He was all of twenty-two inches high and fifteen pounds light, but his need was big.

That's how Stokes had made him—to run on a need. Stokes had learned in an Antique Manuscript brought his way in trading for curiosities how to piece together a little man through a complicated process of manufacture and necromancy. Separate the full and the empty, said this text, by holding a flying bird under water; then the light parts rise and the heavy parts sink and we see that Life proceeds from a lack. Stokes wasn't certain he saw, but the book also contained practical instructions more along the lines of a menu. A gentleman from Cambridge had translated this manuscript from its original Latin into the Queen's English in return for favors done by Stokes. This scholar attributed the calligraphy—found on the verso pages of a treatise sewn in weathered boards on the Last Supper by Origen—to the hand of Dioscorus, fourth-century priest of Serapis at Alexandria; in fact, it was a copy of that precious missing text, the *Physica et Mystica*, not the spurious imitation ascribed to Democritus, but the true original, author unknown—or a copy of it—upon which Synesius had based his commentary, last heard of in the library of Rudolf II and evidently the very manuscript mentioned in Hugo Blotius's catalogue, the *Adversaria Multifaria*—a priceless document thought destroyed for centuries.

Mine, said Stokes. You can't have it.

Start with some *mumia*, or mummy powder, said the text. The best *mumia* came from human bodies, preferably saints', but if those weren't available, then it became necessary to kill birds, stuff them with spices, and grind them to a powder, though the results weren't as good. Further, *mumia* alone wasn't sufficient; it had to be stimulated by a kind of semen born from imagination and hatched out by demons who performed a horrible *actus* with it. The process was painful and secret; you need the blood of a murdered man . . .

Blood of a murdered man? That was no problem, Stokes knew plenty of murdered men. He'd killed a few himself. He could always make more murdered men. Still, he was haunted for months afterward by *evestra*, or ghosts, every night in his dreams.

Place the blood of a murdered man in a stoppered bottle; sprinkle in some *mumia*; after seven days, listen for a knock; open the bottle; put your finger in for the *polong*—a kind of auxiliary demon—to suck, and it will then fly through the air in the shape of a grasshopper and inhabit whatever organic tissue in the vicinity has the greatest need, that's the way to do it. It helped that demons were everywhere anyway, but that stood to reason. Stokes had already vaguely concluded from experience what the Antique Manuscript confirmed with its authority, that if there was a God there was also a Devil, and if there was a Devil there were subordinate powers too. Therefore the air was as thick with demons as it was with flies in the summer. Crows and owls were demons, and so were flies, the ones with red eyes. But most demons were invisible. They spent half their invisible lives tweaking each other's noses, pulling each other's hair, kicking each other's shins, and slitting each other's throats, and the rest plaguing humans. They filled the kitchen, occupied every shelf and jar, unmade the bed, caused smoke from the chimney to puff into the room, and outside they waited at every crossroads and turnstile to trip up people, and made their homes in the heads, necks, and noses of certain animals, especially horses. They animated the leaves, knocked trees down on dowagers, threw darkness in priests' eyes, and caused the genitals of schoolteachers to itch unbearably. The Antique Manuscript even named a few of them: Asmodeus, king of demons; Afernoch; Thauthabaoth; Erathaoth; Suriel; Ialdabaoth; Ogdoad . . .

As for the *polong*, this was a lesser demon, as its sole function was to animate dead tissue. The life it conferred was mostly specious, Stokes knew that, but it would do in a pinch. Life in general was specious anyway, being so ubiquitous. When Bonny stirred and quickened after months of patient stitching of odd body parts together in that workshop on Rotherhithe Street, the first thing Stokes thought of was insects hatching out of slime, manure, wet wood, old hair, horsemeat, and sweat—that sort of thing. If worms and snakes could spontaneously generate in the muck of old wells, and sea slugs, frogs, and salamanders grow from rotten seaweed—not to mention, in Stokes's own shop, all the mice born from piles of discarded woolen clothes—it stood to reason old eyeballs, teeth, and fingers still had the spark of life in them, didn't it? Sure, they'd gone past their highest state of perfection, some had even dried up or begun to rot, but what about seeds? Seeds were dried up too. Stokes had seen enough two-headed calves and six-legged dogs in the curiosity business to know that, if anything, the problem wasn't bringing things to life, it was stopping them from growing. The Demiurge, said his Antique Manuscript, formed the natural from the artificial, which was why you had blue-spotted eggs, strange beautiful fish in the sea, green-striped snakes, swirling complicated coral, intricate shells, and myriad flowers all growing and exploding in fantastic shapes and colors from here to Africa. The book also pointed out that the human body was a chemistry factory cooking up concoctions in the fire of the blood, spewing out everything from the hard bodies of metals to the moist fluids of plants. When it lost blood, it made more. Stokes had supplemented the murdered man's blood with his own in animating Bonny. And he'd made him small, thinking he'd grow, but the package unfortunately proved too tight.

Then when he saw what he'd made he was thankful. He'd done his best. He'd stitched together a little man, a small being, perfect in detail down to the little finger pads, except not exactly perfect. In places the yellowish skin had trouble sufficiently covering the work of muscles and arteries beneath. The glassy deep-set eyes, the lips straight and black . . . With his swag shop of body parts, Stokes had plenty to choose from, but they didn't always mesh exactly, and weren't entirely aqueous enough, despite the oil, water, mucilage, and other such liquids and fats he poured in. As a consequence, Bonny's joints creaked and ground against each other, making movement difficult and resulting in a life of constant pain. Every now and then a piece fell off. If it weren't for the lack that attracted the *polong* and gave Bonny a goal to shoot for, the pain would have sunk him long ago.

The lack was his little manhood; he had everything but that, every organ, vein, and hair. It was at this time that Stokes had first acquired the reliquary, conceiving of its contents as his creature's biological incentive. He made Bonny's ugly face with Napoleon's death mask as a model—it proved too large for his body—and to be cute, dressed his little man in a bicorne and cutaway, whose buttons he'd fashioned from actual sections of Napoleon's rib, then propped him up on a shelf with one hand tucked in his coat. He stood the reliquary across the room, summoned the *polong*, and watched little Bonny's fingers twitch, his eyes pop open. What a moment of triumph! Civilization would thank him. Shortly thereafter Jo showed up and spoiled it all, but Stokes blamed himself for not counting on Jo's considerable cunning. Jo saw right away that that bull's pizzle in its fancy jeweled chest wasn't Napoleon's, you couldn't fool Jo—he knew where the real thing lay hidden too. He ran off with the one item Bonny lacked, but the net effect was like zapping the little man with thousands of volts of current, he had too much life now, it shuddered and yanked his stubby little limbs, and Stokes found he had to cool off his creature by bashing him with a stick periodically. It made him wonder what would happen if Bonny ever actually caught up with that thing.

He proved to be an excitable little man, but he could sit and talk for an evening too, though not terribly well. He could memorize lines for Punch and Judy. He could be a friend, a helpmate, someone for Stokes to pass the time with, besides thugs and dustballs. And from the first he demonstrated other talents bound to endear him to Stokes—he could sneak around, ferreting out this and that, slither up alleyways, crawl in through windows, drop down from piers onto gentlemen's backs and slit their throats before they felt him there. Since he lived in constant pain he assumed the rest of the world felt the same way, so inflicting a little didn't matter; it was part of the general groping through the fog surrounding you out toward the faraway unreachable edges . . .

Together, Stokes and Bonny concluded Jo had crossed the ocean with his stolen prize. Stokes knew Jo still had family in America. Then the call came from one of his long-standing clients, Mr. Barnum in New York, for a shipload of curiosities to fill his new museum and Stokes figured, might as well go myself. He'd never seen New York.

He'd been here a month.

He rocked in his chair, sipping his yard of flannel slowly, and feeling the well-being of it spread through his body. Bonny was searching for Jo on the streets, as he'd done every night since they'd arrived. Stokes had traced him from Baltimore to New York, then lost him in all those tobacco chewing multitudes. New York's bad habits made him long for his pipe, but good pipe tobacco wasn't to be had. Nor was good ale—you had to heat it up with an egg.

At last he fell asleep in the chair with his fake nose sitting on the table beside him.

Out on the streets, Bonny's faulty memory made his searching wasteful—he covered the same territory often—but the blind, groping instinct of the hunt pretty much made up for that. He sniffed out trails like a rutting dog, and spotted old brick drains and iron pipes—some sticking out beneath houses in ditches—which humans of normal stature were bound not to see, let alone fit in. Down there with the frogs and bugs, under alleys roofed off by vaults of bricks, in storm drains through marshes that once bordered Manhattan Island before drainage reclaimed the river banks, God knows why he thought he'd find Jo's spoor, but he did. Some storm drains near Twelfth Street followed diagonal lines, ghosts of streets that once bordered Peter Stuyvesant's old Bouwerie House and farm. You could follow tunnels once formed by wooden pipes—huge logs hollowed out and long ago rotted away leaving just the holes—all the way down to the East River by means of routes branching out from the old Collect Pond drained years ago. Now and then he ran across sleeping forms, street Arabs in pipes near the river curled around half-empty baskets of shoestring, or buried in hay bales piled near the site being cleared for the new bridge's tower. In the alleys, they slept in ash carts; a gang of them once tried exacting a toll of Bonny—as they did to everyone who passed—but quick as a wink he slit the Achilles tendon of the boy with his hand out, right through his boots, and loped off fast and awkward on his small leg stumps through piles of garbage and bricks.

Hardly visible, down at the base of the walls of buildings, he threaded alleys and passages that wound at odd angles through interiors of blocks filled with rear tenements—huge haphazard dominoes—thinking the only unconfused thought of which he was capable: *I wants it.* It wasn't so much a sentence as a loop in his mind he could break into at most any point—*it I wants, wants it I*—the meaning didn't change. He said it like sucking a piece of candy while butting pigs out of the way with his head and slitting the throats of dogs who attacked him. His small toe dropped off in his boot. In the stale beer dives he hopped up on kegs and asked for Jo while the tramps who drank from tomato cans stood him beers if he tried to sing. He tried but hadn't the slightest idea what singing was, thought it was something like cracking words open: *I—wa—nt—sit.* Staggering back from their laughter, he dislodged large flakes of the brown crust covering the wall behind him and watched in bewilderment showers of crawling roaches emerge from beneath and come dropping down.

One by one he singled out those laughing for murder, then forgot to wait outside and commit it.

He was only half aware of what *it* was—some swelling shape in the pain. It made him scowl perpetually. He was good at smells because everything was smell, that is, traces of cravings in the air. In the three-cent lodging houses with tiers of bunks three sleepers high, he looked for Jo. Those were mansions compared to the cellar rooms where sleepers slung in rows by their armpits on clotheslines stretched from wall to wall; he kicked them in the shins. They thought he was collecting the penny charge for hanging there.

Still, he picked up a trail. It was in a sort of a cave near a manhole outside a lodging cellar, a hole in a yard broken for descent where night soil poured under rotten boards through a brick drain. Just a few inches below the flooring overhead on which the tramps strung on clotheslines snored, Bonny found a growler from the docks fallen on hard times curled up on a kind of ledge—cooking tea in a tin can over a fire—who'd heard of such a man, yes he had, and sent him to Cherry Street, to a second-floor dance hall in a flamboyant, decaying converted mansion. From Cherry Street, the trail led to brothels on Greene Street where gaslights blazed in bowls of tinted glass and the girls stroked Bonny's head and tickled his chin, thinking of those legends about the size of dwarves' members. His scowl warned them off.

One young girl with red hair and yellow eyes gave him a room number at the Fifth Avenue Hotel.

The cooks there thought it must have been a stunt—General Tom Thumb himself escaped from Barnum's Museum—when they spotted that creature sneaking through the kitchen, keeping to the wall with his jerky little walk. He was gone before they could toss him in a pot.

He took the elevator—New York's first—as the well-lit stairs were being scrubbed at that hour. On the third floor he found Jo's room and knocked—gently, so as not to scare him off. The lowered gas jets in the empty hallway barely hissed—only Bonny with his keen ears could hear them—but the hiss confused his juggled resolve, so he took out his knife before climbing to the transom, thinking he had to jimmy the lock. He held it in his teeth.

The room was unlit but he knew by the smell that no one was here.

In the light of a match he saw drawers left open, sheets pulled back, torn paper collars discarded on the floor. The heap of puzzled fragments inside that room jogged Bonny's mind for a brief revelation which he kept on forgetting. Why was he here?

Oh yes: *I wants it* . . .

But Jo, who had it, was gone, moved out.

Chapter

❧ 7 ❧

Some time or another, selling rail-
road bonds back in New York, Jo had been told or read about the
snakeheads on rails out west, those straps of iron spiked down in timbers
that sometimes sprang up when the spikes worked loose and stabbed
through the floor of a railroad car impaling whatever poor souls were in
the way. It hardly mattered that the new solid iron rails had put an end
to snakeheads years ago, Jo didn't know that, and anyway, the unpleasant
part was the waiting. He enjoyed the luxury of their Pullman palace
car—solid black walnut inlaid with French walnut, crushed velvet upholstery, crimson curtains, and to top it all off, water heated in pipes and
circulated through the walls according to Baker's patented apparatus,
taking the winter chill off entirely—but outside was a hostile environ-
ment of grizzlies, tomahawks, snakeheads, and hastily laid tracks, and the
thought that it might break in spoiled the fun. He didn't like trains, they
smashed up too often. Smash up out here, and where could you go, my
goodness, some red Indian could jump from a bush and skin you alive!
Rumors had reached back to New York of tracks on the Union Pacific
put down last year before the frost melted and later sinking into the mud,
of poorly graded curves and weak timber bridges, and though Jo hadn't
seen any of this yet—wouldn't recognize it if he did—he couldn't help
feeling it had to be a mistake to ride on the actual physical tracks your
own company had laid if the company was as dishonest as his, because
what better candidate to pay for its sins than someone who'd pocketed
its tainted money?

It gave the promised land a hard edge. Jo insisted Nathan Meeker take the window seat, from which he could marvel out loud at the rich black soil of the Platte River valley, the earth ocean of the plains, the herds of antelope, the cloudless skies of intense and spiritual azure. He didn't want anything to do with it himself. The one herd of buffalo they saw drew the passengers all to that side of the train crowding up against Jo, because it is a dreadful thing to want to see a buffalo and not be able to do so. A few hundred miles west of Omaha, Nathan took out his pen and notebook and commenced writing in broken lines that looked suspiciously like poetry. God forbid he should read them to Jo . . . A family of poets and collectors of reliquaries! Jo tried to see Josie's face in her father's. Yes, it was there, that would be her destiny; claim it now before it grew old. His only disappointment in coming west at last was in leaving behind those pleasant visits to the Meeker house on MacDougal Street, when she answered the door looking down—if she happened to be in. Once, he kissed her wrist before she could bolt.

More scribbling; at least it shut him up, and he stopped gazing everlasting out the window. Nothing to see out there anyway but desolation—monotonous yellow plains, a dried-up riverbed, a few scrawny little towns—Jo preferred the silver-plated lamps and spittoons inside, the gilt molding and scrollwork overhead. At night, the scrolled panels pulled down to rest on the seat backs and made a top bunk well out of the range of snakeheads. Stuffed behind those panels were soft mattresses, snowy sheets, warm striped blankets, nice pillows. He'd arranged all this luxury for the Locating Committee at the bargain rates of emigrant passage—even secured a dining car for the use of passengers all the way through to Promontory. Of course, they weren't interested in Union Pacific land—had their hearts set on Colorado—but they agreed to take a look. Jo himself had to pretend every place they stopped was lovely and full of promise—every isolated station with its one wooden depot house and half a dozen rude adobe huts and tents was potentially the next Chicago. This was land he'd puffed and sold back east, the lots around stations all deeded and recorded and marked by stakes, but he'd had no idea it would look so treeless and barren. And they said Wyoming was even worse . . .

But Meeker seemed to like it. He envisioned busy towns and wagons stacked with produce and grain parading to market, or Jo helped him to. In Wyoming, where nothing grew, Jo planned to point out the valuable minerals just under the surface, especially the coal, which you couldn't actually see. And if all they accomplished was touring the line—if Colorado really looked that much better—so be it, Jo had in his pocket an authorization from John Evans of the Denver Pacific to act as land agent for their half-completed line between Cheyenne and Denver. Across this vast barren Eden he had the committee surrounded. The idea was to sing this or that's praises equally high so they'd hear whichever they wanted. Nathan Meeker, General Cameron, and Richmond Fisk, their heads all filled with utopias and their pockets all stuffed with money, needed little inducement to dump either out. When he wasn't writing poetry, Nathan was spouting Association, and Fourier, and Social Minimums, and Working Not for Wages but Dividends in the Colony—to the confused dismay of Fisk, Jo saw that. Fisk hadn't counted on locofocos.

Jo watched the men in that car watch the West, his pleasant calculations impaled now and then by anxious snakeheads in the brain.

Around them the endless prairie grasses had turned to sagebrush, hard to pinpoint exactly where—someplace back before North Platte—and the empty country had emptied out more. Their snail of a train whizzed motionless, it seemed, it could have been backwards, through land where nothing changed. Not even a buffalo broke the monotony here, they'd mostly been shot. Their rotting carcasses littered Kansas and Nebraska, waiting to make William F. Cody famous.

The sun went down. In the posh dining car hung with ornate mirrors, Nathan ordered once more an antelope steak against all his principles— tried not to enjoy it, welcomed the coming vengeance of his belly. No Graham tables on this train. When Jo Benton filled the room with cigar smoke, Nathan pulled out a plug of chewing tobacco and bit off a small piece, then bit off more. But he'd quit soon, he'd promised Arvilla. She'd made it a condition of coming out west. Of course, she'd come if he didn't quit too, she'd obey him, she always had, but why torture his poor wife about it? She was right to want him to stop. Indeed, why torture himself . . . ?

He chewed and sucked the juices out with bitter pleasure.

Then it was bedtime. As luxurious as their Pullman Palace was, Nathan preferred to sleep in his clothes, since the men and ladies were all mixed together and some walked around in their nightshirts and chemises! He'd rather have no sleeping car at all. Why, just last year, touring for the *Tribune*, he'd endured an emigrant train with its mephitic atmosphere, its smells of unwashed people, its shocking mixture of the races, its red-hot wood stove, its floors slippery with tobacco juice, its complete lack of sleeping accommodations, and its ten-minute stops at trackside for meals in one-story shacks of pine boards with a deal counter inside— no seats—littered with pea coffee and putty pies. Rushing back to catch the train you smelled the mutton tallow lubricating the axles. But at least no one used the lack of privacy at night as an excuse to walk around half undressed.

That night, while the Locating Committee slept, their unending plunge forward got them nowhere, and they knew it. Their dreams emptied out like spigots left open.

But when they woke it was dawn in Wyoming, pink with shredded ribs of clouds in the sky, and pink and blue across the high plains. Then this brief show ended and the wind commenced butting against the train incessantly like a stupid bull, bleaching the air with dust. White dust, white air. They crossed a fork of the North Platte on a new stone bridge and came into Rawlins, where Jo had proposed the colony locate. Pine forests, Mr. Benton? Rushing rivers? Grassy glades? The small riverbed was nearly dried up. Not a single piece of vegetation in sight, not even a sage bush. Actually, things was troublesome to see, the wind and corrosive dust made you squint mighty hard, mebby you missed something . . .

Beside the tracks were piled shaved logs for ties, along with rocks, bales of hay, and rubble. For the hour-long stop here they spent five light-headed minutes outside, then rushed back to the shelter of their Pullman, rubbing their inflamed eyes and spitting. Conductors passed out the boric acid. The town itself consisted of a few railroad workshops and one hundred tents and shacks, with great bare mottled rocks all around. "Beetling crags," Nathan wrote in his notebook. The wind was like a runaway train. Lots of coal beneath the dust, Jo pointed out. Oilshale too; cutting through this land, the Union Pacific workers had built a fire one night and were shocked when the walls of their cut caught fire and burned with a brilliant flame. They used the flames to illuminate their night work. There's a fortune in oilshale under that dust, Mr. Meeker.

Is that so? From the window of the motionless car, Nathan spotted Indian squaws and cutthroat white men, outlaws for sure, living in open commerce.

Between Rawlins and Green River, on a long flat stretch, a caravan of white canvas-covered wagons pulled by mules and oxen trudged along beside the tracks. Again everyone crowded to Nathan's side of the car, for a look-see at the Mormon wagon train. A woman walking beside a wagon carried the rim of a spinning wheel in one hand, a loaf of bread in the other. The sight made Nathan in his comfortable seat feel downright elderly. "The New World and the Old World side by side," he wrote.

"Why don't they take the train?" someone asked.

"Saints can't afford it."

"It don't seem right. They should just grab on."

"Sure; might find them some extra wives around here."

The train sped past. No one waved.

Nathan hadn't made it this far last year. This year the ground was bare of snow, but looked hard as rock. Strange country. Agriculture was out of the question, you couldn't irrigate from dried-up rivers. No trees for lumber. Plenty of lye, though. You could make soap here and ship it back east—that was the best to be said for it. Hard to imagine children sorting peas in Fourieristic harmony in this hellish place, or the Little Hordes with their banners charging into work on Shetland ponies, making games of their chores. In the ideal phalanx, hordes of children, who naturally possessed a contempt of wealth and love of dirt, patrolled the perimeter searching out croaking toads, caterpillars' nests, snakes, and other unclean objects the presence of which would make outsiders scornful of the phalanx and thus cause its shares to fall.

This country would bleach your bones out in a month. Josie should be here—if dry air's good for anything, it's a cough. A deep cough, the mouse in the chest, the thing that scares parents . . .

He regretted agreeing to come this far. Even Jo Benton seemed taken aback, you'd think he'd never seen it before. Of course, there was no extra charge to go to Promontory, then back to Cheyenne. Fifty dollars each, paid for out of funds for the colony, a bargain really, with plenty of sights along the way to store up in memory. They could look at the Utah Central land too. Strange rocks outside—castles, cathedrals, pyramids—Nathan searched for comparisons in his notebook. Certainly not the sublimity of the Alps; more like ruins abandoned by fed-up gods, the Alps turned inside out. I met a traveler from an antique land . . . Colony members could take excursions to these parts to refresh themselves and make their work at home seem more pleasant. Of course, no one *had* to work. The Social Minimum made work not a necessity but a pleasure, and if people didn't see that planting pear trees or cultivating bees was attractive in itself, that was because civilization had corrupted work and made it feel loathsome. With production and consumption on a rational basis, with irrigation carrying water into everyone's backyards, people would work at as many different tasks as they chose, say nine or ten a day. Drudge work too, a little each day. Manufacture out at the edges of the colony just below the horizon where you couldn't see the smokestacks. You could have a sort of colony of the colony out here in Wyoming: a lye factory, say. Workers could spend a few weeks here each year, newlyweds maybe. They could make a game of it . . .

Columbus, Newton, Fourier, Meeker—men who discovered things, men who began things. Handsome men too. Horace Greeley, can't forget Horace. Men careless of dress or appearance, unlike the dandy sitting next to Nathan with his monocle and chin tuft, his stiff military bearing. You'd think he was sitting on a pencil. His nerves seemed made of women's hair, undoubtedly the consequence of civilized commerce. The parasitism of the merchant and the middleman—the chief cause of economic ills—Fourier had compared to the spider, who constructs his web in the most filthy streets or against the most beautiful monuments, wherever it takes hold. He seizes his prey, wraps it in glutinous threads of soft sticky words, and sucks it dry. A head covered with eyes, an enormous belly, but the thorax is wanting. He devours his own kind, even the younger ones. Maybe that's why Jo was smiling to himself, Nathan could see it from the corner of his eye.

But Jo wasn't thinking of devouring anything. In that tiny speck of a train inching west somewhere in North America, dwarfed by everything in and out of sight, his thoughts had naturally led him to Napoleon. He was wishing he'd remembered to take on the train General Gourgaud's diaries, recently published. To ride on a train without reading material! Still, certain passages he knew like scripture.

Everything is matter, the Emperor told Gourgaud.

But sire, without religion, what prevents secret crimes?

Morality for the upper classes, the gallows for the rabble. Who keeps me from marrying my sister? Morality.

Piety as well; concern for others.

Bah! The main thing is oneself. It's a lucky thing to be selfish, Gourgaud. If I believed in a God who rewards and punishes, I would have been timid in war . . .

The Great Man had also compared himself to Christ, who triumphed because circumstances were ripe. Just like me, thought Jo. I'm wealthy because I took advantage of the circumstances. With enough stock, I could become president of the board. But everything in its time—everything discreetly. With Boss Tweed's son and his friendly judge waiting to pounce on the UP's financial dealings, bond sales had slowed down, dividends halted. Selling land was how you raised cash these days, and land was nothing but holes filled with dirt. Whose it was hardly mattered—the UP's, the KP's, the DP's, the prairie dogs'. He could merge the UP and the Kansas Pacific; then add, maybe, the Burlington & Northern. The Chicago, Milwaukee & St. Paul. The Erie. The New Jersey Central . . .

And back in New York he could find this Peter Doyle and reclaim his precious relic of Napoleon. It all added up to one glorious task: to re-member the body of the Emperor.

Beyond Green River, the mountains grew larger and bolder, folded in closer, right up to the windows, then broke into the narrow and rugged Echo Canyon, too tight and fast for Jo's comfort. The beetling walls of rock exposed a little rift of lurid sky above, while far below waited bottomless pits and rushing waters. Then Weber Canyon—they clung to the sides. Jo's fear of snakeheads diminished out here where it seemed any minute, going this fast, the bottom itself could drop out unannounced. He pictured them plunging down the canyon sides . . .

At last they pulled into Promontory, a place nearly bare and empty as Rawlins, though stuck up higher into the sky. Here the plan was to view the historic juncture of the railroads, then climb a mountain just south of the station—Jo declined this pleasure—in order to see the Great Salt Lake and its giant valley, and catch the return train to Ogden where Joseph Young would meet them. The mountain's summit looked a mile away but turned out to be four, and the thin air rattled them, but they made it, and there it was down below reaching all the way out to the horizon, the lake where nothing lived but some brine shrimp. From up on that summit it was huge as the maps said and bluer than the sky, surrounded by a margin of white alkali, with mountains all around quite dark at their bottoms and white with snow at their very peaks.

They ran into some Saints up there hunting bears.

Back in Promontory, Jo presented them each with a piece of the railroad tie that had united the continent, the very one into which Leland Stanford had driven the golden spike back in May—the last one laid to complete the line! Each thumb-sized piece of wood was mounted on a little brass pedestal inscribed with the compliments of the Union Pacific Railroad. Of course, he didn't tell them there had been five or six of these last ties; the first disappeared on the day of the golden spike, carved up by all the relic seekers, and the second lasted barely a week longer. This particular last tie had never actually held up any track; as a matter of fact, it came from the UP offices back in New York, where some smart people figured it was easier to carve it up before it was laid, so as not to disrupt the running of the trains.

From Ogden, they toured the nearly completed Utah Central down toward Salt Lake City, but every place a stream came down from the mountains and fanned out in alluvial meadows the Saints had already planted a town. At each one the train stopped, the children poured out—boys and girls waving banners—and sang a song and cheered Mr. Young, who responded in grateful words of a Biblical tone.

Joseph Young showed them some land not quite as well watered as that in those towns, somewhat rocky to be sure, and hemmed in a bit by foothills on both sides, cutting off a view of the lake—for five dollars the acre. Meeker said they'd take it under advisement.

Then began the long voyage back up the rugged canyons of Utah to the moonscape of Wyoming, back through the towns Jo wanted to sell, where the talk grew serious. Evanston land was available at six dollars the acre if they acted fast, Rawlins at four—he was doing them a favor—but the committee found neither desirable for an agricultural colony. By now, Meeker's dreams had begun to shrink, but he tried not to show it. That bitter taste was just a craving for tobacco, wasn't it? You could buy government land with Agricultural College scrip at ninety cents per acre, but here they were pretty much committed to settling close to a railroad, and these prices were, well, a mite high.

They laid over in Cheyenne at the UP Hotel, then caught a Denver Pacific train south as far as Evans, halfway between Cheyenne and Denver. Jo looked around at the rolling plains of sage and sparse grass powdered with snow near the station, with nary a tree in sight, and thought, what a wasteland. Just standing there shriveled him. But out loud he declared it to be highly attractive country. They'll finish the line to Denver this year. Majestic view of the mountains, he said. You could drop anchor here.

Let's go on, said Meeker.

From Evans they commenced a three-week tour of Colorado Territory, with Jo Benton always at their elbows, more useful than a majordomo. It was Jo who made inquiries, who arranged for horses and wagons, found out when the stages left, even paid their fares. He showed them Denver, scarcely ten years old, once destroyed by fire, once swept by flood, subjected to Indian hostilities too, but nonetheless bustling with so much business the clerks there barely had time to comb their hair. From downtown Denver you couldn't see a farmhouse. Nathan was especially impressed with the city's system of irrigation by which waters from the Platte were made to run along the gutters of every street and into gardens and grist mills and ponds. Coal here was in plentiful supply at ten dollars the ton, and the cottonwood trees, where vigilance committees had once hung villains, now shaded picnic groves next to the river. It was said to be, said Jo, a most law-abiding town.

They considered a location near the base of Pike's Peak, but found it too small and with insufficient water. They traveled to the country above

Pueblo on the Arkansas River, but could find no large body of farming land all together there. They endeavored to reach San Luis Park, but the snow prevented them. Northwest of Denver, they stayed at the ranch of Colonel Craig, agent of the St. Vrain grant, whose own property was several miles square and the envy of all, with its large and elegant house furnished handsomely, its model farm with several hundred head of hogs, its vast herds of cattle and large numbers of Mexican workers. Streams ran by footpaths and around hummocks Nathan was told became flower beds in the summer.

They visited the Poudre Valley, where clear waters poured from the mountains amid box elder trees, but found the soil wanting and likely to give out after a year or two's cropping.

Back in Evans three weeks later, they took a closer look at the land near the railroad station. The mountains along the western horizon, all white with snow, resembled migrating clouds. Why not here? asked Jo. Equidistant between two major outlets for marketing produce, Cheyenne and Denver, both serviced by railroads. Close upon the convergence of two sizable rivers, the Poudre and the Platte. Majestic view of the mountains, bountiful natural resources close by . . .

Let's look at those rivers, said Meeker.

On a bluff overlooking the rivers' convergence, he began to think this place wasn't bad after all. It looked better than he remembered from three weeks ago. They'd even passed a grove of pine trees between the station and here—several dozen spruces at least, not to mention two or three cottonwoods—and besides, you didn't want too many trees because you'd have to clear them before you could plant. The soil wasn't bad if you could water it sufficiently, and the Platte River was especially wide if not very deep. Good grazing land too. Of course, the banks of the river were already settled, but from here they looked like squatters to Nathan. You could irrigate out from the rivers regardless; dry country, sure, but with irrigation ditches picture all the fruit trees, the fields of wheat and beans . . .

Best of all, it was available, said Jo, for three to four dollars an acre, more than Nathan had originally figured, but so much better than Utah and Wyoming, where the soil, let's face it, was decidedly inferior, that it sounded like a giveaway. Why, Jo even knew of individual holdings bordering the railroad land available for a slightly higher price.

Of course he did; he'd purchased them on option.

After several days of negotiations, the Locating Committee, with Nathan's urging, agreed to buy a number of parcels from the railroad and from private hands totaling twelve thousand acres, for which they paid nearly sixty thousand dollars. It was a considerably higher amount than Nathan had planned on, but if he threw all his savings into the pot and asked Uncle Horace for more on loan, they could swing it. He thought they could. They also signed a contract with the Denver Pacific for a refusal of fifty thousand acres more to be held for three years at three, three-fifty, and four dollars an acre, according to the respective dates of purchase. The success of the colony, its productivity and capital stock, would buy this land. And if worse came to worst, they could turn to Horace . . .

Evans was rejected as a town site because the remains of the railroad camp there could not be controlled to keep out liquor by forfeiture clauses in the deeds. So they located north of Evans. And to avoid antagonizing the squatters—some of whom turned out to have title—they went east of the confluence of the rivers, close beneath the Poudre, on a level plain. This eliminated the few trees, but with irrigation they could plant more.

After the signing of notes and the handshakes, they stood there beneath a cloudy sky with the wind picking up and some snowflakes in the air, Jo Benton and Nathan Meeker amid the prairie dog holes and prickly pears. This? thought Nathan. Well, it's all right. No Garden of Eden but no desert either. He assumed a dignified air to mask the confusion best ascribed to the altitude. Jo and the others would go back tomorrow, but Nathan planned to stay on and get started. Search up a house in Denver, telegraph for Pete to bring the family out. Then file incorporation papers and arrange for a survey and start laying out the town. In just a few months the first colonists could come. Main Street over here, church over there.

A blast of snow struck Nathan in the face; it was getting heavier, covering his town.

Post office, hospital, school, town square. Farms around the edges of the city. Number-one ditch, number-two ditch, grist mill, pond, corrals, fences . . . For some reason, things seemed to slide off this place, but Nathan felt confident they'd take hold in time. Maybe it was the snow. Think of Columbus. Aeneas. George Washington. Men in doublets and hose planting flags on a shore while polite regiments of natives looked on. Of course, it never happened like that. There'd be conflict and dissension. Founding fathers had to be steady, couldn't brook doubts—firm but gentle with their children.

"What shall you call it, Mr. Meeker?" Jo had to shout over the wind. His nose was red, he shivered, his eyebrows, mustache, and chin tuft made little ledges for the snow.

Call it? Maybe that's what it needed.

"I submit the name Meeker as most appropriate, most fitting."

Nathan felt his color rise despite himself. Meeker? No, he couldn't. The Lord strikes down swellheads. Still, it had a ring . . . "I think not, Mr. Benton. Only one name strikes me as fitting. If my colony has a guiding light, a patron saint, it is Horace Greeley. I shall call it Greeley."

Jo suppressed a smile. Greeley didn't exactly pluck the heartstrings; it sounded like a cheese. In all that barren land piling up snow, full of wind going crazy with nothing to strike against, he pictured Horace Greeley waving a cane. Over here, the newspaper. Over here, the Graham House . . .

The two stood there like snowmen on the plains. Already several inches had fallen. Neither bothered to brush it off. Nathan didn't move or turn his head, but Jo shivered like a shaved pig.

Greeley.

Jo laid over in Chicago a few days before returning to New York. Then at home, after more than a month out west, under the pier at the Jackson Street dump, the good news was that they'd found his Peter Doyle—in an alley off an alley, a place called Cow Bay. They'd take him there now if he gave them the other half of that greenback.

He'd give them the other half of that greenback if they took him there now.

Outside Pete's hovel Jo stepped back into the smelly shadow of a privy and let one of the growlers knock. "Where's Doyle?"

"Gone!" The voice inside sent up a most heart-wrenching moan.

Jo pushed past his man at the door and looked around, waiting for his eyes to adjust. A bundle on the floor in a corner turned into a woman wrapped in blankets whose face had lost the greater part of its chin. She was waving a fist, but the large man sitting on the cot ignored her. Most of the rest of the room appeared empty.

"Gone where?" said Jo.

Walt's white hair and beard stirred; he lifted his head, hands on his knees, and displayed a face distended like bread dough and streaked with tears, eyes red and swollen, a mouth ripped open in utter grief. "Gone—who knows where? Left me! Disappeared!"

"Get out," squawked the woman, who rolled back and forth on the floor in her anger. "My room! Get out! Go! Off my bed!"

PART
IV
1872

Chapter

❧ I ❧

Dear Miss Dickinson,

I return the poems—found them interesting. Nothing very new or different with me. I have been badly pulled by the heat—sit in my office & keep quiet as possible—for if one stirs two steps, the sweat runs off him.

Grant stock up, Greeley stock down. I am likely to prove a true prophet about Mr. Greeley—he is not expected here at the White House next March.

The heat and the nervous prostration keep me unnerved and generally clumsied—not at all pert—rather kinky. Shoulder grumbles now & then.

All words are spiritual, Miss Dickinson. Nothing is more spiritual than words. Yes, I agree with you—folks want poets to indicate more than the dumb beauty of objects. I shall mind your admonition—it answers my turn—and I guess you'll heed mine. I don't sit in judgment no more than you, but allow the sun to fall around helpless things. The poetical quality is not marshaled in rhyme and traditionary metrical laws nor in abstract addresses to things that go off half-cocked, Miss Dickinson. You put too much over-emphasis on complicated contrivances. Remember that nothing beats simplicity. A man (or woman) fertile in expedients such as yourself profits from simplicity as the earth does from rain. I don't know what you mean by "cooled my *Tramp*"—you say too many enigmatical things—but I do know that beauty grows loosely like lilacs or roses from a bush, profuse and impartial. Be natural. There, I've frankly unbosomed myself. I know you have no more deference for Mrs. Grundy than I—so we make a pair.

I feel it due to myself to write you explicitly thus, though it may seem harsh and perhaps ungenerous. That a disgraceful poet would still be worthy enough to borrow a penny of goes a long way toward making him feel rich. But my dear Miss Dickinson, when you say,

> He touched me, so I live to know
> That such a day, permitted so,
> I groped upon his breast—
> It was a boundless place to me
> And silenced, as the awful sea
> Puts minor streams to rest

I am reminded of some lines which appeared not long ago in the pages of the Atlantic Monthly, if you recall. You can't say you ain't seen them—I sent you my Leaves, in which the same lines appear. This is a delicate subject to kick up a row with, but consider the likeness in a spiritual sort of way:

> I throw myself upon your breast, my father
>
> or
>
> Touch me with your lips as I touch those I love
>
> or
>
> You oceans both, I close with you.

I will be candid with you, my friend, and say I do not hold this resemblance against you. Indeed, I shall bona fide consider you blameless if you pursue it no farther. Nor do I expect you to abandon your verses on my behalf—only to take more care in their inspiration. But I'll raise no more smoke. I wouldn't have undertaken the mentioning of it if I didn't think you would receive it in good spirit. I have to add that often whenever I think of your letters and verses I have the greatest desire to see you, feeling that if I could once take *you by the hand I might be something to you. Do you have a portrait you could send me? In any case, I charge you to construe what I have written here in terms of my declared and fervid realization of our profound moral sympathy and attachment. And so, with that in mind,*

Farewell,
Walt Whitman

Amherst/August 23, 1872

Oh, did I offend it—wasn't I natural?—Daisy—Daisy—offend it—who bends her smaller life to its more lusty and liberal as nature—Natural—Daisy who would have sheltered her Master in her childish bosom—only it wasn't big eno' for a Guest so large— this Daisy—often blundered—Perhaps she offended his finer nature. Daisy knows all that—but must go unpardoned—Even the wren upon her nest knows more than Daisy—being so natural.

If her words don't sting, tell her her actual fault. Then pledge you will forgive sometime before the grave. You say your shoulder grumbles. Daisy's got a cough big as a thimble. Daisy's got a Tomahawk in her side, but that don't hurt—her master stabs more—you say I must be natural. What is natural? I have the heart in my breast— set a little to the left—you know what a leech is, don't you? Is it natural? Sunset at night—is natural—if it don't sting helpless things. But sunset on the dawn reverses Nature. Are eclipses natural? Science bows before them. Is the sun dead, or Jehovah's watch broke? The hen that laid its 6 eggs on my window sill thought it was natural—so I killed it—it was getting tired. Please sir, such an ugly hen, nor profuse nor impartial. All men say "What" to me, but I thought it a fashion till you said I'm unnatural—If you please, it afflicts me. I thought your instruction would take it away. I am honored to be your scholar, sir. Don't smile at me—Don't—and for this—Master—I shall bring you obedience. Are you perfectly powerful? Will you help me improve? It must be so, if you say it is so. I therefore confess the little mistake, for your sake—and say I've done it before, if you think me guilty—but disguised it so nicely even the dead couldn't tell. I shall observe your precept hereafter—I marked a line in One Verse already—because I met it after I made it—and never again will touch a paint mixed by others—even if bought— with so penetrating a preceptor by—who identifies Butterflies from their Worms—when you showed me what my ignorance missed—I blushed for the two of us—ruler my knuckles, Master—then I may see it—you speak of inspiration. What is inspiration? To those who ask for my Mind I'm penurious—the World can't have it—you must feel the same—God made me—Master—I didn't be—myself. I don't know how it was done. He built the heart inside me—Bye and bye it outgrew the casing—Is that natural?—and like the mother—with the big child—I got tired. I wish that I were great, like Mr. Walt. Whitman. Are you really very wicked? If I had the beard on my cheek—like you—and you—had Daisy's petals—and you cared so for me—what would become of you? I'm concerned. I didn't tell you for a long time, but I knew you had altered me. Could you come to New England and see for yourself—would you come to Amherst—would you like to come—Master? If you saw a bullet hit a Bird—and he told you he wasn't shot—you might weep at his courtesy, but you certainly would doubt his being natural.

Could you believe me without a portrait? Yours is in my drawer—in ceaseless rosemary. I am small, like the Wren, and my Hair is bold, like the chestnut Bur—and my eyes, like the Sherry in the Glass, that the Guest leaves. Would this do just as well? It often alarms Father—He says Death might occur, and he has Molds of all the rest.

Because you have much business, beside the growth of me, you will appoint, yourself, when to come—it would be so natural.

Your plagiarist—
Daisy

Solicitor's Office; Treasury
Washington/Sept. 14, 1872

My Dear Miss Dickinson,
I have been waiting for time & the right mood to answer your letter in a spirit emerged from the shelter of my umbrage. I wished to give it a day, a sort of Sabbath or holy day apart to itself, under serene & propitious influences—confident that I could then write you a letter which would do you some good, & me too. I bear you no grudge. I am not insensible to your hurt. Permit me to offer you my continual friendship, and do you feel no disappointment because I now write briefly. In order that there be the frankest understanding with regard to my position, I will tell you that W.W. is a very plain

personage, and as entirely unworthy of your barbs as he is of your dependency. You must not construct such an unauthorized and imaginary Master and call it W.W. and get so worked up. I too have blabb'd, blush'd, resented, lied, stole, grudg'd, had guile, anger, lust, and hot wishes I dared not speak. I too must insist upon my unmitigated self, with all its infernalities and airy talk. My hyena disposition I shall try to check, if you do likewise with yours. But one thing I am not—I am no dainty dolce affetuoso. I've always made the whole demand—won't brook half-way measures. And so, Miss Dickinson, let there exist between us a relationship of trust and mutual affection, accepted by both of us with joy.

I must travel to Boston on a business next week. Are your plans such that I could pay you a visit on the return?

I send you my respect & good will.

Walt Whitman

People's Restaurant & Boarding House
Greeley, Union Colony
Colorado Territory/Sept. 15, 1872

Dear Walt,

Note the new address. Moved out of the Hotel de Comfort as the floor collapsed last week at a meeting of newcomers who landed in the cellar amid the potato bins and barrels of pork. They was having a tip top time before that, tossing pepper on the hot stove to keep everyone sneezing. (Stove stayed put.) That's their idea of a ludicrous time. The grumblers & worseheads find this town dull, dullest in the world. They heard there was two and a half places in town fairly lively, one being the Hotel de Comfort where Colonel Randolph performed The Arkansas Traveler nightly, so they all come down. But of course there wasn't no blacklegs nor grogsellers, no painted women, no cries of "Make your pool, gentlemen," no stag dances played to fiddlers shuffling around in hide boots, no smashing of glasses & oaths & pistol shots. We did get an exhibition of parlor skating some weeks ago, they say it's all the rage back east—you been on wheels yet, Walt? Can you do the Boston dip? No one here took it up as folks is too busy working. No high living & high heeled boots here. Place is growing fast. Since I've done but little of life's allotted portion of my duty, I'm making up for it monstrous quick. Busy all day. No rest for the wicked nor for me. Have full sway over

Father Meeker's newspaper except what he composes on the stick and picks out from the weeklies in the mail. Well, as it's dull, and the Hotel de Comfort with its odor of high living's being torn down, Walt, don't tell no one but I tramp over to the unthrifty dilapidated village of Evans, 4 miles away, for a tipple whenever I can. Enjoy the loathsome miasma of drink. Makes me feel fine, but must be careful of my language & moral conduct tramping back. They don't like drinking swearing bloats in these parts. Sober up walking with glad and gallant step & get home in good season, mud shoe deep all the way. Trip over sagebrushes in the dark. You're lucky the streets back east don't grow sagebrush. Tumble into my gopher hole at the boarding house named above & pour forth my soul in song as the room is unvented except for a crack I got covered with a chromo of some darling little boys with some darling little doggies. I know, unvented rooms give the scrofula—I can just hear you, Walt. But not if you're pickled. Attribute my good health to bathing in cold water privately. Wake up and have to grease my socks mornings just to pull on my new span of boots I'm breaking in which get monstrous hard from the wet mud of the night before. These boots cost nineteen dollars, Walt, which is two weeks' work. They cut quite a dash. Price of everything's down except boots. Buffalo rump at 2 cents a pound. Pails they call buckets now and sell half the price at Monk's Dry Goods. Bootmaker might have to reshape my feet.

Arrivals from the States still constant. Some still depart in a grumble. So this is the wonderful town of Greeley, they say, built in a single year and not a drunken man in sight. I tell them watch the Evans road at night. Watch the shipments from Denver. Some bachelors in town delight in public temperance & private whiskey, and order their kegs from Denver packed in crates of nails. I never told you before, Walt, the first year we had some Blind Pigs and Blind Tigers in sod houses outside of town full of base fellows. Pay 10 cents to see a Blind Pig and the man gives you a free glass of whiskey. Wasn't illegal to give it away. Then Father Meeker passed an ordinance. After that, Flower & Cameron kept whiskey in their drugstore and anyone could buy it for medicinal purposes, but Father Meeker who's bitter against it shipped it all out. So they brought in all manner of ammonia straight, disinfectants, & rattlesnake antidotes to satisfy the thirsty, but Father Meeker preached about that in the paper and some riled-up folks nearly burned down the drug-

store. *There's people here would go on a drunken rampage just to keep the rest of us sober.*

Yes, Walt, I heard all about the immigration fever. But lots of folks take one sniff and keep going. Some come just to look, we're such a curiosity. This is the place cooperation built. Father Meeker's Bible of Cooperation and Reform gets hauled out every day, sometimes they bash folks' heads with it senseless just to make them cooperate. People grab what they can just the same. When they don't cooperate he throws on a tax, that's how they built the fence around the town. Cattle was raging throughout the streets eating everyone's cabbages and turnips, so Father Meeker impounded them, but the cow-boys broke the pound open at nights. These cow-boys call us farmers Meeker's Saints who armed ourselves against the heathen round about. That's because a number of settlers guarded the pound against incursions, but the stock must of opened the gate theirselves, they was all out the next day. At last Father Meeker raised a tax and convinced the government at Denver to let us erect a fence around the colony, and now even the cattle cooperate. This accounts for the bad odor we have from the heathen, which don't like fences. Mr. Greeley predicts the stock business will be pushed to the wall by farming communities settling all up and down the rivers & streams in Colorado Territory.

Father Meeker spoke on "Life in a Fourier Institution" last week at the lyceum, which means I guess this ain't a Fourier Institution no more, as everyone already knows what life's like here. The railroads ship out our goods alright and ship in all manner of rubber pigs, kerchiefs, cakes of scented soap, herring boxes, tinned sardines, and other sundries. By the way, Walt, the freight train conductors are said to have an extensive collection of boys' legs. We got our own dump of tin cans where the hungry goats graze. Mr. Sanborn detected some queer money at his store last month—we ain't immune. Even Father Meeker said in his lecture that cooperation's based on self-interest, which is how you call a fish a horse. The grumblers and soreheads which left the first year and didn't cash in their old certificates can sell them now for double the money, he says. It costs $205.00 for a share in the colony these days, and for that you get a lot in town and farmland off on the moon. Newcomers buy their shares first then grumble against everything from the grass is too short to the mountains is too far away to they can't get a quarter section close to town and they expected when they come to get a quarter section close to town. Most is surprised at the size of the place, thinking before they arrived it was like an Illinois railroad town with a few houses built alongside the track and not realizing all the streets we made & long rows of brick stores with goods in the windows and the flowers and lawns and the two thousand people with parlors and organs and chromos on the wall, which is why it ain't a Fourieristic Institution—it's just another town getting on fast. Father Meeker built a mighty fine house out of sun burnt bricks, but he can't afford it. Too many irons. He says there ain't no aristocracy here and the high works just as hard as the low, but he's in a fine house and I'm in a gopher hole—but I don't grumble. What's the sense of it? It's true you got men with collegiate educations driving ox teams and digging ditches, which is maybe why we need so many lawyers. Educated farmers make disputation a pastime. They're all grumbling now for the third ditch to get dug, as they forever need water, but Father Meeker who writes better about farming than farm himself says some things is better underdone than overdone, for example our porridge and our prayers, and irrigation's one of them. These farmers—something always needs tending to. It's a meager life to get rich on, I say. They're always breaking new ground, building new things, digging new ditches, hammering away—it's a kind of disease. New fences, new furrows, new gardens, new barns, new sheds, new houses, new lawns, new walkways, new trees, all the new things you're supposed to stay put in a while. They put up a house, tear it down or move it aside & put up another, then buy some new land and start all over. Must be they miss those good old days when they first arrived and pitched their canvas mansions in the dirt and had iron rusted coffee & wormy hard tack for supper each night & got rained on when it rained pretty lively. Must be they enjoy moaning and complaining about it all day long. Father Meeker says he understands the trials of Moses now and his stiff necked followers crying out in anger, Why have you brought us out into the wilderness to perish? Well, someone had to make the desert bloom as a rose. Can't let it stand full of prickly pears and prairie dog villages all its natural life. Anytime anyone here spots a tract of barren cactus plain they long to see it converted to fruitful fields waving with golden grain or green & purple with blossomed alfalfa giving bread to the sower and labor to the tramp & all vocal with the buzzing of hordes of grasshoppers. It's an itch folks have. Mr. Greeley came here on a flying switch from his campaign out west and praised this place to the skies, but in private to Father Meeker

*called it a burning disgrace that we still don't have our own milk
instead of trucking it in. Make the people plow and plant, he said,
plus don't trust the railroads and keep the booze out. My humble
self was sitting there in the newspaper office with the two of them.
Uncle Horace plans to retire here after he serves out his term as
President. I didn't remind him he'd best get elected first. I kept my
trap shut. He told Father Meeker to insist on being relieved from
all official duties connected with the colony and instead govern
through the newspaper. But don't give credit on subscriptions. The
paper don't pay yet. Father Meeker pointed out that you have to
reach the land of Beulah by slow stages and up hills of difficulty,
through the valley of the shadow of death and leaving the Vanity
Fairs behind, which he says they haven't been left behind yet—they
got them in Evans—but Uncle Horace says what they really need
is a Joshua, but he ain't come yet, and so they went on like this
slinging the Bible back and forth between them, it made them feel
better. Father Meeker averred as what he'd really like is to be sent
to Europe as a correspondent for the New York* Tribune, *but Uncle
Horace severed his ties with the* Tribune *when he got the nomination, he said. But he'll see what he can do (not much). He loaned
Father Meeker another thousand dollars. You are the colony, he
said. What would Israel have been without Moses? Father Meeker
said, Well, we all come from the ground and was made out of dust.
I say amen to that, some folks smell of it too. Uncle Horace was
agitated that his trees all died. They planted a thousand evergreens
and two thousand larches on the land he bought and built a dyke
over to it, which set some folks off for the special treatment, but the
dyke was made from sandy soil and the gophers worked it and most
of the water run over and got lost before it ever arrived. So all he
wound up with was nuisance trees, the cottonwoods and some box
elders.*

*Then there's the grasshoppers. Walt, you should see them! They
got grasshoppers here to 6 inches deep. Some things they like and
some they don't. They leave a potato field alone if there's any corn
nearby. Sorghum they got no taste for, but they dote on onions and
alfalfa, prefer cabbages to tomatoes, and disdain peas. A continuous
smudge saves some of your precious vegetables & flowers, but someone has to keep everlasting at it, which means me in Father Meeker's
case, as I also assist him with his crops. We tried water, kerosene,
coal tar & different kinds of traps, but made a failure each time.
Seven or eight inventors came this summer showing us machines to*

kill the grasshoppers and left with our money, but we still got the grasshoppers. Turned out the hogs & poultry to feed upon them, but they sickened and died. You kill one grasshopper and a couple thousand come to its funeral. These ain't natural grasshoppers like you got back east, Walt, they're big. They're rigged considerable like a stout railroad man with heavy top boots, corduroy trousers & a fireman's hat which sits upon a mulish head. They look like a mule in a too big harness. Makes you think of a bunch of green harness buckles welded together in Egyptian dark. There's so many of them you wonder how they don't just get lost in a crowd and forget who they are. Suppose you was a grasshopper, Walt, and got lost in one of them crowds of millions they got here, how would you know whether it was you or somebody else? You might feel bad about it.

I trust you ain't still mad at me, Walt. Your last letter sounded miffed if coaxing. I showed it to some people—hope you don't mind—to prove I got a famous friend. They want you to come and lecture at the lyceum. If they offer to pay you in cabbages, hold out for turnips. No, I can't come back east—not yet. Sure I miss you. Do you miss me? And yes, I miss city life too, but you got to remember I was raised on a farm. Here I got not just farming but a newspaper to write on, which is more than I ever had in New York. I ain't run out on you, Walt, not really—just taking a vacation. My vacation consists of rising at dawn with the birds and setting type all morning, then making acquaintance with the grasshoppers camped on Father Meeker's crops in the heat of the day. I can't even idle away my sabbath except by skipping services, which I'm doing right now. I've learned to sweat like a butcher, Walt. It's hot as love in July lately here. Must remember to be extremely grateful to my redeemer for his continual preservation of my sanity. I'm improving myself. Spend time in fixing my person & cramming my mind. Makes a boy long for his Daddy's barn. Josie Meeker gives me lessons in how to keep level. Swear I'll die head up. I'm sure my life would be burthersome here but for her, my truest and warmest friend in this place. She's a good spud—you'd like her, Walt. Stood up in church two months ago and told the preacher she don't subscribe to his heaven & ain't afraid of his hell, which just about knocked the sides as well as the bottom out of their bottomless pit. It was the Presbyterians she said this to, even though it is well known that the Meekers are Campbellites. The farmers here stay close to whatever belief strikes them as narrowest at the time. Kind of like plowing. After that, Father Meeker started a Unitarian meeting in

*his parlor, which proved scandalous. You'd think they was worship-
ping the Devil. Father Meeker dotes on his daughter because he
thinks she got the mouse in her breast, and he lost one son to
consumption years ago. Climate here said to be good for pulmonary
disorders. He prints all the news of the suffragites lest Josie throttle
him. Mrs. Elizabeth Cady Stanton spoke here at the lyceum and
stayed with the Meekers. She favors Mr. Greeley for president. Josie
is only seventeen but she spoke at the lyceum too concerning "Lo,
the Poor Indian." Seems a farmer's dog kept bringing him bones
after he plowed. Had quite a stack of them—claimed they was
cattle bones. But I never seen cattle bones with rounded skulls and
black hair. The black hair on one turned red in the sun. Josie said
he was desecrating a sacred Indian burial ground, and that just
about made everyone furious with her calling it sacred. Walt, if all
the Indian haters here was to act on their principles there'd be a
considerable mortality. People gripe about Indian Troubles, but I
ain't seen any. Only Indians near this place crossed the Platte River
north of town on a hunting expedition three days ago with their
agent along. He was carrying a flag of truce so as not to unduly
alarm the farmers. It's true a section hand on the railroad was killed
by redmen a while ago, but that was in Nebraska. Mostly they're
human too. I saw they got their good luck charms just like me in
little pouches slung about their necks. Sure, they paint their faces and
bark like dogs but that's just for show. You see Bowery B'hoys back
in New York strut a lot worse. Folks claim they ain't civilized, but
I say if being civilized means singing the bass & soprano parts of
"Old Hundred" simultaneously like George Quigley done at the
lyceum last week, who benefits by that?*

*One old timer here says he was scalped years ago by an Indian.
Says the redmen stole his peltries he was taking down river to sell,
so he and some others attacked their camp. But he got tangled up
in a nest of squaws, one of which clubbed him dizzy and while he
was lying there some big buck chief stepped one foot on his chest and
gathered up the hair near the crown of his head. He closed his eyes
to greet his maker and felt the awfulest biting flash round his head,
then it was like his brains had been jerked clean up and out. Took
him three full days to come round with the sorest head of any one
human person that ever lived. He never got the scalp back, and the
hair never growed again on that particular spot top of his brow.
Name's Jack Wilcox. The farmers don't approve of his kind. He was
one of the squatters they tried to buy out when they settled the town,*

*but he never quite sold. Visits at the newspaper office when Father
Meeker ain't here. Walks down the street surrounded by horseflies
wearing a greasy coat made of a blanket, some leather leggins that
creak like the devil, plus moccasins just like a redskin, and a leather
belt from which hangs the knife and tobacco pouch, and the farmers
just turn their heads like they sucked a lemon as if to say how on
earth did that old heap of horse shit with eyes squeeze into our
genteel community? It's more like they had to build the place around
him. He talks like that kerflummoxed bumpkin in "The Lion of the
West," Walt—you know, the ex-flunctified one—the "feller" that's
all the time sayin, "Wake up, snakes, June bugs is comin'." Me and
Jack Wilcox come to an understanding right away; he tells me as
many far fetched tales as he pleases, and I believe as little as I like.
Says he was once in the grasp of a bear. Says he knew a fellow bit
by a bear in the head who claimed he heard the skull break. Says
their delicacy at round up camps was buffalo intestine raw, which
two mountain men ate from either end squeezing the contents ahead
as they chewed. Every time he's been here at the office and left,
Father Meeker comes in and sniffs and inquires, "What's that
smell?" I just shrug. Jack don't say ruckus, he says ruction. A lot
of noise is a catawampus. Whiskey is nose paint and talk is palaver.
He told me how they used to make butter out of bear fat & molasses
and call it Charlie Taylor, but why they called it that he couldn't
recall. When he cinches up his belt on an empty belly, that's his
Spanish supper. Bear meat is pork. An appaloosa horse is skeebald.
Most everything he don't have a name for is fixins or possibles. You'd
appreciate him, Walt. He's a grumbler too. He told me last week,
Nowadays you can't never put an inch or so of knife into a fellow
but the law's slobbering after you. A man deserves some peace, he
says, and not all this interference in his privacies. Sometimes we
tramp off to Evans together. For an old man he walks a good pace.
I told him I plan to stuff him when he dies and ship him back east
for mounting in a glass case as an extinct species. He laughed like
a whore. Kind of reminds me of you, Walt, with that big bushy
beard he got. You should see when Father Meeker spots him—his
face goes cold enough to freeze a newborn babe in the cradle. I think
he considers him part injun—or woman. Jack wears his stringy hair
to his shoulders like a woman. For all his suffragite talk, Father
Meeker wrote a piece in the paper last month which gave his
daughter a violent attack of bilious cholic—called "Woman, the
Natural Savage." Had to do with why the Indians are so nation*

hard to civilize. It's because the women dote on their boys too much, which can't be whipped but must always be coddled. So the boys grow up undisciplined and lazy and become the women's slaves. Josie thought that was so much rot and truck that now she's vowing to go off and live with the redmen and learn them some manners and education so folks like her father won't keep on getting the wrong impression.

Well, Walt. Must learn to abridge my epistles. Do enjoy my new Leaves finely. Thank you for sending. I've been charged by Josie to ask you in particular what you think of Uncle Horace's chances, since she can't squirrel a straight answer out of her father. He fights a battle every day in the newspaper against those who ridicule Mr. Greeley for president, but I think he was flummoxed just like everyone else by the nomination. Folks keep on bringing up the fact that Greeley don't fly with the orthodox political butterflies, that he fancies himself a farmer, that he's a pissen poor farmer—not to mention a closet Fourierite—that he wears clumsy shoes and perverted neckties, and that he bailed Jeff. Davis out from prison. The answer to that is he is the most popular man in America—but that don't mean he'll get elected president. The wave of reform ain't that strong. Josie thinks it the kiss of death that the Democrats nominated him too, but Mr. Greeley said when he came here that if the Lord rejoiceth in one sinner that repenteth, how could anyone object to 3 million Democrats raised up out of perfidy? Well, we in the territories can't vote anyhow, which makes us no better off than women. So long, Walt. Got my Graham biscuit soaking. Like Jack Wilcox says, Keep your teeth sharp. Yours to the backbone,

Pete

Amherst/Sept. 30, 1872

Dear Pete,

I write you from a quaint little Inn in a quaint little village in Massachusetts. Every thing comfortable, but very Yankee—not an African to be seen all day, let alone redmen—not a grain of dust— no smell of coal tar—green grass every where. Every house stands separate & genteel & has quite a ground about it for flowers & for shade or fruit trees, or a garden. Looks like quite a mincing praying life goes on behind those big closed doors. I'm here on a visit to a quaint little gal whose servants have turned me away at the door—

twice—with the word she ain't well. If she don't get better today, it's back to Washington. The truth is, Peter, the gals dote on me. This one is hardly seventeen like your friend of course. But you would be astonished, my son, to see my brass & coolness & my capacity of flirtation & carrying on with the girls—I never would have believed it of myself. Lectured last week in Boston on Lincoln's Death, and spent my time there mainly in the midst of female women, some of them young & jolly. The way in which this aged party comes up to the scratch & cuts out the youthful parties & fills their hearts with envy is absolutely a caution. Sought for, seized upon & ravingly devoured by these creatures—& so nice & smart some of them are, & handsome too—there is nothing left for me—is there—but to give in. Of course, young man, you understand, it is all on the square. My giving in amounts to just talking & joking & having a devil of a jolly time—that's all. Which you will admit, considering my age & heft, to say nothing of my reputation, is doing pretty well.

Went leisurely up the Connecticut Valley, by way of Springfield, through the best part (agriculturally, & other) of Massachusetts. Will return via Albany & down the Hudson by boat. Getting much more strength & vitality lately, Pete, & easier in the head—more like myself. This railroad inn smells of fish, but the room is nice & large, with a fire in it, and the grub suits me fine. Brought your letter with its cheering portraits & prophecies here with me. God bless you, boy—You are the greatest comfort I have. Keep up the good spirits & write me more such letters & tell me everything. I like your letters far better than the solemnified ones some people send. Don't get in any tight spots with those injuns & mountain men. Maybe I'll surprise you & take up that lecture offer. Everything would depend on how it was fixed up & prepared for & put through—Let me hear more particulars. I've never seen the Rockies. The fee would have to cover my western fare and lodging, of course.

Do I miss you, dear boy? I don't miss you, Pete, of course not, I only sit & stare at nothing out the window all day long. I don't feel it, no, don't feel anything more than a stone, or the tree that's standing in the garden all empty & bare that once was warm and green when the birds used to sing in its branches. The truth is I think about you every night, especially in Washington. Reproach myself that I failed to get up to New York & see you more when you was there. If only I could get on a train & go up to see you right now & have some good times with you like we used to! You'd be *surprised at how I'm getting on.* General health *much better than ever, but hard to always keep up a good heart.*

Tell your friend I see no prospect of Mr. Greeley's election. The Democrats look blue enough & General Grant's troops are on their high horses. Last week was about the greatest political show I ever saw in Washington. Sky full of big balloons, letting off rockets & Roman candles way up amongst the stars. The excitement, the rush, & the endless torches & cannons fired all night, gave me great pleasure. As I was on my way home on the cars between 12 & 1 o'clock we got blocked in by a great part of the returning procession. Of course we had to just stand & take it. I enjoyed it hugely from the front platform. They were nearly an hour passing us, streaming past both sides with all sorts of objects, models of ships forty or fifty feet long, cars of Liberty with women, & every body carrying a blazing torch.

Love to you, Pete. I'm off to try the Yankee barricades again. This quaint gal of mine is a poet, dear Pete. Something of a local legend. She seems to have formed an attachment to my bulk. Don't be jealous, son, if you can help it at all. Keep up a gay heart & let the world wag on. Your loving comrade,

Walt

Chapter

❧ *2* ❧

"Yes?"

"Miss Dickinson, please."

"Who shall I say?"

"Same as yesterday. Walt Whitman."

The poet on the steps and the servant at the door eyed each other with equal suspicion. He'd called twice yesterday, hadn't he?—she knew damn well who to say. The whole town knew by now, Walt felt. He was the peddler, the tinker, some kind of tramp or leather man, he dressed funny, his hat was too floppy, shirt collar wide open, watch your chickens, guard the clothes on the line. A network of whispers linked all these houses behind their high fences and hedges. Yankee towns did this to Walt, brought out the ragtag and bobtail part of him, but this Amherst especially, with its large and silent buildings which nothing but a first-class, brass-lined, thousand-ton volcano would stir. It looked like it hadn't changed in centuries. Below the pillars and hedges, the roads in perfect little hollows had been spread with the ashes of God, which settled equally in wheel ruts and alleys and pathways and down beside the roots of great trees. You sensed yourself skirting some downright slippery places here. *Their foot shall slide* . . . And the devil lurked behind every tree. Walking the streets of Amherst—he'd walked them all yesterday deciding whether to stay and try again or head back at once—Walt had sensed the townsfolk giving him a wide berth, though it also seemed they hardly noticed him. Everyone walked across planks in this town. Even down below the train station in Irishtown, down there amidst the hat factories and unpainted shanties, Walt felt under the influence of the town's get-under-my-feet religion, which, as he saw it, gave hell out to the crowd and saved heaven for a few. He detected it in this servant's face too. She could have been anything, Catholic, Jew, Mohammedan, she probably came from Irishtown herself, but in her master's house she took on his church and all its gloom. Hovering there, imposing above him, this fully upholstered Maggie or Molly, thin-lipped and high-browed, appeared no more capable of smiling than the north wind.

"Come in. She's expecting you."

"She's in better feather?"

The woman turned and regarded Walt. The slit of her mouth lengthened. "She feels better, yes."

Walt lumbered up the steps and shut the great oaken door himself. The long, broad hallway with closed doors on either side led to a staircase curving up out of sight. At the foot of the stairs stood a marble-topped table with thick spiral legs and a chair beside it. The servant's broad hand signaled the chair. She stood facing Walt before the staircase like a tree and waited while he sat down, removed his hat, shook out his locks. Then she proceeded up the steps.

He placed his hat gingerly on the table.

Whispers, rustles, and creaking doors up there. Walt looked around at the brown wallpaper, the hanging lamp. The day outside had begun hot and dusty, but this hallway felt cool and dark. The landlord at the Union Hotel claimed she wore white always, lived with her parents, and never went out. No one knew what she looked like, he said, so Walt had been forced to imagine the face she'd described in her letter, the fine auburn hair, the sherry-colored eyes. They must be large. He saw her as small-boned, she'd insisted on that, with a boyish face and large, startled eyes, or maybe just the pupils were big—two dark disks in a flat pale face. Lips of putty, indistinct lips. He felt he was trying to imagine a corpse. He'd made a mistake in coming here, surely. The thought that this bastion would yield up a woman of snap and spirit seemed farfetched now. A pedigree from Amherst, a life surrounded by dyed-in-the-wool Yankee preachers, was bound to freeze your soul. Yet her letters suggested the independent type, hardly narrow, hardly gushing. And just this morning, back in his room at the Union Hotel, he'd found himself nibbling at a notion here and there around the edges, only half consciously. She lay on his bed, arms crossed at her bosom, his Amherst bride. A few light kisses, a few embraces, a reaching around of arms. He with his palm on the hip of his mate, she with her palm on the hip of her husband . . .

What would Pete think?

Walt nearly laughed out loud. From somewhere deep in the house came voices. Muffled creak of a door. Dear sweet Pete. Still, it could happen. He could become the robust husband of a woman. Why not? It wasn't too late, even at age fifty-two, to beget fierce and athletic girls, new artists, the fathers and mothers of sons, and in them the fathers and mothers of more sons and daughters—farmers, artisans, musicians, singers . . . A form all in white lay on a bed, immobile but giving off sparkles like scissors on a wheel. The color rose to Walt's face. That gloomy hallway judged him severely. Then a new thought struck him: maybe she needed rescuing from this place.

He stood up. If Pete could only see him. Pete, if you miss me, come back right now. It's me who needs rescuing, save me, Pete, or I'll get hitched for sure!

Everything was quiet in the house.

He looked up the empty stairs, then sat down. He hadn't lied to Pete—felt much stronger lately. Almost his old self. Had seen through the press a new edition of *Leaves*, and delivered the commencement poem at Dartmouth in June at the invitation of the students there, who considered themselves advanced. Lectured in Boston on "Lincoln's Death." Read the inaugural poem at the National Industrial Exposition in New York just a few weeks ago too, an event that would have been a smashing success had not the very workmen he celebrated in the poem drowned out his voice with their hammers and saws. They had to finish the exhibits before the crowds could be admitted. He'd pretty much gotten over Pete's departure too, though the old wound festered now and then. Be good to see Pete, out of *curiosity*: see his actual face instead of a photo. If Pete arranged that lecture, maybe Walt could whip up a whole western tour: Kansas City, Greeley, Denver, Salt Lake. He could gawk at the bigamists in Utah . . .

"Mr. Whitman?"

"Yes?"

"How are you and the cosmos getting along?"

The voice came from up there, beyond the stairway's curve. If she'd walked to the head of the stairs, he hadn't heard. Had she been lurking up there all this time, listening to him mumble? He held off till she came down.

"The gentleman with the barbaric yawp makes no reply? Perhaps you've had a falling out, the cosmos and you?"

"The gentleman aforesaid prefers talking face to face."

"Mr. Whitman, you'll forgive me, but I cannot see you just now. You'd dazzle too greatly, and my eyes are—finite. You send sunrise out of you, if you recall." This began in a hesitant whisper that gradually bodied forth a voice, but what a voice! It twisted around itself, braided like wire, until sentences that had started out breathless sounded strong enough to Walt to hang a whole sack of potatoes on. "You don't care for me quoting you? I recall you said once the sunlight would kill you if you couldn't send it out of yourself."

"The mental apparatus is slow, Miss Dickinson. Don't talk so fast. My memory—sometimes it fires up, but sometimes it gets so low I have to bust my lungs just blowing it to flame. That's from *Leaves*, is it not?"

"I have the page. 'Dazzling and tremendous, how quick the sunlight would kill me'—Mr. Whitman—'If I could not now and always send sunrise out of me.' It comes close after your marriage to the cosmos."

" 'We also ascend dazzling and tremendous as the sun, We found our own soul in the calm and cool of daybreak.' "

"Evidence of your recovery, Mr. Whitman! I feel the flame up here from my perch."

"Does me good to hear it. Your voice gives it heart. There's more of me, the essential ultimate me, in those lines than any others."

"Oh, I don't know. 'Divine I am inside and out.' There's some of you there. Or none."

Walt slapped his knee. "That's famous! None."

" 'The scent of these arm-pits is finer than prayer.' "

" 'Enough—or too much!' "

"In quoting you, I quote myself."

"Now don't drag that up. I regret the accusation."

"And I regret the ink on my fingers."

Walt couldn't help staring up the staircase. He pictured his words mounting the steps. "That's what my *Leaves* amount to anyhow—that's what I mean them to amount to, Miss Dickinson. There's a certain point in their evolution where they cease to be my creation or possession."

"I am relieved to hear it, Mr. Whitman. Shall I amend my copy? 'I, Emily Dickinson, one of the roughs, disorderly, fleshy, of Amherst a daughter . . .' "

"Wonderful! Famous! That's it exactly."

"But why not Blades?"

"What's that?"

"Before I chase you out of your Leaves—why aren't they called 'Blades of Grass?' The vein asks the artery."

"That wouldn't do. It don't sound right. I got the 'Leaves' bee in my bonnet from the first."

"And it bit you."

"Profoundly true, Miss Dickinson. You've hit the mark."

"You made the arrow. I wondered when I read it what point of contact there could be between us. I thought you were poking fun, Mr. Whitman. Emily Dickinson, learned and accomplished—austere, ascetic and tame—and Walt Whitman"—her voice dropped an octave—"turbulent, eating, drinking, and breeding. Searching for the wand of Circe. Will the gentleman with the low voice forgive me if I say your words are barbaric?"

"Hold your blasts, Miss Dickinson. Leave us a shred."

"I thought it wasn't poetry till my body went cold. There's your shred. If I feel physically as though the top of my head were taken off, that is poetry. Is there any other way?"

"None. There is none. It must scalp you—knock you down. Some shocks knock you down, some up."

"But I thought you the silliest creature alive! I thought if you barked the world would howl. Gentlemen should think twice before they bark."

"Well, I—"

"Then I read what Mr. Emerson said about your poems. He said he had to rub his eyes. So I sifted it twice. And I thought, Why is any other book needed?"

"Thank you. I think I should thank you."

"Pray, don't."

"I only see myself from the inside—with the ordinary prejudice a fellow has in favor of himself."

"We feel no stranger but ourself. Would it comfort you to be poked full of holes?"

"I'm not certain—"

"You might leak. Then what a mess we should have! All that bigness and bravery, all those mountains and forests and church bells and hats. All that unbounded divinity, Mr. Whitman, confusing my floor. I'd be in danger, sir. The rising tide of it up to my roof. How the sailor strains when his boat is filling. So much world I've never entertained here. The papers said Mr. Tennyson wrote to you. I trust his words found you august. I'm tipsy at the thought. I have a little Tennyson with my own name in it. My drop in the sea. Do all the people touch you, Mr. Whitman? Are you the president? Smile, if you please. The world is not the shape it was—before you came. I should think you'd erase it. Please remain clothed. You'd embarrass my dog. Smile—"

"Dammit, I *am* smiling."

"I'll wash the expletive."

"Are you coming downstairs, or ain't you?"

"I feel more comfortable talking like this. It's safer."

"For who?" Walt stood up and scowled at the hallway. A painting on the wall across showed three young children, two in dresses, with hair thin and short, identical faces, and big cow eyes. Down the hallway beyond the staircase an open door with its shutters secured admitted light in horizontal stacks. Above, the silence grew ominous. He *was* leaking—drilled full of holes by that unyielding voice. It kept coming at you. Something knocked lightly above. He looked all around. I could walk out right now . . .

He ducked at the shadow, felt his heart lurch. A bat or a hawk come swooping down—

Just a box, a picnic basket. Hanging from a cord! He spotted a small hand guiding it through the railing on the landing above. Chest high it stopped with the open lid inviting him to examine its contents: two daylilies, a pair of scissors, and a note scrawled in haste. The handwriting looked like fishhooks, like Arabic: "These are my introduction. Forgive me. I never see strangers, and hardly know what to say." He removed the lilies and laid them beside his hat on the table; the basket remained. From above came the voice, hardly a whisper.

"I won't ask for your scalp, Mr. Whitman. You could plunder your beard."

"Don't be so damned cryptical."

"That adjective again! Daisy requests a lock of your hair. The furthest from your mouth."

"Lock of my hair?"

"A hoary lock. Mixed tussle hay of head and beard. I trust the crop is abundant. Could you spare me just enough for a nutshell?" Her voice had reclaimed its strength. The basket jiggled as though to tempt him. "Surely your readers have made such requests before?"

"Never. Never once."

"Then I am honored to be the first."

Standing there, Walt contemplated the scissors. A lock of his hair? That's a good one, that's rich. He sat down and the basket followed, resting itself on the table beside him. The insides of his elbows felt damp. They were dressmaker's scissors, heavy and black.

"The mouse tails dulled their edge, Mr. Whitman. You musn't concern yourself they'll bite someone so illustrious as you."

He looked up at the empty stairs.

"You'd prefer I request you to shave your cloven hoof?"

"You talk with real swing, Miss Dickinson, but God almighty—stop poking fun! I get humors—they come over me, can't help it—emotional revolts against people everlasting regarding me as something to laugh at. How would you like it?"

"I shouldn't presume they were laughing at *me*. Sometimes our tormentors are imaginary, Mr. Whitman."

"And sometimes we're blind."

"The blind can't be hounded—nor dazzled."

"Then you must be one of them."

"But you've dazzled me twice over! Once with your book, once with your tongue. It's the blindness of others that makes us stumble. Ask yourself which is the worst, to be laughed at or ignored."

"What a choice! Ignored, I suppose."

"I disagree. Ignorance is harmless. The worst is to be smothered by upholstered convictions."

Walt slapped his hand on the table. "Exactly!" He found himself nodding vigorously. "You've hit the nail. Refined, bookish, made-up attitudes. I know what you mean. 'You take this advice, Walt Whitman,' they say, 'or God damn you, we'll know the reason why!'"

"But you mustn't take it!"

"Oh I would—I would—but they can't agree as to what they want. Some don't like my clothes, some do. Some don't like my commas, some do. Some cuss my poems, some think them holy. Nothing I've done but a lot of somebodies objected; nothing I've done but a lot of nobodies praised it. What's the use? My old daddy used to say it's some comfort to a man if he must be an ass anyhow to be his own kind of ass."

"Your father read your poems?"

"He died just my entrance year—1855. I don't suppose it would have made much difference to him if he'd read the *Leaves.* The family, they sort of accept me, it's a matter of course, but with a feeling as though of not knowing why or what I am—a feeling, a wish, I might be more respectable, train more in accustomed lines, let myself be stitched in with the cluster of celebrities—you know. The lingo of authorship."

"Your dear mother too?"

"My mother!" Walt smiled to himself and regarded a scab on the back of his knuckles. "My mother. How much I owe her! My mother is illiterate in the formal sense, but strangely knowing. She can tell stories, impersonate. Very eloquent in the utterance of noble moral axioms. Very original in her manner, her style. *Leaves of Grass* is the flower of her temperament in me."

"Is she well? Do you see her ever?"

"She is close to death. Arthritic and weak. Nearly eighty years old. I see her—I visit—every chance I get."

Down the hallway a door opened, and the same thin-lipped servant who'd admitted Walt approached bearing two cups of tea on a silver tray. She set one down next to the basket with hardly a glance at the good gray poet. The voice from above said, "Thank you, Maggie." Walt looked up—then she *was* a Maggie. She nodded at no one. For all her looming presence she moved as noiselessly as an ant. She climbed the stairs with the other cup of tea.

"Oh, Mr. Whitman!"

"Yes?"

"Ginger snaps to speak with your tea?" The basket stirred. Walt's hand got there ahead of his brain, snatched up the scissors, and cut off a long curl of hair behind his ear. Then both hands tossed scissors and hair into the rising basket.

Thank God she didn't thank him. Her thanks could be like worms in a cake. After a minute the basket returned with the lid closed and a card saying "Come in" fastened to the top with a pin. He opened the lid and found two ginger snaps. "You cooked these yourself, Miss Dickinson?"

"Myself and the elves. Has the flair—departed?"

Walt sipped his tea and took small bites of cookie, exactly as though she were sitting across from him. "They are delicious." The basket ascended. He heard her clinking her cup upstairs. This cozy soirée had grown nearly intimate!

"You have brothers and sisters, Mr. Whitman?"

"My share—the usual. They care only about pipes and money. I'm thinking of George. He works in a pipe foundry. He said to me once, with a wink, mind you, 'Say, Walt, what's this game you're up to anyway?' Referring to my poetry."

"I hope you kept the secret."

"In fact, I told him there was no secret. I wrote the books I wrote just because I did it—that's what I told him. What mystifies him is the sheer fact I wrote them. He finds it impossible to realize them as mine. He don't believe evil of me—yet the poems seem to him as something evil. He thinks them of the whorehouse order." Walt sipped his tea. A chair scraped upstairs. Across the hall, the three faces in the painting looked much too adult for the size of their bodies. Was one of them she? "And you, Miss Dickinson? Enough of me. You have brothers and sisters?"

"One of each species. Sisters are so brittle, I'd like more of those. When she's ill, the meaning runs out of things. If it's only a headache it's still important if the head aches next to you. She's far more hurried than presidential candidates. As for my brother, he's slow as a Dutch frigate turning a corner." She laughed. "But I love him. He lives a hedge away. He don't keep the moth part of the family, he keeps the butterfly. He gave me another sister, and she gives me children, and so I have many to test immortality for. And my mother?—she goes rambling in the floods and comes back with a twig. She don't care for thought. Father is too busy with his briefs to watch her, but he's away now, so we lock her up. The doors don't know how to hang without Father. I asked him once what made my door erroneous, and he said it was not plumb. Some rectitude or vigor, I suppose, in which the door was wanting. Father never learned how to play. Sometimes I think his physical life don't want to live any longer, but I hope I am mistaken. He buys me many books but begs me not to read them because he fears they joggle the mind. I live here with my family, Mr. Whitman. The definition of God is home. They are all religious except me, and address an eclipse every morning they call *their* Father. I never go to church—don't go out. Either. My canaries, and my garden—they come to me. *You* talk instead."

"I have nothing to say."

"But you say it so well. Have you read George Eliot?"

"Can't say as I have."

"Then you ain't large—you've missed out on glory." Much of the barb had left her voice, and what stings there were came so fast they hardly stung—went right past him. She talked like a bee circling his head. If she'd only slow down he could picture her face, crawl out along the contours of the words and build up her looks like a house in their subsoil. She was like a pianist whose notes you could *see*, but what he saw was hard to piece together—moist cheeks, sharp lonely eyes, lips made for nothing but chiseled words . . .

What was she wearing? "Your poems, Miss Dickinson—are they in print?"

"No—but they're clothed."

"I've enjoyed immensely those you have sent me."

"That gives me no drunkenness—I've tasted rum before."

"You've written a long time?"

"Just these few weeks."

"You first sent me poems two years ago!"

"Yes—and I still feel the red in my mind. You must understand, Mr. Whitman, we grow newer everyday—not older with the years. Are not all facts dreams when we put them behind us?"

Walt ate the second ginger snap whole, and looked around the hall. All at once he felt immensely hungry.

"Now it is you who laugh at me. Perhaps the whole United States are laughing at me! I can't stop for that."

"Nor should you, Miss Dickinson. If they laugh, thrust another poem in their face."

"And go undressed? That's easy enough for you to say, whose verse requires a lung, but no tongue. I sing like the boy at the graveyard, who was scared. Once I found a bird on a bush in the garden and asked it, 'Why sing, if nobody *hears?*'"

"And what did it say?"

"'My business is to sing . . .' it said."

He looked up at the painting—that could have been her, the one on the left holding a book. But it could have been anyone too; the features had been drawn so vague as to cover any future possibility. The face above on the landing refused to take shape, as though under water. It closed like a fist when she started to speak, then from something thin and emaciated began to swell out, and the mouth grew large—darkness poured out of it, ravines appeared in that birdlike face.

"I sang like a nighttime canary—when they covered my eyes."

"You have—you *are* blind, then?"

"Not anymore. Some years ago I had eight months of Siberia. It was the only woe that ever made me tremble. The medical man said, 'Eyes, be blind.' He might as well have said, 'Heart, be over.' Later he clapped and said, 'Sesame.' The first thing I read—devoured—was Shakespeare. For books I have you—and Shakespeare, Mr. Whitman. Do you have Shakespeare?"

"Homer and Shakespeare are good enough for me—if I can be understood as not closing out others."

"Do you ever read one of his sonnets backwards because the plunge from the front overturned you?"

"Can't say as I have. Miss Dickinson, I must be honest. Shakespeare, or whoever he was—or *they*—some say he was Bacon—read Miss Delia Bacon's account—Shakespeare appears to me much too effeminate. He leans toward taking the fiber and blood out from our civilization. Too medieval for my taste. The gospel of the grand and luxurious, great lords and ladies, plate, hangings, glitter, ostentation, hypocritical chivalry, dress, trimmings, carpets, uniformed lackeys. I am an animal. So are you. I require to eat, drink, and live. But to put any emphasis whatever on the trapperies, the luxuries, the, the—curtains—that were the stock and trade of our great-grandfathers—that I could never, never do. I speak of the plays, not the poems."

"No curtains?"

"Not the richest curtains."

"Well, we are all human, Mr. Whitman. Until we are divine. Won't the plays stand alone for all time?"

"Don't mistake me. They undoubtedly will. I have never questioned his vastness, his space. He was under a contract to produce two plays a year with one of the London theaters—did you know that? Much like my agreement with the *Herald.* So much a year. But the plays do not seem to me spontaneous. They seem laboredly built up. Too rich with satiety—overdone with words."

"You make me tremble." He pictured her trembling. "Overdone with words? I have no tribunal. You rob me of my food, sir."

"I repeat—don't mistake me. He—whoever he was—was a gentleman. He was not a man of the streets—rather of the court, of the study. He was not vulgar. You think me vulgar?"

"The little peacock in me tells me not to answer. But why is it, Mr. Whitman, when we had a Shakespeare club, the tutors proposed marking out the questionable passages? I should add that we told the men, *We* shall read everything—and we did."

"Bully for you."

"It wasn't too rough for our delicate palates."

"Nor should it be." Walt finished his tea in one gulp. "They proposed to expurgate me as well. Emerson said it—he of all people! Down on your knees, Walt Whitman—expurgate! Apologize!"

"And did you?"

"Of course not!"

"Bully for you. You're quite the animal."

"Miss Dickinson—" Walt found himself nearly shouting. "Take my advice: never take my advice."

"I shall. I shan't."

"Let me see you a minute."

"No."

"You should—you should show yourself."

"Should I take your advice?"

"I judge a man by his face."

"But you shan't judge mine."

"Get out—put your coat on. Walk the streets. Ain't you just starved? I mean for living?"

Her voice dropped; she nailed each word with what sounded like disgust. "I find ecstacy in living, sir. The mere sense of living is joy enough."

"You don't feel the want of employment?"

"I never thought"—she paused—"of conceiving"—she took a deep breath—"that I could have the slightest approach"—something was tapping—"to such a want in all the near future." Silence. The tapping stopped. He looked at the stairs. "I fear that I have not expressed myself strongly enough." Another pause. "The crunching cow with head depressed finds me afflicting?"

"You've given me—quite a meal to chew over."

"Do you sing, Mr. Whitman? I mean, sing out loud?"

"In the open air."

"Would you sing for me in the closed? I should be deeply grateful if you would. Lusty and loud, Mr. Walt Whitman."

"Show yourself and I'll sing."

"Sing and I'll show myself—but not just now."

"When?"

"Sometime soon."

"You can think how I look; I can't think how you look."

"Don't think. Sing. Mine is just the thief's request."

"I suppose you want a hymn."

"Anything will do, sir, except hymns. Those tunes make me darken. Something that laughs."

Walt stood up and stretched his legs. Upstairs, a door opened, footsteps crossed the hall. "Just one moment, please, Mr. Whitman. House is being cleaned. By committee. I prefer pestilence." Another door opened, then closed. "Now we're safe."

Sing? Might as well. Pete used to love to hear him sing too. Even drained as he was—wounded too, it seemed, by her barbs, but just a flesh wound, actually it helped, his blood had risen, he felt flushed all over— Walt could sing out a tune just fine. With open mouth, strong and melodious, a song. What do you hear, Walt Whitman? A song! The spots before his eyes weren't dust motes, he knew, they had something to do with his pulse and circulation. He walked a few steps just to limber up. But he did feel drained. Strangely weak and dizzy. Sing or sit down. Singing starts at the soles of the feet. Down the hallway, through the back shutter, he caught sight of trees sliced horizontally, and hummocks of grass and hay underneath them. He walked to the foot of the staircase—looked up—but the small bit of brown wall, the railings, the ceiling, all were perfectly blank. She was there, he knew, still as a rabbit. Something that laughs? He braced himself against the table and threw back his head.

Camptown ladies sing this song,
Doo-dah! Doo-dah!
Camptown racetrack five miles long,
Oh doo-dah day!

Come down here with my hat caved in,
Doo-dah! Doo-dah!
Go back home with a pocket full of tin,
Oh doo-dah day!

'Gwine to run all night,
'Gwine to run all day,
I bet my money on the bobtailed nag,
Somebody bet on the bay.

Silence echoed when he finished. Then small hands clapped overhead. "I pictured your big face singing, Mr. Whitman—and felt as the band does before its first shout. Daisy thanks you. Such a lung! Don't leave yet." How did she know he'd put on his hat? Some trick with mirrors. His eyes on their leash sniffed up the stairs, but his neck had grown sore, he could barely focus, and found to his surprise he was leaning both hands against the table stretched out, while trying to swivel his head in that direction. "Do sit down. Please. One more minute." He slumped in the chair and felt the hall spin.

The minute passed. Something knocked up there. Then it came down again, Pandora's basket. "My song," she said. Inside lay a sheet of paper with a poem. Above the words, a lock of reddish hair had been fastened to the paper by a button of wax. Beneath them in more wax was pressed a dead fly. Walt's hands twitched holding the thing. The basket ascended.

It took him some time to stop the words buzzing round and bring them into focus. When they landed, in order, the poem read itself.

Again—his voice is at the door—
I feel the old Degree—
I hear him ask the servant
For such an one—as me—

I take a flower— *as I go—*
My face to justify—
He never saw *me*— in this life—
I might surprise *his eye!*

"Note the fly, Mr. Whitman. We had a little meeting in my room and voted to remember you, including immortality. This is my vote. Entomological name unknown."

Walt stood up.

"Include me to your mother, please. Come again and see me."

"See you?"

"Next time you shall. The hearts are never shut here."

As though conjured there, Maggie had materialized by the front door and now held it open. Light filled the hall; dust swirled outside. Walt's life felt suddenly full of dark secrets.

"Parting is bleak, Mr. Whitman—like death—but occurs more times."

He walked to the door clutching his lilies and poem, his lock of her hair—his fly. "So long," he said.

Beneath the dust-coated leaves outside, two trotting buggies passed waving on the road.

Chapter

❦3❦

"Yes?"

"Mr. Doyle, please."

Maggie looked this one up and down and found him a good deal more respectable than the last, that creature who'd just left, the peddler or tinker, singer of ballads. He *smelled* better, first of all, and the hair didn't sprout all over his face like some animal in the forest, and—in general— he was natty. Up to the mark. He spoke like a gentleman. "There's no one named Doyle here, sir," she said.

"Peter Doyle?"

"Direct him to the cemetery, Maggie." The ringing voice from above drilled the back of Maggie's neck. "Perhaps there's one there and he needn't look farther."

His stand-up collar and tie, his cutaway jacket with lapels bordered in silk, his gold-headed walking stick, all said money. His handlebar mustache and chin tuft—his smile . . . Ask for Miss Emily instead, sir, why don't you—she's not engaged, never was. Maggie tried to smile. Why is it that the quality come here by mistake and the slime is rewarded from above with ginger snaps? If her father was here he'd have thrown out that ape. Shakespeare indeed! To have no truck with Shakespeare, when Shakespeare was just about king of the world!

This one tapped his walking stick smartly.

"There's a Doyle down in Irishtown, sir, but I doubt as he's the one you want. His first name ain't Peter."

"What is it?"

"I'm uncertain. It's Father Doyle."

"An old man?"

"No, sir. The priest at the new church."

He stroked his chin tuft with the back of his finger. "Black curly hair, blue eyes, a small man, favors a derby cocked forward, small hands and feet?"

"There's plenty of them here—that's the way they all look in Irish-town. The young jackanapes. But none's named Doyle, sir. So far as I know."

His quick eyes searched the hall behind Maggie, then fixed on her face—shot clear right in—one might have winked! They seemed to say, I'll share your secret. What secret, pray? She felt her own eyes widen.

"My apologies. Terribly sorry."

Everything he said had another meaning, and his face, though perfectly composed, seemed to smile.

"Regards to your mistress. Thank you for your patience. Good day."

But he stood there. Therefore, she shut the door slow and gentle, with both hands, regarding him—then scuttled up the stairs to share this adventure with Miss Emily.

Outside the colonnaded portico, Jo Benton looked up and down the house. Yellow brick, freshly painted. White trim. Curtains at all the downstairs windows. He descended the steps backwards, with care, and caught a face at an upstairs window as he knew he would, just a flash— one face or two, human or animal, hard to tell which before it vanished. The house remained silent. Of course Peter Doyle was in there—had to be—but how to make sure? He could unlatch the gate, walk through the garden, and peek in the windows, but that wouldn't do. This place felt important. If Doyle lived here, he'd most likely be some kind of servant or gardener, a groom, stable boy, butler, hired hand. But why would they hide him? He'd changed his name, most likely, Jo should have known.

He turned and stepped through the gate to the path above Main Street. Out here, the house was barely visible—just the chimneys and cupola on the roof—but there had to be an alley behind, a back entrance for buggies. With measured step, he walked down Main Street, hat in one hand, stick in the other. If a squealing thing crossed Jo's path, he'd club it for practice or sport—even beetles. Just to crack the shell of a garden snail would give exquisite pleasure right now, but living things seemed to hide in this town. Mansions and gardens lurked behind hedges. Walking, he made out the shape of a barn looming behind the Dickinson hedge, but stopping to peer through the hedge he saw nothing. What a fortress! And just when he'd all but caught up with his prey . . .

He'd followed Walt first to Boston. Endured his boring sermon on Lincoln, checked out the males and females he visited, all simpering literati, of course. Concluded he'd gone on a wild goose chase until this detour, twenty-five miles off the main track, where Walt had taken a room at the Union Hotel by the station in order to visit someone at this estate—who else but Doyle? Surely Jo's months of surveillance were over! The net he'd thrown around Mr. Walt Whitman, the growlers he'd paid, even Pinkerton men, had finally caught him a Doyle, or all but. Now he had a choice—do it aboveboard, offer Doyle, say, a thousand for the thing, and pocket an inconceivable profit, or just crack his head open, grab it, and run, it was his in the first place, his by blood and family title. Besides, he missed it. A little. But mostly he needed the money.

He'd all but lost interest a year or so ago. In that alley off an alley deep in Five Points, Peter Doyle had simply vanished, leaving a weeping poet behind. And Jo had stocks and bonds to puff, books to doctor, worthless land to sell, investors to gouge, greedy bankers to split specious fees with, all the harried duties of a gentleman of finance.

Then Union Pacific stock plunged and his mother came home.

These two events were unrelated except in the destiny of him they converged upon, humble Jo Benton. Stock in the Union Pacific dropped because the glory days of declaring dividends and collecting fees had finally been succeeded by the necessity of paying contractors. Then the government unexpectedly demanded all its interest from the bonds it had issued the company. So Jo and the board did the only thing they knew how to do—issued more stock to raise more cash. They pooled together to bull their new issue, but couldn't prevent the certificates, those corpses whose pockets they'd stuffed with their own money, from sinking with the weight of it. Then, worst of all, the scandal broke, it was still breaking, it hovered like thunderclouds over all their heads. Just four weeks ago the *Sun* had run its first headlines: THE KING OF FRAUDS. HOW THE CRÉDIT MOBILIER BOUGHT ITS WAY THROUGH CONGRESS. HOW SOME MEN GET FORTUNES. Indeed, thought Jo. Some men get fortunes and lose them just as quickly, and that's when they kick you—when you're down. But he had to be careful; he was walking on eggshells. Just before he'd left on this trip, he'd received a letter from Oliver Ames asking him to destroy a certain note in the company's records upon which the names of thirteen congressmen had been scribbled, with amounts paid each. Poor Oliver. To save his own skin, Jo had turned this letter over to the Select Committee Luke Poland had just formed in Congress to investigate the scandal. Of course, he would have destroyed the note in question—perhaps—or at least kept it for himself to sell to the highest bidder, but someone had gotten to the New York office ahead of him and spirited away all the files, and now it looked like the sort of place one should avoid, with seedy men in black hanging out, bottles strewn around, tobacco spit, herring bones, and peelings on the floor . . .

That well had gone dry.

In the midst of all this, Jo's mother returned from Europe, and he was given the dubious honor of squiring her and her young popinjay—a man Jo's age!—from New York to Baltimore, where she moved in with Aunt Betsey. She'd crossed to America on a steamer which also carried a shipment of Darwin's new book and the commentaries of Schopenhauer. When the Empire fell to the Prussians in '70, when the Bonapartes all fled to England, Jo had received a letter from Jerome, Betsey's grandson, informing him that his mother alone of the court had managed to hang on in Paris. She had ways of surviving. His mother . . . He hadn't seen her in five years, not since his own ignoble departure from Paris for having killed the journalist who'd insulted the Bonapartes. He'd remembered her as lovely, still young—though past forty—flushed with court life and dozens of suitors. Now she'd gained weight, and her porcelain face, still without wrinkles, looked positively Chinese with its painted eyes and lips—its portrait of her face. Put on weight in the Siege of Paris, Mama? Not likely. Not when dogs, cats, and rats caught up rain spouts sold for twenty francs the pound, and all the animals at the Jardins d'Acclimatisation had been auctioned off and eaten. But Caroline Benton claimed she ate peacock and wild boar for five months, as she'd managed to befriend the writer Arsène Houssaye, who bought the Jardins' boar for a thousand francs and its peacocks for four hundred each.

She had ways of surviving.

She'd survived the defeat at Sedan, the surrender and abdication of the emperor, the siege of Paris, the occupation of the Prussians, and even the Commune—even the crowds that toppled a statue of Napoleon I in the Place Vendôme—before finally agreeing to join the rest of the exiled court in Chislehurst, England. There, the Empress Eugénie nursed the broken, defeated Napoleon III, there the Bonapartes sulked and pooled their spoils, and argued the succession to a nonexistent throne. Napoleon III was old, ill, and sad. His bladder contained a date-sized stone. When would the Bonapartes rule France again? A question Jo had no reason to guess would ever concern him, since, surrounded by his American dollars, he'd lost interest in his defeated European cousins.

But it turned out to touch him where it counted the most, in his purse. His mother's consort claimed to be a certain Count Léon-Fernand-Léon, another illegitimate Bonaparte—son, in fact, of Europe's most famous bastard, the Count Léon, whose birth had proven to Napoleon I that he could achieve paternity if he tried, and thus convinced him to divorce Josephine and marry Marie-Louise. This preposterous Count Léon-Fernand-Léon carried an offer from the Bonaparte family to purchase that unmentionable relic of Napoleon's body which Jo had managed to locate, the news of whose existence had drifted back to England. From Caroline they had learned of her son's search for it in London; perhaps he could help them? Did he know who had it now? Rumor placed it in America . . .

They offered Jo sixty thousand dollars for it.

Count Léon-Fernand-Léon wore a monocle on his pimpled face. Tall and thin, with a beak of a nose and the complexion of an adolescent, he appeared not the least nonplussed by the fact that his mistress had a son his own age. He talked from a great height down to everyone of the future of the Bonapartes, the purity of direct descent, a body and a nation restored to wholeness. Then gazing out wistfully at the trees of Baltimore, he acknowledged that France was at a low ebb now. But she would come back. She . . . or He.

He turned back to Jo with a sweep of his arm. This relic he would restore to France when the Bonapartes were returned to power.

Sixty thousand dollars? asked Jo.

He told them he had a pretty good notion of where it could be, but it might take him time to get his—hands—on it. They gave him five thousand on deposit. His mother winked, cracking her porcelain face, and embraced her son so weakly for such a largish woman that he guessed her intent—that *he* supply the pressure, in gratitude for what she'd brought him, for this skinny preposterous count and his offer. Jo set to work on it right away. That relic he'd once prized so highly for purely sentimental reasons had turned to gold, and everyone knew that when stocks plunged you put your money in gold. He hired Pinkerton men, set the growlers to searching, and now here he was, close to his prey, which was holed up—God knows why—in this foreboding house. Did Doyle know its worth? Then that's why he was hiding. But how could he know? Had someone else gotten there first? Ever so slightly, Jo stepped up his pace. He turned left at Triangle Street, left again at Lessey, then cut through a field toward the Dickinsons' barn, fully visible now through the saplings and scrub oak; beyond it stood the back of the house, shuttered against the afternoon heat. Jo found a little stand of trees to lurk in. A well-dressed man in a stovepipe hat standing in the woods as still as a tree would be visible only to prying eyes, but from where he stood he could see the entire back of the house, the barn, and the garden between them. He waited.

At last the rear downstairs shutter opened, but the emerging figure in its white dress was clearly female. Still, she seemed furtive. Jo recognized from experience the signs of someone who wished not to be seen: she glanced around with rapid eyes, then with wringing hands—or perhaps just folded, or maybe they carried something—dashed through the garden to the barn. Once more she looked around—Jo stood motionless trying to see her face—slid the barn door open, slipped inside, and shut it behind her.

Interesting. She hardly looked bent on milking the cows or feeding the horses. Why sneak around just to gather up eggs? Not a servant, either—her white cotton dress buttoned to the neck looked much too fine. Patience, Jo. A squirrel above chattered away. A dog over the hill behind him commenced to bark.

At last a small door back of the barn opened up and Jo's heart snapped like a mousetrap. The young man who emerged in jacket, britches, and a big floppy tam, scrambled through brush, hopped a low fence, and crossed the field Jo himself had cut through minutes ago back to Lessey Street, looking neither left nor right. He was quick as a thief, nearly out to the road before Jo stirred himself to follow.

A tryst? A warning? Can't fool Jo Benton! He sniffed in triumph. He gave his fish plenty of line, no rush now. Emerged onto Lessey Street just as the young man—carrying something, Jo saw it now, a little box or package of some sort!—turned right on Triangle, down toward Main Street.

Back on a public street, Jo walked with snap, swinging his cane. Wealthy once more! He tipped his hat to a passing carriage. The ladies inside it nodded politely. Down Triangle Street to Main, heading east. Train station, Doyle? Skipping town, Peter? Up ahead maybe five hundred yards, his quarry walked like someone haunting dark hallways, too scared or too rushed to look around, walked hunched, with a leap in his stride, as though earth itself were too sharp to step on. Then Jo saw he was barefoot.

He crossed the tracks but passed the train station. Jo followed calmly, feeling the tug. All at once he stopped at the Union Hotel—of course! Jo stepped up his pace. Back to Walt. Of course, of course. How it thickened! And maybe deposit an item for safekeeping? My darling relic? My drop of gold . . .

Walt felt unwell. Chair pushed back at the end of the single long table in the smoke-filled dining room of the Union Hotel, amid the smell of cold ashes from the fireplace and of dead fish rising through the floor—where tobacco spit balled in the sawdust—with a plate of uneaten greens before him, and a tankard of ale half drunk, platters and tureens scattered about, he felt needles on his skin. The stink of fish had caused it, he'd decided. But the landlord disagreed. The occasional sniff of a dead fish never killed nobody, he said. Besides, the hotel business of itself don't pay; therefore, he used the basement to pack shad, cod, whale, herring, and other brain food for local delivery.

Brain food? asked Walt.

Amherstites are a tribe having much brains, and it is well known that fish is brain food, said the landlord.

Walt planned to leave the following day and return to Washington via Brooklyn and his mother. Brain food . . . He thought of Emily's face, that oval rubbed smooth and blank like a pebble at the beach. And the long taut string of her voice with its quavering sarcasm and insistent questionings. How she'd drained his nerve power! Without even seeing him, she'd managed to draw off most of his strength. He knew it wasn't just the odor of fish. Since that interview he'd felt jumbled, disarranged. Lumbering back to the hotel, he'd longed for a Pete to lean on, but why not an Emily? Then he wondered how it would be to live near her. Not *with* her—just near. Powerful magnets consume electricity. She would think you *tired* and always be thoughtful, and meanwhile you went on giving yourself over—couldn't help it. The void of that face . . .

"Can't blame Greeley for falling behind." The man who said this, with slicked-back hair, wore red whiskers trimmed like Grant's to a point. The unlit pipe in his hand poked the air. "Who could run fast with the Confederacy on his back, Tammany in his arms, and North Carolina tar sticking to his heels?"

"The Ku Kluxers swing their bats and whoop for him," said another. The cockeyed, chinless face of this man seemed to have swung nearly upside down as it screwed itself in Walt's direction from across the table. It felt like he'd spoken from one of the plates.

"Why's that, then?" asked Walt. And why feel so annoyed? Most times Walt positively wallowed in hotel talk. Politics, women—he held forth for hours.

"Why—he bailed Jeff Davis out of prison."

"And you count that against him?"

"Of course. Don't you?"

"Don't misunderstand me," Walt answered. "I'm for Grant. I often see him walking down the street in Washington. I always salute him, and he does me. We acknowledge each other. But Horace Greeley's contribution to Jeff Davis's bail, its public nature"—Walt swept one arm through the air—"was sublime. It was a sublime gesture." He looked around. "An attempt, however misguided perhaps, but an attempt nonetheless to bind up the nation's wounds. An impulsive act. Yet consider it—" He opened his mouth, but nothing came out. The others waited. "Philosophically."

Then the door opened and a boy walked in. Or young man—hard to tell his age, with his smooth, beardless face and playful smile. He walked right up to Walt and held out a book. Big hazel eyes seemed to mock him. The eyes looked a size too large, and all the flat, pale skin around them made Walt think of someone who'd misplaced his spectacles. The face was froglike, with full meaty lips and a wide flaring nose, and the gaze unwavering—Walt nearly withered. Then he rebounded. This handsome young man had come solely to him, as though no one else were present. And Walt couldn't stop himself, here he was smiling, a weak smile for sure—he still felt lightheaded—and tilting his head, he curled one arm at his chest bending the hand like a flipper, as if to say, me?

"Could you sign my book, Mr. Whitman?"

Strange voice . . . "You recognized me?"

"Oh yes."

The recent edition too! Walt enjoyed hefting the *Leaves* anytime, but especially moments like this—with this lad. His smallish hands looked white and unused.

"I have a pen."

"What's your name?"

"Tim, sir."

Sounded like gravel, a mouth full of gravel. A deep voice crammed into too small a throat. With his sweetest smile, still cocking his head, Walt accepted the quill from the boy. "Landlord—some ink!" His bellowing surprised no one more than himself—his strength had returned!

The diminutive man who called himself landlord delivered a bottle of ink, clearly annoyed. He'd been setting out bowls of fresh eggs at the bar for tonight's egg-eating contest. Walt signed the title page with a flourish: "Walt. Whitman greets Tim. Amherst. 1872."

The young man stood there regarding Walt. A smell came off him of soap and musty clothes. His eyes widened. They were asking a question. He and the poet stared at each other. Fine spidery lines around his mouth and eyes—he appeared older, yet the curled-up smile looked like a boy's. Barely open, it seemed to be forming a word from below, from a spanking new well just starting to fill. "I—" Walt reached out for his hand on an impulse and the boy jumped back, snatching the book from Walt's lap—"Thanks very much"—then turned and bolted for the door, head down, nearly bowling over the landlord.

Walt stood up, watching him leave, then noticed his bare feet. What would his mother think? Suddenly he felt he'd been blown inside a floating soap bubble. He remained there in absolute and breathless calm. The door slammed and Walt heard hissing, something popping, clouds of needles rising from his chest. A funnel of vertigo and dizziness such as he'd never experienced before in his life spiraled out from the center of his brain like some crazy spring—his arms flung out—he was flying! Or falling. The men at the table caught him and thrust their faces at his as though regarding a fish in a bowl. "Easy, boys." It seemed he could hardly lower his arms; whatever had just snapped in his head had also stiffened his limbs. With two men at each arm, he managed to stagger upstairs to his room, where they laid him on his bed. Waving one hand, he thanked them profusely. "Don't mind me, boys, I'm fine." He sank into a black and empty sleep.

Chapter

❧ 4 ❧

Out on the porch of the Union Hotel, Miss Emily Dickinson fell back against the door clutching her book and fighting laughter. Puffed cheeks released her breath with a whistle. She could crow! But not here. Well, Mr. Whitman, I kept my promise, I showed myself. The *look* on his face . . .

She followed the train tracks outside the hotel through hot dirt and cinders, then ran up an alley past Wescott's house, skirted a wagon, overtook the deaf boy pushing his cart stacked with trays of rancid lard and clapped him on the back. He spit after her. Slag heaps of bottles and empty tins fanned down the board fence behind the hotel. Ash pits, blackberries, skinny catalpa trees. Burnished weeds gave off smells of copper, and unseen crickets somewhere inside them celebrated their pathetic mass.

The overcast sky seemed to swell her eyes.

She watched for flashes of glass in the dirt. Hopped a fence at the alley's end into Mrs. Cashman's orchard—boys could hop fences. Stole a fat apple from one of the trees, a Spy, and bit into it, feeling ready to burst with bad little boys inside her who hollered *mine*, wore no shoes, stole apples, broke windows, tortured cats, smoked stolen pipes, ran off from home, scattered the birds' eggs, and crawled beneath tent flaps to see the fat lady. Behind the orchard she crossed a meadow of buzzing insects. Stubble and burrs scratched her feet. Did he notice her feet? Did he even suspect? The same book he'd sent her three months ago! Tim thanks you, sir, for the name in his book. He carries it next to his unclean heart. Your smile was sweet but you looked so much older than Tim expected, he nearly curled up in your lap, Mr. Whitman—to inspect a face rubbed so much in the world, with its thousands of fractures and stringy veins and hair all kneaded together in clumps. But it slapped itself respectably in line—didn't it?—and flared up like brass when little Tim walked in. Hardly looked like a face used to hiding. What did it feel like to carry a face full of dismal hope parading through the world like a marching band—sir? It ain't *natural*, Mr. Whitman.

Barefoot down the hill toward Whitney Street, where the maples had turned at their edges, Emily pulled at her tam for shade. *Her* face felt like a freshly dug hole. Where Whitney Street bent back toward town stood an apple tree whose side had split open in a perfect Gothic arch. Goldfinches scattered as she approached it. Inside the arch, on dried grass and nutshells, she laid Walt's book. Though this tree had no insides, leaves still grew on the skinny branches pushing like spokes out of its trunk. She crossed the road, practicing a swagger. *That*'s how bad little boys put down the world like a bundle and fly . . .

She liked this boggy acre on her feet. Trees grew here without human supervision. Marshlands and trees unbuttoned by mushrooms led to a stone wall surrounding a wheat field. Crossing this field with its rich smell of wheat dust was like swimming through bread, and made her lightheaded. Pockets of cool air broke at her ankles. Looks like a katydid parked on that stem, Mr. Whitman. Thank you for singing. Gnats and chaff mixed with the dust, and her boy's clothes netted the chaff in its folds, and itched. The field broke off at some pine trees whose needles had softened the ground so it felt carpet-like. When a dragonfly stopped right in front of her face she thought of what Austin had said last week: What if you woke up and everything—*everything*—was twice as large? Could you possibly know it?

She stared at the dragonfly—brain on a stem. Her brother had it wrong. What if everything were half as large? One third, or one tenth . . . *Boo!* It veered off.

If Walt Whitman came back to Amherst she couldn't very well show herself now, could she? But he wouldn't come back—they never did. He might come back to see the *boy* who winked at him purely for disobedience's sake. Not all men with large words looked harmless as you, Mr. Whitman. You looked like a grandma except for the beard, sang like a lonely dog in a barn, smiled like a flower . . . Mrs. Walt Whitman? My "husband," women say, stoking the melody. Betrothed without the swoon. "Wife!" She laughed out loud. Still, his words followed in the dark, eyes on long sticks. She could nurse him back to health and keep him in ginger snaps. What would Father say? Maggie would disapprove of course, and one couldn't marry without Maggie's approval. Being married to a multitude, a walking mob, might prove somewhat crowded without corners to stand in. They'd live in New York on unpainted floors with washtubs in the hallway. Could she please still have her own little room? Her hand reached out and turned at the wrist, one turn of the key—and freedom!

She felt someone watching.

She'd stolen the clothes from Maggie's little brother, who'd left them in the barn. He wore them digging up moles for Father. Boys could steal clothes, being wicked and brave. *Mine!* One boy she'd heard of who stole a fox hid it under his coat when he spotted the owner, then forced himself to endure the creature gnawing at his vitals as he walked down the road. He couldn't cry out. Of course, it killed him . . . Was someone watching? Boys could run faster. Some Irish woodcutter sniffing out trees? Boys ran faster, having more practice, whereas girls stayed at home with their feet in a sling cooking vicious pies, tending the sick, washing and shaving the dead . . .

Piss on girls.

At last came a road, East Street, with more fields below it, and pastures for cows. Beyond was the fairgrounds. Slanted streaks in the overcast sky were sheets of rain that dried up falling. She shaded her eyes. Dust clouds rose from the trotters at the racetrack. Between stands of trees they swung in an arc, and a small roar broke like waves on an island.

The crowds at the Hampshire County Cattle Show and Fair might oppress an Emily dressed in white, but not a barefoot Tim in jacket and trousers. They poured from the grandstand—the final race over—and swelled around in a doughy mass of bobbing heads and buzzing tongues, heading for the pens, tents, and exhibition halls. Their scraping feet raised dust, but boys didn't care. Boys could pull tams down and dodge in and out of slow legs just dandy, squeeze between bustles and walking sticks, run their stiff fingers up surprised dogs' spines. Down there you smelled the hay mixed with urine wafting from the animals' pens, from the shorthorns, Ayrshires, and Jerseys, from the stallions, mares, sucking colts, and oxen, and from the poultry—coops of pigeons and white leghorns—as well as from the one dromedary near the entrance to the Program of Visible and Mysterious Apparitions. Beyond the pens a group of boys with slingshots chased a dog. Boys labored at tag in a ring used for boxing matches, stuffed their mouths with spun sugar, crowded at booths to shoot the air guns, and climbed all over the carriages and wagons displayed by J. Adams & Sons outside the Agricultural Society Hall.

A donkey bearing a stuffed Horace Greeley—with whiskers of steel wool and beer-bottle spectacles—lumbered down the midway, encouraged close behind by a man with a switch dressed like Brother Jonathan in striped blue and red trousers, stars on his coat and tall silk hat, and sporting a sandwich board painted U.S. on the front and GRANT on the back.

In the hall, unlike the rest of the boys, Tim headed straight for the flowers. Mr. Howard's table, rich with verbenas and dahlias, cowered as usual down there beneath Mrs. Gray's hanging basket—five feet in diameter!—huge and bursting with over a hundred colors and two hundred varieties. It hung there like an exploded bomb. Then the woolen yarn and cloth, the stockings, blankets, linen, and cambrics, the city of hats, the fancy work—quilts, needlepoint, laces, and samplers draped over crates or hung on the wall—and the pears, apples, peaches, and grapes, the watches, silver plate, jewelry, paste, the preserves in crocks sealed with hog bladders, the tinware, basins, milk strainers, hand lanterns, flat pans, tater graters—the wallpaper, umbrellas, and corn cures, the buttermilk and cheese, the cage of white mice—the breads! At the bread table before the rye bread baked by Miss Emily Dickinson, Tim thought of sampling a piece, but didn't; too much fennel, he knew—not enough sugar . . .

Still, her father refused to eat any except her rye bread.

It hadn't won anything.

Suddenly Emily pulled down her tam. Hunched up, she squeezed through the crowds toward the door, away from the unsmiling face of Maggie, who was dressed in tentage with something hanging down the front like lungs. Headed straight for the breads, of course. She'd report tonight on Emily's lack of a prize. Maggie, the only one there who would know her, unless Lavinia or Austin showed up, Maggie whom boys instinctively shunned, as well as disgraceful cosmic poets . . .

Outside, the Scottish games had started, but Emily wasn't tempted. Boys who like cunning don't care for muscle. Instead, she strolled, hands in her pockets, toward the dromedary hired out for giving small children rides between its floppy humps. A woman beside it stood on a platform showing not only her ankles but her thighs—in Amherst, no less!—surrounded by doves who perched on her shoulders, arms, and head, pecked at her lips, cooed, and submitted their necks to be stroked by her long yellow fingers. Emily supposed this woman was "pretty." She smiled like a banshee in pain. Behind her a sign on a post announced the Program of Visible and Mysterious Apparitions, for which curious folks paid fifty cents and entered a long striped canopy pitched at the entrance to a sprawling shed, two hundred feet long—Mr. Kellog's chicken shed way back when, before he sold this land for the fair. They'd never bothered to chop up the foot-deep crust of manure and garbage and feed on the floor pressed down harder than Roman cement, and instead put down canvas to smother the smell for the week of the fair. They'd thrown down rugs too—Persians, they looked like, and felt warm as sheep on Tim's bare feet. She'd snuck in, as boys do—squeezed in among an abundant family of fat little boys with their ravaged mother, whose face looked familiar. A childhood friend? An Amy or Mary, something like that. She reminded Emily of those exhausted birds who flap back and forth to feed their greedy young even after they've grown and the branch bends beneath them . . .

Oil lamps inside made things smell closer. Tall men were forced to duck beneath rafters. Canvas tarps suspended from beams divided rooms and hallways like tunnels, through which grinning people groped pretending they were miners. In the first room a man dressed in black declaimed Shakespeare. She recognized it right off—Richard III bemoaning his deformity—but slipped out before the words burrowed in, having no desire to hear Shakespeare bloodied by elocution. The second room, smelling of gunpowder, had drawn quite a crowd, and the calcium lights reflected every surface, making it feel like a brightly lit tomb. On tall upright spindles turned by a crank unrolled a panorama of the Battle of Bunker Hill. The man turning the crank droned on about the destruction of Charlestown, the bravery of Prescott, the perfidy of the British. On Gage's third charge someone behind the rollers lit a string of firecrackers sending up smoke and causing ladies to squeal. Emily ducked out.

Down the canvas hallway on a Persian runner rolled a wooden ball three feet or so in diameter. People skipped out of the way; boys followed and whacked it with sticks. The thing seemed to move of its own power, turned into a room—dragging a considerable audience behind—rolled on a circuit around the room, then up an incline onto a box, down the other side, around and up again, where it stopped. A hinged top opened and a man crawled out, unbending himself to gasps and applause. Impossible . . . Children leaned over to peer in the ball. A bald man with a lisp introduced this rubbery person dressed in what appeared to be a long black stocking as the greatest disarticulated artist of the century, whose bones, he said, rather than joining by means of cartilage, were held together with a kind of fibrous muff, woven like hair, which kept them in their sockets but left them capable of great elasticity.

He stands on his own coffin, said the bald man.

Emily craned her neck to see, then thought, Ah yes, I'm a boy, and shoved forward. True enough, the box on which he stood was a minia-ture coffin with little brass rails on the side, all of three feet long. As the bald man talked, the one made of rubber balanced his neck on the ball, then swung his legs back and over his shoulders, hooking the feet under-neath his chin. Seems he fell into debt from gambling years ago—the bald man explained—and offered to dispose of his skeleton upon his death for a thousand guineas, payable at once—advertised to this effect in the papers—and was taken up immediately by a London doctor, whose address was now painted on the coffin. A paper gummed inside the coffin's lid gave directions for the disposing of the body, to wit—the persons who place Mr. Walter, deceased, into this coffin are begged to inject a solution of chloride of mercury and acetic acid into his veins . . .

The face of Mr. Walter smiled a melancholy smile at this grisly infor-mation, while the nest of snakes known as his limbs writhed around, framing it in various arabesques. Emily stared into his blank eyes, alarmed. Somehow it soiled her, this trick of bones—a bone has obliga-tions. When he poured himself back in the ball headfirst like a piece of smoke, she felt scarcely better. It wasn't so much hauling your own coffin around, she could understand that, as the thought of being unfinished inside. And *paid* for it too . . .

In the murmuring press of flesh squeezing out she found herself spun around on her feet. Inside her rose a compelling obligation to spin the other way, to unwind her spring. She tripped—arms lifted her—then a boy or very large dog racing past knocked her into a booth-sized room. No one was here but herself and a woman seated behind—or in—a neck-high platform, who smiled at Tim, then raised her eyebrows. That proved the face alive, did it not? The uncertain light in the room shifted, shadows passed over the face, and it changed to a grinning skull. Emily laughed, half relieved. Gothic effects . . . Mr. Poe's goblin. When the top of the skull gave off smoke and exploded into a rose bush, she found a beaded curtain and passed through.

"What's a *boy* doing here?" Standing around her were naked bodies, fully naked, with all the proper details, although some possessed extra fingers or toes, and one—the most prominent—the hair of a man, the breasts of a woman, and under the belly in a helpless knot the size and color of newborn mice, the pathetic semiformed confluence of male and female. Its face didn't smile. She saw it was wax—all of them wax. A large man in clothes approached her. "No boys!" With burning face and racing heart, she swaggered out through a flap in the canvas.

No boys! She looked around. More wax figures, these fully dressed. Though they shared the same anonymous face, they were famous people, distinguished by their clothes and the signs hung about their necks: General Washington, John Bunyan, Captain Kidd, Stephen Decatur, Oliver Hazard Perry . . . She glanced back; from the flap she'd just passed through, the man scowled at her, stroking his beard. Above him hung a sign: ANATOMICAL WAXWORKS, with smaller words below it, MEDICAL STUDENTS ONLY, then even smaller ones: SEE THE MORPHODITE. A gentleman approached the flap, placed a coin in the scowling man's hand, and disappeared inside.

Women in *this* room carrying parasols glanced in that room's direction as though gazing with absent longing out a window. Boys dodged around Stephen Decatur and General Washington, whose uniforms had yellowed. Their opaque faces looked scratched—disappearing. In a corner stood the Witch of Endor in a tattered black bombazine gown and pointed hat, brandishing her wand in the direction of Samuel and King Saul with a painted sky behind them. Just in front of Emily a boy stopped to gaze at Cleopatra applying the asp, screwing his probing eyes into her bosom. A froth of laughter erupted inside her—she tugged her hat down. What next? It was easy to tell the wax from the real—wax figures always went clothed, even naked ones—harder to tell the real from the wax, though. Even in this room, eyes dropped when they met yours—faces went empty. You couldn't measure their grief. Narrow squints rounded corners and searched out every public feature of every nameless face, but yours.

She found the exit.

The hallway ran deeper into the shed. There had to be a way out soon. She lowered her head—Maggie again. Emily entered THE ROMAN ORGY, surely Maggie would keep from a Roman orgy. Here, behind a rope, baboons dressed like Peruvian generals had been tied to chairs at a banquet table to which a monkey on a chain brought food. They chattered and squawked at the waxed pears and apples, the empty cups . . .

She pushed through the corridor, squeezing past families, forgoing all manner of tempting attractions—the Salon of Phrenology, the Strong Man, the Display of Magnetism. Some rooms were empty. In one, an armless woman cut silhouettes with scissors held in her toes, but from the door Emily saw that no one was watching. Silhouettes of nothing.

In another, a hunchback, shirtless, passed his hump beneath the skin from his back over his shoulder to his chest and back again, without any effort. Then two empty booths, then a man before a small audience lowering a large sheet of slate to the floor. He pulled a hen from a sack and held its beak flat to the slate. On his hands and knees, he drew a straight line of chalk on the slate out from the hen's eyes. The man stood up but the hen didn't move. He lifted it, threw it up into the air, but it stayed immobile, dead as a rock. Only when he tossed it up and clapped his big hands did it burst into squawking feathers, and land with its legs churning out circles. A comic chase ensued for the benefit of squealing children, but Emily ducked out before sack swallowed hen.

This far down the shed the canvas partitions had all but run out. A few men in knots smoked cigars and pipes by the fading light of a row of knee-high windows. The stanchions here supported heavy beams by means of struts from which rages of webs hung. At an open door, a plump man stood and regarded those smoking. "Interest you gents in a curiosity?"

The soft light outside said dusk, get home soon. One more, she answered—just one. The men stirred. Smoke and dust swirled. "Twenty cents. Dreadful amazing. The genuine"—he lowered his voice—"inti-mate tool of his manhood. The largest which has ever been knowed. Napoleon Bonaparte's very own, what hung between his legs . . ."

She followed the men following this man outside into the warm glow of evening. Colors had sunk—a thrush piped—crickets—and the sky hung close. They were all the way back where the shed reached the trees, back from the midway and racetrack and pens. Twenty or so feet from the shed beneath the sheltering elms stood a small tent. The lamp glow inside illuminated a table, a jeweled chest, a jar—something whitish and smooth floating in the jar . . .

Gone! Her hand searched the dried grass and nutshells inside the apple tree. Books were too heavy for squirrels and pack rats. Around the tree sat lumps of something, but they weren't books. The sky still looked white but most of the light around things on the ground had drained out by now, no more cutting through fields, no telling what you'd step on. Did boys ever get tired of being boys? It was just after dusk, when you couldn't distinguish zigzagging swallows in the sky eating their last meal of the day from bats commencing breakfast.

Someone had seen her put it in that tree. Mr. Whitman had followed her. All at once she felt certain that something horrible was about to happen, and pried at her mouth with her thumb, running her tongue along the nail while the fear crept slowly up her neck—then embraced it, closed around it, strangled it, tossed it in a sack, and left it in the ditch by the road to rot behind her.

She walked up Whitney Street trying to swagger. Austin could buy her another *Leaves*, but who took that one? The leather man, of course. The thought of Mr. Whitman hopping a fence and hobbling through fields to follow her! Some boy had watched her put it in that tree. They steal things purely for sport, because they're boys. Run off to the fair then get tired and miss their homes, so have to tramp back along roads in the dark whistling tunes to let the world know just how brave they are. Still, they feel small as mice with blistered lungs. Uphill all the way . . . Even small feet trudge . . .

She doubled her pace in case someone *was* following. At the edge of Irishtown, persons had thrown a whole mattress out—perhaps it was died on. The house looked dark. Just a mattress, nothing else. Air felt colder now night had come on—the trees filling up—lawns full of north. Thank God the world had no experience at being you. Half the world was sham anyway. The effort to see things exactly as they were squeezed out most glory, but it was worth it. She'd seen that whitish pizzle in the jar back at the fair for what it was—a bull's, not a man's, let alone Napoleon's. Any girl with cousins on a farm could have guessed. When boys grew up they made shams of everything. Paste, wax, dolls, paper cutouts. No golden fleece; Jason sham too. They wanted to put the world on display, but wound up making it obvious and dreary. What if all the skeletons went out of things, causing the world to collapse like a tent? Of everything she'd seen that day perhaps the most disturbing had been the hunchback with his movable hump. She *felt* it—over her back, down her chest . . .

She stopped, out of breath. Had to pee. There, in those trees . . . But looking around she swore she saw someone behind, down the road, and the inky fear bloomed again like a nudged squid inside her. She picked up a rock and threw it at a tree—not at whoever it was, just in that general direction. Boys could throw rocks, couldn't they?

He sagged back into the shadows.

One of those creeping wonders from the fair in search of her bones. He'd suck them from her arms. Ghost of Napoleon. Shabby tricks. A lump of wax. Worms in her brain! The thief who stole fire from the gods—did he know about wax? When the gods themselves turned out to be wax—Napoleon too—you forgot your own problems. Wax souls don't hurt. No gimlets in the nerve. No insides mangled just from looking up, remembering, rubbing an eyelid . . . Wax morphodites and Napoleon's decapitated Gorgon, or Cyclops, close up—its eye froze your liver—carried the burden of too many ideas. When inspection melted them, they still survived. Half the world was idea, the rest creaking machinery. Let it stand around regarding itself, it was made for that, who wants it, they can have it. Let it prance and strut like a panther in the grove. Surely that wasn't *misery* they felt, all those twitching puppets? Was *that* why they danced? Loss scooped the breath right out of their chests—I recall how it feels . . .

Bloody Napoleon bellowing orders.

She turned left on Main Street nearly exploding. Her full bladder made it painful to walk. Wanted to rip off her tam right there, but someone might see her. Union Hotel. Mr. Walt Whitman—the traveling panorama. You'd like that shed back at the fair, sir—it's where the world went. Not songs or curtains, not the clear bell of fear swinging back and forth inside without a sound. Those who can't tell the inside from outside easily grow accustomed to the dark, but I have to grope—hit a tree in the forehead—never learned to see . . .

But thank you for singing.

Is it true boys can do whatever they wish? Boys and men—big burly men. Go where they want? Lucky them. Go. You must know where you're off to, dobbins. So long. Have fun. Bring me back your name for the Pacific Ocean, your chunk of the grail . . . I'm heading home. Up Triangle Street. Closer now—glory. One turn and freedom!

There it was, house—the great dark shape of her home up the hill, through the big trees. She'd had enough world to last her a winter. Body had filled with it nearly to bursting. Down Lessey Street, over the fence, through bushes and saplings, have to be careful here, twigs sting the eyes. At last, in the shadow of the barn, she pulled down her pants, squatted, and gushed—the salt smell steamed up—it wet her bare foot. The world dropping out of her made her feel dizzy. Pants and linen down around her ankles, she tipped, put her arm out, lowered her head. Then closed around that spiral of dizziness; smelled the damp grass. "World" had grown cold. Who took my book?

Unmistakable footsteps out there on the dirt, in the darkness. Pulling her pants up, she sprang to her feet, strong as a cat, made the barn in one leap—slipped quietly inside . . .

Chapter

❧ 5 ❧

Jo's heart dropped at the sight of those breasts, small and round as apples. He wasn't a Pete—wasn't male at all—was a bloody woman, the same one who'd entered the barn hours ago. Pretty little thing . . .

He'd been tricked somehow, thrown off the scent. Still, something was up. Stokes was involved—he'd followed the trail clear from London. Stokes! How it thickened. What were they up to? The item she'd deposited in that tree turned out not to be his prize, but a book, of all things. He'd tossed it in a ditch. Some sort of decoy, no doubt. Crafty people. They'd managed to divert him, but some diversions proved more pleasant than others, for example, watching a pretty woman undress—small as she was—in the glow from a lantern in a barn, watching her hair come tumbling out of that oversized tam. Modestly, she crossed her arms at her breasts and kneaded the shoulders, how cute. Something would come of this yet! She rolled her boy's clothes into a bundle and stuffed them in hay under a feed bin while horses nearby in the darkness stirred. Creaking barn noises, snufflings, snorts, plus something else, a whistled tune. The little fox whistling!

He'd been misled, he knew. Something was up; it could be she'd exchanged something back there in secret with Stokes, maybe that was it. There's a lesson in this, Jo Benton, take heed—if you have the chance, kill them. Don't let them survive and follow you later, they'll catch up for sure and cheat you of your property. Blasted Stokes . . .

He could let her go now, return to the fair, find Stokes, bash his head in good. But who had the prize? A little terror wouldn't hurt at this interesting juncture. Grip her arm and squeeze hard. Hiss like a snake. Stroke her throat whispering, that might be fun. Violate a plush . . . Her skinny limbs looked as fragile as pencils. An elf's beard lay flattened inside each armpit, he noted them when she pulled on her shift. Then the white dress; she rummaged under the feed bin, shook it out, turned, and was in it—she'd be out the door soon—buttoning up from the collar down while smiling demurely, head bowed. She appeared entirely too satisfied with herself. They'd managed to make a fool of him, hadn't they? Well, we shall see . . .

A man preparing to jump in when others least suspect it holds back as long as he can—savors the plot—runs through his brain the explosion of hay dust, the look of horror on her face, the gloved hand gripping her throat, the ripped dress, the squeal. She had no idea demons were watching, but she should have, demons were everywhere, Jo knew . . .

He stepped forward as she snuffed the lantern, but before he could reach her a foul-smelling wing brushed his face, or a paw, and something landed on his shoulders in darkness, nearly pulling him down. She slipped out the door. Some fox or dog—raccoon—or goblin—its sharp tooth probing his neck at the larynx. It felt like a child or puppy sniffing. Jo reached up to tear the demon off, but a clammy little hand squeezed his throat, and the sharp tooth pressed harder—harder—then was in . . .

Jo stopped struggling at once. *It was in, it was in*, just a quarter inch—horrid—it pinched warm and cold, it *bled*. On his collar . . . He froze there supporting the weight on his shoulders in dark air thicker than blindness. "Please . . ."

"He says, 'Please.' "

"No more."

" 'No more,' he says."

A large hand slapped his back, pushing him forward, and Jo couldn't help it, he gagged.

"Take care not to slip, Jo, it's stuck in there good. Ever view my collection of Adamses' apples, Jo? I seed him once slice one clean out, it's a gripping sight. He does it pretty tidy. Better than ripping the bloody thing out, but one way or neither the agony's affecting—you can't even scream." Stokes squeezed past Jo, then his voice grew smaller. A light popped inside Jo's brain and the barn reappeared. Stokes held the lantern she'd left behind ear high, next to his own pulpy face.

Jo felt the creature around his neck stir. It gave off cold like a reptile—

it *hissed*—but all he could see, lowering his eyes carefully so as not to move, and straining the muscles of the eyeballs, was a stubby fist gripping a long knife whose point disappeared somewhere beneath his mustache. It hurt, but he couldn't stop himself from swallowing. What if he coughed? Just the thought of it made him feel compelled to. Lodged in the thyroid cartilage of the larynx, just below the notch—secure in a hollow—the knife tip felt like a toothpick he'd breathed in, pinched like a crab, rose and fell with his swallowing. Don't sneeze, Jo, don't cough. His voice came out squeezed. "What is this—creature—draped about my neck?"

"Friend of mine with a knife."

"Ask him to remove it."

"He don't do what I hasks."

"Tell him, then."

"Why should I do that? Might cramp the business we come here upon." Stokes set the lantern on a railing surrounding the stall they'd gathered in. "Cozy here, Jo. Comfortable like." He thrust his face into Jo's and squinted. "Fancy meeting you here. Like my new nose?" When Stokes snapped it with his fingernail it echoed like an empty shell.

"Pretty."

"Yes, ain't it? Gived me some trouble breathing at first—liked to fog up and sweat something fierce. But I climated to it. It's a far greater misfortune, you'll learn, having to draw yourself double with the screwmatics in the gills, than just losing a nose—you'll see. Or to be caponed neither. When you're dismantled once, that's the limit. One of these won't help you"—he snapped the nose again—"down there." He grabbed Jo's crotch and squeezed. "So have a care of your funny remarks."

Jo swallowed cautiously. Stokes let go. "How did you find me here?"

"Follered you, darling. Or my friend did, what hangs about your neck. *He's* my nose. You've been under inspection these past months, Jo. My critter here is bloodhound related. Name of Bonny, after a certain misplaced relic—misplaced, mind you."

Bonny grunted. Jo sensed this—being—had attached itself for life. He felt it breathing there draped about his neck. It sighed, stirred, and began to move. Stokes reached out and held the knife for it, even twanged the thing once, Jo could have sworn, like a spring or stumpy twig. It actually wasn't in that far—he realized now—but the pressure felt enormous. It had pricked the skin and lodged in the larynx, and just a little push set off alarms. He'd swallowed a beak which had stuck in his voice box, forcing him to talk like a hen. "What relic?" Bawk, bawk!

Stokes pushed at the knife and poor Jo gagged. Squidlike, Bonny crawled all about him, reaching in pockets, removing their contents. His small hands tickled . . . Don't sneeze, Jo, don't *laugh*. "You could save yourself some lemontations if you gave off pretending ignorance, Jo. I wants it especially now, right off." All at once his face beamed with involuntary if spongy pride, and he spoke in a whisper, leaning forward. "Important persons is concerned." He straightened up when a small arm extended itself from inside Jo's coat—Jo's lowered eyes saw it—and handed out a hanky, a chequebook, some bank notes, a snuffbox. Stokes examined each item by the lantern. But the *knife*, Jo—no one was holding the knife! The damn thing just hung there, stuck in his throat . . . Stokes was busy shaking out the hanky, riffling the chequebook, stuffing the bank notes into his pocket, while Bonny continued burrowing around like a mole in Jo's coat. "Where's that item you stole from me, Jo?"

Jo swallowed carefully. "I don't—" The knife hung there.

Next to the lantern, Stokes screwed one eye up and reached for the knife—pushed at it playfully. Again Jo gagged, like a cough in reverse. "Fishy goings-on out there tonight. You've been snooping around to beat creation, I hear tell. Packages in trees. Where is it, Jo?"

Jo felt something clammy on his skin. That thing had weaseled inside his shirt and was mumbling something—*I wants it, I wants it.* In his frightened confusion, Jo half supposed the creature was searching out nipples to suckle. Stokes with his other hand turned Jo's snuffbox over and back in the lantern's small light, then snapped it open and dumped the snuff out in a powdery cloud. Oh no . . . Jo's nose tingled. Don't even *breathe.* He opened his mouth—felt himself panting.

Stokes leaned into his ear once again. "Important persons, Jo. More important than you is. They made me an offer I can't refuse." He glanced down at Jo's coat bulging with Bonny, then whispered. "Don't tell my friend there—he wants it for hisself." Now Bonny was circling Jo's slender waist, digging his greedy little paws into the pockets of his trousers. Coins, a folding knife—a small wooden case. My opium, Stokes, don't take that. The arm reached out again. Stokes's features flared. He reached for the case, snapped it open—glanced at Jo. Sniffed at its contents. "Bad habits, Jo." Stokes dumped the gummy ball on the floor.

Then Bonny felt down Jo's pants to his intimates, poking around all the creases with care. He was *sniffing* too. He started down one leg, head first, feeling everywhere. With a bent finger, Stokes prodded Jo's folding knife. Tapped it on the wooden railing. Hmmm. Looks familiar . . . His other hand clung to the knife at Jo's neck. "You skinned me once, Jo, you won't skin me again." He leaned forward and whispered in his ear.

"A count as claims to be grandson to Napoleon hisself found me out—he's near crafty as you is—knowed the fake in the jar for its true colors right off. Made me an offer I can't refuse if I fetch the real thing tooti sweety, monsieur." He straightened up. "Where is it, Jo? I wants it right now. Where?"

"I don't have it."

"You're mushing, Jo. AIN'T HE MUSHING, BONNY?" The creature worming his hands in Jo's boots made a grunting noise. "Kindly lift up one foot, Jo. Quick-like." When Jo lifted his foot, small hands tugged off his boot. Balanced on one leg, Jo had the urge to look down and see it—some kind of monkey, perhaps?—but his head couldn't tilt while Stokes held that knife, and teetering there he felt like a puppet.

"I'm not—mushing. I don't have it."

"We shall see. If you don't have it, Jo, then we'll kill you for certain. Nothing personal. Mere revenge. Other foot."

Jo lifted his left foot up, felt the boot slide off.

"You'll resemble a blowed-up miner when we're finished. Your dog won't know you. Where is it, Jo?"

Jo's face twitched, trying to get Stokes's attention. His eyebrows pumped. He attempted a wink. "How much—" He whispered. Stokes leaned forward. Finished with the other boot, Bonny had begun the long climb up Jo's leg. "How much did Count Léon-Fernand-Léon offer you?"

Stokes drew back, flummoxed. His eyes widened, then he hissed, clicked his tongue, and one pupil bored in. With the heel of his hand he pushed at the knife. Jo gagged. His whisper barely squeezed out.

"How much—Timothy?"

"How did you know?"

Jo's face squirmed and he lowered his eyes, shaping his lips to form silent words. This was it, his last chance—he grimaced and smiled, opened his mouth in a wide silent scream, tried shaking his head. Ease off, Stokes! Less pressure—I'll tell you.

Stokes got the message. Bonny had crawled back up inside Jo's coat around the back to examine the lining. Stokes spoke sotto voce. "Offered me sixty-five thousand dollars, Joseph. In all my years dealing relics . . ."

The bastard . . . But Jo didn't blink. "Offered *me* seventy thousand, Timothy." His mother's boyfriend might be sly, but what a poor judge of character, to offer Stokes sixty-five and Jo only sixty! Who did they think he was? Maybe Stokes was lying. He might be exaggerating to look good—as Jo was. Then again, he could be taking Jo in, they could have offered him more—seventy-five, say; a hundred, perhaps . . .

"Ten on deposit," whispered Stokes.

"Fifteen for me," said Jo.

Once more, Bonny had draped himself limp about Jo's neck, and now he relieved his master of the knife. Jo felt him sigh and relax, he was home. In front of Jo, Stokes glanced all around the stall; bit his lower lip, opened his mouth—but nothing came out. His face was engaged in collapsing inward, mushroom-like—he was *thinking*, Jo could tell. Don't let up now—it's your neck, Jo . . .

"Timothy. Far be it for me to inform you. But you're being skinned." Then again, so am I . . .

Stokes addressed the thing on Jo's neck. "No sign of it?"

Jo felt its head shake.

All at once Stokes hauled up his face and smiled. "Kill him." He stage-winked at Bonny. "The ugliest way you can think of. Use your imagination."

Jo panicked. "I know where it is."

"Oh you do, do you? Where?"

"I don't know—"

Glaring at Jo, then at Bonny on his neck, Stokes ran his finger across his own throat.

"But I know who has it!"

"Who?"

"His name's Doyle."

"Where is he?"

"I don't know."

Stokes cocked an eye at Jo, then at Bonny.

"But I know how to find him."

"How?"

Stiffly, Jo tilted his head. Set his jaw. "Tell him to remove the knife, Timothy. Make him climb down. If you kill me, you'll never recover your precious relic. I know who has it and I know how to find him. What good would it do you to murder *me*?"

"It's the satisfaction."

"Someone with your talents—and his. We could be partners again."

"I has a partner."

"You need another."

"Not one as coshed me on the boko like you done."

For a long moment nothing stirred in the barn. Then Stokes, peeling one eye at Jo, reached for the knife, and pried Bonny's grip off. Jo felt the struggle. Then it was out, and with shaking fingers he probed his neck, wet and raw. Now the pain began . . . With the knife, Stokes signaled Bonny to climb down. This time Jo watched. The creature looked up, climbing down, with an old man's head on a monkey's body, and seemed vaguely familiar in the flickering light, even crying as he was with a tiny face pinched in bitter disappointment.

Stokes handed Jo his hanky. He brought it to his neck, squeezing the pain. "Now then, Timothy. My chequebook. My bank notes. My little gumball of bliss, where is that?" Under Stokes's watchful eye, Bonny searched the hay-strewn floorboards for Jo's drop of opium. "Now. Let's talk business."

AM

by Pony Express

Dear Sir,

It was reserved for Walt. Whitman to find Dr. Livingstone but for Mr. Stanley to get all the credit.

Will Mr. Whitman come again this morning before he departs and find a surprise? My breath has straightened and my brain has cooled. Old Moses saw "Him" face to face and was not consumed—therefore I could try.

You were so generous to me that if possible I offended you, I could not too deeply apologize.

Emily.

Walt held this letter in his hand, unable to make heads or tails of it, unable even to drop it to the floor, as though someone had gummed his fingers. The enormous pressure in his head drove out comprehension. Something had plugged up his brain, no doubt, the world perhaps—stuffed in his head . . .

He knelt on the floor by the door to his room at the Union Hotel.

The knock had dragged him from sleep all at once and he'd sat bolt upright, eyes wide open, with a horrible throbbing behind his brow. Noted the letter slipped beneath the door, even made out the address: *Mr. Whitman, Union Hotel.* That was him all right, Walt Whitman, but he felt mighty dizzy. Felt such a ringing in his ears and confusion in his mind that staggering out of bed in the clothes he'd slept in—not breathing so much as gulping air—he thought it safest to crawl, not walk, on the plank they'd thrown across this new abyss between the bed and door.

Reaching for the letter, his hand struck the door a foot or so above it. The world was insulting him! He forgot for a minute how one opens a letter. It was perfectly reasonable, then—wasn't it?—that a man in such a state couldn't comprehend gibberish. Who on earth was "Emily"? A man who could hardly focus his eyes, who felt so cold—whose heart beat so fast . . . Pete, where are you? Oh, I'm feeling rather kinky . . .

He lay on the floor with his left side all fuzzy, realizing he'd wet his pants.

How he made it back to the bed, who undressed and cleaned him up, who summoned the doctor, he never learned. The doctor diagnosed a partial stroke with left hemiplegia, and forbade travel. You almost died, sir. But once he remembered where he was, once he could barely stand and walk, with the assistance, for sure, of a strong young man, Walt insisted on making the trip back to Washington. The doctor, shocked, asked, Surely, not alone? No, not alone. The strong young man generously offered to help, since he was going that way himself. Seems he was staying at the hotel too. Heard the commotion when the doctor arrived and rushed from his room to lend a hand. When Walt felt up to it later the next day, this kind man, himself somewhat injured—neck bandaged up—helped him hobble around, up and down the hotel stairs, through the corridors, and out to the privy. With him on Walt's left, and his gold-headed walking stick in Walt's right hand—he'd insisted Walt use it, how thoughtful—they managed to board the train together with tickets for Washington . . .

Chapter

❧ 6 ❧

Mr. Walt Whitman is available to visit Greeley and lecture at the lyceum upon the Death of Abraham Lincoln. We propose to open a subscription in the columns of this newspaper to which civic-minded men and women are invited to make contributions. If the sum of $300 is subscribed, it is presumed that Mr. Whitman may be induced to come.

Mr. Whitman has delivered his lecture in Boston, New York, and Philadelphia to universal acclaim. The crowning touch of the evening, his recitation of "O Captain! My Captain!" is said to bring audiences to their feet.

Though some may regard Mr. Whitman's poetry as depraved, we have always found it to be strikingly presented, neither befouled with the filth nor defaced by the vulgarity that his detractors take such pride at sniffing out. His purpose in Greeley will be to lecture on Lincoln, but he may be persuaded to read a selection of his poems as well. If so, the fair-minded citizens of Greeley will discover for themselves that no one need blush to a crimson when the poet of the human body and the human soul acquits manhood and womanhood from the charge of infamy, degradation, and vice, on account of the true purity of the order of nature.

In the office of the Greeley *Tribune*, Pete regarded this proof with a cold eye. The last paragraph was clearly the wormy one. It was Josie's idea and Josie's wording, her slap in the face to her darling townspeople, who would surely kick back—that's what she wanted. Instead of subscribing they'd leave at the door paper sacks of horseshit. The puritans of Greeley had done that before, dumped coal ashes, offal, manure, and garbage by the wagonload at the door of the *Tribune*, in answer to everything from Father Meeker's proposed fence tax to his endorsement of Catherine

Beecher's notion that healthy women should wear flannel linen instead of corsets beneath their skirts, also Josie's idea. But even Josie would never succeed in persuading her father to run this plug. They should have printed it two weeks ago when he left, but he was returning tonight. The offending paragraph had to go.

He wiped down the last six lines of the galley in preparation for distributing the type. Josie's interest wasn't so much in what Walt had to say as in the potential scandal of his presence. Pete could have told her that dear old Walt was harmless as an overgrown pup, but first they had to raise the money, and they couldn't do that by displaying unnecessary contempt for their fellow citizens. But that was Josie. She hated Greeley and its beastly hypocrisy. Why, even the Unitarians had asked her not to teach Sunday school if she couldn't say something *good* about people. Instead of the Bible, she insisted on discussing the Indian question. The slaughter of the buffalo, she told the children, was really a way of killing off Indians. Their parents wanted to know what that had to do with God. God? she sneered. The unknowable all-being of unknowable character, the God of the Unitarians? He was hardly a fertile subject for discussion. How could anyone worship or influence such a being? How could we get him to listen to our prayers? Pete pointed out if she felt that way maybe she'd like to go back to the Presbyterians, whose God at least gave a roar now and then. Sure, she said—before he gobbled you up . . .

That was Josie—the one who spoke at the lyceum about starting a lottery to finance the new library, only to have her fellow citizens ignore her with icy politeness. She might be Nathan Meeker's daughter, but seventeen-year-olds of no matter what family ought to confine themselves to recitations and doughnuts. The one who'd introduced Elizabeth Cady Stanton as "a savior of women," only to have the pious females of Greeley point out they already had a savior, thank you, of the masculine gender. The one who wanted to go and live with the Indians, to teach them how to read and write. Actually, she'd announced this intention so often that Pete suspected her father's trip had something to do with finding an Indian school for her to teach in. He'd been gone for two weeks somewhere over the mountains, or around them on the railroads, then into them on horseback, deep into the wilderness, far away, said Josie—eyes all agleam—far from these mincing self-conceited people, and Pete was to fetch him at the station in Evans in the Meeker's buggy on his return tonight. Concerning exactly where he'd gone, for precisely what purpose, Josie turned coy when Pete asked. It seemed something was up. Her father had plans, or was solving a problem, or undoing something someone else had done. He'd certainly been glum enough lately, what with Greeley's presidential campaign in decline, and people in town complaining left and right about the price of the canals, the failed stock company, the ravages of grasshoppers, and the unfriendly cowboys. Pete could tell when things weren't going right by the rising incidence in Father Meeker's newspaper of spread-eagled platitudes concerning the fine soil and climate of their colony, designed to make folks feel smart about coming here. He taught Pete how to puff the town with the newspaper, and Pete had observed how well it worked. Worked so well that few people remembered to give Nathan the credit for founding the colony in the first place, or for laying out the streets and canals and discovering what would and wouldn't grow in this soil—only the blame for building such a fine specimen of a house that no common farmer dared track mud on Father Meeker's carpets . . . Half of them never paid their subscriptions. Pete knew he felt the pinch. He looked up to note the accounts in arrears skewered on a spike above the sloping desk at which he sat. But Nathan had their papers delivered regardless, on the theory that reading his *Tribune* was bound to be good for them. From his high-perched stool, Pete's hands flew up and down the cases distributing type. Sure, it was good for them. It helped them digest the venom of their spleens—which ain't by far a healthy condiment. They vilified Father Meeker, but the generality of them at least grudged him his unsmiling honesty. Pete liked him well enough too, but hungered for greater freedom with the *Tribune.* It seemed to him half his time on the newspaper was spent breaking down copy—as now—though this one was of his own volition. At Meeker's insistence last month he'd broken down a story based on the weeklies' description of the Liberal Republicans' heavy losses in the October state elections. Then just two weeks ago he'd composed a personal cribbed from an article in the Illinois *Republican* in which Horace Greeley was compared on matters of personal dress and general philosophy to, of all people, Walt Whitman— naturally that one had caught Pete's eye—but Father Meeker spiked it as demeaning Greeley's dignity. Pete hadn't let Josie know about *that.*

There. Back in the cases, the type and leads were just plugs of metal. Amazing how words could break down to atoms, and then, stick by stick, make up sentences again, sentences containing lovely sentiments, queer notions, staggering curses, or gall and wormwood—everything from the Declaration of Independence to an exposé of the dangers of lead in the pottery industry to a description of ladies' undergarments to the most hair-raising prurient lechery. Pete so loved composing on the stick he spent hours in the office at night writing hoary-headed nonsense and vulgarity for his personal edification, then breaking it down. From the top down, the sentences raveled, and from the bottom up unraveled just as fast. He didn't take proofs, just composed and decomposed, thinking all the while, I *am* pretty clever . . .

A howl came from outside—sounded like a wolf, but Pete knew who it was. He'd lowered the overhead lights in the office, but with dark coming earlier each evening and the floor-length windows uncurtained, Jack could easily tell he was in here. Had to be Jack, he didn't knock—he kicked the door. "Hold your horses." Pete pushed open the gate on the spindled railing separating the public side of the office from the work space with its presses, tables, sloping desks, ledgers, cases of type, and vats of ink. He wiped the words off his hand with his apron, unlatched the door—felt a blast of wind—and regarded the spectacle standing there before him.

"Pete, oh Pete, it's so fucking cold, just let me step in."

"It's only October."

"Horseshit! Feel it yourself."

Jack Wilcox stepped back—it seemed to take an effort, he'd been drinking, as usual—and Pete squeezed past him, surprised at the cold. The stars looked barely ten feet above his head. Up and down the wide dirt street the only lights came from the Greeley Hotel. "Winter coming."

"Sure as hell." Jack had already lumbered inside and turned to face Pete. "Brought you some arwerdenty." From one pocket of his worn frock coat—someone's discard, Pete knew—he pulled a corked jug, smacking his lips. Those lips were the only visible skin in the bottom half of his hairy face, and they reminded Pete of freshly sliced liver. Jack was sixty plus, but his beard still showed color—dirt brown, more or less, hard to tell with all the drippings and juices congealed in its thick fur. He didn't remove the shapeless wool hat, beneath which hung ropes of shoulder-length hair.

The skin around his eyes had shattered, pieced itself together and shattered again countless times. "Here." He held out the jug. He stood there, all two hundred pounds, like an unmuzzled bear giving off odors: rotten cheese, dog breath, hay, manure, mud . . . His voice needed oiling. "Boughten of a Mexican in Evans." The black frock coat showed holes here and there the size of coin slots. Underneath it, his greasy hickory shirt and buckskins billowed out.

A hole in one moccasin oozed a bare toe.

Pete took the jug and tasted the molasses-sweetened brandy. The sugar and the oily fire separated on his tongue and drained into two throats, one burning, the other soothed. He labored at a long pull of the liquor—to make the drunk come, as Jack liked to say.

"You et supper yet?"

"Some beans."

"Here? Like a buck nun? It's froze to hell in here. Didn't you never cook them?"

"Straight from the can."

"First thing we need's a fire, Pete. Here. You take this." From the other coat pocket Jack pulled a puppy, fat and squealing. He tossed it to Pete. Pete set it down and, looking up—showing two red crescents beneath each eye—it made a little puddle on Nathan's wood floor. Pete wiped it up with his ink-stained apron. They'd just oiled it last week, that floor, he and Josie . . . The puppy, splotched like an Appaloosa, with long floppy ears, scratched himself once, fell over, then clamped down onto the toe of Pete's boot.

"That's a hell-pup there, Pete. 'Tain't just a mongrel—it's a complete muxed-up karimption of dog, javalina, and bear cub. It's a scrub. You watch. He won't let go of your toe for certain. You could knock him silly, won't matter. He bit my foot oncet for four months."

Pete took a step but the puppy hung on. "How old's this pup, then?"

"Three months old."

"Fat."

"Well, you want it?"

He looked up at Jack and laughed. "Jack, you are a caution. What would I do with a pup?"

"Warm your toes."

The thing didn't growl—didn't even chew—just hung on to Pete's boot like a bear trap. For the two steps Pete took to return the jug to Jack, it stayed there wrapped around the boot. "What else you got in that pocket?"

"My shucks."

"No smoking tonight, Jack. Nathan's coming back. I got to take his own buggy out to Evans at ninish."

"That train always lags."

"Most like a milk train back east."

"*Milk* train?" Jack had removed a corn shuck from his pocket and quick as a skunk pulled a pinch of tobacco out of the pouch hanging off his belt and spread it on the shuck. He knew how to make himself at home all right. "Now, Pete . . ."

"Damn it all, Jack, go fall on yourself. You know how that stinks. He'll smell it for certain."

"What, he's coming *here*? He ain't going *home*? He won't smell it *tomorrow*!" One hand held his made-up shuck—pinched each end, turning it in his palm with quick meaty fingers—and the other tipped the jug to his lips.

"He sure as hell will."

"We'll make us a fire, Pete, and let some smoke out. Say it backed up. Let the wood smoke mux up the tobaccy smell, he won't tell the difference. Fucking old glue pot. Boiled shirt. Damn a fool nonsmoker teetotaler anyhow, he acts so fool-like." Jack stomped through the gate toward the stove back against the wall behind the presses. "Wood box empty."

"Go fetch it yourself."

Pete stood there in the outer office with a puppy on his foot, not caring to move. Jack was fun, sure—a *compiche*, his word—but could be such a bother. He'd be here all night, and Pete had to go and see Josie before he hitched up her father's buggy for Evans. *Had* to see her, and show her the proof. She'd be waiting, expecting him. Offer him supper as well. That's a royal road, anyway—two suppers in one night. That got pretty close to his ribs. Better than the People's Restaurant and Boarding House, where two communal towels hung from nails on the door jamb, one on either side, for before meals and after, and where Pete's own ground-floor room had served all summer as a shortcut for slugs on their way to and from the kitchen gardens. Had to be careful where he stepped . . . "What's for supper?"

"You'll see." Jack dumped an armload of wood in the wood box then stormed out again, leaving the back door open. "This wood's putrified!"

"It's wet."

"It's froze to hell is what it is!"

"It ain't that cold outside."

"Horseshit, it ain't. Like to freeze my eyeballs."

Pete looked around the office. "What was it you was thinking of cooking?"

"Never you mind just yet." Jack kicked the door shut behind him, and dumped more wood in the box. His shuck hung from his lips, unlit. He might just forget it—he'd done that before. One got lost in his beard last month—worked itself in and never came out.

Pete shrugged. It *was* cold in here. Only October. But who was Jack to complain? The hut where he lived didn't even have a stove. He slept there all winter wrapped in buffalo hides on a dirt floor, cooked his food outside at an open fire, let his dogs and puppies run free on five unpenned acres of prime bottom land all run to weeds right next to the confluence of the Cache la Poudre and Ditch Number One. Nathan and every other town father had tried buying him out countless times. But Jack needed that much room, he said. He had a cow too, some goats, chickens, sheep, and a pig, not to mention the empty bottles, oyster cans, sardine boxes, herring and chicken tins strewn all about. The goats couldn't keep up with the garbage. His shack was just an adobe box with a tendency to run into mud and gravel where one corner met the ground. He carried the young sheep inside on cold winter nights to help warm his body. Had so many dogs and puppies running all around that a new bitch whelped every month or so somewheres out in a chicken shed or hold, he couldn't keep track. Forgot all their names . . .

He'd taught Pete once to eat sheep's head boiled. First the eyes, then the brains, then the meat on the cheekbones and jawbones, saving the tongue for a delicious conclusion.

Pete lifted his occupied leg high in the air, but the pup hung on. "Where's the friedcakes I brought you?"

"It was give to the pups."

"Last time I go to such trouble for *you.*"

"It's just cornmeal mush. I'm accustomed to *meat.*" Jack fumbled at the stove with paper and matches, then clanged the top on lest sparks light his beard, since the slags of sappy pine spit a lot burning, and that beard contained enough fat and grease to burn hours. In front of the stove the wood floor was spotted with tin can lids nailed over burn-holes. Jack tipped the stove lid to let smoke in, then lit his shuck. "Pete. Where's that pot?"

"Under the counter."

Jack was in his element now, bustling about like he owned the place. Under the counter holding the type cases he found an old iron pot and stepped out to fill it from the pump in back. Pete reached down to pat the puppy, and it wagged but didn't let go. The fire spit and snapped in the stove, and the warming metal began to pop. Jack staggered in with the pot full of water and set it on the stove, sloshing some. Caught between the stove and the pot, drops of water spit and snapped.

Suddenly Pete went moist all over. "You look buggered, Pete, how come?" Jack had pulled out a long leather strap and snapped it a few times. "My bosal." Pete backed up when he approached, but proved too slow; Jack yanked the pup off his boot, wrapped the bosal around its neck and tied the other end to the overhead light fixture of cast metal and frosted globes with oil lamps inside. The puppy yelped and *ki*-ed a few minutes, then hung there limp, eyes popping out. Rooted, Pete faced it. The dead eyes accused him. He fingered the pouch around his neck. "You never et pup?" asked Jack.

"Can't say as I have."

"Injun dish. You'll find the flesh a mite greasy, but sweet. Tastes like tarrapin." He unfastened the strap and held the dead pup by the scruff of its neck, belly facing Pete. Then he pulled out his knife, made one quick cut from the neck to the crotch, and with a meaty forefinger yanked out the guts as though cleaning a fish. He looked around quick, then shook them into Nathan's wicker basket before Pete could say, No, not there.

In the outer office Pete sat on a bench.

Jack pushed the pot back toward the stovepipe, removed all four cast-iron lids from the stove, and laid the gutted puppy on the open fire. It was drawing well now, only small dollops of smoke rose up from time to time bearing smells of burnt flesh and fur. He kept turning the thing until all the fur was well singed off, then carried it by one ear to the counter—to Nathan's oak counter!—and cutting off its head, sliced it in chunks of all imaginable shapes and sizes. These pieces he hauled in two open hands to the pot and dumped in. Fed more wood to the fire, set the lids back in place, adjusted the damper, pulled the pot to the middle, wiped his hands on his coat . . . Took a swig from his jug of Mexican brandy and slammed it back on the counter, satisfied.

Jack still hadn't removed his slouch hat. "That's all right, Jack, you just make yourself at home." Pete jumped up, removed his apron, and pulled on the coat he'd left on a hook beside the door.

"Christ almighty, Pete, I'm cooking us *supper!*"

"Mighty glad, Jack, wish I could stay, gotta fetch Father Meeker's buggy right now. It's getting on time. Wish I could stay! Lock the door when you leave, there's a good pardner, I'll look in later."

"You're full of beans!"

"Not for long, most likely."

He slammed the door behind him, rushed out into the street, and threw up all the contents of his stomach in a roily puddle. There, that felt better. He could go back inside and take one more pull at the jug, but the thought of the *smell* of that—food—just the thought, puckered his stomach and doubled him up once again . . .

He hadn't even taken the proof. Had to show it to Josie—but sometime later. Maple Street was empty of buggies and *cold* for a body that just lost its packing. He started off west toward Monroe Street, lightheaded.

"Pete! Come on back!" Jack stood outside the office waving. Pete turned and did a little jig on the street to kick up the dust, but this

Greeley soil went from mud to cement with hardly a speck of dust intervening. The thin dry air excavated the dust. He spit a few times— Jack stood back there shouting—and someone stepped out of the Greeley Hotel to disapprove of the noise, then stepped back inside spreading the news that winter was coming. *Cold* out there . . .

Pete turned left at Monroe Street and headed south. Two years ago some pasha from the Arabian Nights had broadcast the desert with magic seeds and this town sprang up. The trees now were nearly ten feet tall. Brick stores lining the flat, wide streets sold everything from pianos and organs to window glass, boots, baked goods, watches, harnesses and saddles, lumber and coal—even flour for those who didn't farm. The town might grow bigger than Denver someday! Gathered on corners, ghosts of Sioux and Utes waited patiently in clusters for the whole extraneous foreign shape of it, the square, squat buildings and houses, the ornate fronts and sheet-metal roofs, the milled wood, glass windows, and the geometrical waste of the broad streets frozen in some sort of mindless grid, to wash or blow away. This physical town was a spirit world; there was no such place. The waters would rise and bear it away. Already, cellars flooded in spring; the Indians laughed. Water came up from inside the earth—not down from the mountains—as if in protest at being stolen from the river. These people cut the earth and put in water. They surrounded their houses with pastures watered from slits in the earth, then fenced horses out—they didn't make sense. Burial pits would erupt from beneath them and leave the whole town awash in bones—not just bones of buffalo and horses, and the People, but of ancient animals, wooly mammoths, camels, lizards, things with claws, horns, and beaks . . .

But that wouldn't happen, Pete knew for certain. Greeley's farmers were too damn clever by halves. They were nothing if not industrious ants, carrying bits of things here and there. When their irrigated fields and lawns caused the water table downtown to rise, they decided to put in drains along Main Street. He hopped a ditch crossing Main now, with the collared tiles laid out alongside waiting to be installed. Busy, busy, busy. The way to improve things was do them in circles: put the water in, take the water out. Down beyond Main, where the houses began, people's lawns were two acres large, and they mowed them, no less. They played croquet! Made trees to grow where trees had never been. But they grumbled no end, about typhoid autumns from open ditches and swampy drain fields. No pleasing these gentlemen farmers and their wives. Some complained of oil in their wells. No more wearing shabby clothes, living on skim milk and mush and pork fat, they wanted good

houses and decent clothing and money to spend on lectures and concerts—they wanted a new life! All last month, all around the town,
combined reapers and binders had cut the grain and steam engines had
threshed. In the spring, sulky plows would turn the soil and seed drills
plant in rows of consummate efficiency, with not a seed wasted. Of
course, in order to purchase this machinery, most of the farmers had
mortgaged their farms. Once the grasshoppers cleared out, this autumn's
harvest had wound up doubling last year's but now these farmers were
learning that an increased yield meant lower prices for their crops, so
they'd been forced to borrow their new lives from banks. The finest brick
buildings downtown were banks. It was a wealthy town all right, but the
wealth was elsewhere. And what had happened to Father Meeker's cooperation? First the stock association had to sell out, in consequence of a
severe winter, and that put a damper on the cooperative bakery and
laundry he'd planned. If they pooled their capital they wouldn't need
banks, but they'd all run out of capital to pool . . .

So theirs was just another town getting on. One by one, Pete crossed
the streets Father Meeker had insisted they name after Horace Greeley's
beloved trees: Walnut, Pine, Chestnut, Linden. Around the Meeker
house on Cherry Street they'd forgone a lawn—all the rage in Greeley—
and planted trees instead, four or five of each species. Huddled up in the
cold, Pete watched the house take shape ahead, with its pyramidal roof
and the cupola on top. Papery leaves still clung to the scrawny trees
around it. Lights burned up there in Josie's window.

He could hitch up the buggy right now and leave, without knocking
on the door. He wasn't hungry now. Josie was there, but so was her
mother, who roosted up near the wainscoting in the parlor and dining
room, dressed in black feathers, ready to swoop down. She seldom left
the house. Once, in a thunderstorm, Pete had watched Arvilla Delight—
her given names—stand at the black cookstove in the kitchen, snap her
fingers—and fire came out of them! Fire, or sparks. Funny that a woman
whose piety was famous should look so like a witch. For all her black
garb, she was too glum for magic. She sat in exactly the same posture
as she stood, stacked on herself like a pyramid, pelican nose nearly
touching her lips, hands locked across her spreading waist. Mostly she
just stared, and mostly at Pete, as though she'd detected a secret about
him.

He'd seen her once on her knees to her husband. They played out
these little dramas now and then. He turned his cold side to her and she
knelt beside him and held his hand. Cold, black, wicked, and choked,
Nathan sat there and read a book while Arvilla silently wept. He smiled.

"It makes you smile, does it?" Her tears dried up and she walked away hardened, but returned minutes later with a book which she proceeded to read out loud, sitting by the fireplace. The passage she'd chosen declared that some people having the nervous temperament are often cross and melancholy, and nothing can please them—they are diseased. She looked up at her husband. "And so are you, my dear. Diseased." He sat there and silently read, ignoring her. Meanwhile, Pete and Josie on the couch turned the pages of an album of architectural wonders, pretending to exclaim at the Parthenon, the Coliseum, the Tower of London . . .

Pete avoided her when he could.

In the gravel drive, he snatched up some pebbles to throw at Josie's window—they spread like buckshot. Her face appeared—Josie's face!—and mouthed silent words. She pointed toward the carriage house, then vanished. Pete sauntered back there, feeling his blood rise. It might be cold out, but here he was, warm. He stood in the drive straight as a flag pole. *Josie's coming* . . . When the door closed behind him, he jumped. Footsteps approached. She touched his arm but he didn't turn, just stood there letting the touched skin ripple.

"Pete the Great!"

"Don't call me that." He wheeled around as if to start back to town.

"Oh, Pete. Don't be preposterous." Josie grabbed his pocketed arm and dragged him back toward the carriage house door, literally dragged him—his feet wouldn't move. Well, just a little. He did help her out. Couldn't let the poor girl strain herself. Josie was strong but sickly at times with that phlegmy cough, those limbs of a stork.

They slipped inside the darkened carriage house and she kissed him on the lips. There, that was over. He returned the pressure, feeling all moist, melting then icing over again. She backed away, he groped around and stumbled on something in the absolute dark, some harness or saddle, rousing the horses, who whinnied and hoofed in their stalls. "Hey, Josie."

She lit one of the buggy's lanterns and stood there in a high frock dress beneath her open coat, with a modest ribbon at the collar secured by a modest little brooch, smiling at Pete. He knew that one of her teeth had a spot, but it couldn't be seen in that uncertain light, only imagined. Her cough was better, though—the mountain air did it. Still, she practiced it now and then. Climbing into the back seat, she coughed, and lifting the cushion, pulled out a muff. Then she sat there with arms swallowed by the muff, fish-eyes wide open.

"Where are you going?"

"I'm going with you."

"Your pa won't care for that, it's so nation cold."

"We can pile up blankets."

"There's scarce room for us and his bags too, Josie."

"I'll ride up with you."

"Against the wind?"

"Don't be so tiresome."

"Bosh, I ain't tiresome, I'm just—"

"Dreadful vile. We can warm ourselves first. Don't be so foolish, Pete, come sit beside me, it's early yet. You hardly give me room to breathe. What time is it? The train comes at ten."

"Comes at nine-thirty."

"Whose time? That's Cheyenne time."

"Same time in Evans."

"Evans is on Denver time. I know for certain. I picked up Pa when he come back from Washington City and I waited alone on that platform for an hour enduring the jibes and whistles of men so forward you'd think they were steel-headed bankers. They were just railroad men."

"They got a reputation."

"The train came at ten."

"Likely was late."

"Likely the time on the board was wrong too. Likely you'll straighten them out when you get there, I'm certain of that—but it won't speed the train. Ladder's over there beside the chute, Pete."

You could bicker with Josie to lick creation without pulling even. She'd sit there until he left, Pete knew. He supposed she'd be bundled enough if she buttoned her coat and he threw on some blankets. He could go inside to fill up the warmer, but he might run into Arvilla.

Josie's clear eyes reflected the light from the lamp as though they'd run out of oil sometime too. Somewhere inside her were rotted boards—her soul crept across them. Because her duty was to care for her health, so as not to spoil her lungs, she loved the luxury of incautious behavior, which gave her eyes glint. Pete couldn't picture her rotting inside, she'd uproot it first, she'd *have* no insides . . . Her mouth, her thin lips, went straight to his vitals. They looked washed-up on shore, they came from some other place, wanted to go back, and this accounted for their merciless clarity as well as, what?—all the sand and grit . . . But where were they going? Could he go too? He could sit in the buggy like her and not budge. "Where'd your pa go off to anyway?"

"You'll find out soon enough."

"Something important?"

"You'll see. Pa didn't want it bandied about." She was smiling. Couldn't hold it in long, Pete saw that—she was too excited.

"I do dislike being left in the dark."

"Oh, Pete. How would you like to live with wild Indians and wear skins of animals and eat raw meat?"

"Just love it."

"Indian agents have to be brave."

"I'm a newspaperman."

"Not you, you goose. *Daddy.*"

"Your father?"

"They might need a new Indian agent at White River."

"Where's that?"

"Over the mountains."

"Far?"

"Far enough."

"At his age he's going to go live with the Indians?"

"He wants to do good for them."

"Folks only got so much good to hand out."

"And he needs the money. He despises indebtedness. It's a matter of honor. Indian agents make fifteen hundred dollars a year. He don't like counting pennies. Nor do I. I'd rather count injuns than pennies, Pete."

Pete didn't dare ask the next question, not yet. *Then you're planning to go with him?* He'd dragged a stepladder out beside the buggy and climbed toward the ceiling. Around them, the lamp threw a thin cloth of light on the feed bins, gunnysacks, stalls, on the harnesses and saddles hanging from the walls, on the heads and shoulders of horses come forward to peer across their schpriggel bars. Their eyes caught the lamp's glimmer and broadcast a message back to their legs to fidget and paw, to their tails to swish . . . He'd have to feed and water them first, before they left—that would take time. Above his head he clung with one arm to an overhead roller fixed between beams, fishing around in a hole with the other, then came down with a bottle held high.

"How much left?"

"Enough to kill a horse."

Josie liked drinking it straight from the bottle, just like a man. Prime Eagle Whiskey, smuggled to town in a consignment of boots. Pete stepped down from the ladder, uncorked the bottle, took a big swallow— he could smell her mouth on the lip—then reached it to her, and proceeded to shovel feed in the horse bins. They could water downtown at the tank on Main Street.

He climbed up next to Josie.

"You bring peppermint leaves?"

"Hmmn." When it found his stomach empty, the whiskey went straight to Pete's head like a rocket and popped somewhere up there amongst the stars. He blinked his eyes. "How much does your Pa owe?"

"Enough to embarrass him. Pete, please don't mention it. I couldn't bear it if people in this town found out."

Most folks know it already, Josie. "I was sitting in the office when he borrowed another thousand of Mr. Greeley last summer."

Josie looked down. "You should have stopped him." She traced the veins on the back of Pete's hand with her tiny finger. "Course if Mr. Greeley were to win the election, Pa could be something big and important, he wouldn't have to take an agency. If Colorado were a state, and Uncle Horace was president, Daddy could be a U.S. senator . . ."

"He won't win."

"He might."

"Not likely."

"He could."

Pete took another swallow of whiskey. "You want him to win or you want to go live on a reservation with some wild men?"

"I want what's best for Pa."

And you? What about you? "You got such a fine house here."

"Pa could make some money by letting it."

"So you'll go too?"

"Why shouldn't I go? It's not for a surety yet, Pete, don't fuss."

"I wasn't fussing."

"It takes time to make such appointments, and Pa wanted to see the place first and talk with the present agent and get a good feel for it. He might not like it, but I pray that he does. You could go too. We'd make a pair, wouldn't we, dressed up in feathers and beads? I hope it works out. I pray every night for Uncle Horace to lose, if you want to know the truth. I ought to be shot. I pray he winds up defeated and broke and calls in all his debts and quits New York and moves here to retire and rents our house, Pete. Let *him* live in this town that bears his name, I can't stand it. I'd rather live in a tipi than spend one more day in Greeley. I'd sooner dress up in buckskin than walk down the streets of this town and nod to Mrs. Welsh and chat with Reverend Plumber, and have to smile when all the time I'd rather be scalping them. They smile back like they think I'm Sally Brass. Smile like they've got a bug pinching them in a secret place."

"I guess you do too."

"Like to scratch it if I did, right in front of them. Reverend Plumber told me a story concerning him and Mrs. Plumber, when they were first married. They married in New York and took a train to Philadelphia. He disembarked half way there to buy a newspaper and the train left without him. This was before the telegraph, Peter. So he got on the next train for Philly while she boarded one from Philly to New York, and for the next ten years they went back and forth like that . . ."

"Ten years?"

"More or less. I think they're still doing it. I told Reverend Plumber, Well that's marriage for you."

"That's famous! What did he say?"

"He come out with a sort of Moses-in-the-burning-bush look and averred as I might make a speech for *men's* rights. I've thought about that, Pete. I might just do it. Their right to be waited on hand and foot by stupid females. Their right to a home, a wife, children, and love they have no interest in returning." She tipped the bottle and swallowed some whiskey, then smiled, breathing out her nose. Her nostrils made steam in the dry cold air. "Not you, Pete. You're not like that. When *you* marry, don't seek out a housekeeper with no more sense than a horse. Find a friend or companion."

"Why get hitched at all? That's what I say."

"*I* never shall."

"Nor I." Steady now, Pete—you're getting too close to your own spiritual longitude and latitude altogether here. After all, Pete knew something of marriage, having once stopped a man from beating his wife, stopped him cold . . . But with Josie there beside him—most breathing on his neck—he felt the danger of losing his bearings on this important question and getting all bumsquabbled. Here they were promising never to marry. It pinched too much, it sounded like a pact—like a *marriage*, no less.

What did she want from him?

Then again, it was no doubt a way of setting her sights not just higher than him, but higher than anyone else in Greeley—higher than most tobacco-spitting American males, who even with their coffers stuffed walked around with dirty fingernails. But where could you go higher than that?

It was out of the question—he couldn't marry. Well, if you're not going to marry either, let *me* be the one you don't marry, Josie . . .

Pete sat there stiffly, growing a shell.

I could come too. I could live with the redskins and dance and holler and whoop it up famous. Of course, she was planning to teach them in a school. Well, someone had to sweep out the schoolhouse. Someone had to haul wood and water.

Then again, someone had to mind the newspaper, right here in Greeley. Unless Nathan sold it . . .

He felt her unbutton his coat and reach in for the pouch around his neck. Hefting it with her small palm—smaller than a hawthorn leaf—she looked up at his face, kissed him on the chin, just down beneath the mouth, a little to the left—kissed him with *three* lips, it seemed to Pete, one in between wetter than the other—then poked at the pouch with a finger. It was sewn shut so its contents wouldn't spill. "An agate," she said.

"Nope."

She sniffed it. "Dried apricot."

"Course not."

"Smells like it. Ginseng root?"

"No."

"Rabbit's foot."

"You asked that last time."

"I know, I can't think. You said it brought you luck. Brimstone?"

"No."

"A magnet."

"Nope."

"Mandrake root—"

"No—"

"—dead mouse—"

"—nope—"

"—human ear—"

"—no—"

"—chewed-up hunk of oh I don't know, cowhide—monkey's paw, someone's finger, rooster tongue, oh Pete, what is it?"

"You have to guess."

She squeezed the pouch with her delicate fingers, turning it over and back.

"It's a wad of, I don't know, nothing—you're tricking me, Pete. I don't even care. A piece of stiffened cloth. Don't torment me so!"

"You started it, Josie, remember?"

"At least you could tell me."

"You made the rules."

"You're such a stick, Pete . . ." All at once she pulled at the thing, jerking his head forward. He snatched it out of her hand, tucked in his shirt, but didn't bother to button up, they were wrestling now, he was going all moist again . . . Josie was kissing and biting his neck, he couldn't tell which, this was the fun part, but unnerving too. He had a tendency to sink a bit here. Commanded his arms to do this or that, but the bones seemed to struggle *inside* the flesh, to part from the tissue like overcooked goose. It was fun to wrestle, sure, but still—let's go slow here, Josie. He was backing off, he couldn't help it. Had to be careful . . .

With her lips at his collarbone she exhaled in short breaths, moist and warm. She was rubbing his arm just above the wrist. Rubbed it in small rhythmical circles with her first two fingers. "I swear I have more hair on my arm than you do, Peter."

"I singed it off."

She rubbed. It felt pretty good, so regular like that. Seemed to *mean* something . . . He slowly relaxed. She switched from the soft pads of her fingers to her boney knuckles and continued to rub that spot in steady circles, round and round. Mouth still open at his neck, her tongue licked his flesh, probing the soft crease above the collar bone. His arm had gone dry where she rubbed it, and grit or something had formed in the circle, dead skin no doubt. She pressed down harder, rubbed a little faster. Actually it hurt just a bit, but he couldn't very well ask her to stop. "Hey. Josie." She rubbed faster and harder. Skin was coming off, he felt it abrading—she'd seized his arm with her other hand, strong as a vise. And he'd gone all moist! His heart wasn't fluttering either, but thudding, like some huge muscle that ground things up . . . It hurt, Josie, stop! But he didn't cry out. It was some kind of test. This was all meant to be, she'd intended it somehow, the grating, dry pain, she was breathing hard too.

He looked over at one of the horses.

Suddenly his arm was wet. He didn't look down—knew it was blood. Felt he could almost smell it as well . . . Her breath came now in heavy sobs, she shuddered a few times—*he* shuddered too, it rippled right through him, felt himself gasp! Then she stopped and went limp. The carriage house had gone completely silent. He realized now the buggy'd been creaking to beat the band. Ferocious! "Now you do it to me."

"Josie. My goodness."

"Do it to me, do it to me. I've done it myself. See?" She sat up, and pulling her arm from her coat, unbuttoned the cuff and rolled up her sleeve. A row of scabs climbed up her arm, little circles of dried blood.

Snow. And only the third week of October! Little seedy flakes of it halfway back on the return trip from Evans blowing into their faces like sand, and though Nathan made not a peep in the back—no one spoke the entire trip home—Pete knew he'd sunk even deeper into his own abysmal brand of silent fury, directed in this instance at Peter Doyle for his consummate folly in allowing Josie to make this trip. Not a lick of sense . . . She sat back there huddled up against her daddy's rigid body beneath piles of blankets. Nathan's bags sat up front next to Pete.

No one said a thing when he dropped them off at home.

Then, by the time Pete had unhitched the horses and closed up the carriage house, the wind had picked up, a Greeley wind like a runaway horse making the smallest things feel out of control. Snow blew around in large ragged sheets still gritty as dirt, leaving half the streets bare, the other half and the ditches and wagon ruts filling up slowly.

Then it blew out. Stars reappeared. Pete felt more than saw the huge shadows of clouds moving off east toward the prairies. On moonlit nights white ghosts of mountains appeared in the west, hardly breaking the horizon, but tonight wasn't moonlit—just star-dazed. The wind pierced you bad, and clothing felt useless. It looked to the west like more clouds were coming.

He walked up Monroe Street heading downtown close to midnight, could have been later. No one on the streets, and all the lights in houses and stores snuffed long ago. They'd had to help Josie down from the carriage and into the house, but Pete knew she was playing it up. She loved making folks around her concerned, especially her father. Coughed a few times for good measure. How could someone be so sickly yet strong as a horse, and give off such a sweet smell of decay? Tomorrow he'd find her glowing again, eyes all aglint, sharp tongued and sweet, hard and soft both . . .

Her father had seemed gloomy enough even before spotting Josie in the buggy, had waited as much as a half hour, he said. Train come early? No, right on time. Clammed up about the White River Agency when Josie inquired, except to say that the prospects were dim. That's why she huddled against him in back, she was comforting Daddy—herself as well. Surely Nathan wouldn't remove such a delicate daughter to the mountains, regardless. And what about Arvilla?

Maybe Mr. Greeley would win. Maybe Pete and Josie could start a subscription to pay off Nathan's debt—in secret. Maybe Pete could find buried treasure too . . .

Can't I just do what I want?

Averting his head, Pete hunched against the wind. Kicked at some snow. Skipped once too—bare homage to a jig.

On Maple Street, he spotted a pile of something dumped outside the

Tribune office. Another farmer objecting to one of Nathan's schemes had unloaded his manure spreader in protest, no doubt. But the pile wore clothes, Pete saw that getting closer. It slumped there like a load of rags abandoned against the side of the building, and didn't stir. "Jack! Stupid ox." Pete tried to roust him. The skin on his face felt cold as ice. Someone had hung a crude cardboard sign around his neck with baling twine: NO DRUNKS IN GREELEY. "That's all right, Jack. C'mon. Get a move on." When Jack wouldn't stir, a spurt of fear shot up inside Pete, licking at his heart. He stood and looked down the cold, empty street, cursing this town. Some folks make you tired . . . They hang signs on you and leave you to die.

But he wasn't dead. His breath still felt warm. Can't kill an old horse—just let him rot or freeze or get lost. Pete tore off his coat, threw it on Jack, and poked the sleeves up under his arms. He opened the *Tribune* door—unlocked!—anyone could have walked right in and taken what they wanted—then squeezed in between Jack and the building and, grabbing hold of the sleeves, commenced dragging him in. It was hard work, but Pete felt steamed up enough to drag mountains. Jack was no help, he groaned a few times, but wouldn't come around. Inside was cold too, the fire had gone out, the overhead oil lamps burned to their wicks. The place smelled horrible—burnt wicks, putrid puppy meat, stale to-bacco smoke, rancid blood and guts, dead coals . . .

Pete lit the lamp above Nathan's desk.

Of course he'd have to clean up Jack's mess. But he didn't have to like it. Inches at a time, he dragged Jack through the gate to the stove in back, then threw one of Nathan's wool rugs across him. The fire in the stove had long ago died, and on the surface of the water in the pot floated a coating of scum—congealed puppy grease—out of which poked chunks of glutinous meat. Jack hadn't eaten much, too busy drinking. Making as much noise as he could, clanging the lids, thunking wood slabs, Pete started the fire up. Kept one lid off for fresh smoke to come in and kill all the other smells.

Jack barely stirred, lying on his back. Pete looked around. On the floor sat a puddle of greasy liquid, probably spilled when the pot boiled over. Broken glass from Jack's empty jug. A severed head and guts in Nathan's wicker basket, blood on his counter—that would never come out. On the tall slant desk sat Pete's galley of the subscription for Walt's lecture on Lincoln. He carried it over and slipped it inside a stack of galleys for next week's edition. Why even bother to ask permission? Go to hell, Father Meeker. Who gives a damn . . .

He added more wood to the fire, got it roaring and spitting—the cast iron groaned and creaked in protest—then closed the lid and lowered the light. Outside, the snow had already returned and whipped at the windows with a beady fury. It sounded like rat shit thrown against the glass.

What next? He looked around the room, heaved a sigh, and lifted the rug he'd thrown over Jack, then slipped underneath to warm his body with his own.

Chapter

7

"Shift's up," a voice squeaked. Ralph looked around, still shoveling sand. The men around him were shoveling too, caught in some sort of rubbery echo, so maybe he hadn't heard correctly. Seemed he'd only been there two or three hours. Sweat poured off him in the moist air mixed with dust from flying sand and gravel being sucked with a constant roar up the sand pipe. All through the echoing chamber, men, arranged in circles, flung dirt at sand pipes extending down from the whitewashed steel roof above them to within inches of the earth floor. Each shovelful disappeared up a pipe. Some sort of tenth circle of hell—he could write it up that way—with bare-chested souls in a cave being robbed of their work's evidence. The dirt disappeared, it didn't pile up, and the deeper they dug, the lower the steel roof above their heads descended, and the greater the pressure—a pound more of pressure for every two feet gained, like to split your tiny eardrums . . . Ralph's head ached terribly, his brain felt squeezed—nuts too—but still he shoveled. Nothing else for it. Feverish work, you felt sore all over, and all you could do to give it some spice was test how far from the hungry pipe a shovelful might fall short—but then you might have to shovel it again, and someone would laugh, or the foreman shout.

His shout would come out in a high, girlish shriek.

"Time to quit!" Compressed air squeezed voices, eyeballs, eardrums. Compressed air also forced the sand up the pipes, creating the necessity for more compressed air, a continual supply pumped down through hoses from a fleet of steam compressors above. The toilets down here had likewise been hooked up to pipes, which blasted their contents up toward the sky outside in a vapory cloud and away. The chamber was hot. Work dragged. So did quitting work. The air felt thick because it weighed more than the tower overhead—had to, in order to hold it up. Ralph thought he could liken working in here to motion underwater, then remembered they *were* underwater—sixty-five feet under—though more or less dry, except for their sweat, as the compressed air also prevented the river from bursting the steel shoe around them. But how to describe this to readers of newspapers?

Try the second person. You'd disguised yourself as a common laborer, that wasn't you shoveling sand. Was that person breathing twice as hard and weighing twice as much *you* or someone else? You only noticed the whistle to quit after it stopped, like a plugged leak. When you looked all around in the calcium lights, too tired to blink, and dropped your shovel—which made not a sound—you found yourself already trudging in a slow hallucination of movement ("that like a wounded snake drags its slow length along"—try that!) together with the rest of the laborers toward the air locks. You never exactly thought of the weight on top of your head, more like wormed along inside it. The caisson you and your fellow workers were digging into the East River bottom, a huge box nearly two hundred feet long, contained twenty-five courses of foot-square timbers laid at right angles in beds of cement and sheathed all around with iron boiler plate, and this was merely the *foot* of the tower. While you dug below inside that caisson, men and steam derricks on top of it laid blocks of granite each weighing three tons in endless courses which of course kept on sinking the more you dug, so the top of their tower stayed even with the river. Only when the caisson hit bedrock and you filled your workspace with concrete until there was barely room left for the last Irish worker, who escaped up a sand pipe, would the tower begin to climb, and only much later, when both towers were finished—Ralph calculated ten or twenty years—would you (or your children) sling the cables and hang the suspenders and construct the roadway for the world's largest suspension bridge, between Brooklyn and Manhattan, the eighth wonder of the universe!

Meanwhile, someone had to do all that grunt work below, and Ralph Meeker had heard—everyone had heard—the rumors of men dying like flies from mysterious ailments underneath the caisson. The Grecian bends, they called it. But Ralph hadn't seen anyone die so far, they only sweated like pigs with their heads in clamps. One by one they climbed a ladder up to the air lock, having earned their $2.75. It felt slow—as though time itself had stretched—yet Ralph's five-hour shift had seemed half that long. He'd been given no trouble signing up off the docks, as they needed men badly. Name? Adam Smith. The bridge company staggered paydays so everyone wouldn't quit at once. The turnover had proved so heavy, Ralph discovered, that nearly every male over sixteen in Five Points had worked in the caisson at one time or another, and all had stories. Some still suffered pains, dizziness, and vomiting. One young man Ralph had interviewed said that he worked only one shift, came out, felt fine, walked home, ate supper, then standing up felt all at once he'd been shot in the back. He was bedridden for weeks, half-paralyzed and feverish, and hadn't been able to work again since. The general feeling was that it took either heroic courage or sheer idiocy to work down there. The company confirmed that three men had died. But rumors in Five Points said many more, dozens they said—maybe hundreds, who knows? They just disappeared, they walked off somewhere and fell into the earth or drowned in the river. They might have thought their time had come to die, but it hadn't—the caisson did it. They wound up paralyzed or crazy or deaf, and even the remedies of Irish landladies—half a roasted onion clapped to each ear with a bandage—failed miserably. The company's doctor had wounded pigeons and dogs down there and found they healed normally. Therefore, conditions were, for the most part, sound. Perhaps the health of these men left something to be desired? He advised plenty of rest for those going into the caisson. Ralph pictured him wagging his finger. *No stopping off at saloons going home* . . . Yet even the chief engineer was rumored to have been stricken one day, and hadn't been seen since. Ralph had located him resting at home. But he denied that going down into the caisson was the cause; it was nerves, he said, insomnia and brain fever. He'd improved already, he told Ralph, because whatever it was he'd determined not to have it.

The iron door clanged shut with a dozen men inside, all taller than Ralph. They were pulling their shirts and coats on slowly, as it still felt hot, nearly eighty degrees; but outside, they knew, was a cold November day. A man with earmuffs and bald head resembling a pickled egg—he'd been here too long—turned the windlass in the door. "Ready, gents." Everyone clapped their hands to their ears. He opened a brass valve, slowly at first—the deafening screech lasted ten or twelve seconds—then closed it. The men looked down at their shuffling feet. "Ready, gents." He opened it again.

Five or six times he opened and closed it. He checked a gauge mounted beside it, pulled down on a handle, and the iron coffin began to move up—this air lock also served as an elevator. Ralph had expected to feel better by now, to experience some great release of pressure, but no such thing. He felt pale and queasy. The other men looked positively blue, they huddled inside their coats already, one stamped his foot as though to get it moving. They looked angry and hungry. When the air lock hissed to a stop, the attendant grinned, turned the windlass again, then stepped aside for a blast of frigid air to blow the door open. One by one the men slogged out.

Then it happened—but not to Ralph. They'd emerged on top of the tower surrounded by a floating platform leading back to the workyards and sheds. The overcast afternoon sky looked the color and texture Ralph imagined the inside of someone's skull might be, if you could just see it. Around him were huge derricks lifting blocks of pink stone, men pushing wheelbarrows and carrying hods, spikes, and shovels, or sifting sand for the cement, or chopping and sawing and running their adzes over the timbers used as frameworks in the tower. Dozens of steam engines sending up black smoke ran the air compressors, whose hoses disappeared down the tower's innards. A row of pipes roared, spewing out sand deflected by granite blocks into scows tied up beside the platform. These granite blocks were being eaten away by the force of the sand, Ralph could see that, they'd soon have to be replaced. Ropes, hoses, kegs of nails, barrels of tar, stacks of timber, coal and sand, piles of stone, iron rails, sledgehammers, shovels and picks, and general rubble lay on the platform in haphazard clusters with walkways between them. Few of the men seemed to know what they were doing. Ralph still felt tight as a drum, and the noise up here struck his skin like buckshot. Across the river, the half-completed Brooklyn tower, yellowish red, rose massively over the ships beneath it and the city behind it, like the facade of an enormous Gothic church—the largest ever built. Leave it to us Americans to build the largest . . . They'd get there first on the Brooklyn side—to the top, that is. *This* tower was still descending, not rising. Six inches a week—sometimes a foot—the Manhattan tower sank through the platform floating around it, as the caisson descended toward bedrock below.

They had to cross a short scaffold to the platform, and that's when Ralph heard the dull thud behind him. A man lay back there writhing on blocks, hands and feet twisted and curled. His body was too contracted to scream—seemed to be turning inside out. And sure enough, blood came spurting from his nose. Four or five men lifted him at once and crossed the scaffold pushing past Ralph. Wide-eyed men looked all around, caught in the fear. Ralph saw one shrug and pick up his shovel. He felt the fear too—would it happen to him?—but newspaper instincts told him to follow. They jog-trotted toward a whitewashed shed, whose door swung open before they arrived as if they'd been expected, then closed. By the time Ralph got there the place was locked up. He knocked. Not a peep. He peered in a window but the glass had been tarred. Ralph stepped back huddled in his coat and regarded the shed, the first in a row leading back along the pier to the warehouses, streets, and tenements. Reporters had ways. He felt better now. He'd learned long ago the most effective strategy was to knock until your knuckles went bloody.

At last someone opened the door a bare crack. "Go away."

"I'd like to speak to the doctor."

"He's busy."

"That man just brought in here—"

The door slammed again—a bolt clicked at once—but Ralph did hear the voice say, "What man?" He stepped back from the building, made a mental note of its shape and location—in darkness one might cut a hole in the roof—then walked up the pier toward Cherry Street.

Between Cherry Street and City Hall Park, on either side of Frankfort Street, the tenements rose in the midst of decayed cottages and warehouses, even a few crumbling mansions. Rubble in the muddy street made walking a task, but Ralph was himself now, healthy again. He walked with a brisk pace, realizing just how relieved he felt to be back on the earth's surface without all that stone and water on his shoulders. Maybe it was true that healthy men had a better chance of not succumbing to the bends. Ralph allowed himself to feel a little proud. With his father gone west these past two years, he'd returned to eating meat so as to strengthen his blood, maybe give him some height too, though that hadn't shown yet. He attributed his stubby growth and premature baldness to the diet he'd been fed as a child: Graham bread and fruit, Graham bread and water . . . His teeth were weak too, and he was prone to gastritis. But meat eating had restored his strength and color, so much that he even indulged in a tipple now and then, as a healthy person's safety valve. It helped expel poisons from the bloodstream.

It might very well be that those men attacked by the bends couldn't afford a proper diet. Must look into that. First, describe the conditions. Then the health effects, the terrible pain, the rumors of death. Lastly, the attempt to cover it up.

At City Hall Park, he bought an afternoon *Tribune* to catch up on the Beecher scandal, a story Reid hadn't wanted to run, knowing Greeley would frown upon it—but he'd been forced to anyway by the competition. Reid's slant was to barely mention Beecher, to concentrate instead on the arrest of Mrs. Woodhill and her sister for sending obscene literature through the mails. Good thing Ralph hadn't been assigned that one.

He unfolded the paper and right away spotted Greeley's name in the top left-hand column. Horace was back! Less than a week after the election, he was back. "A Card," it said, signed by "Horace Greeley." Ralph sat on a cold bench to read it.

The election hadn't even been close. Greeley took six states, that's all, Grant thirty-one. Grant hadn't budged from his throne in the White House while Greeley scurried up and down the country making speech after speech, brilliant speeches too—witty, homey, wise, honest. A bit intemperate now and then, but that was Horace. He never composed, just spoke off the cuff. Then his wife died a week before the election. The South abandoned him. Negro voters spread rumors, induced by village postmasters in the pay of Grant, that Greeley had sold them as slaves before the war. He hadn't even carried New York, his home. Of the workers Ralph had spoken with down in the caisson, most hadn't voted—because, admitted one, with Boss Tweed in jail, it didn't pay to vote. Greeley kept on speaking right to the end, with that squeaky voice, those waving arms, but by the time the election was over, it seemed that he'd become one of Nast's cartoons, even dressed like one . . .

Now he was back. "The undersigned resumes the editorship of the *Tribune*, which he relinquished on embarking on another line of business six months ago." Another line of business! That was Horace all over. If he *had* been elected, he would have deprecated the glory just as equally. Plain-talking Horace. His defeat would set back the cause of reform by decades unless reporters like Ralph could pick up the slack. Americans would never learn, would they? Ralph clenched his fist.

> Henceforth it shall be his endeavor to make this a thoroughly independent journal, treating all parties and political movements with judicial fairness and candor, but courting the favor and deprecating the wrath of no one.

Bully for you, thought Ralph.

> If he can hereafter say anything that will tend to heartily unite the whole American people on the broad platform of Universal Amnesty and Impartial Suffrage, he will gladly do so.

Cheers!

For the present, however, he can best command that consummation by silence and forbearance. The victors in our late struggle can hardly fail to take the whole subject of Southern rights and wrongs into early and earnest consideration, and to them, for the present, he remits it.

For the present—but don't give it up. Don't give up Crédit Mobilier, the Indian Ring, Seneca Sandstone, the cause of tariff, civil-service reform. Don't give up fighting Grant's spoils machine, Horace! Ralph looked up at the traffic on Broadway and realized he had tears in his eyes.

Since he will never again be a candidate for any office, and is not now in full accord with either of the great parties which have hitherto divided the country, he will be able and will endeavor to give wider and steadier regard to the progress of science, industry, and the Useful Arts than a partisan journal can do; and he will not be provoked to indulgence in those bitter personalities which are the recognized bane of journalism. Sustained by a generous public, he will do his best to make the *Tribune* a power in the broader field it now contemplates as, when Human Freedom was imperiled, it was in the arena of politics.

No more politics, Horace? Please don't say that. Science, industry, and the Useful Arts . . . But politics poisons them as well, I can prove it. Tweed bought stock in the Brooklyn Bridge at only twenty percent, and the managers—hardly content to make fortunes—haven't even taken the most elementary precautions for the safety of the men. Men are dying left and right, and they pretend not to notice!

Ralph's heart had dropped. What did Whitelaw Reid think of Greeley's return? Would he get bumped down? And to whom should Ralph submit his article once it got written, Reid or Greeley? He'd planned on a series running weeks and weeks, an exposé, but not too political . . . Not yet. He could emphasize the bizarre netherworld of the caisson workers, sixty-five feet below the East River, and gradually work up to the health effects. Hook Uncle Horace on the science and industry— then clobber him with the company's outrages. Reporter exposes mysterious ailments of the submarine workers . . .

"Ralph! Have I eaten yet?"

"No, sir."

"How long have I been working?"

"Most six hours."

"What time is it, Ralph?"

"Ten to two."

"Shall I eat now?"

"Perhaps you should."

"I ain't hungry, Ralph. You go along. Get yourself some lunch, some big fat oysters."

Ralph stood at his desk in the outer office, listening to Greeley rustle papers and glue pots behind the pasteboard partition. They were scarcely ten feet away from each other, no need to shout. All morning Uncle Horace had worked in there feverishly, scribbling things, cutting up paper, consulting books—Ralph heard him rushing back and forth—though strangely enough no boy had come to pick up copy, no Reid or Hassard had shown at the door to consult on the next day's edition. He'd worked mostly alone, save for Ralph behind the pasteboard, whose presence he assured himself of periodically by asking the time.

At first Ralph had worked on the follow-up piece to the one on the caisson he'd given Horace that morning, but then he'd hit a snag, couldn't write much more until Horace responded to the first one. If he wanted some changes he'd have to know now. If no bellboy had come to take it to paste pot, maybe they'd forgotten how to get here. This office hadn't been used in six months, and on Ralph's side of the partition stood stacks of newspapers near five feet high, piles of chairs in the corners, huge rolls of paper, spools of string, several broken desks. Greeley's side they evidently hadn't dared to disturb, and its clutter no doubt was the same he'd left before the campaign, though the glue jars had mostly dried up, the scissors dulled, and the scattered papers all been layered with dust. It was cold in here, too—Ralph wore his coat. No one had turned the heat back on. Ralph knew that in Greeley's absence the heart of the paper had shifted to the managing editor's desk two floors above. But where was Reid now?

He peeked around the partition. "Guess I'll go, then."

"You go on ahead, fill your belly." Greeley didn't look up. He wore his coat, the famous white linen duster, its pockets crammed with papers. Ralph noted the pink head, the thin white chin whiskers, the bulk—Uncle Horace had gained weight. Yes, one couldn't help seeing Nast's cartoons in him, especially with his back slouched like that and his head blistered out with hardly a neck. Of all the unfair attacks in that venomous campaign, those cartoons had struck the lowest, hardest blows, and even now Ralph hardly knew whether to worship this man or pity him. He recognized his greatness, sure, but couldn't help seeing Nast's buffoon as well. How could you love someone other folks pitied, or laughed at, or barely respected? If he'd *won*, of course, it would have been a different story . . .

Greeley was frantically scribbling something.

"Can I bring you anything?"

"Bring me my chariot. Bring me the Secretary of War's head on a silver platter." He didn't look up. On one corner of the desk on top of scattered notes and papers lay Ralph's article, "Down in the Caisson," in the same spot, he could almost swear, Horace had tossed it that morning. With sinking heart, he looked down at Greeley, debating whether to go to Reid. Who was in charge?

"What did you think of it?"

"Think of what?"

"My piece on the bridge."

"Excellent. Smart." At last he glanced up.

"Does it need any changes?"

"Not a word." With those bottle-bottom glasses it was hard to tell, but the man's eyes looked moist. His round face seemed out of focus, and the head shook a bit. His white beard grew out, not down—framed his face, didn't cover it. It spread sideways thinly like stuffing pulled out of a ragged chair sat in too much and long past fixing.

Ralph saw that the man was looking right through him. He didn't see Ralph, he was off somewhere else. "I'll go, then." He eyeballed his article. Snatch it up, Ralph. Of course he hadn't even read it, that was what hurt. Hesitating, Ralph turned—turned back—Horace just sat there like a wax figure of a famous and busy newspaper editor. Ralph stormed out on his stubby legs, hungry for meat—not oysters, red meat.

When the door shut, Greeley came back to life. He looked all around, patting his pockets. Articles and clippings, notes, ideas for speeches, blank sheets, cards—not to mention pencils, scissors, erasers, quills—had been stuffed in those pockets in stratigraphic layers it might take an archeologist to comprehend. Actually, the filing system was clear to Horace: enemies, rebuttals, regrets, and projections, in that order, enemies on the bottom. The papers on his desk had fallen into more or less the same categories, though some kept spilling out. What to make, for example, of Reid's last note? Enemy or regret? Out of one pocket Horace snatched a draft of his mushrooming response to Hassard's "Crumbs of Comfort," which Reid had allowed into that day's edition, and out of another the offending article itself, with the sentence he had underlined twice: "Every red-nosed politician who had cheated at the caucus and bought at the polls, looked to the editor of the *Tribune* to secure his appointment as gauger, or as army chaplain, or as minister to France." In his desk, Greeley found a fresh sheet of paper and a stub of a pencil and started over. Stubs of pencils he favored over new ones, as they urged him to scribble faster, before the lead ran out. "By some unaccountable fatality," he wrote, "an article entitled 'Crumbs of Comfort' crept into our last unseen by the editor, which does him the grossest injustice. The article is a monstrous fable based on some other experience than that of any editor of this paper . . ." He stopped and looked up. Somewhere deep in the building's innards the presses were turning. Who knew what calumny they'd dreamed up now, what monstrous slanders?

He snatched up another sheet of paper and began a letter to the paper's trustees, this time in ink. "My ruin is no excuse to ruin the *Tribune*. My enemies mean to kill that; if they would kill me instead I would thank them lovingly. I desire before the night closes on me forever to say that though my running for President has placed me where I am, it is not the cause of my downfall." He paused and scratched his nose. "It is true that office-seekers used to pester me for recommendations when my friends controlled the Custom House, but the red-nosed variety was never found among them." All at once he was searching for the first sheet, his response to "Crumbs of Comfort." A letter with the *Tribune* logo caught his eye. One secret his enemies had never learned was that he couldn't read his own handwriting either. "Dear Ham," this one seemed to say, "Who bought all the nuts and lozenges of the Ecumenical Council? I bought four of the earliest and suffered fearfully indefinable cross-cut saws . . ."

He laughed out loud, a hard, bitter laugh. No sleep last night—nor the night before. He sighed and shook his head. He could write to Maggie Allen—she'd supported him to the last. Maggie, faithful Maggie . . . He snatched up a sheet of *Tribune* notepaper.

My Friend:
I write this because I wish to relieve myself of some bitterness but do not expect—in fact, I scarcely desire—that you should write me

again these many, many days. I am indeed most wretched. As to my wife's death I do not lament. Her sufferings since she returned to me were so terrible that I rather felt relieved when she peacefully slept the long last sleep. I did not shed a tear. In fact I am beyond tears.

Nor do I care for defeat, however crushing. I dread only the malignity with which I am hounded, and the possibility that it may sink the Tribune. *So many of my colleagues hate me for what I have done that life seems too hard to bear. Enough of this. Speak of it to no one, not even Mrs. R., but return to cheerfulness and life's daily duties, forgetting as soon as may be*

Yours,
Horace Greeley

That sounded right, that made him feel better. He folded it up, stuffed it in an envelope, licked it shut, and tossed it on the table. As to the Indians—I scarcely regard them as elegant specimens of humanity—he paused—but that don't mean we should kill them all off. Now. You see the same gentlemen who engineered through Congress this project of making the Union Pacific cost double what it should invading the Indian Bureau today . . .

He looked around the empty room.

I stand for amnesty so thorough that no man be left outside of its circle. (Applause.) No autocrats, no aliens, no proscribed class. (Great applause.) That harpy's nest, the national spoils machine, put forty-two relatives of Mr. Grant on the Federal payroll, forty-two! And they accuse *me* of wanting to redistribute the wealth. (Raucous laughter.)

He found he was standing, waving his arms—one arm struck the scissors hanging from the block and tackle over his desk—but had he actually spoken? He couldn't be certain. In his fingers he discovered a crumpled note which, as best as he could make out, told him in so many words—his own—that his failure was due to himself alone. His horrible record, he'd written, paralyzed the voters who should have most favored him.

Head drooping, he sat. The room had gone white for some strange reason. He realized he'd closed his eyes. White with a sort of orange glow and patches of purple fuzz here and there. Like a rock sunk in water, it rushed away from him, and utter blank despair sifted in, down through his brain to his heart, despair piling up like the finest flour. It dropped through an hourglass. He was going to die and that was it. Nothing else, nothing more. He wouldn't see anyone, God was a story, Mary was dead, he'd never see her again. Ida and Gabrielle would be left without a penny. His eyes flew open, he snatched up a sheet of *Tribune* letterhead and scribbled at the top, "In consideration of the sum of $30,000, which he agrees to pay my daughter Ida, for her own and her sister's use and benefit, I convey to Mr. Alvin Johnson all the stock in the Tribune Association owned by me, being six shares therein, and, in addition, for the sum of $10,000, the following real holdings in my name:

1. Eighty acres of woodland in the townships of Mt. Pleasant and Newcastle near the east line thereof, bought by me of Robert S. Hart.
2. My farm in Buckingham Co., Va., near Gravelly Ford, consisting of 500 acres, more or less.
3. My lands in Greeley, Colo., consisting of one five-acre tract planted with forest trees and one wild tract of forty acres.
4. A mortgage on the farm of my nephew, Horace Greeley 2d, in the township of Jackson, Ocean Co., N.Y."

He snatched another sheet. "To Margaret Allen I do convey my right and title to an undivided interest in the Positive Motion Power-Loom invented and patented by Thos. Norfolk, Salem, Mass." He stood up and looked around the room. *"Ralph?"* This partition, whose idea was that? His office used to be twice as large. They'd taken his benches, his chromos, his almanacs—disconnected the bell pull . . .

At the desk, he wrote: "I, Horace Greeley, finding myself bankrupt without hope, do hereby sell, assign and make over to Alvin S. Johnson in trust for my wife's estate to which I owe many thousands of dollars beyond the value of my property, this being the oldest and most sacred of my debts, the following property . . ." The growing words seemed too large for the paper, and purple ink had splashed everywhere. On *Tribune* notepaper, he wrote to Nathan Meeker: "We are in no condition to influence appointments to Indian agencies, nor do I think we can soon. Our luck is very bad. Nor can any of us buy land. I would much rather sell mine at any price. If there is a chance to sell either piece, let me hear of it. H.G." This one he stuffed in an envelope, addressed, licked shut, and dropped on the desk. Dear Cornelius. Now that I have beggared and forever disgraced my innocent daughters, I beg you to take up those notes of your son at face value, giving the money to my children . . .

On a fresh, large sheet of paper—the better to contain the spiraling script—he attempted to summarize it all. "I stand naked before my God the most utterly, hopelessly wretched, and undone of all who ever lived. I have done more harm and wrong than any man who ever saw the light of day . . ." He tossed that aside and began a new sheet. "I, Horace Greeley, declare that my total vice has been a readiness to believe and trust every flattering, plausible villain. These have come to me in succession with their plausible stories and borrowed from me hundreds of thousands in all, which was often not mine to lend . . ." The pen tip broke, ink blotches spread, the paper ripped. He surveyed the wasteland of his desk, all the oddments and sweepings, indecipherable scribbles, scraps of paper, trash begetting trash. In that desert of scrawls, Ralph's article, not yet buried, looked to be an oasis of neat, upright lettering. "Down in the Caisson." Writing of cofferdams at a time like this? Horace felt wires singing in his neck, but sensed that his shoulders were melting at last. Perhaps he could sleep soon. His back muscles slowly were turning to putty. He picked up Ralph's piece and flipped through the pages, then commenced reading.

To fully understand the peculiar power invested in American industry, as well as the price in human lives we pay for that power, come with me to the bridge now being erected between Manhattan and Brooklyn for a lesson in the war between man and river, every bit as dangerous as that recent one between man and man. You have disguised yourself (as I did) as a common laborer and signed on for $2.75 a day to undertake a task few living men are willing to perform. At the foot of Roosevelt Street, where the New York tower is being erected, you meet with one of the busiest scenes in the city—dozens of workmen, immigrants most of them, hurrying hither and thither, while steam engines puff away, lifting huge blocks of stone with tall derricks, and men wheel cement for others to lay between the blocks, kept steadily at work by an overseer who evidently enjoys his employment. But this is not your destination. Your goal is below, in the depths of the river, in a hell reserved for the dregs of our city, swept down there by the force of necessity . . .

He read on, sinking into the words. Seems you worked down there in compressed air whose weight alone supported the tons of granite and water above. If the compressors failed the whole shebang would collapse, tower and all. But compressed air squeezed your brain as you worked. Your heart had to pump twice as fast and your lungs expand double their width just to breathe. I know something of that, thought Horace—plenty. You sink inside, just collapsing—melting—meanwhile swelling out like a gas-filled balloon. It burst weaker men like swollen-up cows, or like rats that blew up having gotten into the yeast. Try digging your way out of *that* one, boys. The more you dig the deeper you sink and the deeper you sink the greater the pressure. I've absorbed my share of ambition, it's true, but all that time, you know what I was thinking? Of a cottage in the land of my boyhood, where sat my aged mother, gray and wrinkled . . . Friends and neighbors, I'm in the decline of life too, but I have an ear still—I heard the call of duty. I heard the thieving carpetbaggers . . . You don't know how it feels, boys, it hurts. It's not just the pain, it's the pressure. Someone takes a spike and slams it into your ear and says, *now* ain't you sorry? It scares you to death. Sorry you ever stood up for your principles. Slams one in the other ear squirreling your brain and splitting it open for any and sundry to peek in at will. The vultures . . . My God, it's no fun. Your eyes might pop out—blood run from your fingernails. Worst is the weight and the pain in your arteries. You weigh more and more. After a while you cannot stand up, cannot lift your head. You open your mouth and nothing comes out . . . God, make it stop. Some vessel or nerve snaps in your neck—at the base of the skull—and horrible how you feel all those bubbles shoot up in your skin . . . Dreadful . . . Hideous . . .

Ralph returned to find Greeley slumped on his desk in a pool of ink. With the help of the editorial staff, he transported him to Alvin Johnson's house on Fifty-seventh Street, where he came to and demanded something to write with, waving his arms and speaking wildly while Ralph and Johnson's servants watched wide-eyed. Ralph backed up and fled the room, and Johnson, patting Greeley's arm, spoke softly to him of bearing up . . .

Back at the *Tribune*, Ralph retrieved his article from Greeley's desk—he planned to submit it to Reid—and spotted some letters addressed and sealed, waiting to be mailed. One was to Ralph's father. He dutifully supplied postage before dropping them in the letter box outside. It was past suppertime; he could find a saloon.

At Alvin Johnson's, Horace raved about Cornelius Vanderbilt, Smiler Colfax, Whitelaw Reid—they were stealing the *Tribune* out from under him, increasing the pressure by squeezing his brain. He'd slept nearly two hours, that was plenty. All night he babbled and wrote letter after letter, sitting up in bed. The next morning, Alvin Johnson personally transported him in his buggy to Dr. Choate's private hospital up near Horace's farm in Chappaqua. Famous brain specialists probed his head. The *Tribune* reported his "nervous prostration." Dr. Choate himself diagnosed the trouble as an exhausted brain that still might recover. But it didn't. He lapsed into a coma and, at the end of the same month he'd lost the presidential election, died, with his two impoverished daughters in attendance.

Three preachers officiated at his funeral, including Henry Ward Beecher, his presence a defiance of public opinion, as he'd been accused of adultery by one of his flock—news almost as sensational as Greeley's death. He came down from the pulpit with his flowing locks of hair and paced the floor amid mountains of flowers, speaking a low-pitched, tremulous eulogy. Phineas T. Barnum sat in his own pew. William H. Seward helped carry the coffin. The funeral procession passed down Fifth Avenue, then down Broadway, where stores had closed and the bells of Trinity and St. Paul's rang repeatedly. People on the streets stood twenty deep, induced to come out by curiosity, closed stores, and belated respect, now that he was dead. Ulysses S. Grant, President of the United States, followed Greeley's family in the first carriage; then came the governors of New York, New Jersey, and Connecticut, and the mayor of New York City. Down Fulton Street to the ferry they went, and across on a special boat decked out in black, past the new bridge under construction—its Manhattan tower at last just beginning to rise from the water—to Brooklyn, and Greenwood Cemetery.

Chapter

❧ 8 ❧

Storrs and Atkinson
Attorneys at Law
418 Broadway
New York, New York
December 5, 1872

The Greeley Tribune
Greeley, Colorado Territory

Dear Mr. Meeker,
Our examination of the late Horace Greeley's affairs has disclosed
liabilities in your name on three separate occasions for the total
amount of $3,000.00. At the urging of Mr. Greeley's heirs, we
hereby waive compensatory interest, as none was specified according
to Mr. Greeley's generous terms. We call upon you now for prompt
repayment of the full amount, such repayment to fully and exclusively discharge all obligations under the conditions of your understanding with Mr. Greeley.

Between us, Mr. Greeley died embarrassed, drained to the last
penny. Only the rectitude of his debtors will enable his daughters to
preserve the honor of his name.

Yours,
Charles Storrs

The Greeley Tribune
Greeley, Union Colony/
Colorado Territory
December 17, 1872

Mr. Ralph Meeker
40 East Seventh Street
New York, New York

Dear Ralph,

Speak to Cooper and Mitchel now about that appointment. I have
friends in Washington too. Make the best case you can in simple
language, giving my knowledge and expertise. I have gotten what
signatures I could obtain from the leading people here. The current
agent at White River knows nothing of irrigation and farming in the
West. It is a source of amazement that he even holds the position.
The agency is in disarray and demoralized throughout, and the
agent might conceivably be induced to leave once the Secretary
learns that the cattle he purchased for the Indians have died, the
ponies he bought them for plowing are used for sport, and twenty-five
thousand pounds of Ute flour and oats lie in Rawlins spoiling.
Mention these facts. A few settlers who object to the roving bands
of idle Indians have filed claims against the Ute annuity account
for damages to their stock which they ravaged themselves. That's
how bad things have gotten. In your presentation and in your letters
be sure to emphasize my knowledge of farming and raising cattle and
the potential of the surrounding countryside to furnish steady employment for the Utes in the business of timber (millions of board
feet of good pine), fruit orchards, coal, sheepherding, wheat, corn,
oats, chickens, and stock. The possibilities are fairly staggering.

If it is not too much trouble, when you can do it, please stroll by
the office of Mr. Charles Storrs on Broadway, and explain to him
that the business upon which he wrote to me will be settled as soon
as possible. I think you understand what I mean. You might explain
to him that Mr. Greeley never expected to be repaid. I have no
security or property to make over. I do plan to lease the house. I will
write to him soon. All these things take time, and he must be patient.
Honor to Mr. Greeley's memory would honor his generosity to
me—and to our town—but his open heart has stopped beating
forever, and the level of distrust in this robber age has risen all the
higher.

Ralph, never forgo the cause of Reform. These receding tides will

surely swing back. Have you seen the outpouring of grief for Horace?
There is a reservoir of hope still untapped in men. It seems to me
it is but a short bridge to cross into a brighter and more beautiful
land and that we only have to make a determined and well-directed
sharp-cut effort to reach it. But first I must pay my debts, though
in one sense I owe nobody on earth. This appointment would answer
my turn because, in keeping my name unsullied, I might also lift it
up. As you know, "Indian lovers" come and go easily—they are
mostly sentimental—but lovers of mankind *may find it in their*
hearts to guide the uncivilized to a better life.

Your loving father,
Nathan C. Meeker

People's Restaurant & Boarding House
Greeley, Union Colony
Colorado Territory/Dec. 14, 1872

Dear Walt,
Just ate my catamount soup, grizzly on toast, rat pie & hashed
puppy, so can squeeze a few minutes in to write while they decide
yes or no to digest properly. Can you still come and give that lecture?
We run a subscription for a month and raised $85, and I know this
won't cover your fare and lodging like you asked in your last, but
can you come anyway? You might lift this place from the winter
dolefuls. Me, at least. I guess we'd raise more before you come if you
gave us a date. That way we could build up a flutter. We could
charge admission too, but no more than two bits, as the farmers are
niggardly. They might pay more if you belched fire and stood on your
finger, but not likely. They're like the lean boarder who remarked
to the landlady touching her bedbugs, I really don't have the blood
to spare.

Let me know quick, Walt. The harvest was plenteous but folks
are in debt, and the citizens, what with Mr. Greeley's late failings—
not just losing the election, but dying so soon after—talk about
changing the town's name. If they did that you'd likely not be able
to find us. Yours to the backbone,

Pete

Amherst/Dec. 18, 1872

Mr. Whitman,

I believe it is several hundred years since we met. Since the earth is Round, if you roll my side sometime again 'twouldn't be strange.

Your Silence numbs as much as your Song. This is my second, since you came. Where is your first?

Nothing has happened but Loneliness. I've been out with the lantern, looking for myself. Maggie did the wash and accused me of Calicoes. My neighbor's mother was buried last week, so there is one orphan more. A hen with her chickens followed the procession to the graveyard. It is supposed the dead lady used to feed them. Now her dog chases buggies and must be tied up to a long rope, that snaps his neck back. In time, Urge will annul itself.

I have a little chest to put the Alive in.

Vinnie says she can't see why I don't get better. This makes me think I am ill, and I begin to ache. Does Master think of Daisy? Sweet news. Thank Master. If you came again I would hide the Cough so that no one could find it. I should be glad to know that you are well, and still have a Soul, and sing with it.

Your scholar,
Emily

Camden, New Jersey
Dec. 27, 1872

Dear Miss Dickinson,

The possibility of my ever visiting Amherst again has been diminished by a debilitating illness. I write this sitting up in bed—the doctor wishes me to keep as much in bed as possible—but I have to keep in, as I cannot move yet without great difficulty, & am liable to dizziness, nausea, etc. He says there is no doubt of my improving, but I have been laid up nearly three months now, ever since my visit to you in the fall.

That is why I have not written. I don't sleep well. I have a good bed—a fire—as much grub as I wish—but miss my friends, and must live in my brother's house with the help of a nurse who comes in once or twice a week. Gradually regaining the use of my left limbs—very, very slowly, but certainly gaining. But all the blowing, talking, powwowing, and, yes, singing I've done from here to Boston amounts to little or nothing these days.

So you see, Miss Dickinson—I may never see you again. You lost your chance, and I lost mine. It takes a live fish to swim upstream, and it takes a fox to come out of her hole before folks can get a good look at her face.

The doctor says I shall fully recover, but I'm in such a bad sort I don't see it at all. He tells me, Whitman, you are like an old wagon built of first-rate stuff, with the best sort of frame & wheels & nuts—& as long as you are mighty careful, & go slow, & Keep to good roads, you'll get better in time. Don't cut up any capers, he said. With my locomotion just about nil, I had to laugh at that one.

And so, Miss Dickinson, you see what a true loafer I've become. But whether or no I shall sing again—let alone fly—only time will tell.

Farewell,
Walt Whitman

Camden, New Jersey
Dec. 27, 1872

Dearest Pete,

I'm not currently in a prospect to take on any lectures out west, and most likely won't be for a long time. Pete, darling boy, I've had a stroke of paralysis on my left side, and especially in the leg. This occurred nearly three months ago, but a second shock came after that, then a third, and I've been anchored here in George's house unable to write until now. Now Pete, dear, loving boy, I don't want you to worry about me—I shall come out all right. But the idea of going on a train out west, with my locomotion just about nil, makes me laugh right now—if I could laugh. Maybe later. As it is, I have a good square appetite and may pull out of it. I look just about the same as usual except for losing some weight. Dear Pete, dear son, my darling boy, my young & loving brother, I only wish I could see you again. I have a nurse, a young gentleman who acts kind to me—comes in once or twice a week and bathes me, makes the bed, etc. He writes down everything I say. Wants to make a book, "The Sayings of Walt." Sharp young man—up to the scratch—but he's no Peter Doyle. If you was to come out and nurse me full time I'm certain I'd improve. Doctor says it was simmering inside me for six or seven years—broke out during those times temporarily—then went over until now. About one fourth of the time I feel pretty well, but can hardly get out of bed. You mustn't fret too much, but do your work as you should and get on with your life. If you could see it someday to come back east and pay me a visit, maybe stay a while, it would give me a great deal of pleasure and comfort, but you are not, at any rate, to risk your position out there for me. I'll find ways to improve. The doctor plans to use induced current by means of Gaiffe's battery, & says this will regain the nutrition of the limbs. Jo (my nurse) is all for it. Says he's heard of cases of complete revitalization by this means in Europe. I have lost some weight, but if you happen to see the squib in yesterday's Herald you should discount it. The news got out and they made it sound more dreadful than it is. You know they killed me off once before in a railroad smash, & they must always make things sound so woeful dramatic. The doctor says there is no doubt I'll get better someday. You may rest assured that I write the exact facts about my case. I am on the gain every day a little—still have a good deal of distress in the head—Doctor only comes now once a week. You must not feel too uneasy, Pete, as you might get sick and then there'd be two of us. I write the truth—neither better nor worse. The most annoying part is the dizziness, nausea, etc., on trying to move, or some days even sitting up. I cannot move without great difficulty, but am certainly over the worst of it, & really—though slowly—improving. The doctor says there is no doubt of it.

I'm sure you can easily return the money. If I'm better off next year, I might come out then. I may not be able to lecture—voice too weak—feel out of breath—but just to visit you, darling boy Pete, if you can't visit me, would be such a comfort. Say nothing about this to anyone. Explain I am ill, but skimp on the details. I've no interest in having my simple debilities paraded about & held up as an object of gawking pity at second & third hand, especially as the rectification in these sorts of cases never seems to reach those who first gobbled up the bad news. Jo agrees. Says keep it hushed. He offered to act as my secretary too—as I did for those wounded boys during the war—but I told him when I can write I'll do it myself—and you see I have, & with steady hand. So I'm not really helpless, just in a bad case. As long as I can bring a spoon to my mouth & put pen to paper, I can't see but things won't get better. Don't vex yourself, Pete, and don't bandy it about. If you can't come to see me at least send me out one of your good smacking kisses—or many dozen—and take in return many, many, many more from your good loving father, which does him more credit than growling & complaining.

Walt

PART
V
1873

Chapter

❧ I ❧

*T*he Great Man lay dead while the
smaller men and women mourned and the mice in the walls nibbled on
paraffin. Well . . . not really Great—not exactly. In the strictest sense,
one might call him little, as Victor Hugo did in *Napoléon le Petit*, referring
not so much to his height or girth (the same as his uncle's, the first
Napoleon) as to his—greatness. Still, he won a few wars, didn't he? He
fought the Russians in the Crimea because the Tsar refused to address
him as *Monsieur mon frère*, and defeated them—or nearly so—and later
drove the Austrians out of Italy, practically out, most of the way, they
did keep Venice when he unexpectedly offered an armistice after the
battles of Magenta and Solferino, each so bloody and appalling he
quickly lost his stomach for war. It was scarcely pleasant to observe young
men disemboweling each other with dull bayonets or staving in the skulls
of the wounded with their rifle butts, and then realize that *you* were in
charge and might be home lying on a sofa, playing patience, and chain-
smoking cigarettes in an overheated room instead . . .

He'd died in exile in England after a failed operation to crush his
bladder stone, described by one of his doctors as of the magnitude of a
date. The bladder stone had been a special bother. How could he reclaim
his throne—how could he effect *his* Return from Elba—without leading
a triumphal procession into Paris on horseback? But how could he mount
a horse with that irritant in his bladder? At Camden House, Chislehurst,
he blackened his hair, waxed and curled his mustache, and climbed on
a wooden horse each day to accustom himself to the pain. The plan was

devilishly simple: leave England on a yacht, meet his followers in Switzerland, then zoom across the mountains to Lyons. While the deputies of the National Assembly were being packed into a train which would strand them all in the Saint-Cloud tunnel, Napoleon III would set out for Paris accumulating followers along the way, and once there resume the throne by acclamation. No one need be gutted by bayonets during this *coup de théâtre*, no butchery please. The French would always embrace their Napoleon—even if he *had* lost the war . . .

Instead, he died. Dr. Louis Conneau heard his last words. He'd been there in 1870 when, in order to avoid needless bloodshed, the emperor surrendered to the Prussians at Sedan, and bent low to his bed now, summoned by the dying man's eyes. "Ah! Conneau . . . It's true, isn't it, that we were not cowards at Sedan?"

This was the man who, as a child, begged his uncle, Napoleon I, not to go to Waterloo because he had a premonition of disaster—his uncle ignored him—the man who spoke French with a German accent not because his father Louis, Napoleon's brother, wasn't really his father, of course not, absurd, those were vicious rumors spread by cousin Plon-Plon, but because he grew up in Switzerland during the restoration of the Bourbons, who outlawed all Bonapartes from France—

Still, the thought that he might not be a Bonaparte pecked away at his liver for most of his life. His mother Hortense had a reputation. What was it Napoleon I had said? Hortense always gets in a muddle over the fathers of her children . . .

Well, Bonapartism was an *idea* anyway . . .

—the man who wrote *Des idées napoléoniennes*, which claimed that now and then in history a great leader appears who transforms society and shapes the world for the next few centuries, a leader like Alexander, Caesar, Mahomet, Charlemagne, or the greatest of them all, Napoleon. Only by following such a leader and, above all, adhering to his ideas *after his death*, can a nation achieve its destiny, he said. Caesar's nephew Augustus continued *his* ideas—and Napoleon's nephew Louis-Napoleon would continue his. For this was the man who, with the death of Napoleon's only legitimate son, the king of Rome—later the duke of Reichstadt—inserted himself into the line of succession as Napoleon III, and attempted twice to overthrow Louis Philippe's government, the second time landing at Boulogne from England with a handful of followers and a vulture flapping about his head (in lieu of an eagle, which couldn't be found), and storming into the army barracks there while firing his pistol at the ceiling, unfortunately striking a soldier with the ricochet—killing him, in fact—for which he was forced to apologize and leave in embarrassment, claiming the weapon went off by accident . . . the man who then clung to the rails around the statue of Napoleon atop the Column of the Grande Armée outside of Boulogne and vowed to fight to the death, only to have his supporters drag him off and throw him in a rowboat, which capsized. The French police fished him out of the ocean and locked him in jail.

He was dangerous, he knew—he'd once been a Carbonari! Hadn't Louis Philippe's police, a year before Boulogne, plotted to embroil him in trouble—possibly even kill him—by putting up that disreputable wretch Count Léon to attack him by letter in London? He'd returned a testy response, of course, and out of nowhere this ersatz count had appeared and challenged him to a duel. He'd been baited, that was clear; they must have known he was planning a coup. He'd never even laid eyes on the man until the morning agreed upon, and then what a shock his face presented. Count Léon claimed to be the illegitimate son of Napoleon I, and indeed looked strikingly like him. How could Louis-Napoleon fire at the very image of his sainted uncle? Fortunately, the British police prevented the duel and confiscated the weapons on a rainy dawn at Wimbledon Common. Later on, after Louis-Napoleon became elected President of France, the count apologized in an endless babble of letters. And after he overthrew his own government and declared himself emperor, the count issued pamphlets praising him as the Savior of the French, Protector of Civilization and Restorer of Liberty, but the emperor ignored him. Sire! Grant me one small allowance, wrote the count. The great Napoleon, my father, left me the income of his forests in Mosel, of which I've been robbed; who will buy me a bed, feed my children, pay my rent, satisfy my debts . . . ?

He disdained to answer. He required no explanation of the duel at Wimbledon, as his aides had confirmed that Count Léon, in prison for debt at Clichy, had been released by Louis Philippe's police, given the money to pay his debts, and provided with a ticket to England as well . . . Well—it took a Bourbon to sink to such depths, to send a Bonaparte to kill another Bonaparte.

But perhaps only one of them was actually a Bonaparte . . .

Though Count Léon was barred from the perpetual banquet of the Second Empire—not even thrown scraps—the emperor thought he detected his face now and then among the chefs in the kitchen or the gutter boys in the crowds outside. It haunted him, really. No one else's face was such a living repudiation of his own. He'd seen it only once, but that was enough. It followed him through years of bathing at Biarritz and hunting at Compiègne, annoying flotsam on the edge of the flood of Bonapartes into and out of Paris—in the stalls at the opera, or peering forlornly through anxious windows at balls in the Austrian embassy, or suddenly looking up from a fire where bitter soldiers cooked their beans outside of Sedan . . . Pay no attention to upstarts, Louis, you are emperor of the French.

I am?

Bien sûr! One crowns oneself emperor, one is emperor forever.

Even deposed?

Even shamed. Even dead. Even if you were never a Bonaparte. Bonapartism is an idea, regardless, you said that yourself. An ardent idea . . . a fertile idea . . .

Now he lay dead in a rented house, while Count Léon's illegitimate son searched out a relic of the first emperor's body somewhere in America. This relic might assure the dead man a decent burial at least—in the Invalides, say, beside his uncle . . . Eugénie sincerely hoped so. Watching over his body, she nodded regally for both of them—full accord at last!—though in death, as in life, his face masked his thoughts, the thoughts of a dead man—*How on earth did I get here?* . . . A little black dye from his hair had smeared the pale forehead when she'd washed the face, a ritual she'd insisted on performing herself after servants had cleaned and oiled the body as though it were a sideboard. The small gray eyes, large strong nose, hair unnaturally black, thick lips, straight mouth—a mouth that seldom betrayed what he thought, as opposed to what it said—the pointed chin, oval face, waxed mustache, imperial chin tuft, the large shoulders and thick swollen torso, into which the head had retracted—the rounded chest—the uniform of a general in the Grande Armée, which he'd tragically disgraced . . .

At last she could lower the heat. She sighed and shifted in her bony chair, chosen to preclude sleep. In health or in sickness, in winter or summer, for two years of exile, he'd kept the house overheated. It felt like the raft of the *Medusa*, she'd said, soon we'll all begin devouring each other . . . They'd managed to crush half of the bladder stone, Dr. Thompson had told her, but loose pieces kept blocking the urinary tract. She'd examined the urine before they threw it out: cloudy and bloody. She'd inserted herself into that colloquy of doctors, and arbitrated their disputes—presided over their decisions—just as she'd done as the empress of France. She knew what Bismarck had said of her: the only *man* in the emperor's entourage. Together with Metternich in 1863 she'd redrawn the map of Europe, though only the map—its actual borders resisted thoughtful adjustment. So when Dr. Thompson suggested a fourth operation, she never hesitated in authorizing more chloroform, for the emperor's comfort—to alleviate the pain—and afterwards, this morning in fact, when he confided that it was the chloroform which had killed him—one could only take so much—she consoled herself with the knowledge, confirmed by the doctors, that the bladder would have accomplished the deed eventually, or if not the bladder, certainly the liver . . .

Still, she'd done it. She'd authorized the chloral, an overdose actually. She'd put him out of his misery . . . Two years on the raft of the *Medusa*, two years of blaming Trochu or Thiers or Plon-Plon for their fall, and working herself into a state of hysterical resentment, all the more indignant, all the louder, in the face of his instinctive ability to find excuses for his enemies—or his silence . . . He knew five languages, one more than she, and knew how to be silent in each of them.

She shifted in her chair. Out the window, the darkening trees of Camden House, Chislehurst, dripped in the rain. Dreary dusk of England. Those trees held spies, assassins, relic seekers. Once, a year ago, a Frenchman had indeed been found in one of them, with spyglasses no less. Undoubtedly the Republicans in France still feared him, and now that he was dead would fear his son—she'd see to that! Of course, she'd have to act as Lulu's regent if he came to power, he was merely seventeen. He'd been moody and listless in exile, perplexed by the whole business at first. Cried like an infant at his father's death—he'd always been closer to him than to her. He was probably crying now on his bed upstairs, poor baby. She'd forbidden him this death watch despite his entreaties—she alone would watch over the body. She knew what had happened to the first Napoleon's sacred remains, knew of the scattered pieces, including the most essential one. Nothing of the sort would happen to her husband! She touched the dagger in her belt. She'd cut a man once . . . And she'd seen a monk murdered with daggers, out the window of her father's house in Madrid when she was only eight—seen him hacked to pieces by socialist radicals who'd suspected the monks of being Carlist agents and poisoning the wells. This happened exactly one day after her father's own death, from natural causes; she'd gone to the window, though warned not to, and there down below in the Plazuela del Angel, a mob attacked the church of San Sebastian, dragged a monk out the door, and with hundreds of hands repeatedly stabbed him in fountains of blood . . .

Later, she became a lover of the bullfight, and wore her own dagger in her belt—with a whip in her hand instead of a fan—scarlet boots on her feet—a pink moiré dress—to provoke the matadors. The Countess of Teba, Countess of Baños, Countess of Mora, Countess of Ablitas,

Countess of Santa Cruz de la Sierra, Marquise of Ardales, Marquise of Osera, Marquise of Moya, and Viscountess of La Calzada, who was born into all these titles during an earthquake, could afford to dress outrageously at bullfights. The same dagger was in her belt now. Her high-collared dress was appropriately black, but the black silk bodice and black shawl were the same she'd worn to those bullfights more than twenty years ago. And the scarlet boots . . . No one would mutilate *this* emperor's body!

Muffled sounds came from deep in the house. The place was full, but death hushed the voices. Plon-Plon had arrived that morning from Switzerland, too late for the climax. She'd observed right away how he comforted her son, this fat Prince Napoleon who hadn't paid Lulu the slightest attention when the emperor was alive—had disdained him, in fact. Said his legs were ugly, as reported to Eugénie by one of her spying servants. Now he'd invited Lulu to stay with him in Switzerland, though of course Eugénie would never allow it, she knew what he was up to. There were two Prince Napoleons: Plon-Plon and Lulu. For a Bonaparte it took only an act of will to insinuate himself into the line of succession; or, who knows, for good measure the monster might even attempt to poison her son, such things had been done, and not just in Shakespeare—it wasn't beneath him . . . Once he'd refused to toast Eugénie at a banquet, though requested to by the emperor. It was Plon-Plon who'd spread the scandalous rumors about her former lovers after her marriage to the emperor. He favored Garibaldi and a liberated Italy, while she insisted that French soldiers protect what was left of the Pope's shrinking worldly domain. He was a closet socialist, she was ultramontane. He was obvious and clumsy, she was gracious, he had common manners, hers were noble. Certain Bonapartes needed that softening influence of the feminine gentility which she'd brought to the emperor, but Plon-Plon had never received it, and this was undoubtedly why he accused *her* of being coarse. She knew that he'd said of her that if it weren't for the Bonapartes she'd be selling oranges in Madrid. Cornered as he always seemed to be, he had only one brush with which to tar others.

Now his prospects had improved—or no doubt he thought they had. At seventeen, Lulu was too young to lead an imperial restoration, but Plon-Plon could . . .

Over Eugénie's corpse! She'd already spoken to Victor, Plon-Plon's son, about placing him next in line should anything happen to Lulu. The plan was to cut Plon-Plon out entirely; even his own son had agreed. It was purely a matter of convincing all Bonapartes. A symbol was needed.

When the first Napoleon's son, the king of Rome—later the duke of Reichstadt—died, he bequeathed the sword his father had left him to his cousin, Louis-Napoleon. Eugénie had raised this important fact with him when they first went into exile. Shouldn't he, in turn, will the sword to his own son? Yes, of course. He'd dictate a codicil. But he never got around to it. In exile, his tendency to defer everything and accomplish nothing—his reluctance even to dress in the morning—increased at an alarming rate as he grew more ill. Then Caroline Benton told Eugénie about Count Léon's son and the relic whose trail led to America. The women invited the exiled emperor to meet Count Léon-Fernand-Léon, but he declined, not because he remembered the father, not just that, but—so Eugénie interpreted the growing distress in her husband's eyes—because he was apprehensive that something would be required of him, a decision perhaps. If Count Léon *fils* has something to offer us, he said, some plan or magic key to our future prospects, then you negotiate with him, my pet, I'll have nothing to do with it. You never officially abdicated, as I did. You are still empress of the French. Besides, this relic is undoubtedly spurious. Such things stopped with the Middle Ages.

I have proof of its existence!

Your project disgusts me. My uncle is dead. The prospect of buying up dubious mementos only besmears his sacred name.

His sacred name has been torn apart and spat upon.

My son shall restore it.

How impossible it is to make you realize the threat your cousin Plon-Plon poses!

Everyone knows the Prince Imperial is next in line.

But everyone also knows the way a Bonaparte becomes emperor of the French is by declaration, with plenty of guns. That's how *you* did it, my dear—that's how you restored France to wholeness . . .

She had lifted both arms, hands outspread—palms facing up—silently chiding the corpse of her husband.

That's how you restored France to wholeness, only to allow it to crumble around you . . .

For Eugénie, who'd entertained mediums and table turners at the Tuileries, and whose Catholicism was of the spiritual and visionary variety, this concept of a whole France was associated almost blasphemously with the idea of the mystical body of Christ. She and Count Léon-Fernand-Léon had discussed the notion in endless late night soirees at Chislehurst. Just as the Reformation had assaulted the body of Christ—the Church—so the Republicans had dismembered the body of Napoleon I—the State . . . Look at France now, the very center of

Europe. Strikes, riots, mob rule, bankruptcy. Hardly had the conquering Prussians left when a new revolution erupted like a boil, with its own reign of terror. For once, she'd been glad to be living in exile. The communards had shot her friend, the Archbishop of Paris, torn down the statue of Napoleon I in the Place Vendôme, and burned the Hôtel de Ville and the Tuileries Palace, the very place where day after day as empress she'd gazed out at Paris unfolding below her, reassured when the Grenelle–Porte St. Martin omnibus emerged from the Rue du Bac that orderly arrangements everywhere occurred beneath the Second Empire's benign umbrella. Later, after the defeat at Sedan, she watched from those same windows as the mobs poured into the Tuileries Gardens. She was forced to escape through the Louvre, and at first no one could find the key to the picture gallery, and noises behind them suggested that the crowds had already stormed the palace . . . Minutes afterwards, veiled in her carriage, she saw their faces close up, faces of the fickle Parisians who only weeks ago had shouted *Vive l'Impératrice!* The joy in their eyes and the cruel mocking twist of their mouths looked positively diabolical now. They were throwing up barricades, breaking windows, tearing imperial crests from the shop fronts. Hating us is *fun*, she realized . . .

It was undoubtedly necessary though unfortunate that Thiers later had Gallifet shoot thirty thousand of those same Parisians in summary executions to suppress the Commune. Necessary for the restoration of order, but order so slippery with blood! She knew it wouldn't last. It was as though all of Europe had gone incoherent, ruptured, broken, sprung, shattered, and crazed. She refused to believe, as her more cynical and detached British friends had suggested, that this was because Europe's center was shifting from France to—*horreur!*—Germany . . . No, the reasons were more profound. In a nightmare, she'd seen the parts of Napoleon's body spread about everywhere, a toppled colossus: the head in England, an arm in Russia, a foot in Italy, and the very Bonaparte root lost somewhere in America. She woke with a clear sense of her duty . . .

Now she shivered. Outside, it was dark, and the windows reflected the room. Eugénie felt unmercifully tired, as though she alone had been lugging the burden of Europe's future up an endless hill. In her chair, she sought the least comfortable position—spine erect, hands gripping the armrests—but her eyelids sagged, she couldn't help it. She drew her knees up and leaned to the side, head awkwardly thrust out toward the bed, and forced herself to look at Death. We all had to die, Bonapartes died, but the Bonaparte Idea lived on forever. Even dead bodies lived, in a certain respect . . .

She shook her head, forced herself to stand. Cold in this room; she embraced herself. He'd died at sixty-four, almost twenty years her senior. After Lulu's birth they hadn't once slept together. In that difficult birth she'd felt as though the whole bottom half of her body was being ripped from her soul, which seemed to swell like something raw . . . She knew of her husband's little distractions, knew each one by name—the famous Rachel, Miss Howard, Frau von Zeppelin, Madame Saunier, Marianne de Walewska, she'd met a few too, and wondered in private how they could bring themselves to submit more than once to his clumsy caresses . . . His thick body, cold, pale, and slow, his disgusting mustache, his eyes of a pig . . .

Even standing up she was falling asleep! She'd been awake since four that morning, with only a sip of broth for lunch. All at once the entire room creaked, and she brought her hands down on the footboard to keep the bed from flying away . . . Assassins were coming—relic seekers—vile mutilators—and she was so tired she couldn't prevent them. They'd crawl through the windows and squirm down the chimney and plunge into their dirty work the minute she dropped off . . . She approached the body; he lay on his back. She pushed down on the mattress beside him as though to test it, but really just for something to do. The room seemed to tilt. Rain struck the windows; the wind had shifted. Footsteps in the hall, a scratching in the walls—mice, of course. All English mansions had mice . . . The room had grown unbearably cold, but no servants would come to rekindle the fire, as she'd ordered them on pain of dismissal not to disturb her until the dawn.

She lay down on the bed beside the dead body, to test how it felt. Hadn't slept with a man for seventeen years, had refused all lovers, in addition to her husband. This close up she realized how fat he'd become, despite his wasting illness. His chest seemed to have swelled up unnaturally, and she touched it gingerly with a tired finger, half expecting it to deflate like a pudding. Curled up at his side, she felt chilled to the heart. He gave off cold as an oven gives off heat through its unsealed openings. Beneath the smell of cologne was another smell, something unmentionable—just beginning . . .

She couldn't stop shivering—the whole bed shook! There was nothing for it but to climb off the bed—still bent over, in a room listing like a ship in a storm—throw back the covers and crawl underneath them, then curl up against his icy body, not embracing it, to be sure, but fetally grazing it—one hand gripping the other's wrist locked in between her knees—so that any disturbance would be sure to rouse her. Her presence of mind was a hinge in the darkness: no matter what dreams she'd fall into, as long as some part of her body touched his—her knees and forehead—anyone who came to rob the dead would be bound to wake her . . .

A knock at dawn brought her back so completely her eyes flew open as though she'd just died. She'd been dreaming of throwing herself down the stairs. A woman could change herself into a man by throwing herself headlong down the stairs . . .

Without looking at him, she slipped from the bed, tidied the covers, brushed at her dress, adjusted her hair, and unlocked the door to let Lucy in. Good morning, dear . . . She smiled sadly. Head bowed, Lucy curtsied, and held out the breakfast tray. While Eugénie gestured her in, and Lucy deposited coffee and biscuits on the marble-top table, while the room brightened with the growing dawn, she wondered about the nameless disquiet closing around her. What exactly was it? It felt different from the other anxious feelings, more flat and tasteless. She made herself glance at her dead husband lest Lucy discover some obvious aberration, but he looked just the same. Lucy slipped out the door with a curtsy.

Then she knew what it was: disappointment. She shook her head, looking down at the body. Disappointment, disgust, it widened out . . . Even in death he'd let her down, for no one had come to rob him of anything, not a button from his shirt, not a lock of his hair, not a finger, not anything.

She thought of Plon-Plon in this very house—upstairs with her son. Without touching her coffee, she walked to the dead man's desk in the corner and scribbled a note, then summoned Lucy back.

Authorize treble offer for relic as requested.
Apply funds Gould's Bank N.Y.C.

She folded it in half and wrote on the outside, "Count Léon-Fernand-Léon, c/o Elizabeth Patterson, Baltimore, United States." Lucy was to give it with a ten-pound note to Banks, the gardener's brother, who would run it by train into the telegraph office in London, fifteen miles away, which would in turn relay it via overland lines to Valentia Bay,

County Kerry, Ireland, and—broken down into electrical impulses swathed in layers of gutta percha—zap it through the transatlantic cable laid just seven years ago, past blind prehistoric fish dreaming of stone on the black ocean bottom all the way to Heart's Content, Newfoundland, and thence by telegraph to Baltimore, Maryland, U.S.A.

Chapter

❧ 2 ❧

"Ladies—make your toilet!" One
grimly determined matron had removed her glasses, rolled her sleeves to
the elbow, and tucked up her hair, so Ben showed his whites—teeth and
eyes—and added cheerfully, "Nothing like a good wash, ma'am."

Goodness me, she ignored him. Maybe he needed more singsong in
the *ma'am*, or a break-down shuffle while tipping his hat . . . When the
last white lady in chemise had marched past, he spit on the fine Brussels
carpet behind her, still showing his teeth. Then, when the train lurched
into a bend, he cracked the panel on the first upper berth with his
splayed-out hand—as though regaining his balance—and made the ladies all jump at the sound, served them right. They cooed and squawked
like hens smelling fear . . .

Something inside the berth thumped back.

He'd heard tell of one lady on the Burlington and Mizzoo who'd stored
her infant up there in a closed berth where it slept all day—everyone
said—rocked to oblivion by the motion of the train . . . And pets—
sometimes these ladies smuggled their lap dogs on the train and hid them
in sleeping berths! Problems with ventilation, sanitation, doggy smells,
hunger, and bowels never occurred to such people. He checked them
bunched up like sheep behind him at the entrance to the damask partition, with its marble and walnut washstands inside, its palatial roller
towel and silver taps—then unlatched the panel, which swung down
on chains, locking into place. Nothing inside on the bed but a hand-

bag, galoshes, shawl, umbrella, tin of biscuits, corset—small flask of bourbon . . .

"Need some more soap back there, ladies?"

Muttered declinations. Ben pushed the debris aside and made up the bed, humming. They liked to think Negroes were happy . . . Funny thing, he *was*. After all, the train had made it to the territories, and he always felt safer out in the territories, ever since the war. The territories was where deserters went, white and black both, and he'd deserted a month before Appomatox. Not that he couldn't see the end coming, anyone could—just that a year of horror and shame gets to a man, snaps a wire connecting his brain to his gut . . . Did it trail behind those ladies like it did even now behind him, that war? It freed his brethren, sure, but poisoned their well with bitter resentment . . . My husband fought for *you*, Mr. Bones?

Shucks, I fought too, ladies.

Lord, don't remind us. Be happy, Ben. Get lost . . . Whistle . . .

Whistle? Let's see . . . Mebby "Camptown Races"? I could mouth the *doo-dahs* just like you like it . . . He lowered the folding table below, swung the seats together, and made up the lower bed next, all the time whistling and humming while faint thuds and bumps came, now from the second berth. They were somewhere west of Omaha in the dark. These upper berths made a slanted row of fancy, heavy walnut panels embellished with a marquetry of scrolls and sleeping cupids, eight linked compartments along both sides of the car. In good times, two conductors made up both sides at once, but this train was only half full due to the financial collapse back east, so Ben had the chambermaid's task to himself. First he'd do the ladies' side while the men smoked and chewed in the parlor car—then pull all the curtains and slip out for a discreet smoke while the ladies snuggled in, and come back later to make up the gentlemen's berths.

More thumps and stirrings—now behind the third panel. Whatever it was had found a passage from one berth to the next, so it had to be small. Some squirrel they'd picked up back in Chicago perhaps, feeding on the biscuits and tinned sardines they insisted on stinking up their beds with at night . . . Please, not in August. He slapped berths two and three hard all at once to knock some sense into whatever devil or ghost had decided to haunt his train, then swung down the panels lickety-split in succession, but the creature or demon had managed to scramble on ahead, it seemed. Rats on his train? Might be hearing things. He could swing all the berths open in a jiffy, even the last two unused ones, but the prospect of a disease-bearing rat biting some lady's toe at midnight somewhere in Nebraska—and one of the *gentlemen* getting the blame— warmed Ben's heart. He whistled louder. *Yes'm. Yes indeedy!* Then he glanced back to check the line at the washroom. They were gathered in knots talking politely, waiting for him to finish their beds. Who needed ghosts on a train full of white folks? Don't stare, Ben, those fraus might report you . . .

Above, in the last berth, Bonny huddled folded up, clutching his booty—two chaste pantalets of his favorite soft chiffon. He grew extra choosy when it came to ladies' underpants; white cotton was preferable to flannel, but chiffon and silk took the prize by a margin. He brought each to his nose in turn, sniffing deeply and rubbing his cheek along the dainty fabric. Beneath the virtuous smell of French chalk lurked something else, something faintly corrupt—rotten leaves and decaying kelp . . . All those centuries (it seemed) of wandering through the universe muttering words whose meaning had grown progressively fainter—blips in the night—*I wants it, I wants it*—hadn't diminished his desire for *something*, associated just now with these delicious pantalets. They also made good bed linen. The history of his desire had reverted to a confused, discontinuous pulse fading in and out, though more than ever now if he came across a mirror he primped and fussed, stuck his hand in his waistcoat, turned his face to the side, frowned a bit—adjusted his bicorne—and assumed the Napoleonic posture. It filled him with the power of unrequited hankering. Whenever he could, he climbed up a chairback and tweaked someone's ear, usually Stokes's . . .

He stuffed the pantalets inside his shirt—they were larger than him, but crushed up fetchingly—and crawled forward, squeezed between the coverlet and roof of the berth. For someone so strong—a little Napoleon—it took nary a pinch of effort to push through the flimsy partition separating the berth from the men's washroom, itself just a booth of damask curtains at the entrance to the car. It was empty now. The men would stay smoking another hour at least, since ladies needed more sleep than they did. Bonny squirmed out and crawled down the curtain like a plump little mollusk or bat, then hung by his hands from the washstand and dropped to the floor.

He sagged along the wall to the sliding door onto the platform outside. The blurred earth skidded past in the dark below. Before the violently lurching platforms could catch him in their jaws, he jumped to the parlor car, slid the door open a crack, and squeezed inside. Down there at the foot of everything, he poured himself along the far wall, half hidden behind the tasseled curtains that hung everywhere. Cigar and pipe smoke filled the car. From the pantry, a Negro waiter dealt out sour mash cocktails, mint juleps, and every manner of iced drinks, while toward the middle of the room a group of buzzing men, including Stokes, had gathered around a sort of couch or love seat made up as a bed, where a half-naked bearded man reclined and held forth. Stokes hadn't seen him, had he? In a slumping flutter, Bonny half crawled half skipped toward the back of the car avoiding blind feet, hoping Stokes hadn't seen . . .

Once more he jumped across the swaying platforms while dirt and dust washed up at his face. His bicorne hat flew off in the wind, but the cord attached to a shirt button saved it. Up here, this close to the engine, the soot and smoke swirled in between the cars, and the bubbling engine and clattering wheels made a horrible squawl in the night. He slipped into the baggage car and made his way in the comfortable dark past trunks, craters, barrels, sacks, and a row of ice boxes against the wall. Hot in that closed car—but it was home. He'd already stabbed a few rats in here, for the practice. Before leaving New York, Stokes had reinforced the puppet theater with hardwood slats, added wheels to the bottom, and now had a combined theater, cart, crate, and bed. Bonny crawled through the stage opening, on top, past the words PLAYED BEFORE ROYALTY and FANTASINA, which he couldn't read, and which therefore appeared to be necromantic signs, little diabolical yellow hats and intestinal thingies and red forking bridges, derricks, or pumps. Often he'd traced them with his stubby fingers.

Snug in the theater, he took off his clothes, shook out the larger of the pantalets, and crawled inside its silky caress as though into a sack made of laminated air . . . The other one he stuffed with wigs to use as a pillow. The props around him made a padded cell—wigs, masks, costumes, Punch and Judy, the baby, the Hindoo—everything was here except Toby the dog, who'd run off or died just days before they left New York, having observed the preparations for departure. Bonny's friends were here though, the ones who consoled him whenever he wound up beaten, hung, and bleeding, out of breath—lumps on his calabash—three times a day and four on Saturday, victim of Mr. Punch's endless cunning and hickory stick, oh the shame of it. He wasn't made for that. It wasn't the pain, pain he could stand—he was made for pain—it was the humiliation. Just thinking of it now brought tears to his eyes, falling asleep in that comfortable nest to the sea roar of his own breath and the fainter blast of the engine outside. The silky soft pantalet did it, he knew—invited him to indulge pity for himself. He pictured the snail tracks down his ravaged cheeks . . .

"It was strictly understood you wasn't to leave this place."

All he could see was a candle flame. "Hungry."

"You're a falsehood."

"Not a bit! Desperate hungry."

"Where's your sustenance?"

"Ate it."

"Obtained where?"

"Dining car."

"Munjari?"

"Cruster bread."

"Falsehood! He's mushing! Little tatter box." The flame danced in the blast of Stokes's shouting, then a fat hand seemed to nudge it aside—he was feeling around inside the theater. "Where's your clothes?"

"Too hot."

"What's that you're wrapped in?"

"Pillowcase."

"Gammon and spinach! Them are ladies' drawers. You've been at it again!" The hickory stick flailed in the candle flame, but none of the blows landed, as Bonny had burrowed deep into the theater. He laughed up at Stokes, a rattling laugh like pebbles in a can. All at once Stokes seized him by the neck and jerked him clean out of the theater and pantalets, both. "What a horrible display. So dreadful disgusting. I should make a wry face if I was you. Be ashamed, you creature." Stokes whacked him with the stick on his bare behind. "You haven't even got a doodle to dash. I'll learn you a lesson. You look like a china doll, you do." Bonny hung there kicking and squirming with nothing but a pinch of wrinkled skin between his legs, while breathless Stokes beat him mercilessly about the head and bottom with Mr. Punch's hickory stick. Candlelight was good for punishing Bonny—you couldn't see the seams where he'd been stitched together . . . "God send you wasn't seed out there."

"Wasn't."

"Well I spotted you. You might have been catched. Tell me *that* wouldn't crab our business."

"Bleeding!"

"*I'll* bleed you."

Stokes raised the stick again but Bonny kicked loose and dropped to the floor. "Please, sir. Oh, please . . ." He ran out of the flickering candlelight half bent, hiding his shame. "Please. Won't never do it again. Just hungry . . . Oh, please." Stokes roundly enjoyed Bonny's pleading, even if he did put a mocking edge on it. Bonny skipped and loped like a child caught outside barefoot and barebottomed, while Stokes whacked the side of the theater hard with his stick for the effect, then stalked his creature with the candle in one hand and stick in the other—teeth clenched, spongy jaw straining—in the clattering baggage car lurching through darkness. "Please, sir—oh, please . . ."

Five minutes later Stokes slid the door to the parlor car open with a hanky in one hand wiping his brow. Bonny lay in his box, sound asleep. He hadn't received such punishment in days, since leaving New York, and Stokes knew how restless the little man grew without their rituals of discipline—how unmanageable . . .

Besides, it gave Stokes's own blood a good workout; he walked with style, like the cock of the yard, chest billowed out and buttocks on display. From the Negro waiter he ordered a mint julep. These American concoctions! In lieu of British ale he was forced to drink a sort of greenish sweetened slime, not to mention accepting it from Ethiopian hands . . .

"I call this extreme negligé, gentlemen—but it's comfy."

In the middle of the car against the wall their pigeon held court from his couch.

"You tell them that Walt Whitman has a right to make a damn fool of himself whenever he pleases. Have you written that down?"

"Yes, sir."

"What do I look like out there? Is it seriosity?" He'd caught Stokes's eye. Of course, Stokes wasn't supposed to know him. On a chair next to Walt, leaning over the open trunk full of jars and wires sticking out every which way, Jo glanced up and chanced a faint wink.

"You looks like some kind of Roman Job, as I may say, with that happaratus at your feet . . ."

"Say that again."

"A Roman Job, sir."

Walt cocked his head and looked down at Jo, who was back to wrapping wires around a sort of jar. His shoulders seemed to twitch. "That tops everything," Walt said at last. "You mean Jove, of course. Zeus to the Greeks. It sounded silly to me when you first said it, but as I turn it over in my noodle I begin to see how subtle it is. Zeus on his couch! And these are my thunderbolts." Draped with a sheet across one shoulder and waist, half reclined on the couch—with flowing white locks and beard—Walt gestured down toward the jars and wires Jo fiddled with beside him. The plush Empire ottoman, with one raised end upholstered in red, set off his white skin and the scraggle of white hairs crushed on his chest, making him look otherworldly. Along his arms and legs milky folds of skin hanging down seemed the apotheosis of flesh. It was see-through skin. Half hidden behind the sheet, Walt's stomach made a vague purple shadow, and had the heart been uncovered, he knew, they'd see what a powerful muscle *it* was. He'd stared at it naked before a mirror himself, with an oil lamp behind him, and watched that reddish shadow opening and closing inside his chest like a fist—scarred and wounded, to be sure, but powerful still . . .

The couch was framed with a tasseled curtain, making him look like someone on stage. The conductors had moved a parlor organ out of this spot and replaced it with the ottoman for this demonstration. A reporter sketched the scene on his pad. He'd boarded the train in Omaha and intended to ride as far as Cheyenne, having learned the good gray poet was a passenger. "Your health, Mr. Whitman," he said. "Has it improved?"

"I'm still cheery, though badly whacked. I'm like a tree with the chief limbs gone." Still, he was beaming—he couldn't help it. He felt pretty good when it came right down to it. He was on his way to see Pete, dear Pete! "I *am* having a spell of good weather just now. Not entirely ready to pass in my checks. I can read, write, and work. That's enough. I suppose I shouldn't kick because I can't climb mountains. I have to keep myself in executive session most of the time. That is, sit with closed doors. I am a prisoner. But this man you see here is not my jailer." He gestured down toward Jo, who looked up and smiled at the assembled company. "Indeed, he is my deliverer. He encouraged me to make this trip. He assembled the apparatus you see on the floor, with the help of Dr. Drinkard, and the inspiration of Messrs. Galvani and Kelvin. At least with their help my locomotion ain't nil. Fetch me some more of that Vichy water, Jo, before we begin. It corrects the too much uric acid."

Jo looked up at Walt.

"The Vichy water, Jo."

Slowly Jo stood, holding the smile.

"He's built slow," said Walt. "Made on the Dutch plan."

The men laughed politely while Jo snapped his fingers and signaled the waiter. "Boy! Vichy water."

"Right now the bowels are the seat of the difficulty with me," said Walt. "Not the source—the seat. Was it Frederick the Great who said, 'Keep your bowels open and your powder dry'? Jo, who said that?"

"Frederick the Great." Jo handed the glass of bubbling water to Walt and returned to his case of wires and jars.

"And your head, sir? Has the stroke affected your thinking at all? Is your memory intact?"

"I've forgotten the question."

"Your memory, sir—"

All the men laughed.

"Considering the condition of the rest of me, the immunity enjoyed by my topknot is staggering."

"You continue to write?"

"My wings ain't been clipped—it's my backside that's laid low. I've been tied to the wharf for almost a year. This is my first chance at trying out my sails. For most of a year, I got up, ate my meals, went to bed again—not getting up very far and not without assistance, not eating much to speak of, not sleeping enough to brag about. Now look at me: I'm west of the Mississippi, and eating decently hardy meals. Whatever trouble there is with me lies not so much in what I feel as in what I don't feel. There's still some paralysis on the left side, and general discomfort. Discomfort, gentlemen, is worse than pain. Pain is life—its absence may mean death. There's a tidbit for your archives, Jo. 'Pain is life—its absence may mean death.' "

But Jo failed to look up from his work.

Walt stage-whispered to the group with his hand to his mouth. "He's writing a book about me."

They all stared at Jo, who refused to look up, still tinkering with the wires and jars in the case. No doubt right now he was memorizing that tidbit, and naturally planned to write it down later . . .

"And your business out west, Mr. Whitman?"

"To visit a friend. And I might deliver myself of a lecture or two if I feel it in me."

"Not likely," said Jo.

"That's the nurse in him speaking."

"How long will you be?"

"We'll drool along for about a month."

"You like the Great West?"

"My first visit, son. But I've warmed to it already. I am very much like a man who feels something toward certain people he meets with and warms to and hardly knows why. I suspect I've found the law of my own poems out here. One wants new words in writing about these plains. The terms 'far,' 'vast,' 'large,' don't suffice. You don't look at it—you breathe it in. And the men, the western men. The cowboys. Not without a certain racy wild smack all their own."

Someone said, "What about the women?"

"Well, the women. I'm past that." General laughter all around. "No more parlor gallantries for me. You see my condition. But as we're all friends—and all from the East—you'll forgive me if I say the women disappoint. They are fashionably dressed, and genteel enough, but dyspeptic-looking and generally doll-like."

"Gentlemen, the demonstration is about to begin." Standing there in his tie and swallowtail with the silk-lined collars and silver stick pin, with his handlebar mustache and imperial chin tuft—not to mention the gold-headed walking stick—Jo looked less like a nurse than an undertaker, though maybe his scowl invited that impression. Then the scowl flowered into a lofty smile.

Eight male passengers had gathered in the parlor car, all in swallowtails, save for a few like Stokes stripped to their waistcoats. Ben and the waiter stood by the door. In the absence of women, all smoked and chewed, for it is the height of barbarism not to be allowed to smoke and chew on a train in America. The Union Pacific ran no ladies' car. As Jo began, a tall man with a large, bony nose and dark masses of hair parted at the top and falling to his shoulders entered the car and nodded at the assembly, with a separate nod for Jo. For a moment everyone forgot Jo Benton, pinned to the spot by the sight of this dandy in his cutaway suit of elegant black velvet, his snow-white shirt and Byron collar with a flossy yellow neck scarf, his knee breeches, low slippers, black stockings—the glittering cluster of diamonds on his lapel . . . One of his shoulders seemed higher than the other, and that, combined with his tall, thin appearance, made him resemble a bird on one foot. "Gentlemen. I hope I do not make an interference?" His French accent buzzed like a bee among flowers.

Murmured denials. Have a chaw, sir? "Soyez le bienvenu," said Jo.

"Merci." Someone vacated a seat directly in front, while the others, standing, parted instinctively, and Count Léon-Fernand-Léon sat in the place of honor, every bit as though it were his right. He appeared to be smirking at Jo and his patient.

"The principles of faradism," Jo began, "require a current between twenty-four and thirty-six volts regulated in order that a weak current may be gradually increased until a sensory effect is produced on the patient. Our batteries"—he gestured toward the trunk on the floor filled with glass jars connected by wires—"are constructed according to the priciples of Lord Kelvin, with the zinc plates immersed in dilute sulphuric acid and the copper in copper sulphate, the two being separated by wet sawdust over which more sawdust has been sprinkled, moistened with a solution of zinc sulphate—upon which is placed the zinc plate. The wire covered with gutta percha has previously been soldered to the copper plate underneath."

"Have you tried sand, Mr.—?"

"Benton. Yes. We've found sand too heavy for these portable cells. The sawdust works reasonably well to prevent the formation of a hydrogen film on the negative plate, which causes—as you know—polarization." The gentleman nodded. "With sand, I'm afraid, carrying this trunk around, I may become a"—pause—"candidate for a stroke." Murmured laughter. Meanwhile, Walt lay there glowing—the center of attention without lifting a finger.

Jo droned on with a voice wrung dry of enthusiasm, befitting an amateur medical scientist—gentleman too—who couldn't care less. Of course, he'd never hauled that trunk around himself, he'd left that to porters. Miracle that none of the jars had been smashed. Back in Camden, Dr. Drinkard—whose interest in the process was nothing if not passionate—had designed the trunk out of wood lined successively with lead and velvet; the lead brought the weight up to seventy pounds. Jo pretended to himself he was selling the apparatus—that made the juices flow just a bit. Of course he'd ditch the whole thing, and Walt along with it, once they got to Peter Doyle . . .

He demonstrated the interrupter, made from a steel spring attached to a hammer, which vibrated directly against the iron core of the primary coil, and the galvanometer to measure the current, and the electrode covered with padded webbing in the shape of a hand—that was Jo's suggestion. Made from a lady's mourning glove in his collection, it resembled a monkey's paw on a wire. The padding prevented the skin from being burned. He explained that the current, slowly increased, induces the muscle to contract by stimulating the motor nerve. In the case of stroke patients whose muscles have atrophied, the induced activity, combined with a modicum of exercise, assists the patient to gradually regain the power of his affected limbs. "Were we not on this train, you would hear a slight buzzing." Jo had removed the electrode from its glove, and held it against his own wrist. He glanced at the meter. "Ten volts. We may safely start there."

He dipped the electrode into a basin containing sodium bicarbonate, then slipped the monkey's paw on it. Using a washcloth, he moistened Walt's left leg below the thigh with the same solution, fiddled with the primary coil, then brought the padded electrode to Walt's leg. This was the part perhaps most distasteful—kneeling before this living icon with his beaming smile, his smug face full of grandfatherly indulgence . . .

"Lower, Jo, lower. A bit to the left."

"More current?"

"Not just yet. We'll go slow."

Jo had knelt a little to the side so all could observe the muscles twitching. As for Walt, he surveyed the audience once, then closed his eyes to enjoy the sensation. It felt like a cool breeze across his flesh . . . Of course, Jo hadn't touched on the true principles involved, the vast electric fluid flowing through everything. Animal magnetism! Walt's new poems explained it, the ones still in the process of being erected in the cells of his brain. The universe itself was a battery of sorts—of immense proportions—and all things were sending and receiving stations, not just men and women, and not just the genitals, but houses, railroad cars, mountains, rivers, birds, trees—the smallest atom . . . Poems too possessed a juice that flowed through them, and words were charged with magnetic attraction. A poem was a kind of magnetic telegraph. Picture them speeding across the prairies, modern poems—not the words, but the *current*. Great poets generated the greatest voltage . . .

"Increase the voltage, Jo—just a smitch."

He was going to see Pete, after three years without him, or nearly three years. And not just Pete—the vast West too, with Pete in the middle of it. The complex internal processes working in Walt's soul felt like a swelling engine, a new alignment of forces and currents, new shoots and growths resembling tubes and charged wires. Already, he'd begun a new life. His diet had improved. He'd resolved, whatever happened, not to yield to sloth. He thought of death more often also, as a healthy man should, because of course he wasn't getting any younger, he could never count on complete regeneration. His own blessed mother had died in May with his name on her lips—holding his hand . . .

The monkey paw moved in soothing little circles on Walt's lower thigh. "More current, Jo. Ahhh . . . There. Perfect."

What would Pete think when Walt showed up? Would he be properly astonished? At Jo's suggestion, they hadn't warned him they were coming, to sharpen the surprise. Once there, he'd convince Pete to return east with him. Oh, it might take a while—Walt knew that. He'd encourage Jo to go back without him, since Pete could nurse him now, dear Pete. Jo had his own life. He might be disappointed—Walt hoped not—but what could you do, you couldn't very well keep *two* handsome young men close by, they'd wind up jealous of each other . . . Back in Camden, Jo had looked in three or four times a week and spent most of the day with Walt. He'd mastered Walt's faradic therapeutics and also jotted down his *bons mots*, as he planned to write a book. It was his theory, he said, that the world would want to know all about Walt after he was dead.

He wrote down his sayings, asked to see manuscripts, quizzed him about his past, and requested access to his correspondence. Walt drew the line at the correspondence as too much snooping in his personals and privates. It was Jo who mentioned Pete—he'd learned of him somehow. Where was he now, Walt?

Oh, somewhere in the West.

Whereabouts in the West?

Out there in the territories . . .

Walt's instinctive coyness on this matter stemmed from his personal rule of thumb to insulate his close friendships from each other, lest they fall into envious competition. And Jo *was* a close friend now—most a savior. Handsome too, if a smack too dapper. Moody as well, but that was a privilege of fine young men with their own lives to live . . . The West, said Jo, I know something of the West. Over the summer, as Walt's health improved, Jo made the suggestion that they pay a visit to this Peter Doyle. Walt's rehabilitation had exceeded their fondest hopes—Dr. Drinkard said as much—and a western jaunt might just complete it. Jo could procure reduced fares too, having once been employed by the Union Pacific.

The challenge to design a relatively portable faradic apparatus in order to continue Walt's therapy away from home enlisted Dr. Drinkard in Jo's exhortations. Travel was healthy in and of itself, and the air of the West might do wonders for the body, not to mention the soul, where true healing begins. Hadn't Walt always wanted to see the endless prairies and the Rocky Mountains, the backbone of the continent? Come to think of it, yes. He needed little persuading. Already in three days his outlook and general constitution had made immense strides. He'd seen a buffalo today! One, to be sure—pursued by three saddled hunters. Most of the large herds, Jo sadly explained, had disappeared or moved up north due to increased hunting brought on by the railroad.

He'd seen entire herds of antelope, though. He'd walked through Omaha—assisted by Jo—and viewed its famous stock market plaided in patriotic squares of red, white, and blue. Crossing the Missouri, he'd spotted barges hauling entire buildings of Chicago construction up the river for the new settlements there. Above all, before the sun had set tonight, he'd contemplated the ample prairies unfolding silently everywhere, for which mere words were insufficient. They were out there now, those prairies, in the dark—so were eagles and bears and redskinned Indians—dwarfing their little insect train, which seemed from inside to be traveling so fast, but in fact barely moved in such infinite space . . .

Well. If Pete proved reluctant to come back east, perhaps Walt could just settle out west. Why not? He opened his eyes. "Jo, more current. Is it functioning properly?"

Jo had gradually guided the monkey's paw up Walt's thigh to his left arm and shoulder, talking all the while. He ignored the question. "It may interest you gentlemen to know that faradism also enables long-standing cases of constipation to be resolved." Raised eyelids and murmured approvals. "I mean those where the muscular failures of the large intestine are so attenuated as to have no power over the intestinal—contents."

Walt scanned the audience quickly. "But, of course—we shan't . . ."

"Of course not," said Jo.

"Why not?" said one of the gentlemen. "The ladies ain't here." This produced much laughter and puffing of cigars and rocking back and forth on booted toes and heels. "How does it work?" asked the reporter.

"Well," said Jo. "The procedure is simple. Introduce one electrode into the bowel—" He moved the monkey's paw down Walt's back. "Well insulated, of course. Smeared with grease. Apply a second electrode to the abdomen." Now the monkey's paw crawled over Walt's middle, down below his stomach, disturbing the sheet. Walt readjusted it, looking up at Jo. "The patient will feel nothing at first until, with a gradual increase of current, a faint response becomes discernable in the abdominal muscles." The monkey paw circled below Walt's navel, and Walt struggled to sit up on the ottoman, but Jo gently restrained him with his free hand, it didn't take much. "Of course, we only have one electrode, and such a procedure is conducted in private. But I think I can give you all an idea of its—efficacy. As the current is increased—" Still describing gentle circles on Walt's flaccid abdomen with one hand—half outside half under the sheet—Jo reached down with the other and made a quick adjustment to the primary coil. Walt's body jerked as though he'd hiccupped. His mouth fell open. "As the current increases, the outside electrode, moving along the course of the large intestine, beginning at the right iliac fossa, releases the appropriate muscular contractions." He stroked Walt's abdomen now with the paw. Walt appeared to be struggling on the couch, and pushed himself up. "The results," said Jo, "are often remarkable."

All at once Walt cut a long honking fart, then deflated, it seemed, back down to the couch. The guffaws of the gentlemen were something to hear. "Remarkable ain't the word!" Walt closed his eyes, then opened them, then looked over at Jo, whose poker face regarded the audience. But he glanced once at Walt . . .

The men wouldn't stop laughing. Jo began the complicated process of dismantling his apparatus and packing it up.

"I'll bet, Mr. Whitman, you're regular as a woman." The man who said this was lighting a meerschaum whose curved bowl depicted a smiling burgher.

"Not too overly so," said Walt at last, deciding to smile. "We're a gassy lot, we poets." The men laughed and nodded. "It's true we don't go for half and half things. It's constipation of the *words* we fear most. But you never can tell"—he adjusted the sheet, swung his legs forward, and sat up facing them—"to what dizzy heights our loquacities might lead us!"

Laughter and applause. The reporter stepped forward to shake Walt's hand, and others lined up to do the same, while the rest examined Jo's apparatus, including that dandy with his outlandish togs and his buzzing French accent . . .

Half an hour later the parlor car was empty except for Stokes and Count Léon *fils* seated at a table beneath a lowered oil lamp. At the end of the car the door slid open and Jo walked in. "He'll sleep tight tonight," said Stokes. "All aglow like that."

Jo pulled a third plush chair to the table. "He wanted to know—in his words—what I thought of the Roman toga effect."

"Smashing," said Stokes. "Uncommon handsome."

"I can't stomach his pomposity."

"Won't have to stomach it much longer," said Stokes.

"You're certain this—Pierre Doyle—has the—item?"

Jo turned to the count, who, though he'd asked the question, appeared to be indifferent to its answer, since he'd glanced away, raising his hand in a sign of protest. With the other hand, he removed a chocolate from a box in his lap to feed his pimply face.

"Pass them around," said Stokes.

"Oh, most certain." He held the box out at a distance perfectly calculated to make Stokes heave up from his seat. When Stokes grabbed hold of the box, Count Léon failed to let it go, so Stokes chose one, which he popped into his mouth and gobbled down.

Count Léon *fils* took smallish bites and chewed.

With his eyebrows, he offered the box next to Jo, across the table. Jo glared. "Be so kind," asked the count, "as to hand me that newspaper behind you."

Jo slammed the newspaper onto the table.

"Push it this way, would you? S'il vous plaît."

Jo pushed the paper across the table.

"*Merci*. Of course, you won't kill the man, will you? This Doyle? If you murder him you will be hung, and if I marry your mother"—he pronounced it "moth*air*"—"that would inconvenience me *beaucoup*, to be the fath*air* of a hung man. I would—I would be—expelled from my club!"

Count Léon-Fernand-Léon had boarded the train in Chicago, having taken the central route from Baltimore. Since leaving Omaha that afternoon, Jo hadn't seen or heard from the man, and sincerely hoped he'd fallen from the train—until he showed up for the demonstration. He'd evidently scrubbed his hands thoroughly, but couldn't quite remove, Jo noted, the reddish ring from around each wrist. Jo knew the ankles had such rings too. The count had been visiting the day coaches, no doubt to view the cowboys, farmers, miners, hunters, and Indians all herded together in their ragged garments hauling dirty bundles, and perhaps with revolvers stuck in their belts, and before entering the coach had suffered his wrists and ankles to be painted with red sublimate of mercury as a vermin barrier; Jo had done the same on previous trips. After all, he was elegant too, and elegant men cultivated aesthetic contrasts, as long as they could protect themselves. But the count out-primped everyone else, including Jo; he carried a lavender-scented handkerchief! It disgusted Jo—his little flourishes, his hand raised in protest, his knee-length breeches, his cultivated indifference. Sure, indifference was always a sign of good breeding, Jo knew that, but not such garish indifference—such a manufactured product . . . Jo wasn't used to being upstaged, it made him feel positively *American*, and provoked him all the more because the count, he knew, was a bastard. He'd *assumed* his title, as his father had before him—Jo had met the father in Paris—but since Count Léon *père*, also a bastard, had raised in addition three legitimate children, surely one of them should have inherited his own specious title?

He sat across the table from a British shopkeeper and a fictitious French nobleman, and debated just how he'd cheat them of their spoils. He'd vowed to keep the relic for himself; it was his in the first place. He'd sell it in England without them and collect the entire amount himself, though precisely how to shake loose these disgusting partners—not to mention Stokes's sadistic little monkey—he hadn't quite decided . . .

Count Léon had raised his offer to seventy-five thousand American dollars each for Jo and Stokes, and made the mistake of flourishing the telegraph from Chislehurst authorizing him to do so. Jo calculated that Eugénie was therefore willing to part with at least two hundred thousand for the ugly little thing. He'd once been fond of it! But that was before he'd grown used to luxury, before he'd run through his own little fortune, before Congress subpoenaed him—just last month—to appear before the Select Subcommittee investigating the Crédit Mobilier scandal. All the more reason to journey out west . . . And if he had to drag these—*creatures*—along, he didn't have to pretend to like it. He sat at the table, legs crossed without moving, his small white fists folded in his lap, glaring at the men who'd hitched themselves to his cart.

On top of it all, he feared an accident. These trains, he knew, overturned all the time, or plunged through the flimsy trestles his former employers had hastily thrown across western gorges. Out west, head to head crashes occurred with a greater frequency than anywhere else, because of all the single-track lines. Frightful cases of engines colliding, of cars smashing to pieces and people scalded to death, or drowned, or crushed flashed before Jo's eyes nightly in his berth, making sleep nearly impossible.

He'd been Walt's nurse for nearly a year now. Was it worth it? Selling bonds had been larking by contrast. When he finally learned where Doyle was, he deeply resented the irony. The land *he'd* puffed, out there on the plains! Amazing that they'd actually built that town. Without condescending to ask Jo to join in, Stokes and the count had begun a game of euchre. He did the dirty work while they played cards! He wondered what sort of schemes they'd cooked up. He could murder them all if he had to—and he might . . .

Then his thoughts drifted back to his mother, in Baltimore, stuck back there in a decaying mansion with ancient Aunt Betsey. Everyone was harnessed to someone else . . . Her betrayal—her alliance with this slimy count—had been the hardest blow of all. Why, she'd once served Jo cake at the Tuileries! His sainted mother—a whore—his mother . . .

Jo stood up. Napoleon had said that every woman is a whore. Only money didn't care who was legitimate and who wasn't. With money you've got Lady Luck on her back. You could buy respect; it was always for sale. Besides, the absence of pain is death. Who was it said that? When I die, Jo thought, when I kick off, I'll leave my money only to those who agree to cut up my corpse and consume it piece by piece . . .

He noted that the small white hands by his sides had made two fists and wondered how he could sleep tonight. The closer the prize came the more taut he grew. Predator instincts . . . He paced the room, then stood there regarding their womanish game. No one spoke. He could visit the day coaches, as the count had done, and watch the rustics packed in together making their vain attempts to improvise out of their pathetic two or three feet of space a position to sleep in. He knew how a body falls asleep: by imitating the posture of a sleeper, then waiting. He knew how to wait, he'd waited all last night, eyes wide open, listening in his berth for the telltale explosion or squeal of wheels that preceded a smash.

"Hand me that newspaper, Count, would you please? If you're certain you're finished with it."

"Oh, most certain." The smirking count handed Jo the newspaper, a Springfield *Republican* way out here in the West. Jo opened it and read of the ongoing Congressional investigation, scanning the columns for his own name. Not there this time . . .

Across the table, Count Léon-Fernand-Léon waited until Jo was well buried in his paper then winked at Stokes, a wink you could almost hear. Jo was right—they had their understanding. Jo would lead them to the prize, they'd agreed, but never so much as touch it himself. It was theirs to sell, they'd shaken hands on that. They'd divide the money and kiss Jo good-by. But what Stokes hadn't learned yet was that the count wouldn't really sell it. Not exactly. He would accept Eugénie's money, of course, then provide her with an ample substitute—Stokes had plenty of ample substitutes—and give the genuine item to his father. After all, Eugénie was the widow of a doubtful Bonaparte. Her husband had scorned the count's own father, the living image of Napoleon I. Count Léon *fils* had served as his father's secretary and written endless letters on his father's behalf, to General Gourgaud, to the emperor and empress, all to no avail. He'd watched his father and his family sink into poverty, and now his father's legitimate children slept three to a bed and shared two pairs of shoes among them, so that one stayed at home when the others went out. Napoleon's own son! Count Léon-Fernand-Léon himself, having ɔeen raised by his mother—his father's first mistress— never actually lived with the man, but visited him often and bestowed small gifts, whatever he could manage to relieve his sufferings. In gratitude, the elder count bestowed his title on his illegitimate son. It gave him an edge in certain uncritical Parisian circles, to be able to call himself a count.

His father now lived in a hovel in a farmyard at the base of a cliff in the village of Pontoise, just north of Paris. He spent whole days in his premature dotage sitting in an armchair before the empty grate with hardly a coin for a bit of tobacco, while his grown children gleaned nearby fields for turnips and potatoes. Oh, the injustice . . .

Count Léon *fils* had fared better in life. He'd dealt in paintings, exported oil lamps to London, and purchased stock in the National Debt and the Northern Railway that left him—comfortable. He'd insinuated himself into the Second Empire in ways that his more impetuous father had never been able to. He courted Jo's mother but gagged at the thought of ever marrying the woman, she was merely his link to the empress—and to Jo, as it turned out. Once he'd paid off Stokes and rid himself of Jo, he could carry both his relic and his fortune back to France, make his father comfortable—fathers should always be comfortable—and resume his life of pleasure and luxury. Rid himself of Jo? Well, not really. He'd leave that distasteful business to Stokes, who had his own methods. He could trust Stokes. He thought he could.

Stokes dealt the cards, Jo read his paper, the train plunged into the American West. Count Léon-Fernand-Léon glanced at Stokes, whose spongy face resembled a piece of taffy someone had grabbed at the jowls and pulled. He dealt out the cards with clumsy fists. Why, the man didn't even cheat at euchre! Of course he could trust him. And if he couldn't—he had a few resources of his own . . .

Then he regarded Jo coldly scanning the newspaper. "Jo, *mon cher*. Let us be—*comment dit-on*—*coopératif?*"

"Cooperative."

"Ah! Yes, of course. We are—associated! We have a common goal."

"Yes. We do."

"I offer you my—grip—upon it." He dangled a limp flipper of a hand before his chest. Jo too extended his hand, American style, across the table. They hung fire like that, regarding each other—hands in the air—each refusing to move, until Stokes gripped their hands in each of his. The count pulled back, then went limp, and suffered his long pale fingers to be mangled once more by Timothy Stokes, who lifted his partners' hands in the air with a wet laugh and, tipping his head like a grapefruit bruised and half filled with water—popping his eyes—snarled out, "Mates!"

Chapter

3

*T*he rock that had chased them down the red mountain was back up on top when they returned to get Piah.

They'd left him up there at the start of the summer; now, three months later, everything was yellow. He'd spent all that time alone on the mountain hunting eagles, and his eyes looked a little funny now, Siwapi saw that clearly when they first rode up and Piah hopped out from behind the rock like a bug and laughed. Nicaagat told Siwapi he'd have to get the old man to knock him on the head with a stick when they got down the mountain so he wouldn't go crazy. Look at him, he'd lost his nostrils!

It was true. Piah's nose had closed up. His horse had run off. He was getting skinny. The rock was a picture rock, and Piah had stared at it all summer. Now the old man would have to poke holes in his nose with a stick so he could breathe right again. His mouth opened and closed without talking. That rock always chased them down the mountain, crashing through trees and sagebrush and scattering them all on their horses before it fell helplessly into a ravine where they thought it would die, but it never did. It crawled back at night . . . Siwapi looked up at it: men made of sticks threw out their arms, insects swarmed, chicken tracks, suns, and zigzags flew everywhere. One huge man hanging upside down with his prick flying up flung sand from his arms.

From that picture Siwapi had received his name, Clean Sand Flying in the Wind. A woman's name! It happened like this: when he was just a boy, his mother and father both died. He nursed on a sheep because his mother was dead and none of the women were nursing at the time. Everyone noticed he liked to play with the girls and act like a girl when he was growing up, so when he started to become a man, Nicaagat and some others took him up this mountain and showed him the rock and made a fire. On one side they put a woman's dress and cane, and on the other a bow and arrow, and told him to choose. He scooped up a handful of sand (as the old man had told him) and tossed it up, and behold, it flew toward the bow and arrow, but as he made his choice someone shouted out, *Naaci kaci kati papasa siwapi*, clean sand flying in the wind, and he looked up and saw that picture . . .

Everyone laughed. He chose the bow and arrow, yes, so now he was a man, but with a woman's name, Siwapi. His job was to help Maasuwini around. He didn't like to fight, and he couldn't hunt, since he acted as the old man's eyes, because the old man had none. He guided him around by the arm, helped him onto his horse, and led his horse on the hunt. He had to stay with Maasuwini just about all the time, while the others shot buffalo, antelope, deer, elk, and mountain sheep. One of the new hunters had asked this time why they had to go through the bother of taking that old man and his assistant along if one couldn't see and the other couldn't hunt, but no one answered him. Then, up in buffalo country, Siwapi led Maasuwini to some buffalo chips, and he climbed off his horse with Siwapi's help and mumbled something to the chips. He was asking them where the buffalo had gone, and sure enough they informed him. The next day they killed three buffalo. Everyone knew buffalo were scarce these days. So that young man had his answer.

Maasuwini's name meant The Other One.

Now Piah's mouth, still opening and closing, was making sounds, and his arms pointed back to his camp. This mountaintop was all rocks with just a few lumps of sage bushes and sand and some scrub cedar scattered about. Far below, across two ravines, they could see the others: twenty or so tiny *carniva*—tipis—and thin lines of smoke curling up. Beyond them, the wrinkled hills and buttes, blue in the distance, folded into the sky up to buffalo country, a hundred miles away. The blue sky was completely empty except for the sun, which wasn't too hot, having slipped in the sky. To get to buffalo country from here, you went a hundred miles north, climbed a mountain, then went another hundred miles, east this time, and kept doing that until you came to some buffalo. They'd traveled like that for eight or nine months, making villages along the way, trading with the *Maricat'z*—the Americans—and storing their dried meat in caches dug in the sides of hills when it grew too much to carry. Now they were going back to the Agency.

When they'd left Piah here, snow still filled the crevices between rocks, in sharp piles formed by sun-heated stone. White water sliding down the mountain divided into rivers below. Now everything was dry, including Piah. His harvest was packed in bags behind the rock shelter where he'd made his camp: two parfleches of eagle feathers, and one of bones, to carve into whistles. Beside them were two willow cages, each with four eaglets opening and closing their mouths like Piah, and beside that a basket of dead mice, lizards, and baby snakes swarming with flies. It didn't matter that they'd gone bad and stank, eagles would eat anything. Piah laughed when they walked toward the cages. He picked up a stick and whacked a cage, but Nicaagat took it away. Near the far edge of the mountaintop about twenty feet away was the pit he'd used for catching the eagles, its brush roof collapsed. To catch an eagle, he had to climb into this pit, cover it with brush, leaving a piece of deer meat on top, and wait for days, even weeks. Eventually an eagle would come. Then he had to reach up and pull it down by its feet and wring its neck lest it tear out his eyes, but just before, Piah always asked where its nest was; then he could go and take the eaglets, even if he had to climb down a cliff with a rope . . .

Between living all summer on this mountaintop, sitting in that pit half the day, and staring at the picture rock the rest of the time, it might take Piah a while to get his thinking back, but everyone expected that. It happened every year. Meanwhile, he was rich. He would get the best horses for his feathers and bones and all the meat his family could eat. Siwapi helped him mount one of the extra horses. He didn't smell at all, and his arms felt like hardened pieces of wood. He acted a little afraid of the horse. Maasuwini might have to poke him full of holes—not just his nostrils—to give him an odor again . . .

Before they left, Siwapi walked over to the picture rock and stared at the man upside down throwing sand. Clean Sand Flying in the Wind. In the middle of his belly was a circle growing smaller, flying into itself. Other parts of the rock showed things spurting about that resembled tadpoles, snakes, four-legged creatures, feathers, horned devils, ladders, and hands. They were spattered across its entire flat face. It looked like some crazy dream the rock had trapped, but the old man had told him it wasn't a dream—those were things that their fathers had seen. If you closed your eyes you could hear them whispering. He'd asked Maasuwini why he couldn't see the same things, and the old man pointed out that he could—exactly the same—by looking at the rock. That's what it was for. He looked disgusted. As for why it liked to chase them down the mountainside, that was a trick. The rock was playing games. Still, Siwapi asked it silently not to chase them, as Piah's horse might bolt and he might fall off. The rock made a kind of humming sound . . . Inside his mind, Siwapi saw his soul—his own soul—sitting in a *carniv*. His soul was watching a small, round bug, the kind they called a coyote's fish, and it said to the bug, "Now you little bug. I think you could jump from where you are up through the smoke hole and make your escape. If you can do that, I can too. I can escape when I'm in a bad place."

The bug made the jump and got away.

When they got toward the bottom of the mountain, the others relaxed and started laughing. They looked at Siwapi. He sat a little higher in the saddle while pretending indifference. He looked around. That's how I know I can get out of trouble—just like that coyote's fish. I'm the one who gets us all out of trouble; I made the rock stay where it belongs. He pictured himself sitting straight on his horse—the ornaments and rings on his arms . . . With the old man's help, he'd eventually become a *piikati*, a doctor, and spend the rest of his life curing sick people and helping others to get out of trouble . . .

At the camp, the old man had emerged from his *carniv* and was walking toward the returning party with his staggered gait. He walked precisely in Siwapi's direction, so the stone must be working. One of his feet was larger than the other. He didn't wear much—just some leggings and a breech clout—and from his belt hung the small bag made, it was said, from a human scrotum, where he kept his things. The scrotum came from an enemy killed in battle. His long arms hung low at his sides as he staggered forth, hands open and palms facing out—fingers slightly curled—veins like old cords. His sunken chest looked as fragile as a bird's. The sockets of his eyes were completely empty, but cupped in his lower lip, as though in a sling, sat a round stone of nearly pure turquoise, and with this he claimed he could see. When Siwapi dismounted, a boy took his horse off to hobble it. Maasuwini staggered right up to Siwapi and placed his hand on his shoulder, staring with the eye-stone in his mouth. Siwapi held up three fingers.

"Three."

The old man spit the stone into his palm and slipped it into his scrotum bag. Siwapi led him back to the *carniv*. He'd managed to roll up the sides of the *carniv* while Siwapi was on the mountain fetching Piah, still more proof of the power of the stone. At the farthest reaches of buffalo country just last spring he'd dreamed of where to find this stone and given Siwapi precise instructions. Over a hill, past a rotten stick, down a cutbank to a dry river—at the bottom of a rock in a cave . . . It was north country turquoise, whose blue-green colors held tiny black veins. Siwapi described it for him, because of course Maasuwini couldn't see his own stone with his stone.

Maasuwini had begun cooking some meat. He and Siwapi acted as *piwán* for each other. Inside the *carniv*, Siwapi poked the fire with a stick, and the cedar snapped and whistled and shot. Sometimes a stick of cedar said *pssst*, and he bent down to listen . . .

He'd once watched an ant crawl into one of the old man's empty sockets while he was sleeping, then crawl out again. The loose eyelids looked like a *piwán*'s cunt, and sometimes children at the agency taunted him by calling him Cunt-Eyes, but even back then—before he'd obtained the stone—his aim with a stick was good. He liked to tell the story of how Coyote went blind, to account for his own misfortune. Coyote saw some birds in a willow tree take out their eyes, juggle them and throw them up in the branches. Then they shook the branches and the eyes fell back down into their places. So he tried it too—he pulled out his eyes and threw them up in the willows. But the crows waiting there ate them. The crows told him they liked the gizzard, the liver, the brain, tongue, entrails, and kidneys—but most of all the eyes . . .

Others told another story. Assuming Maasuwini had done something bad to deserve his blindness, they thought of the story of Coyote and his daughters; it seemed to fit better. When Coyote was a young man he pretended to die. He scratched himself and smeared the wounds with pine pitch to make them look worse and said his enemies had stabbed him. His family laid him out on rushes which they set on fire before moving off. But he was a powerful man, and though the fire killed him, he woke up again and became alive, and began crawling over the earth in pursuit of his family. He sneaked up on them in the night and fucked each of his daughters. They didn't know who it was, so to make him stop they pushed sticks in his eyes. The next morning they saw he was their father.

Of course, no one around claimed to be Maasuwini's children or grandchildren, and no one could remember when he'd had a family, but this story seemed to haunt him. Even bugs in the grass taunted him: "*Maasuwini fucked his own daughters . . .*" He was old—some said over a hundred. He preferred Siwapi to a son or wife, and had taken charge of him since his childhood. Siwapi himself didn't know whether he'd ever get married, though he'd fucked girls during the Bear Dance. The old man told him a doctor shouldn't marry. His job was to care for Maasuwini and to help people get well and stay out of trouble. He wasn't a hunter. How could he feed a family?

Maasuwini had poked a stick into one of his nostrils to make the blood run, then let it drip into the kettle in which their meat was boiling. This meat was from Chepah's first buffalo—a young man on his first hunt. He'd shot him in the leg, and the animal bellowed, limping in circles, so he had to run up and shoot him in the brain, spoiling the material the *piwán* used to tan the hide. Colorow suggested they use Chepah's brains instead. On that part of the hunt, after three or four buffalo, they camped for a week to dry the meat and tan the hides. It was at this camp that things began to go wrong. Nicaagat had gone off with his own band into the mountains hunting for elk, and Maasuwini and Siwapi stayed with Colorow's band—a mistake. Colorow's belly hung down over his saddle horn. When Colorow came to an American's house, he went in and sat down at the table and ate right along with them. He made the women cook for him. At the Agency, he ate the agent's food. He ate things all day, but at night a green dwarf cut open his belly to take out the food, so the next day he woke up hungry again . . .

This time, in the middle of buffalo country, someone had put some cattle on a meadow and built a house and planted wheat. Colorow went to the house to tell him to leave. The hunters turned their horses out in the meadow and the *piwán* set up the *carniva*, then someone started breaking up the man's tools and rakes for mowing. It was trouble spreading like a stain on water. First, just a few started tearing down the man's fence, then, laughing and shouting, everyone joined in. Colorow told the man he wanted money for his ranch. He must pay the Utes for it. But the man said the government had already bought that country from the Utes, so Colorow made the American get down on his hands and knees and eat some of the grass. You like the grass of our country, he said—now you may eat as much of it as you want . . .

They went off after that, taking some coffee and sugar from the house. Colorow led them into the mountains, and no one chased them. He told everyone the story of the man who ate grass, the man-cow, though they'd all been there. Later on, the bands came together and he told it again, making it funnier each time. He told Nicaagat he'd turned a man into a cow. They'd stripped him naked and burned a mark on his back . . . Nicaagat just laughed. But Siwapi knew this meant trouble, and thought of the bug jumping out through the smoke hole. Smoke sometimes covered half the sky now: trouble. Some days the trouble went away. It broke into bits, flies carried it off . . . Nicaagat had grown up with the Americans and knew they were crazy. They told you to leave, then made you come back. They gave you presents, then took them away. They tried to make you work and farm and kill all your ponies. Their new agent, Nicaagat had told them, made Quinkent's band move all the Agency buildings downriver. They put them on rafts and the river took them down. So when they arrived at the Agency tomorrow, it wouldn't be in the place where they'd left it, but instead in the place where they turned out their ponies. Everyone laughed at this joke except Colorow. He knew it was true. So did Siwapi—he'd dreamed of the Agency chasing after them. Then Nicaagat told them that the new agent had forced those Nupartka who were stupid enough to stay at the agency during hunting season—that is, Quinkent's band—to dig a ditch to carry water to the fields around the agency. He talked all the time about ditches and water. He gave them all red wagons, then said the wagons were no good because they were painted red, so he took them away and gave them one green wagon. One green wagon for fifty people . . .

Nicaagat said that sometimes the agent didn't give out the presents, and everyone laughed, except Colorow. They were going back now to be given their presents: not just the flour and coffee, but the blankets, shoes, knives, hats, and shirts the government gave away once a year. He had to give them out because Washington told him to.

Siwapi set out the meat on some buckskin and put some coffee on the fire, then he and the old man ate reclining inside their *carniv* with the sides rolled up. A breeze came through the willows behind them. Somewhere outside, a meadowlark sang, and a blackbird twanged the spring in his gizzard. Maasuwini was singing. He gummed the meat, pulling with his fingers. As quietly as possible, Siwapi pulled some *kwatinapi*—a cake of mashed currants—out of his parfleche, and took little silent bites between bites of meat. Was Nicaagat right? He'd lived with the Americans a long time ago and worked as their slave in one of their cities. He drove a wagon carrying ice. What good was ice in the summer?—it just melts. The Americans were crazy . . . When the wife of the man he lived with whipped him, Nicaagat pulled out his knife and stood there, then threw it to the floor and walked out of the house, refusing to kill a *piwán*. He escaped and walked all the way here. That was years ago. He said the Americans were like two animals, coyote and wildcat, who decided to scratch each other's backs. So they scratched and scratched, going deeper and deeper until all the sinews were torn off their backs and there was no more skin and the flesh was in rags . . .

A white flash sent Siwapi reeling. His ears rang. Before him the old man knelt with a hard chunk of cedar in his hand. He felt ashamed. He held out the cake of mashed currants for Maasuwini. The old man took it and dropped the piece of wood. He knelt there with that stone hanging loosely cupped in the bottom lip of his mouth, broke the currant cake in two and gave half of it back to Siwapi. With a hollow pop he spit out the stone and slipped it in his bag, then reclined again, gumming the currants.

The next day, led by Nicaagat, they all rode down in a snaking line from the narrow canyon into the wide park of the Smoking Earth River. It looked strange. Sure enough, none of the buildings were there any-more—just logs and rocks that used to hold them up, with weeds growing in the exposed ground. Scattered here and there were some Agency cattle. The Agency was down at the winter valley now, beyond the yellow cliffs, too far to see from here. As they descended toward the meadow, some pack horses, smelling the grass, bolted. The two cages with Piah's eaglets snapped off the back of a horse to the ground, and one broke open. But Piah scrambled down off his horse and gathered the eaglets and fixed the cage. He was better already.

They headed straight for the river to water the horses for the last few miles to the new Agency. The trail to the winter valley was wider, with ruts on both sides made from wagon wheels. The ponies dragging their *carniva* poles had to go last because of the dust. Ahead, Nicaagat and some of the hunters began galloping, but Siwapi stayed back with the old man and the *piwán*. Already he felt their names changing. The Americans called Nicaagat Captain Jack. Quinkent was Douglas, and his son was Frederick. Canavish was Johnson. Siwapi himself was called Jim, or Henry Jim, and the old man was just the Old Man—no one called him Maasuwini. Even the Smoking Earth River had an American name—the White River. Tomorrow, when they were given their presents, they would have to make a mark with their thumb beside these American names, because the agent didn't want to give presents to Utes who were from other Agencies, they had their own presents—and their own American names . . .

Tonight Nicaagat had said they'd have races. There were some good things about coming back. Maybe Pausone had set up the sweat lodge. You stuffed your nostrils with dried sagebrush bark, tied up your prick, and sang in the heat about hunting and battles . . . Then someone says, I think I'll put water on the rocks now, and the steam comes and everyone burns. They sweat so much they almost die. But the brave ones stay till the steam dies down and the boss of the group lets them go and take a swim, even though they can hardly walk to the river, they're so weak from sweating.

Everyone had stopped. Maasuwini popped his stone in his mouth looking ahead toward the winter valley, but it didn't seem to work—his head kept on shaking. Siwapi pulled on the old man's horse by the rope attached to his own saddle. "Describe it to me," the old man said. He slipped the stone into his bag, and Siwapi suddenly understood about the bag: it wasn't made from a human scrotum at all. Just some wormy buckskin taken from a fawn—the thin part, back near the haunches . . .

He described the new agency for the old man. Children ran around there below them. The people's *carniva* were down across the river. Between the river and here were seven or eight Agency buildings made of logs, more than ever before, and a large field growing corn and wheat, with horses fenced off outside it. There was a big corral for hay, and small gardens down by the river, and just beyond where they stood ran that ditch filled with water to feed more fields. It curved around back to the river. Two roads intersected at the Agency, one with a signpost attached to a horse trough. On the porch of one house were crates for people to sit on. Outside another house a corral held some cows, but most of the cattle dotted the hills far away across the river. Dust was everywhere. Children ran past the Agency buildings up toward the rise where Siwapi and the others had stopped. One led a tame bear on a rope. Crows cawed, chicken and roosters pecked at the ground, and beyond the large fenced-in fields, the horses had sensed the excitement and were running—bays, yellows, blacks, roans, sorrels—moving through the meadows like pieces of smoke.

Everyone began to go down into the Agency. Siwapi led Maasuwini's horse. Some of Quinkent's men were wearing straw hats, and one carried a hoe. People were saying *maiquas* to each other. Outside the largest building, Nicaagat vigorously shook hands with an American with a very pale face and skin like dust. Siwapi thought he looked like a woman. His mouth was open and he talked at a gallop, pointing out things. For no reason that Siwapi could see he was smiling broadly. Standing before him, Nicaagat said nothing. This was the new agent. His white hair looked sick, and the black coat he wore was coated with brown dust. From his horse nearby, Colorow shouted down to Nicaagat, "You better do what that agent says, or else he'll spank you!" Everyone laughed, and the agent looked around, confused but still talking in American. His mouth was open and the words galloped out. They realized he couldn't understand the People's language, so someone else shouted, "You should see his *piwán*. She looks like Colorow's grandmother."

"So does he!" Colorow said.

The laughter spread and the agent seemed pleased that everyone was happy. He took Nicaagat by the arm to show him something, then it seemed as though he was going to fly. He almost fell down. Arms and legs flapping buglike, he shouted at the *piwán* setting up their *carniva* down by the river. He looked all around and pulled at his hair. Now he wasn't smiling, but the words still came out. Siwapi looked at the others like himself who had just arrived, but they were just as confused. A few of them laughed. Maasuwini said something. Across the field, Nicaagat's *piwán* had just lashed together his *carniv*'s poles, and the agent was running toward them and shouting. Behind him, Nicaagat stood stiffly and spat. Other *carniva* were sprouting up all around the Agency, too many for the agent to keep up with, but he ran from one to the other anyway waving his arms. He pulled on the arm of Wausits's *piwán* as she was lashing her poles, causing Wausits to gallop over on his horse. The agent pointed across the river, and then up the river, and Siwapi understood that he wanted them to erect their *carniva* further off, not where they always had. The old man was laughing. Away from our horses? You might as well cut off our heads, he said. People started laughing. Cut off our heads! Of course, the agent couldn't understand what they were saying, so he swiveled his face looking all around and tried to smile. Some children started taunting him, but the old man dismounted to make them stop. Siwapi noticed smoke in the sky, way off to the east, just above the horizon. That trouble again . . . Things were calming down. Nobody seemed to know what to do. If they erected their *carniva* where they always had, would they get their presents? Nobody knew.

"Tell him that these people, who are his friends, have become my friends too. There's no reason he can't as well. All I ask is some cooperation." Nathan Meeker gestured toward Douglas and Johnson at the words "these people," but fixed his gaze on Captain Jack while the boy translated. Of course, Jack understood English. He'd been raised by the Mormons as a household slave in Salt Lake City, though luckily had escaped castration. Some Mormons preferred their slaves castrated . . . He'd fought for General Crook against the Sioux, even wore his Army scout clothes now—the fringed jumper and buckskin pants, the cowboy hat and boots. Around his neck, for this special occasion, hung the silver medal presented to him by President Johnson when he'd visited Washington back in '68—back when Nathan lived on MacDougal Street.

They were gathered in the windowless warehouse. Light slanting in through the open door, a solid block of it, tipped the room up toward Nathan. Next to Jack, seated on the floor, Douglas wore his usual work shirt and blue denim pants and American shoes. Cropped at the ears, his hair hung straight, whereas Jack's had been pulled back in braids. Faintly edging Douglas's mouth was the trace of a mustache, rare among the Indians, and a sign he had to be on Nathan's side—he'd slid just that much into ways of the whites. He spoke English too, Nathan knew that, but for this formal occasion they'd brought an interpreter. It gave them more time to compose their lies . . .

"What does he say?"

"He say nothing to that."

These Indians were expert at pointing out the obvious. No sense of irony . . .

Next to Douglas sat Johnson, Nathan's strongest ally. His clothes were a compromise: the green flannel shirt was government issue, but the buckskin leggings were Ute. Around them he'd strapped an army blanket, and on his head sat a plug hat. Johnson owned three cows—from which he obtained milk, cheese, and butter—as well as poultry, goats, a house, a table, crockery, and dishes. Nathan had caused a log house to be built for him, first among the Utes. Eventually they'd all have houses, then maybe stores, barber shops, churches, meeting halls—a civilized town! If they learned to cooperate. Johnson had a truck garden too, and just last week had hired a slew of women to dig his potatoes while he supervised like a New York businessman, bustling around smoking cigarettes and giving orders. He was wealthy; he paid wages in money, and was said to own more than one hundred horses. Of course, the horses would have to go in time. Since the days of Lot and Abraham, the conflict between horses and cattle for the best part of the range has existed in all pastoral countries, and eventually the horse must give way . . . Sitting there, Nathan composed in his mind his next piece to send to the Greeley *Tribune*: You see, Johnson is one of those men who lead from the savage to the barbaric life on the way to civilization. He is not quite as far advanced as Cedric, the Saxon, the master of Garth, in Scott's *Ivanhoe*, but he is probably equal to the best among the British chiefs who tried to withstand the invasion of Julius Caesar . . .

Should he mention that although Johnson had his own house, he didn't actually sleep in it? He'd pitched his tipi outside the door and slept in that on buffalo blankets, but used the house for meals, social gatherings, and—Nathan knew—status. He was thought of by his people as a medicine man, what they called a doctor, which may have accounted for the backsliding way, for a man half civilized, he painted his face: crimson streaks on the forehead, bands of red, yellow, and blue on the cheeks, and a yellow band running diagonally from his left eyebrow down across his nose to the right corner of the mouth. He looked like a species of French harlequin.

Next to Johnson squatted the interpreter, whose name Nathan had missed. The four of them sat there silently before him while their agent, half seated on a barrel of flour above, scribbled notes in a daybook.

Of the three leaders, Jack was the problem. He and his bands had been gone for eight months off the reservation annoying settlers, though of course they'd returned for the general issue of annuity goods—they thought it their due. Those who stayed at the Agency acknowledged Douglas as their chief, as did the government, but Jack commanded the loyalty of more, including the troublemakers. How much easier it would be to lead them to wealth and a happy, productive life, free of sin, if it weren't for the troublemakers! Of course, they were human—like Nathan. They had their good qualities. The men loved and protected their wives, delighted in music, and worked when they had to, though they must be driven to it by almost galvanic force. But anything akin to abiding care, conviction, and foresight was completely foreign to their ways. Even Josie thought so, though she always defended them. They live for the day, she said—which was why, said her father, they'd managed to conceive that the white man was created to wait upon them.

Jack spoke up. His words were surprisingly soft and melodious. Nathan looked down at the interpreter.

"He say, Why you move the Agency? He say the place for the Agency was settle by treaty."

"Tell him I moved the Agency to better grow things in the earth. Tell him the previous agents were men who knew nothing of farming, but I do, and with the help of these men"—he nodded toward Johnson and Douglas—"I moved it to where some farming could be done. Tell him that each of these men has been given a piece of ground to raise his own crops, as they are important men, and that he will be given one too, since he is important as well."

The young man translated. Johnson had already raised his eyes at the word "important," and raised them again when it came out in Ute. Of course, they were rivals. Johnson had status, but Jack had followers.

Jack nodded politely when the translator finished, then spoke in a stream of musical syllables, scraps of sound scattered like seeds. He didn't seem angry; so far so good . . .

"He say, How can you give him a piece of ground which already belong to him? It doesn't make sense. He say, All the Ute have many horses and they pasture them here during the winter."

Horses again . . . He should shoot all their horses. Then where would they be? Nathan gazed out the door through clouds of light in which insects spiraled. Utes out there were bending over to peer inside the

warehouse. Councils like this improved affairs for a day or two maybe—
then they reverted to form again. He couldn't help wishing he were back
in Greeley, the wish he'd vowed never to succumb to, for at least another
year.

Turn the screws a bit, Nathan—you have to be firm. "Tell him if he
stayed on the reservation like Washington wanted him to and not go
running all over the place getting into trouble and committing depreda-
tions—if he stayed here and worked he wouldn't need so many horses."

Jack didn't flush. "He say, Ute ground, Ute horses, Ute people, and
Ute agent. You are paid to work for the Ute."

"No, I'm not. Tell him that."

Nathan watched Jack's face. His black eyes slowly closed, then opened.
They never blinked; they were like a moth's eyes. They appeared to be
set too close together for either party to gauge any depth, the one peering
in or the one gazing out, and the long ridge of his nose barely parted the
eyes, slanting up into his slanting forehead, so that his face seemed
arched back gazing at the ceiling—but it wasn't. It looked right at Nathan. "He want to know what are you paid money for if not to work for
us."

"I am paid to show you how to work and to help you."

"He say he already know how to work. We work as hard as you do.
Did you ever try skinning a buffalo?"

Nathan smiled and scribbled in his notebook. *Did you ever try skinning
a buffalo* . . . "Tell him his friends here worked to dig that ditch outside.
How can he expect to be given his goods if he doesn't work for them?"

Jack stared at Nathan, mountains of silence looming inside him. Nathan sensed how much Jack's face resisted his own considerable knowledge of faces. For a giddy moment he realized how little he knew about
these people. They were utterly foreign.

The face made some sounds. "He say the goods belong to the Ute. The
government bought them with the Ute money."

"Ask him if that's why they come in here and steal them."

That did it, that brought a reaction—Jack's eyes opened wider. "He
say he don't know what you mean." The interpreter's voice had risen
with Jack's.

"Tell him that since his people returned, someone has come in here
stealing blankets, jackets, and other things. The blankets were hanging
to those rafters before, but you see they aren't hanging there now."

"He want you to show him the holes or what other way Indians have
entered the warehouse. It is always locked."

"You must have a false key. You are too much around the Agency buildings altogether. You people are always lying around the Agency and nothing can be left out that you don't pick up."

At this, Jack brought his hand to his mouth and pushed it out suddenly with two splayed fingers, the sign for liar. But he spoke quite calmly. "He want to know whether you wish him to leave. You just told him he should stay on the reservation."

"Tell him that's a good joke."

Nobody laughed.

"Tell him I do not wish him to leave. I wish him to stay here and work. Tell him that a man must expect some trouble in life and must face it in a manly way without complaining."

Jack grunted something. "Trouble?" said the boy.

"I mean bother and work. Nobody ever bettered themselves without making an effort." Nathan stood up and tried to smile, but the pulleys and ropes wouldn't haul up his cheeks. He walked toward the door looking out at the sunlight, where Ute squaws and braves had gathered in ever thickening numbers. Behind him, Jack conferred with the other two, then raised his voice.

"He want to know why his people could not set up their tipis where they always do."

"Because that is land I wish to plow up. Why do you think we dug that ditch?"

Jack conferred again with Douglas and Johnson, and Nathan turned to them, watching their faces. "He say you better plow up some other land. You should plow on the hill. The land you want to plow is land you said you would give to the important men. We need that for our ponies."

"Tell him I'm the one who must say what land will be plowed and what won't. I know what Washington wants me to do. My words go to Washington, tell him that. The words he speaks don't go very far. Washington wants me to plow that land, and if you don't want to let me do it, then Washington will get heap angry and send out soldiers. Tell him that."

The boy commenced translating, but Jack broke in suddenly. "I am good friends to soldiers," he said in English. Nathan strolled back to retrieve his daybook, staring at Jack. Then he smiled—it worked!

"You can stay there and talk if you want to. I'm going home."

"You leave the Agency?"

"Don't you wish it. No. Not to my home-over-the-mountains, as much as I'd love to." He was conscious of speaking as though to a child. "Just to my house around the corner, Jack. You discuss with my friends here what I've been saying and let me know if you decide to cooperate. I'm good friends to the soldiers too, and if they come here we'll see whose friends they'll be." In four long strides he was out the door.

Outside, nearly the whole tribe had gathered, and all stood as Nathan passed. Half of them wore blankets like Roman togas. No one greeted him. You make the most of a bad thing and what do you get? Vilification. It was for their own good, of course, and he had no choice but to be constant as the northern star, unassailable . . . Was his shirt untucked? His birthmark visible? The purple stain up and down his side had begun to itch in this dry fall weather. He felt like exposing himself to the heathen multitude and watching them avert their eyes and flee. They were a superstitious lot when you found them out . . .

Arvilla stood when he entered the house, hands clasped at her waist. "How was your council?"

"We'll know soon enough. Where's Jane?"

"Gone off."

"Don't they always go off when you need them?" At the door to his room, he turned to his wife. "Dear, could you do me a service, then? Fetch Mr. Price and ask him if he's ready to plow." Nathan tried another smile; with his eyes he infused some grit in his wife, trying not to think of what some Utes said: she looked more like his mother than his squaw.

She seemed so resigned she was almost happy. Her nose very nearly touched her chin. She scurried out the door surprisingly fast for a woman past sixty.

In their bedroom, he sat down at his table. Of course, he shouldn't have mentioned soldiers. They bristled at that. But they needed such shocks to get them moving. He dipped a pen in his inkwell and wrote. "Where is the cause of want of success? Hard luck. Refusal to dissimulate. But men are unconscious of the power they possess. When compelled by circumstance to make a strong and even desperate effort, the greatest difficulties vanish—the mightiest obstacles are removed—" And? The most powerful something . . . "The most powerful opposition disap-pears."

Out the window, some Ute boys pretended to shoot at each other with longish sticks. A Ute child, sex indeterminate, swung what looked like a rope about his or her head, but Nathan knew it to be a deer's intestine, slit at the top to make a whistling sound. The children weren't like their parents. Perhaps because they were always indulged, they never seemed to be stubborn or willful. Of course, their parents doted on them. They were remarkably good with their children, with the result that Josie's school had attracted a mere three pupils, despite the teacher's popularity. Their mothers didn't want to give them up.

Precisely how such children grew to become the obstinate adults Nathan found himself dealing with day in and day out was difficult to fathom. They did something with the boys when they reached puberty—fed them on rocks . . . Was there ever such a world? It had to be the horses. His ditch had become one long watering trough. Their horses took the best range and scared off the cattle, since a Ute never walks his horse—always tears off at a gallop, even for a mere hundred yards. So the Agency, most of the day, was a haphazard snarl of horses shooting this way and that, panicking the cattle, ripping up meadows—worse than Broadway and Fulton at noon! To get such fellows to work and continue at it when they'd rather be off hunting or racing was like trying to help a spring-poor calf to its feet. But they'd have to learn. The government demanded it, as did civilized society, whose foundation was farming. Speed the plow! To make homes and establish therein the domestic hearth, to educate families in economy, cleanliness, household arts, and household industries—what a glorious task!

What thankless drudgery . . .

If only they could read what the Denver papers said about them: the Utes are exceedingly disagreeable neighbors, with a disgusting habit of ranging all over the territory, stealing horses, killing off game, and carelessly firing forests in the dry season. Sure, Nathan wanted to be their friend, but he couldn't help but acknowledge a degree of truth in these charges. The governor wanted them all shipped out to Indian territory. In Denver, the single most common graffito on brick walls and board fences was THE UTES MUST GO! These Indians didn't know that Nathan was their savior. Grubbing out sage—plowing up rocks—he was the only one who stood between them and dispossession of their lands. The Denver merchants would love nothing better than to open up this reservation to mining. Miners were lined up now to get in. Every once in a while two or three came through with their blackened hands and smudged eyes full of wild hope, and Nathan had to remind them to keep on moving. This was Ute land, and Father Meeker was the Utes' protector. If only they'd learn to cooperate . . .

From Nathan's window, the view to the Utes' racetrack down at the far end of the meadows was partially obstructed by the storehouse and Johnson's cabin. They'd gathered there, though, he could see the crowds. Dust was rising. Was Josie with them? On either side of the section of track visible from his window, braves were spreading blankets on the ground—Agency blankets! One laid down a blanket, and another across from him did the same. Then a buffalo robe—a buckskin—moccasins . . . These were the bets for the day's first race. No doubt, Johnson was there,

and Captain Jack and Douglas. If their council had upset them, that
wouldn't stop the races. Utes never nursed their displeasures for long.
They'd rather be racing—gambling—smoking. And the boy jockeys
raced in the buff! He'd forbidden Josie to attend, but she was even more
willful than her Ute friends. Her position as big sister to the tribe—*pa-
veet'z*, they called her—demanded it, she argued.

Nathan once had observed a squaw offer Josie a cigarette down at the
racetrack. Tobacco? A Meeker? Her attitudes were just as worrisome as
her cough.

Tired—it made him tired . . .

"Nathan? Dear." Arvilla stood at the door. Her meek voice knelt
before him in apology. She wasn't supposed to disturb him at his table.

His own voice roused to exhibit annoyance, just the proper, expected
measure. "Yes?" He sat there waiting, looking away—rubbing his forehead.

"Dear. Mr. Price is at the door with his team and plow."

White River Agency
Colorado Territory
August 30, 1873

Dearest Pete,

*Where are you? Father awaits his mules and I my Pete. Perhaps I
miss you. If you haven't been scalped or kidnapped yet, and haven't
yet left, Father charged me to tell you that as our stock of all kinds
of paper bags is nearly exhausted and none came from Rawlins in
their last shipment, could you see fit to bring some?*

*I'm a little surprised at missing you so much, since you hardly
deserve it. We have passed a pleasant summer at the new Agency,
and hope to be snug and warm in the winter. Everything turns
golden here now. The Agency swells with prodigal Indians we hardly
saw hide nor hair of before who come by for the general issue. And
no paper bags! I wonder if any kingdoms ever fell for the want of
paper bags?*

*These new Indians all in their colorful costumes seem jealous of
those that stayed behind to look after me. They have races every day
and ride their horses buck naked and when they cross the finish line
simply fall off and lie on their backs and laugh at the sky. Father's
afraid my morals will suffer, but you know me. I have all the evil
qualities and vices already.*

I'm worried for Father. He won't brook rebellion in bettering the lives of our Utes. His concern for their welfare tops all, but they think he is continuously against them. I can hardly tell yet whether my next four years' work is among them or no, but if it is I am determined to make it a success. I like the Indians very much, most of them are agreeable, they come into our rooms whenever they feel like it, and if there are no seats the bed suits them quite as well, so we do not get lonesome any. They dote on Flora Ellen Price— Shadrach's wife—who is only sixteen. One named Pausone has asked me to marry him—twice! Father didn't find that altogether funny. I only have three pupils now at my school, and two of them are orphans. The Indians seem to think that if their children learn to read and write we'll want them to learn to be carpenters next— then to build houses—then live in the houses and learn to farm and break up the ground, which would cripple their horses by its uneven course, and if they gave up their horses they might as well be civilized and have done with it quite. I try to explain to them that as the white man's gain is the Indian's loss, they ought to at least learn geography and mathematics, in order to have some tools with which to fight back when white people try to take away their land. I carried a globe to my school to explain that the earth is round and to show them where we are. I tell them I'm on the Indians' side, but Father thinks it unseemly to say so. Leaders, says he, should stand above and apart—like the famous oak.

Well, I can't follow any but the higher law. Father always used to say, if the majority of the world believed 8 plus 3 are 2 and it was heresy to say they make eleven, then we must be heretics. So I secretly prepare them to reject our yoke. Each day I think less of the great mass of mankind and more and more of these human beings in their unadulterated state free from the influence of society & hereditary predispositions. Pete, I do think I've pondered on life and death and the universe more than anyone else alive! It must be because I'm so green, so old, so youthful, so big, so small, so spontaneous, so stagey, so bulging with vanity and so crowded with affection. At 12 I was a freethinker, at 13 a Buddhist, at 14 a Mohammedan, at 15 a follower of Carlyle, at 16 a Darwinian, at 17 a skeptic, and now at 18 a red Indian. These are the rough landmarks, I daresay. I glory in having no unalterable opinions and in my superb contempt for custom. The only idea I fight against is the idea of fixed principles! It does beat all how I find myself laughing at the smallness of this little earth, Pete. With my thumb at the

PETER DOYLE

North Pole & my finger at the South Pole I could pinch it altogether.
So much for the realm of earthly clods!

Father wants me to say it was ten mules—not nine.

Now I must go to the races, dear Pete. I hope this finds you well,
or at least finds you. If it makes you feel better, I'm lonely without
you—kind of shipwrecked.

Your squaw,
Josie

Chapter

❦ 4 ❦

"I'll teach you!"

"Leave off, I say!"

"No, I won't!"

"Very well, then, it's my turn to teach *you*!" Mr. Punch chased Judy around the stage to the hoots and shouts of the cowboys, desperadoes, and railroad firemen gathered at the Eagle Saloon waiting for the juicy parts. He'd already pushed her to the floor and mimed a quick *coitus*, interrupted by the cries of a baby, which, in this version—the Real Punch and Judy, Stokes called it—he'd jerked out of Judy's belly from between her legs and tossed to the audience as a sop. The baby suspiciously resembled a sausage . . .

Now Punch was clubbing Judy with his stick in the venerable tradition of all Punch-and-Judys, but in deshabille—with his member exposed— and Judy suddenly seized the weapon and knocked off Punch's thing, huge and erect. It flew into the audience, which howled and spit, shouting encouragement. "Take that, you limey pig!" *Wagh!*

"Oh my thingy!" Punch grabbed his crotch. "My thing, my poor thingy!"

Judy faced him wielding the stick. "Now, Mr. Punch . . ."

"I needs another stick!" He was leaning over to shout down below. "My kingdom for a stick!" Quick as a wink, a human hand popped up and handed Punch a stick. Right away he commenced beating his wife about the head and shoulders. "I'll teach you!"

Poor Judy dropped her stick. "Oh pray, Mr. Punch—no more!"

"Yes, one more little lesson!"

"No, no more!" She began to whimper.

"I thought I should soon make you quiet!"

"I don't like that kind of teaching!"

Punch beat her about the head and bottom until she lay lifeless upon the stage, face hanging over the platform. He leaned back against the side, panting. "Now, if you're satisfied, so am I." He puffed and heaved with a rasping sound like a cracked kazoo. "There now, get up, Judy my dear. I won't hit you no more."

"She's a gone beaver, mister!" someone shouted from the front.

"No, she's just achy. Get up, I say . . . Well then, get down!" Punch pushed Judy's limp body down below with the end of his stick, then swayed back and forth holding his crotch. "Oh my poor thingy! Nurse! Come quick, Nurse!"

Enter Polly the nurse.

"What a beauty! What a pretty creature! Nurse, Nurse, I've been caponed! I've been killed!"

"Oh no, Mr. Punch. Not so bad as that, sir."

"Not killed, but speechless."

"Where are you hurt?" She reached for his head. "Is it here, sir?"

"No, lower."

Polly stroked his chest. "Here?"

"Lower still."

"Then is your handsome leg broken?"

"No, higher."

Polly bent forward and Punch all at once removed his large nose—it came off quite easily—and attached it between his legs. "Mr. Punch—it's enormous!"

He seized her by the shoulders. "Come, Polly, come."

"Do you really love me?"

"I do! I do!"

"Then I must love you!"

They wriggled and squirmed up there on the stage like children pretending they'd been set on fire. Evidently, Mr. Punch had difficulty fitting his prodigious tool into Polly's opening, and pushed at her desperately.

"Mr. Punch, that hurts!"

"No, it just tickles!"

They struggled, turning, and fell to the platform with Punch on top. One disconcerting aspect of this scene was that leprous cavity where Punch's nose had been, through which the audience clearly made out several fingers fat as slugs obscenely fluttering . . .

Out of this cavity emerged a string of sausages. "Squasages, Polly?" A fry pan appeared, and Punch commenced frying them.

"Smuggings, Mr. Punch! You smugged them, I daresay!"

"You say you want to smuggle?" Punch embraced Polly.

"Oh no, let's eat first!"

Somewhere in the audience on the undulating floor, where tobacco juice had gathered in puddles, a beer mug smashed, raising howls of execration. Amid the clouds of tobacco smoke and smells of sweat, leather, sawdust, tap drippings, and onions, below the zoological specimens peering down from the walls—heads and horns of deer, antelope, and buffalo mounted on puncheons hung between cattle brands burned into the paneling—a man swung his fist at a bearded face which collapsed like dust. "Bardog! More popskull!" Punch rapped his frying pan up on the stage to regain the attention of these queer backwood folks. Another Friday night at the Eagle Saloon . . .

Some claim the name Punch comes from a stock character of the *commedia dell'arte* in sixteenth-century Italy, Pulcinella—one of the *zannis*—whose name, in turn, was a corruption of Puccio d'Aniello, a vintager in Acerra near Naples—a real person! But others assume that the entire family of Italian Masks derives from the characters of the Atellan Farces, or *Osci ludi*, which in turn descend from Dorian Mime via the Phylax Comedy—lost in history—and that Punchs particular ancestor is none other than Maccus, a.k.a. Pullus Gallinaceus, a hooknosed hunchback with spindly legs. And Maccus's prototype? Undoubtedly Priapus, the phallic god, whose wooden statues guarded orchards from thieves with threats of painful sexual cruelty for both male and female—behind, in front, above . . .

"Mr. Punch, not *there*!"

"Tumble up, Polly! Backside to heaven!"

But Polly refused to turn around. Instead, she popped her blouse open to reveal, of all the horrid things, a huge grinning mouth where her navel should have been. She seemed to speak from it—the nasty engastrimyth! "There—this'll fit you!"

"Goodness me, Polly!"

The phallus of Priapus, whom sailors invoked in distress, and fishermen prayed to for a big catch, later came to be regarded as protection against the evil eye. Young brides-to-be sometimes mounted the wooden statues so the god would claim their virginity first. Shards of Priapean braggadocio and license scattered through history turned up in Jack Finney and Big Head of the Mummer's Play of St. George, in Vice of the Mystery Plays, in Pulcinella of the Italian Masks and Polichinelle of the puppet theater in France, where they acquired Punch's large ruff and buttons. Polichinelle crossed the channel with the Huguenot refugees, and later, as Punch, emigrated to America, which sanitized him for children's birthday parties. But Stokes thought he had the real thing with this fellow up there on the end of his arm. He'd carefully altered the puppet according to the spotty rags of history he'd managed to pick up in the relic trade, filling in gaps with his own shameful dreams, and had fitted Mr. Punch with secret holes and a hollowed-out hunchback stuffed with sausages, snakes, and other phallic things, all for the crude delectation of American cowboys in the Wild West . . .

Punch: "Where's my stick?"

Stokes (below): "At the pawnshop."

Punch: "I wants another stick!"

Stokes: "You can't have one. Now get on with the preformance, please."

Punch: "I wants another stick!"

Stokes: "No."

Punch: "I wants one!"

Stokes: "You can't have one."

Punch: "Give me a stick!"

Stokes: "Very well . . ."

This could go on all night. You could stretch the show at just about any point, break in and deflect it here or there, since it ran on principles of *coitus interruptus* and *coitus resumptus*. Stokes's right arm, the strong one, held Punch overhead, while the left reached up a short thick stick, handing it to Punch. Around Stokes, the puppets hanging upside down resembled so many tortured and executed victims. Through a peephole before him, he surveyed the crowd. Soiled and grizzled, with foam on their beards, they gummed their beer mugs in anticipation like overgrown children—he had them where he wanted them. The smutty parts had softened their morals. To the left, where the room jogged out, the faro players had looked up too. Count Léon-Fernand-Léon stood there in his fancy duds, unsmiling—somewhat tipped to the side. Above him, the faro lookout in evening dress perched on a high stool surveyed the game, he couldn't look at Mr. Punch, might lose his job. To his right was the closet where, for twenty-five cents, you could view the head of a Ute Indian preserved in a barrel of Old Gideon rye. Some fandango girls along the back walls in scarlet dresses with black bands around their skirts marked the crowd, smoking long thin cigarettes; one of them pointed at the count. He'd just laid his hand on the dealer's arm, a breach of the rules. The lookout said something.

"I wants a bigger stick!"

"What's wrong with that one?"

"It's too little!"

"It'll do."

"I wants a bigger stick!"

"You can't have one."

"I wants it!"

"No."

"Give me a bigger one!"

"Oh, very well . . ."

The trick of this little dialogue between Punch and his master lay in the skillful use of the swazzle on the roof of Stokes's mouth. When Punch talked the swazzle squeaked, but for the puppetmaster's lines, quick as a flash his tongue pried the thing off his palate and held it—then plastered it up there again when Punch spoke. It was second nature, this creasing and slicing of sounds from each other, but more than once Stokes had spit out the swazzle—and long ago, in Covent Garden, had managed to swallow it, a sure sign of bad luck . . .

This new stick was impossibly long, and Punch swung it down below the stage at Stokes. "Too long!"

"Oh, will you behave?"

"This stick's too long! I wants another one!"

"You're getting no more."

"I wants another one!"

"No, you can't have one."

"I wants it!"

"No."

"Piss on you, then!"

And that's what Mr. Punch did. Stokes had already wormed the tube up through his puppet into the nose hung between his legs—his dummy pizzle—and now squeezed the bulb shooting beer through his puppet's snoot back down below the stage, out of view, into his own open mouth. Then he faced Punch out and gave the gentlemen seated in front a quick squirt. They howled with delight.

A battle ensued between Punch and Stokes, the latter remaining down, out of sight. Punch bent over swinging his stick and squawking out insults. "Lick-twat! Barge-arse! Gully-butt!" He jumped down from view and Stokes tossed things up from below—sticks, wooden phalli, false teeth, a shirt, an old pair of trousers—a limp Mr. Punch . . . He flung some long johns up through the opening out into the audience. At last he said, "Here then—take your bloody stick."

"Aye, that's the way to treat 'em," screamed Punch, who leaped up and caromed back and forth off the sides of the stage and shouted, "Huzzah!" He whacked his head against the platform, then stood there and thrust his hook-nosed penis out at the audience, swinging it from his hips back and forth like a crane.

The cowboys roared with glee. At the faro table, on the other hand, all was calm, Stokes was glad to see that. The count sniffed at a hanky in his fist pressed to his shoulder. Scented with lavender, Stokes knew. He looked the picture of melancholy, but Stokes understood that beneath his carefully composed exterior billowed rage. The perfume barely checked it. The count was incensed that they hadn't found Doyle. They'd arrived in Greeley hot for their prize only to meet with an empty room nearly cleared out at the People's Boarding House and Restaurant. What possessions and clothes he'd left behind they ravaged minutely, of course. Even ripped the heels off his shoes . . . Walt was no help. The proprietor of the boarding house hadn't the vaguest notion of where Pete had gone, or when he'd return.

So Bonny and Jo were out there right now sniffing out spoor. Leaving Walt to pine away at the Greeley Hotel, they'd all tramped back from Greeley to Evans, where the trains came and went. They'd consulted the stationmaster's book of receipts. No Peter Doyle. Evans at least had a few saloons, all within pissing distance of the Denver Pacific depot. You could get a drink here—put on a show . . . Stokes nursed on patience. Nearly four decades in the relic line had developed in him a kind of sixth sense, a palpus of sorts. He knew he was close when his mouth started watering. Meanwhile, he could perform the Real Punch and Judy, since going for too long without a show made him feel almost dead inside.

Because Bonny was out searching for Peter Doyle, ending the show with the hangman wasn't possible, so Stokes opted for the body-counting scene. Mr. Punch had murdered three people so far. He carried them up and laid them on the platform for the counting of the bodies. "One . . . two . . . three." Then, mentally exhausted, he leaned against the side of the stage to rest. Wait a minute—when he turned around, there weren't three, but *four*, and they were right behind him, not across the stage where he'd just left them . . .

The culprit was Joey the Clown.

Punch examined the bodies with care. His phallic snoot poked at their intimates. He pushed the entire pile of them stage left across the platform and counted by dragging each one stage right. "One . . . two . . . three . . . four . . . five . . . *six*!" Now he exploded, sputtering and squawking.

He didn't even notice clever little Joey, who kept sneaking around to the end of the line for recounting.

Poor Punch turned his back in despair. Joey removed himself. Now there were three. Punch counted them, satisfied. He turned away—turned back—counted again . . . Just two! To see Punch so outwitted made you think all his brains had perhaps dropped out through that cavity in his face. He was coming apart. When he leapt and danced around in a rage, the big thing between his legs fell off and Punch had to duck down below the stage for Stokes to reattach it, thus doubling the laughter of the audience, who thought they'd caught the puppetmaster out. Actually, it was planned. Stokes took the opportunity to stuff Punch's nose with sausages, snakes and other foul things . . . Punch jumped back up and counted again. "One . . . two . . . three . . . four . . . five . . . six!" He whacked his wooden head against the platform. "This one's alive!"

"No I'm not."

"Yes you are!"

"No I'm not, truly!"

"I'll soon find out!" Thrusting out his nasal phallus, Punch approached Joey. "I'll treat you!"

"Not me. Try that one. She just moved!"

"Which one?"

"That one there."

"She's dead!"

"No she ain't!"

"Yes I am!"

"See? I told you . . ."

Stokes's arms were growing tired. Arthritis, muscle fatigue . . . His throat was sore too, since the swazzle required a volume of air just slightly below that of a scream. Still, standing there with both hands up high, making all those funny squawks and different voices—shouting them out—he felt prodigious . . . Absolutely manifold . . . Sometimes the show just took over and whipped around up there on its own. *He* was the puppet, hanging down. He felt a tug on the leg of his pants and kicked out. "Get!"

With hand puppets, aping sexual activity was more or less like percussive applauding, and Stokes liked to throw himself into it. Good show, Punch! The cowboys roared and hooted. Scanning the crowd through his little peephole, he noticed Jo next to the count. Something was climbing up Stokes's leg. Not while Mr. Punch was having such fun!

PETER DOYLE

"Going time," said the voice in his ear. Bonny clung to his shoulder like a pet. "Pack it up."

Stokes pulled the curtain while Punch was still at it, then, so as not to waste his preparations, thrust Punch's nose—still hanging from his hips—out the breech, just the nose, spouting sausages, rubber snakes, gum drops, and other sundries. They made a little pile on the floor. The cowboys cheered and stamped their feet.

Packing up was easy. The stage swiveled down on its wheels and, presto, became a cart. Bonny had already snuggled inside. Stokes took his hat off and bowed at the men, who were surely a more than appreciative audience. One pressed a mug of beer in his hands—American beer! Stokes declined politely. Behind him the next act was just beginning. A Mexican señorita who'd come out to dance had spotted a spider up on the ceiling. Judging from the way she crossed her arms and ducked, the spider was descending. It somehow managed to land on her clothes, making her jump, squirm, twitch, and kick, while entangling her in its huge sticky web. She was frantic! More spiders came down, hundreds of hairy, ugly spiders—you could tell by the fear in her eyes—and attacked her in various delicate places . . .

Hands and arms numb, Stokes waddled toward Jo, who held up some tickets. Rawlins, Wyoming. The train left in less than an hour. He'd made his inquiries, they'd located Doyle—at last they were hot on the trail!

> Greeley Hotel
> Greeley, Colorado Territory
> Sept 6, 1873

Dear Miss Dickinson,

You will be surprised to get a letter from me away off here. I have been taking quite a journey these last few days—have come out to the Rocky Mountains and Colorado (2,000 miles) to visit a friend. Enclosed find a rude map which will show you the line of my jaunt. The red lines are of my present trip, while the blue ones are of former journeys when I didn't get so far as this.

Well, this is a wonderful country, and nobody knows how big it is till he launches out in the midst of it. Large herds of cattle— settlements 15 or 20 miles apart. No improved farms, no fences (I mean along the way to this place) but 600 miles of rolling prairie land. I do believe I have found the law of my own poems out here. Far glimpses of a hundred peaks, titanic necklaces, stretching north and south. The pure cool mountain air is delicious to breathe. New senses, new joys, seem develop'd.

I am holding my own in the recovery of my half state of health. Hope you may say the same for yourself. My condition is very tantalizing in its fluctuations—still having electricity applied, as my good doctor back east constructed a portable apparatus especially for this western tramp. Still feel I shall pull through, but O it is a weary, weary pull. I put a bold face on, & my best foot foremost. Sometimes I get the blurs, & sometimes feel all the while ready to have them, confusing me and affecting the eyes.

A B Alcott is expected here to talk, and I may see him. May deliver myself of an oration too if I can see fit. Greeley is quite the place I hear for the most toploftical Hegelian transcendentalists. They come from the East to view the transcendental mountains, and some find they are like the philosopher who, gazing at the stars, tumbled into a well.

You might be interested in the enclosed piece from an Omaha newspaper regarding my views of the West.

I now await the friend in question. Have just seen the mountains at sunset, a bang-up sight—shall never forget it.

Best wishes,
Walt Whitman

Propped up in bed, Walt folded the letter, addressed it, and waited for Jo to return with Pete. It might take a few hours, he'd said—but it's been all day! Each time footsteps approached in the hallway, he perked up expectant, and each time they passed, sank back, inexpressibly tired. At least Jo could bring him some news. Nothing for it but to wait. Teetering on the fence between sleep and waking, Walt pictured Pete and Jo running off hand in hand across the prairies and leaving him here helpless beside the snoring wallpaper salesman in the next bed. He lowered the oil lamp, nearly settled into sleep, but surfaced all at once. His eyes flew open. He knew where he was—in the great empty West. But Pete—where was Pete?

Chapter

❧ 5 ❧

Pete was climbing the St. Vrain Canyon from the prairies below along a thin wagon road with big Jack Wilcox and a string of mules bound for the White River Agency still two hundred miles to the west—across three ranges of shining mountains, through valleys, canyons, rivers, brush, rock, dust, and grass galore. You could tell it was a wagon road from the wagons smashed down the slopes below, as well as from the one they'd encountered earlier that day descending the canyon with a group of asthmatics and consumptives just heading back to Greeley after their summer camp cure in the mountains. Some sported a dollar-sized red spot on each pale cheek, the mark of consumption. They reminded Pete of Josie. He was going to see Josie! Across endless mountains with ten mules for Father Meeker and a last-minute consignment of paper bags . . .

It was slower than taking the train to Rawlins and dropping down from Wyoming Territory into White River, but ten mules on a train cost nearly as much as ten people, thus consuming their profits, and the scenery in Wyoming was rumored to be dull. This route shortened the distance and lengthened the trip, forcing them up and down instead of around, but the mules had all the free forage they wanted. In Wyoming they would have had to resort to chewing on each other's tails.

As they climbed up the canyon, Jack pointed out streams where he and his friend Mountain Jim Nugent had trapped thirty years ago, before fashions in men's hats shifted from felt to silk, and the beaver trade collapsed. He remembered these mountains before white folks came, excepting himself and Jim Nugent, of course; Jim still lived up at the head of this canyon. Now people trekked all the way from Denver and Greeley just to look at the scenery, and the consumptives told Jack another party had preceded his and Pete's by two days: a survey team in two wagons filled with tripods, brass barometers, photographic equipment, pencils, clipboards, compasses, and parchments, the chief triangulation party of Mr. Ferdinand Hayden up from Denver to map the territory. They'd already plotted a six-mile base line from the foot of Long's Peak down to Estes Park.

Surveyors! screamed Jack. First come the prospectors and cattlemen, then the gentleman hunters, then the consumptives, then the survey-ors—then the taxes, the laws, the damned police, the city fathers, the teetotalers and farmers. By the time the women and children show up it's a lost cause for sure . . .

Pete filed Jack's rantings away in his memory for the Greeley *Tribune*, as he planned to write this trip up when he returned. He could make it a series! He hoped to meet the famous Mr. Hayden in Estes Park, but by the time they got there the surveyors were gone, the mountains had swallowed them. At Devil's Gate, gazing down into the wide Estes Valley, they spotted several large herds of Texas cattle among the scattered pines and lemon-yellow aspens. Across the way, the valley was dwarfed by huge gray mountains with gorges in their folds—the mountains they'd cross the next day, said Jack. A river ran through it, and one orange lake reflected blue peaks. To the left, Long's Peak had snagged a huge cloud which the setting sun was igniting red. Blue shadows crept out of canyons on their way to do some kind of nightly mischief. This was bosky land, and its colors kept changing: blue to yellow to green to black.

"I do believe there is a God!" shouted Jack.

"Looks empty to me."

"Empty, Pete? You are a piece of work. I wouldn't send *you* to tell shit from honey. Folks that cross mountains should keep their eyes skinned." Jack pointed with the rifle he carried across his saddle horn out of mountain-man habit. Sure enough, back there up above the meadow they'd just ridden through, set up toward the trees on a darkening hillside, stood a cabin, a corral, horses, and goats, not a quarter mile away.

They turned and rode back. Before the dogs could bark and the horses panic, Jack began shouting, "Halloo the house!" The place looked black and half caved in. Smoke curled out of the roof and window. A dog outside with the head of a mastiff and body of a collie growled at their approach. The rear half of a steer hacked up with promiscuous abandon lay outside amid rusted tins, horseshoes, furs, antlers, and horns of deer and elk strewn in the hardening mud. A cone of glistening offal flared up just then in the setting sun with magnificent splendor. "Halloo the house!" The mud roof was covered with furs laid out drying, and a whole beaver skin had been nailed to the door. To Jack, of course, it looked just like home . . .

The door swung open on leather hinges and Jim Nugent stepped out.

The cautious greeting of Mountain Jim and Jack Wilcox surprised Pete at first. Jack swung off his horse and these two old friends who hadn't seen each other for more than ten years looked askance and sniffed around warily like dogs. Jack had described his friend to Pete as eight feet tall and over five hundred pounds, but in fact he stood about middle height and weighed considerably less than Jack. He'd once cut off a living man's head during a fight, according to Jack. A chunk of his forehead and side of his face had been removed by the operation of an axe or bear paw, and as a result one eye appeared as a loosened rip across the top of his cheek. But the nose looked handsome, the eyebrows were thick and black, and his hair, like Jack's, hung in long curls down to his collar beneath a crushed wideawake. He was ten or more years younger than Jack. Pete counted three ragged waistcoats on his torso, the first buttoned over a worn leather shirt. His buckskin trousers were stained with blood, but his boots looked brand new. He grinned at Pete, showing wooden false teeth as brown as weeds, then pulled off his hat in mock gallantry, and offered his hand to help him step down from his horse as though he regarded Pete as a girl.

Jack acted nervous and skittish around Jim. They'd trapped together, sure, but that didn't mean they'd always gotten along—he recalled that now. They'd once split over ways to cook rabbit. Jim couldn't see any way but boiling, with the head still on and the guts intact . . . An eerie cry came from the cabin, and a peacock ran out. Jack looked over the valley. "Whose cattle?" he asked.

"The earl," said Jim.

"What earl might that be?"

"Earl of Dunraven. He regards this whole valley as his."

"I didn't see no settlement."

"Can't see it from here. He got some affidavit men out to Denver and Longmont who swore homestead claims and sold him the claims. Says he owns the whole valley."

"That so?" said Jack. "I was thinking we could blow it all up."

"Might find gold."

"Not by a long jump."

"What's the mules for?"

"White River Agency."

"Scurvy beasts."

Pete looked back at their string of mules, who just stood there in line. They'd have to be hobbled. The thick-necked, hairy-legged, mouse-colored animals twitching their ears and flaring their nostrils tried looking as ugly and stupid as possible for Jim. Out of perversity, Pete walked up to the nearest and rubbed his head and neck. His long ears lay down and his eyes winked shut.

"What's for supper?" asked Jack.

"Beans and whiskey," said Jim.

"You serve lunch at this time?"

"Beans and whiskey," said Jim.

"How about breakfast?"

"Beans and whiskey, you donkey!" shouted Jim Nugent.

They walked inside while Pete hobbled the beasts. Something felt wrong here, Pete decided. He could jump on his horse and just keep riding, but where would Jack come in on that deal? And their string of mules bound for White River . . . As he led the animals down to some grass and tied their forelegs with thick leather straps, he thought of Josie. She was lonely without him! He pictured her picking beans in the kitchen garden at the Agency, watched over by half-naked Indians who, one by one, asked for her hand. She was sweating; loose strands of hair escaped from her twist and hung across her forehead. The muslin sleeves of her high-buttoned dress had been rolled up like a man's, revealing muscular arms. She'd fallen in the world, at least for a time, and Pete had risen—a newspaperman—so maybe there'd be a ledge in the middle large enough for the two of them to meet on. Not that they'd marry. Pete couldn't very well *marry*—could he? He looked up at Jim's hovel growing black in the dusk, then down at his arm—his own sleeves were rolled up—at the faint pink circles of newly healed skin on the back of his wrist, then broke into a jig on the grassy slope, but had to stop right away, as the thin mountain air made him dizzy. He clung to a mule's hairy back for a moment and felt for the lucky pouch around his neck. Mules were all right. Like portable trees. The air had turned cold—he was breathing needles—and the looming mountains across the valley had put on their cloaks. No, they wouldn't marry—out of the question—but they could maybe tread water together . . . He saw it in Josie—her difference matched his. Come weal or woe, fame or dishonor, success or misfortune, ain't we in it together?—most up to our necks . . .

That night he and Jack lay side by side beneath layers of buffalo robes on a straw tick thrown against the wall, fully clothed save for their boots. The stone fireplace ten feet away spit out stars of burning pitch pine. It seemed to give off more light than heat and more smoke than either, so Jim left the window unlatched. By the light of the fire, Pete could make out a long pine settle next to the fireplace on which Jim sat sipping his whiskey. In front of it stood a table covered with black oilcloth and some arthritic chairs, thrown together with a hatchet. Antlers hung on the walls, rifles stood in the corners, and five or six dark bundles of men lay thickly strewn about the room wrapped in army blankets on the bare floor. These men had barely said a word to Pete and Jack, or each other, all the long evening—just sat around cleaning their rifles, casting bullets in long-handled molds at the fireplace, rubbing grease on their boots, and sewing patches on their jackets. Winter was coming . . . Then, when Jim snuffed his candles and bitches—tins of bacon grease with wicks made of rags—they knocked their pipe ashes into the fire and curled up like dogs wherever they could manage to find a spot. It wasn't the most comfortable floor either, made, as it was, of thick disks sectioned from logs laid directly on the bare ground. Smaller disks filled the spaces between them, but still there was plenty of damp earth exposed. Shivering Pete under buffalo robes felt rather spoiled, though he'd surely been warmer sleeping beneath the stars just the previous night. It was evident that Jim had given them his bed. What about you? Jack had asked him.

I'll be outside leaning up against the wall.

You sleep here, said Jack. I can sleep anywheres myself. Give me the floor anytime above a bed. I can sleep lying down, standing, doubled up and hanging over, twisted, pinched, jammed and elbowed, snored at, sat upon and smothered, long as I don't get too awful cold.

You sound like a mattress, said Jim.

That I am. Here, you sleep beside Pete.

No thanks.

Jack snorted. Pete kept his trap shut.

Lying there in the shivering night he listened to the howls of wolves outside, the snores of the potter's field of cowboys on the floor—all employees of the Earl of Dunraven, as it turned out—and the endless talk of Jack Wilcox and Jim, who finally, after their beans and whiskey, had warmed to each other. Jack faced the fire, propped up on one elbow. Pete lay on his back beside him, watching shadows on the ceiling. Jim spit in the fireplace and fed it with pine logs that cracked like gunshots. A dark shape stirred and flowed across the room, threading the sleepers, either peacock or dog. "Heard from Sam-Art?" Jack asked.

"Gone under."

"Where's Clancy?"

"Gone under."

"If that don't beat all."

"A clever man as I ever know'd."

They both seemed to think about this for a while. Reflected light from the fireplace flashed overhead amid clouds of trapped smoke, and the room smelled of wood smoke, tobacco, and beans . . .

It shocked Pete to suddenly wake up—he hadn't felt tired. Jack and Jim were swapping stories about Indian battles which were a perpetual rain of ribs and vitals, or so it seemed. It was hard in Pete's half-awake state to tell voices from pictures, harder to know if evaporating scenes of violence had wafted from his mind or theirs. His eyes flew open. It seemed that a crow or some clumsy shadow had opened its black shape outside, and one fat wing was brushing the cabin . . .

Jim's stories favored severed heads and torture, whereas Jack's were partial to episodes of survival in which brave men were forced to such extremities as frying mule's blood or eating live ants. They'd told them all before, Pete knew. Inside the words more words hatched from slippery eggs, and more inside those.

Jack began a long one. He'd been living with a tribe of Utes, he said. One Ute ran off with an old man's wife and took with them his daughter from his first wife, who'd died. So Jack led a party of angry Utes in pursuit of the eloping couple. He detailed the various kinship ties between the search party and the wife, but Pete lost track. They crossed starving deserts, they humped it through canyons. One by one his party fell off, dead of ambuscades or distracted by hunting. It seemed the runaway couple had their allies too, and soon Jack found himself the one being chased. Someone touched coup: a hand out of nowhere ketched at his shirt, and then they were on him. One took his shoulder and one his leg. They had a tug of war, and damn if they didn't manage to tear off most of his clothes. But he scratched and gouged and effected his escape with a hundred screaming injuns clamoring after him up a narrow confine in the mountains. He grabbled up the sides but came down in a slider. He shot three of the varmits right then and there, and gave two more red devils the quietus with his ax, but still they flew at him. He was running blood from dozens of holes in his back, the canyon narrowed and closed to a pinch, it turned out a box canyon, that made him feel queersome. He couldn't go further and couldn't turn back! He made a raise of his rifle and pulled the trigger but nothing happened. Empty. They was screaming and barking coming up fast, he threw the rifle down, feeling the damn cliff hugging his back close as a toucher—someone put a ball into him, he felt gone under, he fell down chewallop. He figgered they wasn't anything for it, so—

"So?"

"So. There ain't no backout in *me.*"

"So what happened?" asked Jim.

"I like to die right there. Almost did."

"What happened?"

"Keep your shirt on, Jim. I don't care to be hurried. You got wood ticks on your Johnny?"

"Spit it out, Jack. What did you do?"

"I was younger then. Had more funk in me."

"So? What happened?"

"More funk than a bull with its tail up."

"*So!*"

"So I clum to my feet, screamed in their faces, and—"

"And—"

"Scalped myself!"

Jim held fire. He hawked from his nose and spit on the floor. "That kills me right up, Jack. Tell that one to your pretty friend there."

"Don't be so squamptious."

"Don't I see through it?" Jim stood up. "You think to come it over on *me!*"

"I *scalped* myself, Jim. You seen the scar."

"You seen *this* scar?" Jim was pointing at his forehead, leaning out toward Jack, but the fireplace behind him left his face in shadow. "*This* child scalped himself ten years ago. Someone tole you that story, Jack, after they heard it from me."

"Fact! Scalped myself."

"Not by a long chalk. No pissant on earth scalped himself and lived to tell it save *me.*"

"Well, *I* done it, Jim . . ."

Pete closed his eyes. What next? They'd pull out knives, they'd roll around flailing on the floor. He thought of the story Jack had told him back in Greeley, and whispered in his ear, "I thought you said—"

"Shut your fly trap," Jack whispered back.

Pete closed his eyes and felt himself shrivel. He curled up like a bug, squirming into the covers.

No one pulled a knife. Instead, Jim stormed out. A few minutes later, a blast of gunshot had Pete and Jack pulling on their boots. Outside, the stink of gunpowder hung sharp in the air. The sky overhead still held enough pale light to reveal Jack down there leaning against a mule. "Help me give this one a shove." The three men heaved and the mule keeled over, with a crash like they'd toppled a mountain. Then Pete realized it was dead.

"That mule cost me twenty-five dollars," he said. He found himself fumbling in his pocket for the bill of sale.

"Worst waste of money I ever heard."

"How come you shot him?"

"Damn fool mule wouldn't get off my foot. I came out to piss on him."

"Is this a private quarrel," asked Jack, "or religious belief?"

"I hate mules. They're as scurvy a set of quadrupeds as ever demoralized any community."

Pete was waving his papers around with such distraction that Jack had to take his arm. He'd borrowed from the bank in Greeley to buy those mules, confident that Nathan would pay up pronto. The death of one wiped out half his profits. "I wouldn't care to be so extravagant myself of other people's goods."

"You don't say? Why, you must not be a base fellow."

"You didn't have to shoot him."

"Best idea I had all night." In fact, Jim seemed to have calmed down somewhat. "That mule was slumped anyway. He'd of stoved in halfway to White River." They started walking back to the cabin. Jack had inserted himself between Pete and Jim, but that didn't prevent the latter from reaching around and, of all things, pinching Pete's buttocks. "Don't be so chopfallen."

Pete clammed up. In the dark he felt himself blushing. Some folks make you tired . . . He could tell him to put it in his ass, then run off, but run to where in these endless mountains? And what about the other nine mules? Must steel my feelings . . . He could knock him upside the head with a poker when he wasn't looking, he'd done that before back in South Carolina—he'd stopped a man from beating his wife. Cracked him with a poker and pinned him down with a chair while the knife went in—

Pete felt small and far away.

Back under the covers next to Jack, the certain knowledge that Jim could just as easily kill *him* as any mule spread across Pete and shrank his moist skin. The drunker Jim got the more he baited Pete. Of course, Jack would protect him—wouldn't he? In a bad, disagreeable place, the main thing was to last long enough to get yourself out. You could scarcely afford to indulge the natural outrage anyone might feel when some stranger took an irrational disliking to you, for no reason at all. For your looks, say. It was uncontrollable, like a bad dream. Jim sat on his settle beside his fire looking into his jug. Pete hoped it was empty. "One thing I can't stand," said Jim, "is when a growed-up man looks like a girl. You kallate me, Jack?"

"Sure, Jim, sure."

"Men shouldn't look like wimmin. They shouldn't. Sweet-scented fop and pomatum-perfumed dandies. You're trying to converse with some sheer dog-mean mule, and a little ketch-fart interferes with your privacies. Some foofaraw. That's just like the girls. They don't like wine bibbers and rum suckers neither, now do they, Jack?"

"They sure don't, Jim."

"Little work plugs, so dainty and sweet. Little toothpick hands. Makes me feel tired. Little piss quicks. Pop nuts. Daisies. Dinky little poofballs for feet . . ."

"They don't care for whiskey neither, do they, Jim?"

"They sure don't, Jack."

"Not like you, Jim. Not like a man."

"Not by a long jump."

"You love your likker better'n your God, now don't you, Jim?"

Jim stood up and stepped toward the bed. He was leaning over, staring at Jack, whose whiskered face barely poked from the covers. Staggering back in a slow double take, he stammered out, "Fact. Jack—that's audacious! I love my likker better'n my God. That's so—that's so—that beats all off hand. That's—*some*—Jack—that's *some* . . ." He crashed to their feet.

He still lay there at dawn in the tea-colored light when Jack woke Pete. Quiet as girls, they slipped out of the covers, took their boots in hand, and tiptoed around all the sleeping bodies to the slumping door. Cold—it was freezing! Puddles outside had turned rock-hard. They had to unpack their buffalo robes to wrap themselves in for the trek through the valley. Then up—up so high, Pete felt little springs singing in his blood, spring-tailed creatures snapping awake. His heart didn't beat, it fluttered like a duck's. They climbed all morning through hoarfrost and ice, up past the tree line into full sunlight where mountains inflated, unfolding around them into the cold sky itself.

Jack led the way, then came the mules in a single line, while Pete brought up the rear, looking back now and then, half expecting that Jim had followed them. The smoky plains back there merged into clouds sixty or seventy miles east somewhere over Greeley, too far to see. Between here and there, the foothills and mountains—gray and blue folds—trapped hidden parks surrounded by mountains whose lateral valleys and gorges shot down out of sight. The winding, humpbacked ridge they were on shrunk Pete, Jack, and their remaining nine mules, who crawled across it like aphids. Just nine, thought Pete . . . To his left, the ridge dived into a gorge so long and deep it had to be the place where all the blue shadows that crept out of canyons at sunset were manufactured. Across the gorge, a line of mountains posed, arm in arm, fat and skinny, cone-headed, bull-browed, like politicians on the courthouse steps. Their gray faces reflected the passing clouds, but they weren't faces—Pete knew that—they weren't human at all, only blank massive cliffs and escarpments and talus slopes and peaks. You could tell you were somewhere you shouldn't be up here in the sky when the cold wind sucked the air from your lungs, the highest, thinnest air Pete had ever breathed.

They lunched on jerky, raisins, and hardtack.

By evening they were starting down the other side toward a basin of puddles and salt ponds hovering just above timberline. The mountain sheep gathered there struck Pete for sure as what God must have planned mules to become before he lost his concentration. Beyond this basin the trees began again, and down in the folds of the land ahead of them, Jack had told Pete, was Indian country. Oh sure, they'd see white men maybe, a few miners and prospectors, a rancher or two, if they saw anyone at all between here and White River. But mostly this was where the Ute wandered, though they wandered so much and blent in so well they might not pop up until the Agency itself.

Fine, Pete thought. Fine . . . They'd met enough savages to hold him a while. He fingered his pouch. Least I'm still alive . . .

They hoped to make that tree line by sunset. As the sun sank ahead of them, the night began rising in waves below from the shadows and canyons. At least the wind had died down. Lucky me—lucky! thought Pete. I'm alive! It struck him that what Jim Nugent didn't realize was how much he and Pete actually had in common. Jack Wilcox too. All three were self-created. Why, Pete had scalped himself too in a sense, but he didn't brag about it. If they only knew! Self-created men recollect the past gingerly, and if a memory doesn't fit, they rearrange it, chuck it, or invent a new one. They become the persons other people see. But they don't lean on others—they rely on themselves. Of course, Pete hadn't hacked and clawed his way through life as Jim and Jack had, more like darted here and there, dodging giants' lurching feet, or buzzing loops around their outstretched fingers. He'd always known when to fly off, and just what opportunities to cling to. He was quick. He believed in himself— even the lies—and thrived at other men's feasts. It took wits, pluck, and luck, or just keeping your mouth shut. He'd been scared last night, sure—not for the first time. He'd focused on the exact location of the iron poker beside the fire, in case he had to scramble out and use it. He would have used it—wouldn't he? He'd done it before . . . Fact was, you got *more* scared later, when the danger blew over. Even now, at the end of their long string of mules, he felt that a bullet or flying hatchet could just plow up his spine out of nowhere. Instinctively, he leaned forward on his horse. Going downhill made your belly slosh around. He thought he heard a click back there—shotguns loaded with nails could blast you forever into rabbit squeal—but he wouldn't look back. Days from now— years—he'd still be moving with a twitch and a jerk like a headless chicken out of harm's way . . .

Jim had narrowed considerably Pete's calculated profits from this trip. He could hike Nathan's price up to forty dollars a mule, to make up for the dead one. Sixty-seven fifty for him and Jack, plus two more each for the paper bags. It was government money, after all. Fifty dollars a mule! But he couldn't do that to Father Meeker, who'd given him his newspaper to mind, even if he'd also spirited his daughter away . . . Pete spurred his sorrel to catch up with Jack, as the line of tan and black mules now seemed fixed for all of eternity. The tundra below them had flared up red beneath a red and blue sky, and the beautiful gray and white mountain sheep—each carrying proudly on its handsome head a kind of granite fist—were sniffing the wind with flaring nostrils, as though mistaking mule smell for something more randy. "I *do* believe," shouted Jack. "I *do* . . ." For no reason he could think of, Pete felt himself blushing.

From Jack's saddle hung paws and tails of beaver, mink, and marten. A black rag of some sort also hung there in front of Jack's leg which Pete hadn't noticed till now—because it hadn't been there before.

"What's that?" he asked.

"This?" Jack fingered the thing and hardened his face. He squinted at Pete to curb his reaction. "It's my *scalp*, you lackbrain . . ."

At the White River Agency, Shadrach Price, at Nathan Meeker's orders, had been plowing up sections of the Utes' horse pasture for the past week or so. He was cautious at first, and merely nibbled the edges along strips looping down from the Agency's irrigation ditch, taking special care to steer well clear of the Utes' beloved racetrack. But gradually the strips shrunk the forage for horses and encroached sufficiently on Canavish's land—Johnson to the whites—that the Indian complained to Josie. At least she listened. First he wants us to dig a ditch, he said, then plow up the pasture, then plow the corrals for our horses. Then the land where we put our *carniva*. Then the land where he said our new houses would be . . .

Josie approached her father uneasily as advocate for the Utes. Daddy had their welfare at heart, after all. He wanted to do good, to improve their lives, to lead them by gradual stages into civilization, if civilization would have them. Not that civilized people were any great shakes, Josie knew that. She pointed out to her father that the cause of reform might be furthered if white people studied the Utes for a change. After all, their lives had been guided by principles of cooperation predating Mr. Fourier by centuries . . .

Then let them cooperate, huffed Nathan.

Rumors flew among the Utes that Josie caught wind of. The agent was always writing to Washington, writing bad things about them. He wanted to kill all their horses. A wagon was on its way right now full of handcuffs and rope to hang them all with . . . Josie assured them that none of this was true. Father would never consent to such doings. She brought the two sides together for negotiations, and they agreed that Father Meeker could plow half the horse pasture and fence the rest off. Or did they? Nathan thought they meant all the horse pasture as far as the racetrack, while Jack assured Johnson and Douglas that only a strip one hundred feet wide would be cut by the big curved knife dragged behind Mr. Price's oversized horses. So when Shadrach Price's team made their turn and the strip grew considerably wider than that, two of Johnson's sons shooting at marks let one of their shots sort of wander near Shadrach. It kicked up some dirt and the mules stopped plowing. Next to where they stopped something glittered between hummocks of earth, catching the afternoon sunlight. The only way to tell what that was was to shoot at it, boys. Good targets were hard to come by . . .

At the second shot, the big curved knife yanked loose from the ground, and Mr. Price and the mules ran off across the fields, dragging their empty harnesses behind them . . .

More negotiations. Nathan was furious. He wanted the culprits caught and punished. For shooting at targets? Utes can shoot at *targets* . . . The plowing went into temporary remission.

Meanwhile, life at the Agency went on. At Josie's boardinghouse and school, she and Flora Ellen Price—Shadrach's sixteen-year-old wife— showed the Ute girls how to lace up corsets and make themselves sweet with eau-de-cologne. They played hymns on the Meekers' ornately carved organ, recently arrived by wagon from Greeley—the same organ they'd shipped by train from New York to Colorado three long years ago—and taught the braves and squaws to sing "Come Ye Sinners, Poor and Needy" and "When I Survey the Wondrous Cross." They administered Graftenberg pills to sick Utes, fitted them for shoes, and induced the young braves who liked to hang around and cast sheep's eyes at the two of them to apply a coat of fresh white paint to everything inside the school and boardinghouse—walls, floors, furniture, cupboards. Nathan had built this boardinghouse for Greeleyites he hired to work at the Agency, and for the Ute children who would be Josie's pupils and whom he thought best to separate from their nomadic parents. Now enrollment was down to one pupil, who didn't board anyway . . . They held classes the way the Indians ate, whenever they felt like it. With the Agency full for the general issue, more braves than ever came by during the day to watch Josie teach her one pupil or to pester Flora Ellen for food. The girls played Spanish monte in the kitchen with them, unbeknownst to Nathan or to Shadrach Price. The women had turned brown from the summer, and both favored loose cotton dresses which clung to their legs above the boot tops and stayed open at the necks. Flora Ellen's two children, one a mere toddler, liked to spin like dust devils through the rooms of the boardinghouse out onto the porch, down the steps and through the pastures.

Josie felt ready to sprout in the sun. She worked in the kitchen garden digging fall potatoes with her sleeves rolled up, sweat running down her arms, and dust clinging to the sweat. For someone so thin, her forearms were strong. The veins on her hands stood out like cords. Beyond the milk house, across the river, the green hills in the afternoon sun looked ten feet away. At the base of the hills the aspens had started to yellow, and the reddish tinge of oak brush and chokecherry scrub spread like a rash on the slopes above them. In a fencelike chute down near the river, one of Johnson's daughters had tied a cow with a tendency to kick and was crouching down to milk it. The September sun put things on display. The least bit of dust appeared sharp and visible. This sun dried you up from the inside out, turning your throat to raw silk in the process. If it blackened the logs on their houses so quickly, it likely did the same to hemorrhaging wounds tucked away out of sight in Josie's blackened insides. It turned blood clots to powder . . . Her dry nostrils sucked in two streams of sunlight, and her lungs, over time, turned to layers of paper like a pair of wasp's nests. That was surely why—Josie reflected—some older Ute women looked every bit like Egyptian mummies. They were rumored to be well past one hundred . . .

Utes were gathering for the afternoon races. Josie figured she'd dig one more row, then join her friends—Pausone, Tim, Serio, Jane—at the racetrack. They liked to ply her with cigarettes, and Daddy couldn't very well spot her smoking among those clouds of reddish brown bodies. They stood closer together than white people did. When they shouted and stirred in the growing twilight, with sunlight slanting through chinks of skin—narrow hallways of flesh in the crowd—she felt inside a living tree with swaying limbs and clattering leaves. Sometimes they broke into song around her. They seemed to have no secrets. They had no insides distinct from their outsides. They didn't—as she always had—submit all their motives to a high-powered microscope and become that much more selfish in the fanatical effort to root out selfishness . . .

She could be like them. With her inner eye she'd watched the spot on her lungs growing smaller all that summer. What would Pete think when he saw her! Sometimes the wind blew right through her body, and at first she'd felt horrified at this violation—then realized how much she'd once cherished her own vile impurities, hugged them protectively. The larval death she'd nurtured inside her, stuck underneath a niche in her lungs, had withered like a raisin. Death seemed laughable. How did people die? It seemed so far away. Oh yes—they began in the morning feeling well as ever, turned sickish in the stomach by afternoon, ate little or no supper in the evening. Then sat before the fire saying next to nothing, then went to bed—woke up in the night in a feverish chill as though all their limbs had softened to jelly. Went out doors—saw the cold stars—came back to bed shivering, dreamed bad dreams, failed to rise the next morning, felt themselves sinking . . . The doctor called, and a few days afterward the coffin arrived . . .

With her dry mouth wide open, Josie laughed and stood up, too quickly as it happened. The little stars popping in her eyes made her feel dizzy, but she shook it off. Something rang in her ears and insects swarmed up. She bent down to lift her basket of potatoes, then felt herself moving. The ground seemed to tremble. Her mouth opened up and noises came out—shouts, laughter, shrieks, jabbers. The part of her she left behind wanted to admonish the Utes for trampling her garden, but she let it go as the crowd surged past pulling her with it. They'd all left the races running up here . . . Down by Johnson's house a fence was cut open and two bewildered mules stood there watching. Behind them a plow lay tipped in the grass. Josie looked around for someone she knew, but the faces shining with excitement ignored her. In the midst of the crowd as it surged ahead, Johnson took the longest strides, emerging from the others with his own inviolable armor of air. People backed away even as they followed him, saying his name with awe—*Canavish*. His face was painted. At the ends of his arms swung glutted fists. Josie felt the excitement in the air and something else—confusion—slate shattered with a hammer. When Johnson leaped up onto Nathan's porch, swinging his long arms, the crowd fell back. But Johnson knocked, he was being polite . . . Josie pushed forward to jump up there with him, but the weight of the crowd held her back. Arvilla ushered Johnson inside and the crowd waited nervously, uncertain whether to explode or go home.

"Your father plow again. Johnson angry." Pausone stood by her side. His eyes wandered over her face searching for a way inside. Josie felt her own gaze narrow and dart here and there, like jittery beads. Pausone stood close, as though to protect her. He'd asked her to marry him twice that summer.

The door flew open and Nathan came out backwards, his long strides matched by those of Johnson, who seemed to be pushing him with powerful hands gripping Nathan's shoulders, maybe lifting him up, it was hard to tell. Josie flushed and grew angry; something tugged at her innards. Beneath its yellow and blue painted stripes, Johnson's face looked beet red, while Nathan's had turned gray as cold water. Johnson pushed him across the porch to the crowd's growing laughter and shrieks. "Can't you make him stop?" She found herself shouting. "Someone stop that man!" She knew his name, yes; still, he'd grown strange . . .

A ripple went through Johnson's arms, his muscular form surged forward in a wave, and Nathan slowly rose, as if floating backwards. Johnson pushed him back off the porch. Behind, a hitching rail caught the small of Nathan's back, and his feet shot up in a swinging arc, making the Indian jump back quickly, arms still extended. Nathan raised a cloud of dust landing. The Utes laughed and shouted, but parted for Josie rushing forward to help her father. Then it was over. They just walked away. Johnson strode off to repair his broken fence. Nathan Meeker looked up at his daughter as if from the bottom of a well, hardly recognizing her. His confusion seemed to have cushioned the fall—or maybe the fall had spilled the confusion. All at once he became an old man. Arvilla had rushed down from the porch and together they helped him to stand. He looked around at the Agency buildings as though he'd been dropped there from a passing cloud. His wife and daughter commenced brushing him off. Shadrach Price rushed up with two other white men. Angrily, Nathan spit out dust— as though eating dust were the true indignity—and the color slowly returned to his face. Then he smiled.

White River Agency
Colorado Territory
September 10, 1873

Hon. L. A. Hayt
Commissioner, &c.
Washington, D.C.

Sir: I have been assaulted by a leading chief, Johnson, forced out of my own house, and injured badly, but was rescued by employees. It is now revealed that Johnson originated all the trouble stated in letter September 8. His son shot at the plowman, and the opposition to plowing is wide. Plowing stops; life of self, family, and employees not safe; want protection immediately; have asked Governor to confer with General Pope.

N. C. Meeker,
Indian Agent

Chapter

❧ 6 ❧

South of Rawlins, Wyoming Territory, the wagon road to White River Agency crosses sixty miles of rolling desert spotted here and there by islands of reddish eroded hills before the gathering earth tumbles up into mountains in Colorado Territory. This was the route Pete and Jack had forgone for their beeline, the one-hundred-and-eighty-mile trek from the Union Pacific depot in Rawlins down to White River. It was also the Utes' main avenue up to buffalo country from the reservation, but no Utes were on it. Jo hadn't seen one, despite Stokes's insistence that red men lurked behind every hill. Stokes claimed to have a sixth sense about these matters; his purchase in Rawlins of five genuine Indian scalps from a desperado named Liver-eating Johnson—that's *human* livers—had qualified him as the Indian expert of their little party, or so he thought. He planned to take the scalps back to London, along with, of course, his Napoleonic trophy, as fresh stock for his neglected business.

Jo had also made a purchase in Rawlins. From a Chinese druggist in a board-and-bat shack on the edge of town—his residence and business—he'd obtained a stoppered decanter of laudanum whose high concentration of five grains of opium per spoonful enabled him to indulge a preventative without the bother of avoiding a habit. A spoonful a day assisted respiration in that air-starved climate, promoted regularity as well, and warded off everything from consumption to diabetes, syphilis, cholera, and rheumatism. He'd already taken his teaspoon that morning . . .

Now he sprawled in the back of the wagon driven by Stokes, gazing up at the enormous blue sky with its high cirrus clouds resembling starved fish. Ghosts of fish bones and fossilized ferns. His mouth felt dry but his mind was well oiled; that most pleasant medicine smoothed out wagon roads too . . .

Stokes manned the reins, and Count Léon-Fernand-Léon, legs crossed—half turned away—sat beside him. They'd purchased this wagon and two ghastly horses from a half-pint supplier in Rawlins for the outlandish sum of three hundred dollars, and Count Léon, their banker, paid every penny, adding the cost with a public flourish to the debit column in his expense account. Already Jo and Stokes had spent a thousand dollars each of the money promised them, including train tickets with luxury accommodations from New York to Colorado. From the same supplier in Rawlins, the count had bought a pony for Bonny, a Shetland barely three feet high, and induced a saddler to devise a harness sufficiently small to hitch it to Stokes's Punch-and-Judy wagon. Bonny sat back there now, out of range of their dust, thirty or so feet behind, perched up on the edge of the portable stage like a teeter doll tipping this way and that. Every now and then he lurched forward with a jerk. Poor little man had the hiccups . . .

He wondered where on the wide earth they were. White rocks stuck up out of sickly yellowish-orange hillocks, and one long ridge on their right gripped the desert with stubby knuckles, between which dried arroyos fanned down. Far to the left, where the land went perfectly flat, dust devils like crazy wire springs flexed back and forth before dissolving into air. Between clumps of sage and rabbit brush the wagon ruts ahead looked cracked and dry. Felt like they were climbing, the land seemed to tilt—yet everything around was level as water. Behind, Bonny felt them dragging a tail like some many-sectioned prehistoric beast, and at the end of that tail he sensed his own little brain with its half-empty thimble of memory slowly trailing parched drops. A train—he remembered a train in the night. The canyons and towers and tunnels of a city . . . Ahead, he sneezed in the lingering dust and felt like a creature with both nostrils plugged whom nature had nonetheless somehow managed to interest, let's say, in mating . . . He breathed through caves in his windy skull. In that barren landscape—barren with a vengeance— Bonny sensed a kind of fulfillment just across the horizon, a promise of completion. It wasn't unlike slipping into a bath; you felt that your body might possibly be—of all things—a source of comfort! And that buzzing sound—it came from the sky—though he knew it was also his own straining throat offering to hum the lingering words, *I wants it, I wants it* . . .

Their trip so far hadn't passed without incident. Though the country was empty, with neither a house nor a person in sight, they'd distinctly heard a gunshot yesterday, and Bonny had felt something whistle past his head. Just one shot, not a flurry or exchange. It shrank so immediately in that huge, silent land that five minutes later each of the men realized he must have imagined it, each except Bonny, who possessed no imagination distinct from his buggered-up senses, only nebulous wants . . . If it weren't for wanting, he'd have had no feeling for time passing either; the gunshot lingered, it didn't recede—it stayed right there as a scratch upon space . . .

Then, sometime after the gunshot, a tremendous, thundering clamor shook their wagons, and Bonny noticed that Stokes up ahead had pulled off the faint road into the sagebrush. Bonny himself was slower to react. Events stuffed his brain, they didn't occur and then unwind. Suddenly, lathered-up horses roared past on all sides, carrying men in blue uniforms of every shade with two days' growth of whiskers spiking their dust-coated faces and hats cocked forward to breech the dust. Little Bonny and his trembling pony, surrounded completely by thundering giants, remained there stunned when the troops were gone just as quickly as they'd come, heading south. Like the gunshot, they hung in the air. They didn't pass, they piled up forever—always happening—then faded slowly like patches of light still cocooned inside closed eyelids . . .

Later, a white owl at dusk lunged at Bonny from a hillside, apparently mistaking him on his cart for an incautious prairie dog on its rock. And sometime before or after the owl came the man in green goggles, pushing his handcart. In thousands of miles of empty country, their paths met at their only intersection with another wagon road, the old Overland Trail. He was on an east-west axis, while theirs was north-south, so they made a great X and converged in the center—though of course he might have been waiting there . . .

He wore large green goggles, to prevent the alkaline dust from burning his eyes. His nose looked filthy. Bonny thought his disgusting mouth was maybe bleeding, but the man told them he smeared tomato sauce across it every few hours, to counteract the caustic dust. Dressed in skintight bell-bottom pants, an old army coat, a tall silk hat, the metal frame of which showed through its worn edges, with a large red label stuck in the band reading "Superior Cocktail Bitters," he stood there at a crossroads in the middle of the desert with a coffee pot full of hot coals in one hand and green goggles on his face.

All up and down both sleeves of his coat were pink and blue garters.

His large handcart was piled high with boxes containing—he showed them—all manner of garters, along with washboards, meat cleavers, belt buckles, scissors, Reina Victoria cigars, witch hazel for mosquitoes, and Holland gin and lemon extract for the ague. Mosquitoes? Ague? In *this* climate? asked Jo.

Never can tell when it might get damp. Folks heading south had rivers to cross . . .

As for the garters, those he sold to fandango girls in the various saloons along his route. He was coming right now from Bug Town, below Hahn's Peak—where some placer gold had been found—and heading for Rock Springs and then Fort Bridger, a mere two hundred and fifty miles between saloons . . . Cigars?

How much?

Two bits each.

Stokes and Jo each paid without question that inflated price for the rare sensation of smoking a perfectly fresh cigar in the middle of nowhere. Count Léon-Fernand-Léon turned away, refusing to acknowledge this unseemly mirage. They lit their cigars at the stranger's pot of coals—which he offered to sell them at five cents the coal—but Stokes claimed he had plenty of fuzees.

"They tend to dampen," said the man with green goggles.

"In *this* climate?" laughed Stokes.

The man laughed along with him, a sputtering laugh, hardly social, entailing as it did some reddish dribbles. His indistinct eyes looked trapped in those goggles. "Washboards? Meat cleavers?"

"No thankee. We're fine."

"Scissors? Fine scissors . . ."

"No need for scissors," Jo shot in. He'd jumped back in the wagon puffing his cigar, and sat on a plank nailed across the sides, leaning forward impatiently, as though they were holding up traffic out here.

"Best be going, then."

"How much cost the scissors?" Count Léon-Fernand-Léon had turned on his seat to address the man.

Around them, the desert seemed raised on a platform. Bluish mountains far to the south just managed to poke up from beyond the horizon. Shadows of clouds moved over sagebrush hills and ridges, lingering in the dried creek beds. Five ants stood at a crossroads and talked . . .

"How much cost the scissors?"

"One American dollar."

The count tossed his jangling purse down to Stokes, who paid the man a silver dollar, enough to buy ten pairs of scissors back east. "Scissors?" said Stokes.

"I am needing a haircut."

The man rummaged in his cart for the scissors, coming up with a little fan-shaped box, which he handed to Stokes—who passed it up to the count—who opened it and peered inside. "These are—satisfactory."

Then Stokes jumped back up and took up the reins, while the salesman gave his handcart a heave—it seemed they might crash—but he let Stokes go first. Waiting, he dipped two of his fingers into a blackened tin hanging by a cord from the back of his cart, and wiped more tomato sauce across his grinning mouth, coating the teeth as well as the lips. He tipped his hat at the departing wagon, then bowed low as Bonny drove past with his little pony and his puppet cart with its bold red letters painted on the sides: PLAYED BEFORE ROYALTY.

By the fifth day out, Jo had upped his dosage of laudanum to two teaspoons a day. Each morning he held the decanter to the light, pleased at the quantity remaining. Why, he'd hardly made a dent . . . They breakfasted on dried fruit and biscuits, as Stokes's Lucifer matches had somehow spoiled. The count, however, dined on oysters and paté, from a private reserve of tins he maintained under lock and key in a chest in the back of the wagon.

The count still dressed splendidly. He wouldn't allow a mere wilderness to alter his habits. To be sure, his black velvet cutaway had grown a bit dusty, and his yellow neck scarf soiled and stained, despite the efforts he made to dry his sweating throat with a white pocket handkerchief which he carefully removed, unfolded, folded again, wiped on his neck, unfolded, folded again, and replaced every hour or so. His knee breeches, black silk stockings, and low slippers were nothing if not practical in that desert heat; because water was scarce, he washed his nails with lemon, his hands and feet with bran, and cleaned his face each morning and evening with a dry sponge. When the alkaline dust proved too much to bear, he held a scented hanky to his nose.

He sat beside Stokes picking oysters from a tin. Behind them, Jo had slumped back in an opium reverie sprawled across three carpetbags and some blankets, clutching his gold-headed walking stick. Jo's natty clothes—single-breasted jacket, collar and tie, trousers of broadcloth—displayed an unpleasant tendency to wrinkle, as he slept in them evenings, whereas the count always changed to a nightgown once the sun went down, despite the cold. But the count wished he'd brought a valet for this trip. Sleeping in blanket rolls was bad enough—worse was to do it without assistance. He'd resolved not to give up anything to the wild outdoors—not his comfort, his taste, his charm, his condescension, his four delicious meals a day, his toilet, his beauty sleep. He had nothing but disdain for so-called pioneers, those rootless good-for-nothings whom civilization would never miss. He searched through the tin in his lap for the most promising oyster—the fattest and juiciest . . .

"You look like the little girl as gathered the eggs to bake her first cake."

The count regarded Stokes with disdain.

"Shall I flower his majesty a waistcoat?" Stokes laughed. "I shouldn't make a wry face, sir. You look stunning flash. You've done it up brown. You've not to stress you."

"Fool."

"But how do you know them are oysters, not pig nuts?"

Count Léon-Fernand-Léon tilted his head back and swallowed an ear-shaped oyster. "I could hire you as my taster. You would recognize pig nuts anywhere, monsieur."

"You're up to the business!"

The count held out his tin. "I suppose you would like one?"

"One! A lick and a smell . . ." Reaching over, Stokes looked behind: Jo lay there in the wagon bed with closed eyes and a blissful smile. "I'll have his share too, he don't need 'em." He winked at the count while mauling the delicate oysters with his fist, emerging with a dripping cluster he stuffed all at once in his mouth.

"*Cochon!*"

"A mite gritty."

"You must swallow, not chew!"

"Makes a cove thirsty. Makes a cove long for his favorite river."

Their wagon road skirted a dried-up creek bed whose cutbanks made brown canyon walls ten or more feet high. These canyons in turn wound and twisted inside wider canyons, whose walls, to their left, erupted in outcrops of pink and white rock like open sores or boils. The horses strained; they were breasting a ridge.

"He's poppycocked," said Stokes, pointing back.

"*Comment?*"

"Opium. It pots him proper."

The count turned to look at Jo.

"We could," said Stokes, "dispose of him now. Let him starve in the desert."

"Before we have the—item?"

"Ain't you 'ticed? I'm tired of his face." Stokes turned to wave at Bonny, so small back there on his cart. "He could help."

In his mind, the count exorcised Bonny, who struck him as an odd little devil, not to be trusted. He'd read the *Malleus Maleficarum*, which permitted the Church to burn necromancers and witches. Why not gremlins too? Mentally, he crossed himself, then glanced back at Jo in the wagon bed. "He has brought us this far. Let him finish the job."

"He's a burden to carry."

"We will soon be there."

"Them scissors you bought. They're terrible sharp."

"The better to cut my lovely hair."

"The truth of it is, they can cut more than hair, and save the extra outlay of gunpowder."

"Monsieur Stokes," said the count, "you must learn having patience." The count tossed his head; that shoulder-length hair, parted neatly in the middle, flared out like a skirt, then settled gently back. "The truth of it is—I need a haircut."

"Shall we pause at the next tonsorial parlor?"

"In the absence of civilization, one of us shall do."

"Who, might I ask?"

"Why—you!" said the count.

The wagon creaked forward beneath a hot sun. Sprawled behind the two men, Jo studied their swaying backs with half-open eyes—the walrus and the crane; the horse collar and the mop . . . Yes, scissors would do. The cunning bastards . . . The count was right, one must be patient, patient and cautious. Close your eyes when awake, and sleep open-eyed. We shall see who disposes of whom.

At the top of the ridge the horses paused, and Stokes saw something strange down below—trees and a valley! The land had turned green. The mountains were closer, a river appeared, with green smears of cotton-woods, prairie grass, and willows in its rolling drainage. The Little Snake River, Stokes announced. They were through the desert—halfway to the Agency . . .

Jo climbed up on the single board seat in the back of the wagon and audibly yawned.

"Bon joor," said Stokes.

Beside them, Bonny pulled up in his cart buzzing and humming. The buzz sounded familiar—a Mr. Punch buzz . . .

"My swazzle!" Stokes shouted. "You was strictly forbidden to place it in your mouth."

Bonny's voice buzzed with a nasal whine. "You was strictly forbidden to place it in your mouth!"

"You swallow it and see!"

"You swallow it and see!"

"It's bad luck!"

"Bad luck!"

"I know, as I swallowed that very one once."

Bonny seemed to think about this. His face began to drop. Jo laughed, the count brought his lavender-scented hanky to his nose and turned away . . .

"What's that?" said Jo. He'd stood up to peer down the faint road ahead of them. Between their rise and the river valley, the gently sloping land lay traversed by ravines shooting down to the river. These ravines were folds in the land, hard to tell how deep—but in one beside the road something large stuck out, a dark monolith tipped at an oddly skewed angle. It hardly looked like a natural occurrence, though your eyes played tricks in that wasting country. Stokes flicked the reins and his horse pulled forward; Bonny followed behind still buzzing and humming, but with the strangest taste in his mouth . . .

Whatever it was, it hardly grew closer. It jutted from the earth like a ship going down. From the back of the wagon Jo thought he saw something move up ahead, and reached into one of the carpetbags for a pistol, Stokes's pistol—a dueling pistol, of all things . . . Actually, it was Jo's. Stokes had brought with him on this trip the same dueling pistols he'd sold to the late Edmund Angelo Atkinson years ago in London, originally Jo's . . . Jo held it cocked in his lap and waited.

All at once they were there. A man approached them waving his arms. Pulled off the road were a wagon and horses, with a gleaming steam engine of iron and brass in the back of the wagon. Behind it, a huge, wooden, boxlike trailer fifteen or more feet long, all lined and webbed with nickel and brass and hung with pulleys, wheels, drums, belts, beaters, chutes, blowers, bins, platforms, shakers, and reels stuck out of a gully tilting up with its front hitch suspended in the air. "Can you give us a hand?" The man who said this, hardly more than a boy, sported lynxlike whiskers on his upper lip. His red checked shirt looked black on those high plains, where colors tended to run out to their farthest extremity.

A trap, thought Jo. "What is that thing?" From behind it, another man emerged, shovel in hand, face smudged with grease. "Threshing machine," said the boy.

"What's it doing out here?"

"Bound for the White River Agency," he said. "We was backing off the road to make room for some soldiers in a terrible rush. Backed into a gully we overlooked. Damn fool thing lifted the hind ends of two of our dray horses clean into the air. They whinnied like crazy. It was quite a sight! Had to cut their harnesses to free the horses, but now we can't budge it. Need more to push." The boy rubbed his mouth and stared at Bonny pulling up behind. Then he looked at the count—then slowly scanned the horizon as though trying to imagine what it might cough up next . . .

The other man, short and broad as a tree stump, walked up and tossed his shovel aside. The suspicious eyes in his mossy face regarded one at a time Stokes gripping the reins, the count sniffing his hanky, Jo sprawled in the wagon bed, Bonny humming and buzzing . . . "Where you gentlemen headed?"

"White River Agency," said Jo.

"Fine. We are too. Help us out of this gulley, we'll band together for protection."

"Protection?"

"Indian trouble," said the man.

"Haven't seen any Indians."

"Pray you don't neither. Them soldiers was flying. Must want a good reason for not stopping to help what they pushed off the road."

"And just—what might a good reason be?" asked Jo.

"Oh . . . Say, a massacree."

"Oh."

The men all stared at each other. Then the count perked up. "Is it quite—safe?"

"Safe as tearing the roof off from hell."

"I see," said the count.

"We could turn back," said Stokes.

"No need for that." Jo slipped his pistol back in the carpetbag.

"No need for pissing into the wind neither."

From the wagon behind came buzzing laughter. "Where's my stick?" shouted Bonny. "My kingdom for a stick!"

The count refused to help, and Bonny couldn't, so fragile and small— but with four men pushing, the thresher lurched forward out of the gully back onto its wheels, Father Meeker's prized threshing machine! Made at Battle Creek, Michigan, by Nichols, Shepherd and Company, designed to be belted to the ten-horsepower portable steam engine in the wagon pulled by the other horses—capable of threshing up to six hundred bushels a day . . . The two men explained to Jo and Stokes that the agent at White River considered it the better part of his mission to convert the Ute Indians to farming. He'd ordered this rig most a year ago now. The Indian trouble they'd heard of in rumors concerned the Utes' resistance to farming. The agent had plowed up their horse pasture, they said. So an injun attacked him—him, the agent. One of their chiefs!

Kill him? asked Jo.

Give him a sore back. The troops had been sent to restore law and order, but these freighters weren't really especially worried. The Utes were good Indians—friendlier than most.

Jo turned to Stokes. See? he said.

Stokes rolled his eyeballs to the sky.

The alliance of their two parties proved somewhat advantageous to Stokes. Once across the Little Snake, their road petered out—the road he was told back in Rawlins to follow—and he might easily have lost his way without these freighters who knew the route well, having hauled supplies from Rawlins down to the White River Agency for several years now. They carried hot coals in a coffee pot too! The land was greener now, and they'd entered the mountains, but entered them via a long broad valley. Mountains to the east, high mesas and ridges to the west, and straight ahead, much further south, still higher mountains rising gradually in layers. One knobby, spiny ridge to their right resembled the backbone of some prehistoric animal. A few cottonwoods and aspens clustered in the valley along their route beside a muddy creek, and the land folded down before them as they climbed.

On their seventh day out, they forded the Yampa River, then followed beside it through a deep, gentle canyon thick with cottonwoods between broad grassy fields. It rained for the first time since they'd left Rawlins, but the cottonwoods still clinging to their leaves made adequate shelter. Then they left the canyon. They climbed up a switchback on a faint wagon road, and followed across a series of ridges through high sagebrush country and sudden mountains. One yellow tower hard on their left broke through the trees in escarpments and cliffs. The freighters said Utes trapped eagles up there. They were close to the reservation border, they said, though still a good thirty miles from the Agency.

Near dusk they approached a gradual rise. Already, shadows crept from canyons wedged between mountains, but clouds in the sky straight ahead looked red. A huge lump appeared on the road before them. They approached it with caution. It proved a dead ox, with a hole in its head. Something popped in the distance. They found some expensive trash on the road—an abandoned saddle, a crate turned over and spilling out, of all things, fine china dishes broken in pieces strewn on the road . . . Flashes of light lit up the far mountains. Gradually in the growing dusk they realized they were smelling smoke. Acrid clouds of it blew in their direction, and out of the clouds came a clamor of hooves, then a riderless horse showing its eye whites. It galloped straight at them, veered off the road, crashed down a ravine . . .

Gunshots were plainly audible now.

They slowly creaked to the top of the rise, steam engine first, then the threshing machine with its folded straw stacker bouncing up and down, then Stokes's truck wagon and Bonny's puppet theater. Gradually the whole valley below them opened up in a panorama, with mountains and hills rising up on all sides and smaller hills rippling the valley floor. Snaking lines of fire sent up curtains of smoke around patches of already blackened grass. Bands of half-naked men, some on horses, rushed back and forth in every direction whooping and shouting; a few carried others on their backs up a ridge toward a stand of trees. Light from the fires glared up through the billowing smoke, while rays of the sun setting off to the right—behind tilting mountains—slanted across it. In the midst of the fires, a circle of horses, apparently dead, had been piled up as breastworks beside a gully around knots of besieged blue-coated soldiers. *Tak! Tak!* Puffs of white smoke rose up from their guns . . .

Chapter

❧ 7 ❧

Arvilla Delight Meeker didn't care for Pete. It was something about him *unnatural*, yes, something contrary to the order of things. Sure, he cheered Josie up, and Lord knows Josie needed cheering, what with her Indian friends gone across the river, or the squaws anyway—the braves had moved off north to the mountains. Josie had improved from listless brooding to brittle glee since Pete's arrival, but Arvilla suspected an unholy cause. He had a dark secret despite his good spirits—she saw right through him. His soul was black. Don't be fooled because he's a Pretty Man, Josie. Talkative was a Pretty Man too, and Talkative was a spot upon Christians! Talkative and Obstinate: Peter Doyle and Jack Wilcox. They'd done it all backwards, they'd crossed the Mountains of Difficulty by the Path of Danger only to come to this place of Destruction, and God knows where such brain-sick fellows will lead you, Josie . . .

Arvilla lay across her bed fully clothed, propped on one elbow thumbing through her favorite book, a cabbage-eared copy of *The Pilgrim's Progress*, by the light of an oil lamp and half a dozen candles. The others were gathered out there with her husband. Impossible not to hear Nathan through the door. "Well, if we have to treat them with kid gloves," he was saying, "for fear they may explode and go off, I say let them go off."

"*Father,*" said Josie.

"Where'd they go off to anyway?" A squeaky Pete-voice.

"Oh . . . somewhere else," said Nathan. "God knows they'll be back soon enough."

"I hope so," said Josie. "Pete's never seen a wild Indian close up."

"Well," said Nathan, "you don't know what you've missed."

She pictured his bitter smile as he said it, smudging the words. *You don't know what you've missed.* Since Johnson's attack he wore that smile all the time, the expression of someone whose fate, finally set in motion, was out of his hands. He'd done the right thing, let his persecutors act . . . He knew where the Ute braves had gone as well; he'd told Arvilla, but not anyone else, so as not to unduly alarm them. They'd painted and armed themselves and gone off to meet the troops coming to the Agency. How they'd found out soldiers were on their way Nathan wasn't sure. They had spies everywhere . . . Now who could guess what would happen next? Nathan had sent by secret runner a message to the troops that the Utes would be waiting at the reservation border. Let the soldiers negotiate, he said to his wife—he was tired of it himself. The Utes loved to talk and argue and dispute. The best that could happen was they'd come back convinced or chastened and take up the plow, but Arvilla hoped they'd be chastened so much they'd just stay away. Let them find what they deserved. I have the Mark on my forehead, she thought, I have the Roll sealed to comfort me by reading . . .

She thumbed back to her favorite passage, in which Christian warns his wife and children that their city will be destroyed by fire—but she hardens her heart against him. Well, Arvilla hadn't hardened her heart against Nathan, not this time at least. Thirty years ago at Trumbull Phalanx, when Nathan was a fire-breathing leveler, abolitionist, and Fourierite, she had—she withheld herself from him—and look what it got her: ten long years of cold silence and stubbornness . . . At Trumbull Phalanx, with two young children, they lived in a cramped log house with straw on the floor shared with two disagreeable families who wiped their hands on Arvilla's towels. There was no place to wash but the creek—no butter, no sugar, no tea, no coffee, no milk, and no wheat. Still, it was Ohio, she could visit her family—not like this place at the end of the earth. And the strange thing was that at Trumbull Phalanx, where they'd lasted six years, she hadn't once been ill, not for a day, though all those around her grew sick with the ague, or worse, died of fever. One by one they moved out or died. It had made Arvilla perversely proud to be strong enough to outlast what she hated so fiercely—but she'd been young then too. Four years after they left Trumbull Phalanx she finally relented, and Josie was conceived.

Then came Nathan's long pilgrimage, from the store in Illinois to the newspaper office in New York, to the house in Greeley, and finally here. What kind of man leads his wife through the Valley of the Shadow at age sixty? Why, he walked with a stoop—or had in recent days. Only she knew about the birthmark on his side, the long purple stain of his life of sorrow. He'd told her his mother had never allowed anyone else to see him naked, not even his father. No one had known. Arvilla had been so frightened at first she wouldn't allow him to touch her with his hands, let alone press against her. She wore her nightgown and he wore his. Later, after their ten-year abstinence, she embraced his naked body as a sign of the filth and abomination one might just as well give in to, since it was life on earth. A man of darkness entered her in darkness and she told him not to hurt her, though she wished he would . . . She grew to like filthy things—they filled her with inner sweetness, she decided. Like Saint Hedwig, who'd kissed the seat of a chair still warm from the leper who'd occupied it, she found dirty towels and discarded rags and kissed them, or bathed her face in the water in which her husband had recently washed his feet. What abominations she endured for the Lord, what filth and disease. What fornications and lies and filth and scum and corruption. What vomit and uncleanness and spit and shit and piss! But she offered it up . . . It was honey from a corpse.

If the way to Heaven lay by the Gates of Hell, as *The Pilgrim's Progress* said, then she must be on the way, but Lord, it was difficult. She'd never been ill a day in her life before coming to White River, and now look at her. She'd begun to shrink. Her spine had curled up like a green stick on fire. It was the climate did it—cracked your fingernails, made you lose hair, raised scales on your skin. The sun even dried out the springs in your eyes, the sun and the wind. She'd grown ugly too, she knew that. Some people thought she had no teeth because of the way her lips folded inward, pulling down on the nose and up on the chin until they nearly touched, but she had every single one, every shrunken yellow tooth. She just kept her mouth closed. Why speak if you had nothing to say? She preferred to stay indoors mostly, to lie on this bed when her husband was out. However, even retreating from unholy people had its hazards. *A Christian Man is never long at ease, / When one fright's gone, another doth him seize.* Often, when she'd gone off to be alone, someone or something stepped up softly and whispered shameful blasphemies in her ear, in such a way as to make her think that they issued from her own mind. She couldn't help thinking those horrible things—thinking how God must be laughing at her, for example. This was all his doing, this exile in the wilderness. He's abandoned us here. He's a coward, he's heartless. If he meant to torture us, then what was justice? A tyrant's justice . . . whimsy . . . madness.

Arvilla climbed off the bed and stood up. They were saying their goodnights out there already. Long past the stage of politeness, she didn't bother to go out and join them. Listening, she folded her hands at her waist and watched the closed door. She knew their ways. Younger people and public people all felt compelled to pretend they were happy and wise and enjoyed nothing more than each other's company, then the hand-shake and the hug sent them off beaming back to the Slough of Despond whence they'd come. Quickly, she changed to her nightgown and cap, extinguished the lights, and slipped under the quilt before Nathan could enter. She lay there in darkness, eyes wide open, and thought of the time her father had died, the year before she and Nathan met. He—her father—was then her age now, sixty-three. She'd thought of him often these past few weeks. She'd been the last of eight brothers and sisters, most of whom were gathered in the parlor one evening when he an-nounced out of the blue that something was wrong with him. He felt kind of funny . . . Six hours later he was dead. He'd taught her to spit in the first full pail of milk of the day. He'd taught her how to replace a cow's cud if it was sick and you saw it had nothing to chew, by stuffing an old piece of greasy dishcloth in its mouth . . . Where was he now? Did he walk in white with a crown of gold beset with pearls upon his head, in a place of bliss, with a harp in his hand?

"Arvilla?"

She lay there in darkness with both eyes open wide. The stale smell of sweat from Nathan's day wafted from the door when he closed it. He slowly undressed and climbed into bed.

They lay there breathing.

Then she turned to him, lifting his nightgown, and felt for the mottled stain on his side. The skin felt different, harder and smoother; his birthmark had never wrinkled as he'd aged, nor had hair ever grown on it. She traced the edge of it under his armpit down beneath his chest to his belly, this wondrous, milky, thin, rough skin, warmer and darker than all the rest of him. Her hand felt hot circling down. Suddenly, she lifted her own cotton nightgown, seized him by the shoulders and shook him hard, climbing on top. Lanky Nathan was over six feet tall, and Arvilla had shrunk in the past five years, so she squatted above him curled like a troll, feet at his knees, lips at his nipples, hands reaching up to hold on to his shoulders. Her nightcap tickled Nathan's neck. He wasn't fully hard yet, she had to stuff him in. She whispered abominations in his ear shaking him violently up and down, making him stiffen, making his darkness lengthen inside her like a growing tree . . .

When Arvilla latched open their bedroom shutter early next morning, she saw that the squaws had removed their tipis from across the river. Beyond a rise to the south, smoke curled up—so they'd relocated there—a mile or so away. More smoke came from the men's camp down beyond Johnson's tipi and house, which meant they'd returned, or some had. She remembered hearing horses in the night.

The morning sun slanted through mist rising up from the sluggish river. A crow in the cottonwoods cawed at nothing.

Her husband lay on his back in bed staring at the ceiling. "The men have returned," she told him.

"I suspected as much."

She dressed herself in that chilly room: chemise and pants, a single petticoat, summer corset laced up loosely, calico dress—her own mother's shawl.

"I have a good feeling about this," he told her. "I imagine they talked. After much disputation and chopping of logic, they smoked a pipe and agreed to come back."

"And the soldiers?"

"I sent them a message last night inviting the major-general here with a handful of men—say, four or five. The rest to camp out in the Milk Creek Valley. I suppose there's nothing for it but to talk some more. We shall talk until our faces turn blue. Fix this, fix that. More flour, more blankets. We'll beat up the bush till the game is found, then go back to normal life. They'll take up the plow and I'll issue their goods."

"Do the others know yet?"

"Josie suspects."

"Have you told her?"

"No."

"It's just as well, then."

She left the room, letting him dress. Shy Nathan always locked the door and dressed alone.

At the smell of cooking, the Indians came. Nathan was right, things were back to normal. Douglas walked in with one of his sons and went straight for the cone of sugar on the table. He filed some off with the rasp for Freddie, then for himself. The boy sucked on his, making it last. They loved to beg food, thought Arvilla, except they didn't beg, they just walked in and took it—their own perverse manner of showing friendship. They seemed to think white folks were put on this earth solely to serve them! Arvilla shook her head like a schoolmarm when Douglas ate one of the uncooked fritters she'd lined up on the oilcloth. "You could wait till I fry them."

He grinned. "Like him raw."

She spooned out some stewed peaches in bowls from a pot warming on the stove, and set them on the table before Douglas and Freddie. "These are Mr. Meeker's own peaches, from his trees in Greeley—away over the mountains. A friend of ours brought them yesterday."

"Brought many mules."

"Yes, he brought all those mules."

"Good for plowing."

"Yes—they are."

Douglas laughed, as though someone somewhere had made a joke. He was nodding his head, tasting the peaches. "Very good!" He stood up and shook Arvilla's hand, laughing out loud. She looked in his eyes, but couldn't get far. He seemed almost ready to wink at her. She turned to start some lard in a pan.

This winter, Nathan had said, they would build an ice house. She could order an ice box and cook with butter all the year round, instead of lard when the butter spoiled. Lard upset her stomach . . .

Douglas and his son sat eating the peaches in rapid spoonfuls. "When shall you put Freddie back in school?" she asked.

"This afternoon!"

From the stove, she waved her spatula at him. "You had better."

He grinned.

At the boardinghouse, Josie and Pete rattling together in front of the spacious black cookstove fried up a new round of buckwheat cakes, this time just for themselves. Arthur Thompson, Frank Dresser, and Shadrach Price had eaten already and gone off to spread dirt on the roof of the new Agency building over near Johnson's house and tipi. Flora Ellen Price had walked her children down to the river to wash out some clothes, and Jack Wilcox still lay in bed sleeping. While Pete visited the Meekers last night, Jack had drunk himself to oblivion, in thanks for arriving safely at this place of refuge after nearly two weeks of crossing endless mountains with nine ugly mules . . .

Josie offered Pete a corn-shuck cigarette.

"No thanks."

She lit up her own.

"What'll your pa think?"

"Why should I care?"

"He might be miffed."

"He's got more important things to think about."

Pete flipped the cakes while Josie blew out smoke. He sensed her insides contracting, determined not to cough. She was smoking to shock him, he knew that, so he vowed not to pay the slightest attention. Why would a kitchen need five rolling pins? He stepped to the wall where they hung to inspect them beside the black stovepipe—fascinating tools . . .

But he couldn't keep from looking at her. Women's forearms grew strong with their use, but surely not as strong as Josie's, the beauty of whose long white muscles—like delicious fillets—had gone staight to Pete's heart. They were cunning arms, hard and sleek—she seemed to have polished them. Surely she knew how attractive they were, as she'd rolled her sleeves up to exactly the point where her forearms bulged, trailing dimpled depressions just inside the bend of the elbows. It wasn't flesh, it was gold! When Pete touched her arm he could swear his fingers left little craters . . .

The red spots once on her cheeks had spread and gone tan. She'd put up her hair, but strands of it hung down teasing the cords up and down her neck. She looked pretty good in deshabille. She was taller now too, at least by an inch. It scared Pete just to stand beside her, being shorter and, what?—less sure of what his body might do. It might break into uncontrollable jigs . . . Been digging ditches, Josie? Just the thought of her working, sweating, straining, set off mousetraps in his stomach. He shook his arms—glanced out the window—tried not to picture her lovely neck glistening . . .

All at once Josie exploded into a storm of hacking, gritty coughs. She dropped her cigarette. In a jiffy Pete retrieved it, lifted a stove lid, threw the thing in, and *shlanged* the lid shut.

"You, Pete! How could you?"

"I can't stand to see you suck on that thing. You'll rot out your lungs."

"Don't be such a bug."

"What'll your ma think?"

"Don't catechize me! You've narrowed down some in the last year, Pete. You were born for a preacher."

Pete bowed his head. "Have I fallen so low?"

"I guess you have. You and every other moralistic jackanapes who comes along. The trouble with preachers is they want all your keys—the closets and the bedrooms included. It's not funny, Pete." Pete held his spatula out at arm's length, prepared for a duel, while Josie with her finger and thumb pulled buckwheat cakes out of the pan, jerking her hand back. "Ouch."

"Use this."

"I'll use what I have."

"You'll burn yourself."

"Why should I care?" She loaded two plates with buckwheat cakes then filed off some sugar to sprinkle on top. "Oh Pete." He was tipping, he knew, as he took his plate—leaning into her—nothing for it. "Don't be such a nursemaid, Pete. I hate to have anyone attempt to drive me."

"My growl is worse than my spring—you know that."

"Then don't even growl."

"A fellow gets worse jittery seeing his own sins in someone else."

"What sins?"

"You've changed."

"Is it a sin to change? You've changed too."

"You ain't happy—I can tell."

"Some people are so much sunshine to the square inch—not me."

Pete sat down at the table. Josie poured out some boiling coffee from the pot on the stove and sat there too, not touching her food. Pete cut into his buckwheat cakes and stuffed his mouth, as though talk needed fuel. "Well, you never seemed exactly optimistical. But you *was* more fun."

"Oh, Pete—I'm all right. It's the world that's gone wrong."

"That's generally the case."

"I don't suppose you realize the danger we're in."

"Your pa seems to think everything's swell."

"There's troops on the way—unless something delayed them."

"What might delay them—a landslide?"

"A landslide of wild Indians, perhaps."

Pete drank his coffee. From the boardinghouse, with the window latched open, you could clearly hear the river rushing—always carrying itself away . . . "Your pa did seem slumped—despite what he said."

"Daddy is—Daddy will never compromise his principles. He means to improve their lives or be damned."

"Maybe they don't regard being farmers as much improvement."

"He knows what he's doing. I *know* he's right. It's just—I don't know. It's all gone to smash. They can't plow or chop wood or do heavy work—it's out of the question. Sometimes they seem like creatures of nature and sometimes they seem more canny than a bunch of Philadelphia lawyers. I thought them my friends—I meant them to be—"

"Could be they think you're on your pa's side."

"I am. I'm not."

"Can't have it both ways."

"He's on their side. They just don't see it."

Pete glanced around at the whitewashed kitchen. The log walls and chinks looked freshly painted, causing the black stove and stovepipe to swell. Black iron pots and pans hung from the wall to the right of the stove. Not a cobweb in sight . . . Drysink, cupboards, work tables, spice racks, all painted white. This entire kitchen resembled a freshly laundered apron with numerous pockets.

His plate was empty, so he helped himself to Josie's uneaten buckwheat cakes with his fingers. "What sort of danger did you have in mind?" he asked.

"Oh, the usual. Brute scalpings and disembowelments."

"Wake up Jack. He knows all about it."

Josie turned in her chair, one arm on the table, one on the chairback, and looked at the window. She looked back at Pete, then hung her head, pinching the bridge of her lovely nose. "They're my friends," she said, "and I don't know who they are. I don't know what they'll do."

"Why don't you ask them?"

"Father thinks them depraved."

"What do they think of Father?"

"That's just it, Pete. You know what they think of him. I see very plainly now how the notion of depravity got into the world. Some people made up laws without ever noticing how wantonly unjust they were. Others enjoyed their natural state of anarchy without ever recognizing where their appetites injured those around them. I've thought about this a great deal, Peter. Both sides regard the other as depraved. And both sides are right."

"Seems like that covers it."

"No, it don't. What's left is nature, which is worse than the whole cocked hat gang put together. If we knew the truth of it—*really* knew the truth—we'd throw ourselves off a cliff for sure. Everything in nature is selfish. That's the natural state of things. All creatures and plants are concerned only with themselves. Why should it be otherwise? Caterpillars eat flowers, frogs eat caterpillars, snakes eat frogs, wolves eat snakes. They torture, they kill, they devour. They suffer, they die, they get eaten. Nature is a vast machine fashioned on purpose to bring forth evil."

Oh Josie, Josie. You don't know the half of it! I stopped a man from beating his wife . . . Pete felt the springs creaking open in his eyes and yawned to shut them. His jittery nerves made it a big yawn.

"I can see I'm boring you."

He brought his hands to his throat and popped his eyes. "Is there any hope? Quick!"

"I eat hope. I devour it."

Josie's face had been honed to a glistening point. Around either end of her fine, pursed lips were two curved lines like small fishhooks—but she wasn't smiling. They framed an expression of resigned disgust, and it withered Pete, as the sun withers flowers . . . "I know what you mean," he said, "about nature." Josie's eyes raised a notch; go ahead, talk. "A man I knew in South Carolina, he swallowed a frog—"

"Oh, *Pete*."

"Let me finish. He swallowed a frog which lived in his stomach for fifteen years. Seems he went to the springhouse and took a drink of water and inadvertently swallowed this frog. In South Carolina they call it 'inside frog.' Some folks die of it."

She stared right at him. Fixed her stony gaze . . . Why not?—he took a bite of buckwheat cake and swallowed, as though to demonstrate. "Thing ate twice as much as he did," he said. "Woke him up at night croaking for his mate. He croaked during silent prayers at church, so they barred him from the church." Josie's lips didn't move, as far as Pete could see. The fishhooks still quoted her mouth, but somehow they'd changed. The line of her mouth had slackened, for one thing—it seemed to waver. It floated on her face like a stick in a back current, unsure of which direction to take . . . "Quaker church, Josie. Meetinghouse, that is. So he got himself a stomach pump and shoved it down, but this frog was smart. It hid on a ledge."

"I thought it wanted its mate."

"To come *down*. It *liked* his stomach. Wanted company. When frogs were in season, he'd fish with a fly, this friend of mine—stretched out on his back. Held the rod at arm's length, like this. But the frog refused to rise."

She was smiling! Hallelujah! Head bowed, shaking her head. You could tell she didn't want to. Then again, she did—even metaphysicians required a little joy, otherwise the world might just fall apart . . . "Pete. You donkey. Sounds fishy to me." Her face glowed right at him.

"That's how he got him. He swallowed a fish, which swallowed the frog. The fish swam back up his throat, to spawn. He kilt it with a fork . . ."

"Wawhaugh! What's for breakfast?" Jack Wilcox stood at the door like a human bed, unmade. He'd slept in his clothes. His slouch hat pulled down pushed the flaps of his ears forward like a dog's.

"Beans and whiskey," said Pete.

"I feel all atwitter. Snort, snort. What are you two jawing about?"

"The state of the crisis."

"What crisis?"

"Someone drank all the likker last night."

Jack lumbered into the kitchen. "I smell coffee." Josie handed him a cup. He addressed her, looking at Pete. "He's some for his inches, ain't he?"

"Yes, he is."

He slumped down at the table winking at Pete. His dirty hair hung in clumps from his slouch cap, and the hair on his beard below one eye stuck up, exposing soiled skin. Pete caught a whiff of his foul breath and winced. "Whatever drank that likker," said Jack, "must have been what I heard mushing and sawing 'neath the floorboards last night. Felt it pushing up."

"That's the pinch bugs," said Pete, "trying to get at you."

"More likely our skunks, Mr. Wilcox. But they're teetotalers."

"Like everyone else in this starving country."

Josie started mixing a new batch of buckwheat cakes. Pete leaned back and sucked at his teeth. Jack stood up and stretched his whole body, every muscle and capillary head to toe. You could just about see him filling with blood. When he finished and sat down, his eyes were pink.

"What were you two jawing about?"

"Asking Josie on her catechism."

"Ask me on mine."

"I was born for a preacher—did you know that, Jack?"

"Ask me on mine."

The lard popped in Josie's frying pan. An Indian walked by outside the window. "There's one," said Pete.

"What?"

"A wild injun."

Jack lit up a shuck, but Josie refused to display any interest. She poured dollops of batter into the pan, then pulled the pan back where the stovetop was cooler.

"All right, Jack. Who made you?"

"God."

"Who redeemed mankind?"

"Jesus Christ."

"Who made your hat?"

"The Holy Ghost . . ."

An Indian boy walked in the kitchen. "Why, Freddie," Josie said from the stove.

"Need matches."

The boy stood there smiling. His buckskin shirt looked too large for his frame. Even the Indians wore hand-me-downs . . . Pete studied his face: brown eyes, reddish-brown skin—bumps on the skin around his chin. His wide eyes looked flat, as though painted on the face. Well, he don't look ferocious. Pete found himself wondering: What about me? What do I seem to him?

The boy smiled at Pete for an uncanny moment as though there were no one else in the room.

"What you need matches for?" asked Josie.

"Going to smoke."

Josie said something in Ute, then in English. "You're too young to smoke." But she held a mug full of matches out for the boy to take a handful. He left without so much as a thank you.

Pete stood at the kitchen window watching the boy walk away outside. Other Indians walked around out there. One led his pony down to the river. Flora Ellen Price, a child clinging to either hand, was just returning up the same path, and they stopped to talk. Down by the river, her sheets and clothes were spread out on willows.

Outside the new log building, two or three Indians had gathered to talk with the Agency workers hauling pails of dirt up to the roof and spreading it with shovels. One man worked with his shirt off. The sun had climbed higher in the sky—not a cloud in sight.

Josie served Jack his buckwheat cakes. "I warrant he'll burn himself," she said.

"Who?"

"Freddie."

Jumping up, Jack turned to Josie at the stove, whipped off his hat, and stood there clutching it bunched at his chest. "Much obliged for the slapjacks, ma'am."

"Next time," she said, one fist on her hip, "you take that hat off *before* you eat." She poked her spatula at his shoulder. "And you wash those hands!"

"Aw shucks, Miss Josie . . ."

Outside, a tall Indian walked up to the men spreading dirt on the roof and said something that appeared to make them laugh. He stood there a minute, then wandered down to a group gathered by a fence bordering Douglas's corral. Two or three of them walked back to the building, and Arthur Thompson pitched forward diving off the roof. Pete heard a crack. "Something funny's happened."

Jack's chair crashed to the floor behind him. More popping cracks came from outside. Up on the roof, Shadrach Price was holding his belly and had dropped to one knee. "What's that shooting?" asked Jack.

So that's what it was . . .

Flora Ellen Price rushed into the kitchen holding in two arms her screaming children. "They shot Shadrach!" Josie relieved her of Johnny, the youngest, but the boy squirmed so much all the time screaming that she nearly dropped him. Jack ran down to his room for his rifle. Outside, no one seemed especially animated. A few horses whinnied in Douglas's corral. Nobody was running, and the shots had stopped. A handful of Indians started up toward the boardinghouse carrying their rifles across their chests.

"Here they come," said Pete. Standing at the window, he felt strangely detached.

"This way!" said Josie.

"Wait." From outside came a loud, hoarse shout. Jack had found his rifle. He exploded out there around a corner of the storehouse waving it in the air, hardly regarding where he went. "C'mon, you red niggers!" The Indians stopped about thirty feet away and raised their guns. He hesitated, turned left, ran right, hoisted his rifle, tripped, and fell forward. The air cracked open and puffs of smoke escaped. Jack went down corkscrewing into the earth, face twisted back in Pete's direction. Hard to see his features, though. He lay there twitching.

"Pete! Come right now!" Josie tugged Pete away from the window. Johnny still screamed in her other arm. Pete looked around at the kitchen, confused. Josie pulled him out the door.

They ran down the hallway to Josie's room and crawled under her bed, Pete, Flora Ellen, Josie, and the children. There was nothing for it but to hold their hands over the crying mouths of the children to shush them. Pete felt silly. The picture of Jack falling down haunted him. Flora Ellen sneezed. Josie, of course, had neglected to clean underneath her bed. They lay there, breathing and holding their breaths. In front of Pete's face, pressed to the floor, sat a tiny button in ludicrous close-up. "Josie?"

"What?"

"Did you lose a button?"

Gunshots came, and the sound of glass breaking. They heard bullets thunking the walls above their heads. Then they smelled the smoke. The bullets had stopped. First Josie crawled out, bending low, to inspect the room. Then Pete, Flora Ellen, and the sobbing children. Smoke drifted lazily at shoulder height. Pete looked around the room—Josie's room! Soft things lay about on the chairs . . .

They couldn't leave Jack out there, he thought—he might get hurt. "Put this on," Josie said. She tossed him a calico dress—blue, with hundreds of little yellowish-brown fleurs-de-lis—then turned back to rummage in her dresser.

"What's this all about?"

"They won't shoot you, Pete, if they think you're a girl."

Dress up like a girl? he thought. My goodness . . .

"Put it on, Pete. Here—put on this." She tied a muslin bonnet on his head. Josie looked calm, but her face was flushed. Then she did something strange—she kissed him. A short dry kiss, right on the lips . . . Johnny and May now were sniveling, not crying. Flora Ellen stood at the door in anxious impatience, looking back toward the kitchen. The smoke had thickened, and more gunshots came from somewhere outside. He pulled the dress on over his clothes—it dragged on the floor around his boots. She helped him button it up the front while Flora Ellen scooped up the children and ran down the hallway toward the rear door. Josie and Pete followed behind . . .

Outside, the sun was as hot as midsummer. The gunshots came from the front of the boardinghouse, so they scrambled around the back of the granary, trying to keep low in the coppery weeds. Someone lay on the ground in the horse pasture. They ran up onto the agent's porch, into the house, and found Arvilla sitting in a chair, hands folded in her lap. "Where's Daddy?" cried Josie.

"Gone out."

"Out where?"

Arvilla stood up as though she'd been waiting for them. She was staring at Pete in his dress and bonnet. Now she knew, he thought—knew at last who he was . . . He fidgeted there while Josie searched the bedroom. "In here!" she shouted. In the bedroom, Josie held the unlatched rear window open for Flora Ellen to crawl through, then handed her children out one by one. "Pete, help Mama."

"I can do it myself." Arvilla, scowling, lifted her skirts, and crawled out the window. She was clutching a book in one hand—The Pilgrim's Progress. Then Josie crawled out, then Pete.

The back of the agent's house faced the plowed fields beside the Utes' racetrack. Beyond those fields, straight ahead, were sagebrush hills, blue and green in the sun, with cattle scattered here and there. Voices came from somewhere behind, back by the boardinghouse. Shouts and gunshots . . . They ran for the field, scrambled over the fence, heard a series of cracks. But they wouldn't shoot women . . .

The air snapped around them. Pete found it clumsy to run with that dress on. Dirt clung to his boots in the freshly plowed field, but the tall sage wasn't too far away, they could hide there. They scrabbled through the field like singular insects, drifting apart by instinct or cunning. The children ran fastest, on stubby little legs. A wasp or nettle stung Pete's hand. He glanced back at Josie helping her mother, but had to avert his eyes for the sun. Where was Father Meeker? Jack had been shot. His consciousness felt like a smear across things—the field, the Agency buildings, the sky.

Utes on horseback found them in the sage, out of breath, huddled like scared little rabbits. Pete's hand was all bloody—shot through the palm. "I am sorry," one of the Utes said to Arvilla. He climbed off his horse to help her up. "Very much sorry. Can you walk?"

"Yes, sir."

"Come with us. We have to ride a long way."

Someone grabbed Pete's wrist and held it up. "Very much sorry." He hung his head, as a girl should. But his hand didn't really hurt that much. They were being herded back to the Agency. Smoke poured from the boardinghouse, the granary, the agent's home. Outside the storehouse, whose door hung bashed open, Utes were piling up sacks of flour, dried fruit, coffee and sugar, blankets, shoes, saddles, and cooking pots. People lay about ignored on the ground, Indians and whites. Hard to tell who . . .

They marched toward some horses near Johnson's house. Pete felt terribly thirsty. The mules he'd brought had all gotten loose, and braves ran around trying to chase them down. He looked over at Josie. She walked by herself, head erect—eyes straight ahead—lips pursed—arms swinging.

Late that afternoon, smoke still curled up from the charred remains of the White River Agency. It rose from each separate building, flattened out, merged, and hung like a mist above the entire lower portion of the valley, hung indifferently over fields, pastures, river, and trees, over dead bodies, scavenging dogs, wandering cattle, loose mules and horses, scattered flour, smashed wagons, broken plows, pieces of fencing, wheels, rakes, mowers, barrels, and furniture strewn in the dirt and ashes with articles of clothing, books, and shoes. Crows had already flapped down to inspect the cooling flesh in the afternoon sun . . .

Jo first spotted the smoke a good five miles away, and later, rounding the yellow cliffs where the valley curved, made out the columns rising from smudged blackened patches surrounded by green fields two miles off. He felt far too exhausted to discuss with the others a few columns of smoke, however. They'd marched the last fifteen miles in silence, each on foot carrying his carpetbag—Jo, Stokes, Bonny, Count Léon-Fernand-Léon, and Julius Moore, the younger of the two freighters. His partner, Carl Goldstein, had stayed behind to guard the threshing rig and wagons, which couldn't very well be hauled through brush and marshes in the dark. They'd walked all night in a great arc, skirting that fire-lit valley where blue-coated soldiers fought bare-chested Indians, up steep slopes over broken terrain whose sagebrush snagged the count's fine leggings, then down through ravines, over creeks, through bogs, until even the count gave off complaining, his knees hurt so much—he was chilled to the bone. A savage might jump out and crack their heads open at any time, but they stopped caring. Stokes puffed and coughed and Jo's feet swelled up, despite the assistance of his gold-headed walking stick. Only Bonny seemed indifferent to the hardships, due to his cozy rapport with pain. Besides, over the rougher parts he rode up on Stokes's shoulders, fists clutching his hair . . .

They had descended into the White River Valley at dawn, fifteen miles above the Agency, and collapsed to sleep curled up in a ball—all save the count—in a field soon warmed by the rising sun.

Now they approached the Agency through acres of dry grass alive with grasshoppers beneath the hot afternoon sunlight. Dogs barked. Steers ran off. Crows lurched up heavily into the sky. Evidently, thought Jo, there's been a disturbance . . . They sleep-walked into the aftermath of rage. Then a bright thought occurred to Jo Benton, rousing his spirits: could one of those dead bodies be Peter Doyle?

Julius Moore had dropped his carpetbag and stood there with his rifle across the crook of one arm, shaking visibly. His face had collapsed into quivering sobs. He'd never thought it would come to *this* . . . They wandered through the smoldering ruins. With his foot, Jo turned over a body, then wished he hadn't. Ants had already attacked the eyes. One whole side of the face was flattened, and the crown of the head was a bloody mess where the scalp had been taken. He'd been lying in a pool of dark blood. Jo beckoned Julius. "Do you know this man?"

"I knew him—knew them all."

"Who was he?"

"Father Meeker's assistant. Mr. Post."

Jo turned him back over, to spare Julius the sight. "Help me," he said, "identify the others."

They strolled side by side through a garden of death. Shadrach Price's shirtless torso exposed the hole torn through his stomach. Between the boardinghouse and granary a large, older man had piled himself up in death like a buffalo. His head was twisted unnaturally back under his shoulder—top pointing down—and Jo, looking closer, saw that the top, crushed in the dirt, had been blown away. It looked like an egg smashed to stand on one end. At least this prevented them taking his scalp. Dressed all in buckskin, with bloody whiskers, this man was the only one in the Agency whom Julius Moore failed to identify.

Jo searched his pockets—just in case—and came up with, of all things, an old moth-eaten scalp.

They found Fred Shepard, the fiddle player, Harry Dresser, and George Eaton, whose face had already been nibbled and chewed by animals or crows. Arthur Thompson's gun still lay beside him. In a field behind the storehouse a body lay with its shirt stripped off and a barrel stave jammed down its throat. Around its neck was a chain used, they guessed, to drag it by horse around the burning Agency. Jo recognized Nathan Meeker right away. He'd been shot through the head, and half of his body appeared to be burned; then he realized that blue-black inkstain on his side was a birthmark. Someone had hacked with a knife at its edges, as though attempting to surgically remove it. He turned away with a shudder.

He wanted to know if that was everyone in the Agency.

"Not the women and children. Mrs. Meeker, Mrs. Price, Josie Meeker."

"They took them prisoner?"

"Must have."

Julius and Jo looked around at the Agency with admirable calm. They were at that state of structural fatigue just before the molecules either seize up and crack or surrender and relax into blissful serenity—it could go either way. Jo's mind insisted on its right to analyze everything minutely, with care, despite the hot sun and the world turned over and the ghosts trapped in each lonely cell of his body howling for sleep . . . All the fences in the Agency had been broken open, and five or six horses and mules wandered freely, most in the grass down near the river. Around the two men, cooling fires snapped, transforming the smell of wood smoke to something more black and lasting. In the middle of the Agency, amid leveled buildings, close by a wagon that looked nearly intact, Count Léon-Fernand-Léon had found a barrel to sit on whence he could stare into the hills with his lavender-scented hanky to his nose. Poor Count Léon—his dignified clothes had been torn and smudged, he looked in a daze. An American flag flapped on a pole outside the leveled storehouse above burst sacks of flour to his left. Beneath it, Stokes was counting the dead, starting with three fallen before him.

"One . . . two . . . three." He turned and scanned the burnt-out Agency, pointing as he counted. "Four . . . five . . . six . . . seven . . . eight."

"No, seven," said Bonny. "That's a dog."

"Seven—or eight . . ." Stokes scratched his head, then started over. "One . . . two . . . three . . . *four!*" Gasp—"Now there's four!" He kicked at the last one. "This one's alive!" Bonny jumped up and scampered off buzzing. "Mudlark! Guttersnipe!"

The creature darted behind a smashed dresser. "Oh no, Mr. Stokes! Please, sir . . . no!" His voice fluttered out in a cracked, nasal whine.

"I'll teach you a lesson!"

"Please, sir, oh please . . ."

Julius turned to Jo with a look confusing horror and disbelief. "What are they—doing?"

"Playing a game."

The boy shook his head, near tears again. His jaw slid forward and twisted grotesquely, chewing one end of his scrawny mustache.

Stokes chased Bonny past the broken-down fence of a horse corral, running with feet splayed out like a clown. They ran past Count Léon, who turned on his barrel, adjusting his posture to face away. Bonny doubled back and darted beneath the count's storklike legs, peeking around from behind the barrel to watch from which side Stokes would come. The count blessed himself, jumped up, and walked off. His scraping feet kicked up little dust devils just as a wind whipped through the Agency, stirring the ashes and dust together . . .

Jo poked his walking stick in some charred timbers. His mind like a spider stretched its long legs trying to span cracks growing wider and wider. The thought of searching this whole blackened mess, and the fields around it, profoundly depressed him. Bonny could do it—he had a sixth sense . . . Then again, Doyle had either escaped, or gone off with the savages. "Would they take other prisoners?" He turned to Julius. "Young men? Males?"

"I suppose. There's no telling."

"Hostages?"

"Perhaps. It could be. I don't know." He shook his head, breaking into violent shrugs. "How should I know?" he snapped. He bent down to pull the barrel stave out of Nathan Meeker's mouth, as though that were the source of all pandemonium, the lever that pried the world off its course—

but it wouldn't come out. They'd jammed it down hard. It seemed to weaken him instantly, and he hung there a moment like a wilted flower.

Bonny's shout came in a harsh loud buzz. "Count this one?"

"Missed it entirely." Stokes approached a body nearly hidden behind a stack of blankets. It lay curled on its stomach, one arm across its head. "Nine." Stokes turned it over with his foot.

It jumped up at once and seized Stokes by the neck, grinning fiercely with its painted face.

Jo ran for his carpetbag, Julius raised his rifle to his shoulder, shouting something in Ute, but the Indian crumpled back to the ground, holding his ankle. He grinned at Bonny in fear.

Bonny folded his knife and returned it to his pocket, eyeing a dog who stood barking nearby. Julius ran up, shouting, "Filthy savage . . ." He pointed his rifle at the Indian's head.

"*Pitukupi.*" The Indian sat there staring at Bonny, holding his foot. Jo came running with a dueling pistol. Stokes rubbed his neck. Julius cocked the rifle at his shoulder. "*Pitukupi!*"

"What's he saying?" asked Jo.

"It means dwarf," said Julius.

"Ask him where the others went."

Julius asked him. He pointed downriver. "He says they followed the river," said Julius.

"Did they have any prisoners?"

"Yes! Many prisoners!" The man looked up at Jo, grinning as though his arm was being twisted. His face had been painted with reddish clay, and over that, a bright yellow band across the forehead.

"A young man?"

"Yes! Many young men . . . Went downriver, there."

Half turned, he was pointing at the river when Jo shot him in the head at point-blank range, snapping his neck and splattering brains and blood. Even Bonny turned away . . .

Then they all looked around, as though the echoing shot would bring the mountains tumbling down upon them. From over by the broken fence of a corral Count Léon-Fernand-Léon walked toward them, stopped, then approached again. He stopped and turned around. He sat down on the ground.

They found the wagon outside the storehouse to be in working order. They couldn't go back, not through that endless brush, those steep ravines—not back toward that raging battle—though Julius was all for it. Julius wanted to return to their wagons. Jo insisted they start downriver. He was thinking quite lucidly now, the shot had cleared out his head with one stroke—woken him up! Killing someone like that quickened your heartbeat and flooded your brain with a storm of possibilities. They could *ransom* Doyle—with the count's ample cash . . .

Julius and the others agreed to part. Surely help was on the way, and Julius could guide it. Even if all those soldiers had died, more would be coming. He'd go back to Rawlins to fetch them if necessary, it wouldn't take long . . .

He helped them patch up a harness for the wagon, caught a horse for himself and two for the wagon, helped them load it with flour and extra blankets, a sack of dried fruit, their precious carpetbags.

At last, when he galloped off up the valley, Julius muttered a desperate prayer of thanks. Savages were one thing, desperadoes another, but these men—and that midget—were from hell itself . . . He'd promised Bonny to see that his cart made it back to Rawlins, and the count to take care of his tins of fine food. He'd send help, yes, of course—he'd promise them anything . . . Still, he didn't tell them the Indians had never gone downriver. That Ute told a lie. There was nothing there for them. They'd crossed the river and headed south—he'd seen the fresh tracks. South into the mountains.

He'd send help, oh yes . . .

> Greeley Hotel
> Greeley, Colorado Territory
> Sept 15, 1873

Dear Miss Dickinson,

Still cribb'd up here—dark, rainy, glum today, warm but lowering—keeps the sun off—Haven't heard from my nurse in more than a week—sit up waiting for the friend in question—any friend—in the same monotonous way next the window, in a big chair, with wolf skin spread on the back of it & the woolen foot-cloth in front on the floor—a lap-spread on my knees—in my shirt sleeves but a merino wool undershirt on—reading the Sunday papers—

Live on mutton-broth & dry toast—some farina pudding—digestion power very languid—partial bowel action this morning (first in five days).

Am getting fairly staled with this long wait. Inquiries produce no results, as I can't hoof it outside myself to pursue them—I require a shoulder. A young man here does assist me, but he's out selling wallpaper all day. You don't know what it is, in your cocoon, to be forced to depend upon strangers.

Miss Dickinson, should you ever decide to see the wide West, don't rely on your friends to take you—they have wests of their own to see, most likely. We New Worlders are in danger of turning out the trickiest, slyest, most cheating people that ever lived, these qualities worming into our business, politics, literature, and most essential national character. Pray you provide against them in Amherst, lest a friend break your heart.

2 young deaf mutes checked into this hotel yesterday—hear them thumping about—

You may as well write and no special hurry as I could be here until the four trumpets blow. Which is the best singing, Miss Dickinson—the first or the lattermost? Ask your birds, I'll ask mine. The man who assists me might call upon you one of these days, when he returns to the states. You will forgive me if I gave him your address. He sells wallpaper especially favored by the ladies.

And so, Miss Dickinson—I wait—

Walt Whitman

Chapter

❦ 8 ❦

*T*ik-tik-ta-ta-tik.

The spider turned to cross the other threads. He worked up there by the smoke hole somewhere. Inside the clicking of his legs came a rubbing brushing sound, the pull of the filament out of his anus. The lack of birds in this canyon, and the fact that light came here late, straight from above and down through the smoke hole, made it easier to listen to the spider than see him. Was it night or day? Just close your eyes . . . *Tik-tik-tish.*

Outside, grunting horses chewed the sparse grass. They sounded pretty far away. Siwapi's own breathing rattled with particles of sand or bits of dry lung broken off. Inside himself, he saw his own heart squatting like a toad with a dent in its side: *limp-lump.* The distant roar of water through canyons was in fact the blood rushing through his veins, out toward the remote tunnels of his fingers and toes. He didn't move—it was part of his punishment. When the others woke up he would wait their permission.

He made it a test of his self-control to allow his lice, as they awoke, to bite him freely. One crawled through his hair toward the ledge where his ear attached. He pretended he was dead. He could hear very well the spiders, ants, grasshoppers, lizards, and mice rustling through the grass and dirt just outside their *carniv*, beginning all the work they had to do. A grasshopper sleeping next to your head could kick your brains out in the night . . . He opened and closed one eye only. The light up there could be dawn, or the moon. Each night the moon came rolling down the canyon with the skin of a person tied around his waist . . .

Siwapi's insides were sliding. A fly buzzed above him—two flies. One bird sang outside, and he knew from the song it was the only one coming that day, a meadowlark. Its feet scratched a branch. One fly buzzed with his mouth shut, the other with hers open. How come you're always singing, flies?

We're always that way, we always sing.

Siwapi realized the flies were children. When they grew up they wouldn't sing so much. Right, flies?

They sang: What are you lying there for? Go eat breakfast.

No, do it yourself—go spoil some meat.

No, they sang, the eggs we put down on meat are salt . . .

Siwapi held his eyes tightly closed.

Why am I up here on the smoke hole? asked the spider. What do you think of it?

I don't know.

I hold on to my web, shut my eyes, and see everything over the world. That's why I'm up here.

That's new to me.

Don't you want to see everything?

Yes, I'd like to.

Then shut your eyes and hold on to a web . . .

Siwapi's eyes flew open. The old man stood above him, eye-stone in his mouth. At the door flap, Quinkent watched impatiently, then nodded permission and walked off. But Siwapi lay there a few minutes more, still not moving. Your body has to feel itself to live . . . He put his fingers in his ears to clean them, the first thing he always did in the morning, then threw off his blankets and stepped to the door flap, so all could see the mark of his shame. To him, it was pride: he was dressed like a *piwán* in a doeskin skirt embroidered around with porcupine quills. Under the dress were buckskin leggings with beads and fringes, and above he'd put on the kind of flannel blouse the *piwán* always wore. Hardly anyone was awake. A few *piwán* walked to the creek for some water with one of the captives, the old one, the agent's wife or mother, he forgot which. Limping between them, she carried the jug. He watched them disappear behind some horses.

Above, the blazing sun had already struck the top of the canyon wall. The band of blue sky high overhead was long but not wide. Smoke climbed up from just two *carniva*, Quinkent's and Pausone's, where the Americans were. Two dogs were fucking behind Quinkent's *carniv*. Couldn't wait, could they? They fucked on empty stomachs . . . Some children emerged from another *carniv* and stared at Siwapi. Then the *piwán* came out, pointed at him, said something, turned away. He went inside and found their water jug. Squatting by the fire, Maasuwini turned with his empty eye sockets and the blue stone of turquoise slung in his lower lip. He looked him up and down . . .

Outside, getting water, the cold air felt good.

After they ate—fried potatoes and coffee—he lay beside the fire for the old man to delouse him. Squatting, Maasuwini mumbled as he searched.

How were your dreams, lice? he asked.

I think you are going to kill me, said a louse.

You are nothing but eye-dirt, said the old man.

Siwapi thought, what's the best thing for me to say this morning? He told Maasuwini about the moon. Every night it comes rolling down the canyon.

The moon makes you do crazy things, said Maasuwini—as if that explained the past few days.

Siwapi asked if the Americans were chasing them.

What's the matter with you? They're always chasing us . . . The old man probed Siwapi's long hair with the fingers of both hands, and when he found a louse, cracked it between his thumbnail and finger, careful to get the legs and the belly.

I hear someone coming, said a louse . . .

Maasuwini told a story about the Americans. Wolf found a bloodclot hanging from a tree and pulled it down, but it hopped away. It jumped into a kettle of boiling water and became an American. Now I've done it, he thought . . . The American ran off. He made other Americans. Later on, Wolf climbed up a ridge and spotted a group of Americans below, laughing so hard they sounded crazy. One cut his wife's shoulder open and said, "Through this you shall talk, not with your mouth," then did the same to his son. The Americans were playing with their scrotums. Two young men and two girls were playing, and the girls were laughing because they'd removed the boys' balls and were throwing them up in the air . . . When they came down they put them back in their scrotums. They threw up arms and legs and the other parts of their bodies. The girls plucked out their own cunts and threw them up, and that made them laugh with high shrieking yells. The woman and her child laughed through the holes cut in their shoulders . . .

Wolf couldn't shake the Americans from his mind. His brother, Coyote, came over and noticed that Wolf lay in bed all day covered up. So when Wolf went to sleep Coyote made a fire, then called out, "Your blanket is burning!" Wolf jumped up, throwing off the blanket. Coyote spotted a pair of white legs. Wolf said to his wife, "He has already found you. You better get up and not remain hidden." So the American woman got up.

After that, Coyote and Wolf went off hunting, but Coyote circled back. The American woman had squawbrush splints in her hands for plaiting baskets. Coyote said, "Let me eat my brother's food." He threw the woman down and tried to fuck her, but she crawled along the ground with Coyote on her back. She crawled toward an oak tree and struck it with her head. The trunk cracked open and she kept right on crawling into the tree, preventing Coyote from having his will of her. The tree closed up, catching Coyote's prick. He hung there. It hurt! He grunted in his throat. All day he hung there. Wolf returned. Coyote said, "Hurry up, Brother, cut down the tree, I'm caught here."

Wolf replied, "Here's plenty of meat for you to eat, Brother."

Coyote said, "Can't you see I'm caught here!"

Wolf said, "Did you have a good hunt?"

At last Wolf walked up and cut off his brother's prick. Coyote said, "Brother, you can call me Short-Mentula after that."

Siwapi laughed. But the story wasn't over. Coyote made his prick into a baby and put it in a cradle, then pretended to be a woman with a baby. Wolf figured it out. He told Coyote to gather some wood. Coyote returned in his woman's dress and couldn't throw the wood down because it stuck to his arm. Wolf took the wood from his arm and sighed. Coyote went back to get wood with a basket, but it clung to the basket when he tried to unload it. "Brother, what causes the wood to do that?" He tried to wipe the sweat from his forehead and his arm stuck there. "Brother, you can call me Peering Under His Arm." He was squatting down. When he tried to stand up he couldn't because his calves stuck to his thighs. He found himself rolling around helpless, legs stuck together, arm stuck to his head. Wolf picked up a knife, grabbed Coyote by his hair, cut off his head and threw it to one side. Coyote died.

Siwapi waited. The story was over. So—did Coyote come back to life? The old man had stopped seeking out lice and gestured to Siwapi to delouse him now. He half reclined on the buffalo blanket, and Siwapi squatted, bent over his head, and searched through his hair for the seedlike bugs, not speaking with them, he couldn't bring himself to . . . He thought of the Americans tossing things up. Well, they weren't laughing now. Why couldn't they just have stayed where they were? Why did they have to come and bother us? Now there was so much trouble that things would never be right again . . .

He'd refused to go north and fight against the soldiers—then refused to kill the Americans at the Agency. Instead, he stayed with the women across the river along with Maasuwini and some other old men, who could be excused for their age—but not him. So now he had to wear a *piwán*'s dress, couldn't rise in the morning without the men's permission, and, like the captives, had to carry water and gather wood—in other words, do *piwán*'s work.

He cracked a fat louse with his yellow thumbnail.

At the councils, he agreed with the leaders: the Americans were crazy. They plowed up our horse pasture and told us to go kill our horses. They sent letters to Washington full of lies about the Utes, withheld our presents, and summoned soldiers to cross our borders—a declaration of war. Still, Siwapi thought they shouldn't fight. Wasn't Nicaagat himself always telling the Utes to live good and not get into trouble? Don't go over there and quarrel with anyone, he said, stick with your own tribe. Don't tease the old people, stay away from the Americans, but if anyone comes, give them food. Then they'll say, There's a good person, he treats me the right way . . .

So Siwapi refused to fight, even though Nicaagat said the soldiers had already killed twenty Utes. In this case, he said, we have to fight to make things even. Well, if that were so, then it was right to fight and kill, and equally right not to. So no one knew what was right anymore.

In Maasuwini's thin hair the lice were easy to catch. Most, like him, were old, blind, and slow-moving. This was the time to get them, when they were all together. At the top of his neck, behind the left ear, was a family of lice: father, mother, grandfather, grandmother, and three young children, little nits. He let the children go. They'd be easier to kill after they'd grown up. He began throwing lice into the fire, but Maasuwini slapped his hand. That's not the way to do it . . .

They ate some more breakfast.

The old man told Siwapi to leave and closed the tent flap behind him. While he squatted in the dirt and dug holes with a stick, the braves out there paid him no attention. At the other end of camp where the horses were hobbled was some kind of commotion, and people began drifting in that direction. Well, let's see what it is. Siwapi lingered behind or off to the side nowadays, he didn't care—he felt proud of what he'd done. He didn't care if they mocked him either, let them laugh and mock. He felt no emotion.

In a grassy meadow where the canyon wall curved but the creek went straight the horses grazed, and one of them was bleeding. He recognized it as Pausone's. Pausone and his youngest *piwán* were shouting. She gestured with a spear at his horse, pointing its tip at the wound in its haunch where it bled profusely. The horse was excited, and tried backing up with its front legs hobbled, tossing its head and showing its teeth. Siwape knew what had happened. She was jealous because Pausone had taken a new *piwán*—the agent's daughter—and she'd come out here to stab his horse. Pausone stepped forward, wrenched the spear from her hands, broke it over his knee, then grabbed her by the hair. All the women screamed. He struck the side of her head until she fell, then stormed through the crowd back to his *carniv*, where the new *piwán* waited.

She sat there where he left her wailing in the grass, sat there all morning . . .

A little later, a new commotion occurred. Nicaagat and some others came galloping into the camp on foaming horses, waving army rifles they'd taken from the soldiers. Nicaagat wore a blue army cap and leggings he'd made from a soldier's blue pants by cutting the hips off. Hanging from the end of his rifle were two scalps.

Everyone wanted to know if the soldiers were coming. Even Siwapi pressed in close. Nicaagat just laughed. The soldiers were still trapped in that valley behind walls of rotting horses whose stench was enormous. When night came, they tried burying the horses under breastworks of dirt, and that's when they became easy targets. Or when they went for water. He laughed. It was boring. We wait on the hills to pick them off, and sometimes we just leave them alone, because it's so easy.

Was everyone at the Agency dead?

Everyone at the Agency was dead. Plus two new dead people, two freighters with wagons they'd hidden off the road containing machines designed to kill Indians. Containing other things too. Nicaagat reached into his parfleche and pulled out a brightly colored doll with a big hook nose, a hunchback, pointed cap, and wobble eyes shaking back and forth like beads inside a rattle. Everyone laughed. Those Americans were crazy . . .

He'd taken the scalps from the two freighters, and some of the older Utes looked away when he held them up. They'd known those two men, who often came to the Agency and gave them gifts. Well, war was like that—you killed people you knew . . .

Nicaagat's two *piwán* then took the scalps and brought them down to the creek to dress. With curved knives they scraped out the fat, and formed small hoops out of willow branches, stretching the skin inside the hoops with thread taken from the Agency supplies. They cut a small hole near the edge of each scalp and hung them on thongs tied to long poles, then paraded them about for people to spit at and wave their fists, fixing the poles next to a fire at the center of the camp so they dangled in the smoke. Excitement spread like a dust storm rising. Boys rode around bareback on frantic ponies, circling the fire where the two scalps hung. *Piwán* sang, addressing the scalps with the harshest of words, and waving their fists—you killed our husbands, our children, our horses . . . They threw rocks at the scalps, ran forward and struck them with sticks, even bit them, while the men laughed and sang boasting songs of triumph.

Siwapi hung back, watching the madness.

Then he saw the old man. He'd emerged from their *carniv*, both arms hanging down, staggering forward on uneven feet, the eye-stone slung in his lower lip. He walked through the people, who made way for him. The boys slowed their horses, the men's singing stopped. One by one he pulled the poles out of the ground and laid the scalps down in the fire. The burning hair stank in a cloud of black smoke.

It was crazy—nothing was right. No one was sure what to do anymore. They acted as though they knew, but in fact no one did.

Maasuwini had dressed in a splendid blanket of blue and red stripes around his waist, an old vest of wolf and bear skins, and beaded earrings reaching down to his breast. From his shoulder hung a bag of beaded parfleche. He grunted at Siwapi, who followed in his woman's skirt, head erect, looking straight ahead.

In Pausone's *carniv*, one of the Americans was sick with a fever. She'd been shot through the hand. They crossed the clearing to where Pausone waited outside his *carniv* with another captive, the young woman with two small children. Pausone nodded back to the opening and led the young mother and children away.

Inside, Patika, Pausone's oldest *piwán*, sat by the fire. To the right, the agent's daughter had curled up on Pausone's blanket, facing away, and didn't move when they entered. On the left, the sick woman lay on her back in a dress and bonnet, pale, sweating, shivering—but watching them closely with frightened eyes. Beside her, the injured hand looked swollen and torn, like a dead skunk's mouth. The wound was black. Maasuwini took off his vest, exposing his birdlike rib cage, sat down beside her, and lit up a shuck. He nodded to Siwapi, who undid the top buttons of her dress. Strange—she wore a man's shirt underneath it . . . He unbuttoned that—though her good hand flew up attempting to stop him—and opened the dress and skirt just above her small bosom, pushing aside a leather pouch hung around her neck. He reached up to remove her bonnet, but her hand clamped soft fingers on his wrist and she shook her head, begging with her eyes. So he left the bonnet on.

She was pretty in a strange kind of way. American girls often had round, small noses. Drops of sweat stood out on her forehead, and a white crust had formed around her lips. He stood up and found Pausone's water jug to the right of the door flap, and offered her a drink. Her body shook; he helped her sit up. She seemed to weigh hardly more than a branch. The jug he held to her lips spilled water out over her chin and down her neck, but she drank from it greedily. He lowered her back to the buffalo hide.

The old man had spat out his eye-stone to chant a song without words which began up high: *eee-ee-e-e-eeeee* . . . From his parfleche, he pulled a peeled cherry wand and waved it above her while his voice grunted gradually lower. Leaning over, he blew smoke across her face, then threw his shuck in the fire. He felt with his hands to locate her shoulders, felt down the arm to the wounded hand, and squatted above it. His earrings hung down. The chant came out muffled. He sucked at her hand and came up with a mouthful, nodding his angry head toward Siwapi, who leaned toward him over the girl.

Maasuwini felt for Siwapi's face, then spit in his mouth. The bitter poison spread clouds in his mind, twisting funnels of dizziness . . . This was the hard part. He held it there tightly shut in his mouth while the old man's chant grew lower and lower, descending into his gurgling throat.

Then Siwapi spit the poison in the fire.

Maasuwini waved a feather around, to the four directions and over the girl. Again, he leaned down and sucked at her hand. She shook like a rabbit—her eyes rolled up shut. Siwapi saw—exploding stars. The old man spit the stuff in his mouth and Siwapi held it there again, then spit it in the fire.

Siwapi discovered the song in his throat. Something was pulling it out like a rope, gagging him: *eee-ee-e-e-eeeee* . . . His head tipped back when he opened his mouth.

The old man poked around in his sack. Beside the fire, Patika sang as well. Pausone's new *piwán*, the agent's daughter, still lay there curled up, but facing them now with stony eyes. She watched their activity without reacting. She stared at Siwapi, a man in a *piwán*'s dress, with a man's voice . . . His song came out stronger.

Scrambling fast like a mouse on all fours, Maasuwini crawled around to the head of the wounded girl, felt for her face, and blew on her brow with big gulps of breath and puffed-out cheeks, interrupting his chant. He leaned down and put his mouth to the skin at her open dress, just below her neck. Siwapi chanted, *lu-lu-luuu-lu-lu-luuu* . . . The girl's eyes flew open, she lifted her head, but Siwapi gently forced it back down. She thought something was drilling her chest, he knew. The sensation there felt cold as ice . . . When the old man removed his head, smacking his lips, gurgling the chant, a pile of hailstones sat on her skin between the folds of her open collar.

He scrambled around for more sucking at her hand. The chanting grew louder. Maasuwini sucked, lifted his head, and spit out a stone, two stones. Moaning now from down in his belly, and leaning over her hand while making a sound like water draining deep in a hole, he sucked at her hand, then stood up, facing the others. He staggered a few steps back from the girl. His face looked like webs were passing across it. His fleshy eyelids opened and closed like the mouths of fish with nothing inside, and the whole bottom half of his wrinkled face had puffed up obscenely. Something long and black grew out of his face; it hung down twitching back and forth. He turned to spit it out, then stomped his feet, chasing it off. The quick lizard slithered under a blanket. He turned to Siwapi—where is it?

I'll get it.

Siwapi lifted the edge of the blanket, grabbed the lizard by its tail, and stepped to the door flap. He threw it out, running with his feet to make sure it got away from there. He kicked some dirt at the crawling lizard, the illness the old man had sucked from her hand. Don't you ever come back . . .

Inside, the old man had lit another shuck. The agent's daughter said something in American to the sick girl, who already looked better. The hail had melted on the skin below her neck, and her eyes were wide open. She replied with a kind of choking word, shaking her head. That bonnet looked funny.

Maasuwini's chant died in his throat. He sat there smoking. Patika put some coffee on the fire. The sick girl actually seemed to smile, although she looked dazed. She sat up with a shiver and glanced around the inside of the *carniv*.

The old man wasn't interested in coffee. He put on his vest, took up his parfleche, and left with Siwapi.

By that evening, the girl was completely cured. But she wasn't a girl. That's what people were saying. Quinkent's son had seen her dressed as a male at the Agency boardinghouse before the killing started. Siwapi had noticed a faint swelling of her chest, though—it could be a girl's bosom. He wasn't sure. It could go either way.

Did Americans have what the People called *tuwusuwici*? Half men, half women? That's what he was now, Siwapi. He was strong like a man and did women's work well, and wore a woman's dress. It made him feel proud. Soon he'd be a doctor, when the old man died . . .

To celebrate their bravery, the men built a huge bonfire that evening outside the camp in a clearing against the high canyon wall. To get there, you waded through moonlight on the canyon bottom, past tall reeds and willows and skeletons of bushes with indistinct shadows. The moon hung straight overhead with a frog on one eye. The round moon burned a hole in the sky when you stared directly at it . . . In the clearing, off to one side, a row of men played the hand game, beating their sticks on a log and chanting while trying to guess where the marked bone was. At the fire, Canavish scraped on a morache, someone else drummed, and a few braves danced. They wore their best plumes and fur dancing caps made of skunk and bear skins with ornaments of eagle feathers on their wrists and arms, and breastplates and chokers made of pipe bones and hair around their necks, and soon a ring round as the moon had been formed. Everyone was excited. Siwapi stood off to the side with Maasuwini leaning on his arm beaming his eye-stone from left to right as he scanned the dancers. The captives were there, and each time a *piwán* threw some article of clothing taken from the dead soldiers onto the fire, she looked at the captives and screamed out an insult. They huddled together to one side of the fire: the agent's daughter, her toothless old mother with long nose and chin, the young one with the two children, and the woman they'd cured, still in her bonnet. Someone had bandaged her hand with strips of cloth.

The agent's daughter put her long thin arms around her mother, cradling her closer. Colorow stood near them. Because he was fat, he seldom danced. He was talking too loud, telling stories about the soldiers trapped in that valley north of the Agency. They had no anuses, he said. That's why we shot them—to help them out. A few braves laughed. With a blue cap taken from one of the soldiers cocked on his head, Colorow shouted in American, "*Attention!*" The word made him stiffen, rifle erect—held at arm's length—and his foolish face cramped with mock solemnity. More laughter and shouting. Quinkent walked up to the agent's daughter and made her stand up. He pointed his rifle right at her face and said he would kill her.

She said something in American and turned away.

He lowered the rifle and raised it again, then spoke to her in American. She looked directly at him and spoke this time in the People's language: "Go on, shoot. I don't care if I die."

He lowered the rifle and told her to follow him. The dancers had stopped. The drummers held their sticks above their drums. Pausone walked over to Quinkent, grabbed the rifle, and told him to leave. Quinkent shouted something incomprehensible and they pushed at each other. Quinkent wrenched the rifle away and raised it again to the agent's daughter, who looked right down the barrel and said, "Go on, shoot. I want to be shot."

He lowered the rifle and looked around blankly. No one knew what to do. Pausone took the agent's daughter by her arm and seated her again. Quinkent scanned the captives, gave a little shrug, and pulled the agent's wife to her feet. Everyone laughed when he walked off through the brush dragging the old woman behind him by the hand.

Canavish had crouched down beside the young mother whose two children huddled in her arms. After a while she walked off behind him, carrying one child and leading the other.

The morache and drummers started up again. Some braves danced, some crowded around the remaining captives. To the left of the bonfire, babies laced up in buckskin hides and lashed to cradle boards leaning against the canyon wall followed the movement and noise of the dancers with their wide eyes. The boys' penises hung through a breech in the buckskin in case they had to piss. For the girls, a narrow piece of curved bark fixed between their legs stuck out of the buckskin; urine slid down the trough of one now like water through a flume.

Some kind of commotion raised up dust. The braves around the captives were shouting, and Maasuwini felt curious—he wanted to see. Siwapi helped him walk toward the group. A semicircle had formed around the girl with the bandaged hand, who had removed her dress and bonnet in order to prove she was a boy. She was dressed in boy's clothes. They were laughing at Serio, who had claimed her for his *piwán*. That doesn't prove anything, Serio said. You still look like a girl. Show us more. Show us you are a boy.

The agent's daughter translated.

The braves waited to judge the proof this strange person would offer. He—or she—looked around and seemed to smile, then turned his back to them. His hands went up to his neck, of all things, as though fumbling with his collar, though they couldn't really see. They could make out his arms dropping to his waist to unfasten his pants, lowering them a little. He turned to face them.

For a crazy moment, no one said a thing. Then everyone laughed—they couldn't help it. It was hard to see because he faced everyone with his back to the fire, but surely something hung there through his unbuttoned pants, between his bandaged hand and his good one—some small blackened thing like a shriveled calf's ear . . . "That's the smallest prick in the world," someone shouted. The men laughed so hard they could hardly breathe, all except Maasuwini, with the eye-stone in his mouth—he bent forward to peer intently . . .

Colorow laid his hand on Serio's shoulder. "Do you still want to marry him?"

As he stood there, the boy's face looked both shameful and proud. He was trying bravely to smile even though he looked like someone who'd just stepped off a cliff. Then he turned back around to hitch up his pants. He sat down next to the agent's daughter. "Wait. Stand up," Colorow said. "You look better in this." He threw him the dress. "You must wear this all the time," he said. He pointed to Siwapi. "Just like him."

The agent's daughter translated for Colorow.

"If you don't wear that dress, we'll kill you," he said. "You can live with those two, Maasuwini and Siwapi. You belong with them. You can be their slave. You are *tuwusuwici*. I knew it all the time." Colorow laughed, and the others joined him.

But the next morning no one was laughing. News came with the dawn that soldiers were coming. Not the ones they'd surrounded, but others, arriving from the north, from the railroad, marching down now to relieve those trapped. The scouts said five hundred men—maybe a thousand.

So they had to break camp. Everyone was angry. People kicked at the dogs as though they'd brought the bad news. Siwapi noticed Maasuwini striking the grass around him with a stick, and knew what was happening. The mice and grass bugs were taunting him again. "*Maasuwini fucked his own daughters . . .*"

Siwapi had to show their new helper in his dress how to pack up the buffalo hides, take down the *carniv*, lash the poles through holes bored in their tops to either side of their horses—*piwán*'s work. No one ate breakfast. The new helper was given the job of carrying the fire on a slow match of braided sage bark. Siwapi showed him how to blow on it every now and then so it wouldn't go out.

He had to be helped onto his horse because of the wounded hand. Once seated, he took the braided bark from Siwapi, winding the length of it around one arm three or four times. Then Siwapi helped Maasuwini to mount. The old man on his horse stared at the American man-woman intently with the eye-stone in his mouth—watched him awkwardly seated on his horse, trying bravely to smile. He wore that dress as Colorow had told him, but not the bonnet on his head, as everyone now knew he was a man—wasn't he? Maasuwini scowled.

Then the entire encampment watched Pausone kneel to help the agent's daughter onto her horse. Some of the braves laughed from a distance, as Pausone had never done that with his other *piwán*. She spoke to him; he handed up her hat, a wide-brimmed felt hat to keep off the sun. She said something to her mother, already mounted up near the front with Quinkent's family. Looking around, she noticed her friend in his calico dress and nodded her head. She looked ashamed or afraid. She watched him with eyes full of confusion.

Chapter

❧ 9 ❧

Working away inside Josie's suffering, like a pebble in a shoe, was a nagging distraction—who or what was Pete? On the trail, she watched him trying to be Pete, trying to nod and smile—even wink at her once—but she had her doubts. Some deep shame like a fever had licked him and caused him to slump on his horse in that dress. Yes, she'd spotted him taking that thing from his pouch . . . Horrible possibilities formed in her mind, in this season of horror which had permitted her to see mutilated bodies, bloody scalps, her dead father with a barrel stave in his mouth . . . The canyon they rode through doubled back around spurs and feet of cliffs, bringing her face to face now and then with her mother, Flora Ellen, and worst of all, Pete. They clopped through her brain in a snaking line of horses through dust so thick you could almost write their names on their faces. *Pete.*

He gave off winking. He avoided her eyes.

He vexed the terrible purity of her suffering, the power to be strong and not yield. She was full of dull silence, dispirited, hopeless. She tried to remember her father's face and keep it in her heart, the only place he could live now. It was lonely, so lonely, when your father died . . . Her pain felt so *old*, thought it wasn't—just two days. Each night she spit in Pausone's face and he laughed and rolled off her, then rolled back on. He'd once been her friend. She responded to him in blank monosyllables and accepted his body with unblinking resignation, curled up larvally inside her skin as though all she wanted to do was sleep, though her eyes were wide open and hideously awake. The disgust scoured her soul. It wasn't his fault. Outside their tipi he watched her unceasingly. He was short and muscular with a delicate nose, large brow, small chin, and yellowish eyes. His other two squaws were offended and frightened by this new marriage. They berated and reassured her at turns: Look what he did, he opened you up, no wonder you bleed . . . You should be grateful, they said—he protects you. Nothing was the same anymore, they understood that, while appearing to resent it even more deeply than she did. Pausone slapped Patika to make her stop scolding him. With them, he sought out excuses to explode, but with Josie he acted polite and gallant, he helped her on her horse, brought her the best meat, though she refused it. She hardly ate a thing. Pausone was suffering too, she could see that—he was deeply in love and thought he might lose her . . .

Every waking moment now Josie's stomach sank as though perpetually draining. All things had been drugged with the awareness of death. She fretted for her mother, who also had seen her dead father, and who sat on her horse now curled like a shaving. Douglas had had to lash her to the saddle so she wouldn't tip over. Her mother's brave stoicism appeared eroded by age, had an element of blankness. In those few moments when Josie could be with her, she barely talked. Instead, she read her book out loud, and sometimes the Utes gathered around to listen. As for Flora Ellen Price, she jabbered away all the time or cried—one or the other—and her children had made a quick inner adjustment that enabled them to play and have fun with their Ute friends, though timidly, to be sure. It was like the play of sick children, half envious—like those who can't swim standing in water up to their knees watching those who can.

They rode on their horses through up-and-down country, over ridges, humps, and knolls, up arroyos fanning down from steep hills, stopping to eat or talk with the scouts racing back and forth between them and the soldiers. The new soldiers had relieved those trapped. They were forty miles back now, still in that valley—but they'd be coming soon enough . . .

More braves departed to fight the soldiers. Not Pausone, though—he stayed. Their shrinking party was mostly squaws and old men with some lingering braves to guard the captives, maybe fifty or sixty people in all. They snaked past hills of yellow sandstone with holes pecked in their sides, it seemed to Josie's fancy, by huge prehistoric birds searching grubs. Then they skirted a hogback ridge and the earth opened up in a wide, yellow-green, grassy valley, with smoke curling up from two or three tipis beside a winding river, tipis of braves who'd arrived there ahead of them. This valley was wide and went on for miles; the land seemed to tip on a plane toward the south. Across the blue and green mountains around it, huge shadows, themselves as large as mountains, raced over slopes, in and out of folds. The clouds crossing the sun weren't really that big, but everything swelled in this outstretched valley.

Josie had to help Pausone's squaws erect their tipi. Patika laid a pole across the cover, tied the top edge to it, then stooped to lift, while Josie and Susan pulled with a guy rope. They staked out the guy rope and carried more poles from the dray horses nearby, two for each of the ears at the top which regulated the size of the smoke hole. More poles widened Josie's house of pain . . . Nearby, Pete helped the old medicine man and his berdache to raise their tipi, just a stone's throw away. He refused to glance in Josie's direction, though. His eyes on a tether were staked to the earth . . .

She watched the two men in skirts work like squaws.

Hard to tell how long they stayed in this valley. Time felt stuck. The braves who were healthy left to fight the soldiers, including at last Pausone. The old and the injured stayed to guard the captives, who at first weren't allowed to speak to each other. But after a day or two, no one seemed to care.

Josie's cough came back. She hardly ate a thing, drank no coffee, and ignored Pausone's scolding squaws, who'd been charged with keeping her healthy. That first day, when talk was still forbidden, she managed to clasp her mother's hand, and—at the river, filling their water jugs—declared under her breath, to Pete's surprise, that the valley was beautiful.

"So it is," he said aloud.

She could live here forever. To her horror, she almost missed Pausone. If she had her own knife she could stab him in the dark when he came back—if the soldiers didn't kill him . . . The grass in this valley was two feet high. She ate a few rose hips to keep up her strength and thought of the knife slipping through his ribs . . . The mountains around their spreading valley, patterned with piñon and six-foot-high sage, looked beautiful enough to break anyone's heart who'd just lost nearly everything she loved. They were terribly precarious, those mountains, they could simply deflate like hot-air balloons. The earth looked mummified, and the only true thing in Josie's vicinity seemed to be her hand, which she held before her eyes. This is my hand, the blood runs through it, I can move it up and down . . .

She spotted Pete sitting on a log before his tipi, watching her, and shrugged. She looked right at him and he looked at her. He brought two fingers of his bandaged hand up to his forehead and flipped them out in a limp salute.

Pausone returned that night after dark, then left her again the next morning at dawn.

Arvilla read to the captives and some squaws from *The Pilgrim's Progress* the next day by the river. High cirrus clouds made the valley feel small. The mountains looked mouse-gray. Then the clouds blew out and the valley flared up in the slanting sun, which changed brown to yellow and gray to blue. The green earth blew hard across the horizon and down through the sloping valley . . . *As to thy burden, be content to bear it, until thou comest to the place of Deliverance; for there it will fall from thy back itself.* The squaws all nodded; they knew about burdens. Flora Ellen started crying. Her four-year-old daughter strutted around with a huge cradle board strapped to her shoulders which one of the squaws had given her to play with.

The funny thing was, the place felt like Paradise . . . Josie's scars were all in her knowledge. She held them in and closed around them, feeling almost as if she could just float off, she was lighter than air. Her mind had been hollowed out—it didn't matter. Her heart had received so many blows it could scarcely feel a thing. She and Pete found an aspen tree at the edge of the camp full of golden leaves, a burst bag of coins flung at the sky. They sat beneath it saying nothing at first under the scornful gaze of Pausone's squaws, who were tending a fire in the center of the camp and scraping out hides.

At last Josie spoke. "You look silly in that dress."

"It was your idea."

She realized that both she and Pete stank. The close, heavy, fetid, fecal smell of the insides of tipis clung to and dizzied them even in the open air. Josie seemed to be falling . . . Their legs and arms had been torn by briers, and both now had lice. Pete scratched his neck. Josie removed her hat and settled back in the crook of his arm, gazing over at Pausone's squaws in defiance. What did she care? Patika said something to Susan; both laughed. Beyond them, two boys wrestled in the dirt. A dog had found the foreleg of a deer and ran off dodging legs and bodies as though any moving thing might kick it.

"Well, I guess Pausone got his wish," said Josie. "He married me."

"I shouldn't jest about it."

"Why not? It's all one to me . . ."

"You don't feel that in the least, don't pretend."

"Susan told me the first night that Pausone had conceived it his duty to be my protector."

Pete squirmed against the tree—it hurt. "What did you answer?"

"I said I didn't think much of his protection." She could feel Pete's insides struggling to speak. There was something he wanted, and didn't want, to say. What are you, Pete? She strained her eyes up; that pouch was still there, tucked into his dress—she'd spotted the thong . . .

"I could protect you," he said.

She laughed.

"Don't scorn me, Josie, not now."

Oh, but Pete—everything's changed. Nothing will ever be good again . . .

"I once stopped a man from beating his wife."

"You did?"

"Stopped him cold."

Two hawks flew in the sky overhead. At the same moment, Josie's cough broke open, and she pictured her ugly, misshapen lungs, two collapsed puffballs spewing out dust.

"Josie, I can't get comfortable here. This tree's gotten my back fairly riled." Pete squirmed forward and Josie stood up. Without a word, she walked to Pausone's tipi with long strides that felt like a bow unbending. Pure defiance! She stared down the two squaws, slipped inside, and gathered up Pausone's best buffalo blanket, the soft one he pressed her down into at night. Beneath it, some willows piled there for comfort clung to its tanned side. She brushed them off, folded it up, and stepped out boldly into the sunlight.

She wedged it between Pete and the tree and glanced again at the squaws. Susan's eyes narrowed. Her lips vaguely smiled. Josie settled back against Pete's arm and bosom . . . "Tell me about the man and his wife."

Pete squirmed and fussed, though his back felt fine now. "I shouldn't have mentioned that, Josie, it's nothing. You don't want to hear it."

"Certainly I do."

"No you don't. It's hardly pleasant. It's a longish story."

Josie looked around. "Well, when we finish all our many chores, I suppose then you might manage a snippet? I realize we've both got better things to do, such as brood on our losses."

Pete looked around too—and saw absolutely nothing. Of course, he shouldn't have brought it up at all, but it was too late now. Then again, part of him had been dying to tell . . . The man and his wife. Well, here it is. It's come to that. "Okay, you asked for it."

"You make it sound like dreadful torture."

"It might be. We'll see."

"These were friends of yours?"

"Patience, Josie. This could take a while."

His name was Twig, in respect of his body, all bony and thin, and hers was Peggy, a girl of sixteen. This was back home in South Carolina eight years ago—around '65, the last year of the war. You would have liked her, Josie. A young bride, but a good spud for young—just like you. The only two things which Peggy ever feared was a cow and a drunken man, said Pete.

Josie felt Pete's voice through his chest, the fleshy part next to the armpit, where she'd settled her head. It was squeaky but deep, and it vibrated plenty—even seemed to be shivering. It was dropping a plummet, measuring a chasm. It came out in gulps, he was swallowing air! Hang in there, Pete. Settle down. Easy . . .

The War. How to describe what *that* felt like? It felt like the world come apart at the seams, just like now, Josie. A terrible dark time, even where they lived, Peggy and Twig, at the edge of a swamp, with hardly no roads. The war spread everywhere in the South like malaria. It infected your heart—turned it dark and bitter—just like now. Twig was a swamp rat and yeoman farmer, a wiry thin man with knobby joints and big stumping hands given to the amiable weaknesses of drinking to distraction and beating on folks . . . He was strong for his size. He beat poor Peggy, then called down the wrath of the Lord on his head in spasms of remorse. "Lord, I know I am wicked, but spare her!" Often he said he'd give a thousand dollars to rid himself of his evil temper. She was just a child, a frail young thing skinny as a boy, and he loved her so but his head had been joined to his shoulders backwards. He was dumb as a stump but a foxy man. After he black-and-blued her eyes he cooked a big meal to make it up to her. He went out and stole a neighbor's hog or caught some rice birds . . . This was a country of rice plantations, but Twig and Peggy lived upriver, where rice fields gave way to cypress swamps. It was in the South Carolina low country, said Pete—where I come from before I moved north . . .

They married in the war, then Twig went off to fight, as a substitute for a man whose daddy owned huge rice plantations with hundreds of slaves. He went off with his squirrel rifle . . . Two months later he come back, and whipped poor Peggy when she asked him what happened. They didn't have much—a brag cow and some chickens. The ordnance men had already passed through and torn down his still to use the copper for percussion caps. There was shortages everywhere. Salt went to fifty dollars the bag and flour to ninety dollars the barrel, even there, near the coast. They'd been having bread riots in Georgetown, the nearest thing to a city close by. So Twig went off to fight once again, giving the money paid him to Peggy. At one time substitutes got six thousand dollars, but that was Confederate dollars—near worthless. He went off to fight, then deserted and came back, not conceiving so much an interest in the war as in the money he collected for bounty jumping like that. Why should he fight to defend rich people's property?—meaning their slaves . . . One time he told Peggy of how, in the midst of a battle, a slave run up with a tin pan full of rice and ham for his master, telling him to eat up for his strength. But all dead soldiers turned black in a day or two, regardless of their former color. He'd seen their dead faces, swole up and shining black as charcoal. The only real nigger was death, said Twig.

He kept on going off to war then returning to his wife. At first he come back all sweet and thoughtful, but then he beat her, as if *she* was his substitute. He had to get likkered up first, of course . . . He shouted things at her like, *Shut yer gash, woman!* She was plucky though, Josie—a strong gal, like you. She vowed each time to endure her suffering, but to save up the interest. She knew what he owed her—just like you know, Josie . . .

Josie asked: Were these people your kin?

In a manner of speaking, said Pete, and continued.

"The war got on fast. It was shoe-deep all over. Nothing was normal, everything gone crazy—just like now, Josie. It didn't rain rain, it rained vitals and blood. Even in that swamp where folks all knew each other you couldn't tell who to trust and who not. The war was inside you. Life was a nightmare—like I said, just like now . . . Bands of deserters came through the swamps stealing what they could and raping the swamp women. Runaway slaves came through and murdered white folks. There was talk of slaves revolting on plantations. Some killed the widow on a nearby plantation then broke into the smokehouse and took all the meat. There was no more white overseers—they'd gone to war. Then word came through that Sherman was coming to level the whole state of South Carolina, as he'd done to Georgia. He had a reputation. His bummers stole valuables and burned what was left. They burned whole cities. They raped women and children and tied them to trees and threw bayonets at them—"

"Oh *Pete* . . ."

"So folks said. And on top of Sherman, more Northern troops were coming up the coast—closer to us—which folks said they was black. The

Fifty-fourth Massachusetts Infantry—Foster's Negro troops—were coming to Georgetown. Their ships had already landed on the coast. The Union troops just pushed with their finger and forts toppled, cities gave up. I'm exaggerating, Josie, Fort Wagner hardly budged. But folks started leaving, those that was left. They saw which way the wind blowed. Twig ran off to see what was up, but vowed to come back for his wife, pretty Peggy. It was always a blessing, him going like that. She was just a young thing. She lived in fear not of Sherman but of her bulldozing husband returning to beat her senseless again. He would. He always did. *He* was the war. When he ever showed up, things just came apart. She planned what to do, but doubted her capacity for such sheer dog meanness as it might take to kill him. She hadn't the strength . . . But she waited and watched. The war let you do things you never thought possible. Evenings, she wandered deserted rice fields next to the river to watch for his boat. All the trunks was up—that's the floodgates, which we called them trunks—so the banks wouldn't break while the planters were gone. In better days, Peggy and Twig used to camp on these banks with a fire to watch for rice thieves. The plantation owners paid them to do it . . ."

"Where do you come in, Pete?"

"You'll see, hold your horses. One night at twilight she spotted something—not a boat, nor her husband. A body of a man floating down the river . . . He washed like a big chunk of wood through a trunk right into the rice field, which held three feet of water at least sitting on it. Couldn't tell if he was living or dead—just carried like that by the rushing water. It was freshet time. The trees were leafed out, making it darker, and with night coming on it was some hard to see. Smell of violets and yellow jessamine all about. He washed into that rice field, swirled in a circle, then, just like he was coming to life, grabbled hold of the bank and climbed up. She hid in the bushes so's he wouldn't spot her. At first she thought he was Plat Eye himself—ghost of a man who haunted that area. But he was wearing blue—Union blue! And his face was black—a black soldier, Josie. She figured he was one of Foster's troops, the regiment come to occupy Georgetown. He ran up the bank and slipped into the woods.

"After that, things began disappearing from her house. It was just a swamp house on upended logs with some sheds and smokehouses and pens all about in a clearing near the river. The cow was long dead—butchered by thieves. She had some shad which a neighbor had smoked and give to her earlier and it just disappeared from the back kitchen. Winter turnips out in the garden vanished overnight. It was starving times but not a starving place, as food was abundant if you knew where to look. Cooters, shrimp, catfish, oysters . . . Peggy was spunky—could take care of herself. But not with a thieving soldier about. She found him at last in the woodshed one day, behind the last stack of winter firewood, where he'd made a little nest for himself. They just looked at each other. I think he was more scairt than her. Turned out that he'd absquatulated from the Fifty-fourth Infantry. Jumped in the river when they took Georgetown . . . Even Northerners by then—even Northern black soldiers—were fed up with that war, which they'd all but won.

"She began leaving him food by the woodshed—"

"Pete—"

"Hold on, Josie. We're close to the meat of it. You sure you want to hear this? I shouldn't be telling it."

Josie just stared at him.

"She left him food. Took him fritters in a basket. He hardly said nothing at first, just crouched there. Always waited for her to leave before he et. Plate licked clean when she came back for it, and on a full stomach—after a few days—she cleverly coaxed him with her good cheer to talk. She could blow out a perfect gale of good spirits when the need struck her, Josie—just like you used to could . . . Seems he'd somehow failed of his duty in the war—gave her to understand that. Begged her not to turn him in. She assured him she wouldn't. He was from Boston, a free Negro, name of Ben. A caulker, Ben was. Joined Colonel Shaw's troops for the war effort, partly to prove that black men could fight—black men were brave . . . Well, she didn't doubt it. Course, she'd been raised to believe that folks in the North were all infidels and freelovers, not to mention bloomer women and amalgamationists. As for the Negroes—they were all runaways. But this Ben was kind, and well spoken, and pleasant . . . She let him continue on in that woodshed.

"Then after a week, maybe two, surprise!—Twig came back, just like he promised. At first he was good. He laid not a hand on her, treated her famously. He was there to retrieve her. Sherman's bummers were coming, they'd made it to Florence, just forty miles off. They had to pack up and clear out, right away. Things might have gone fine if Twig hadn't managed to locate a jug, I think it was one he'd buried outside . . . While she sorted their things he got drunker than ever. Fell down somewheres and came back in the house with this huge gash on his cheek? Right about here? Thin, spindly man. He stood there before her. Her husband, she thought. There he stood, with his shoes untied, his shirt buttoned wrong. Remember, Josie, this Peggy had spunk. She'd married him up-country before he brought her down there to the rice coast, pretty far from her family back in the mountains. Cute little thing, of Irish stock.

Her daddy was Irish and her mom just a cracker. She couldn't have been more than five foot four. Had a child's sense of justice. Twig was terrible unfair. When he'd courted her just a few years back, he was sweet and almost shy. A churchgoing man! Now look at him. He stood there before her, pale and trembling, hair kind of slickered down to his head. Beard filthy dirty. He'd been drinking and sweating, doing something outside. Constructing a cart for their travels, before he found that jug. Now he slapped her hard. Said, there's *bummers* coming. Let's go, said. He was trembling awful and applied his fist to the side of her head like a sledge-hammer, hard. Her chin started wobbling. Something hard cracked. He never hit her so bad before, she was down, and the room gave a jump like a wrecked ship sinking. On all fours, sobbing, woozy, and bleeding, she tried to remember her careful plans. The ax or the poker . . . With a stick broken off of a shovel or pick he clubbed her about the head and shoulders, the slimy monster . . . Lying there limp, she told herself to forgive him, like she'd been taught. Thought she understood the poor brute. He was calling down the wrath of God on their heads with one fist in the air and his tiny walnut brain—she could picture it almost—bumsquabbled somewhere lost in his skull . . .

"He toppled down to the floor like a tree, just missing her a grain. Behind him stood that Negro soldier Ben with a poker in his hand. Her head cleared out pronto. They had an old rocker made from some kind of iron wood, which she got up and threw it acrost Twig sideways, pinning him there. He was slow, anyhow. Bleeding from the head. Ben disappeared into the kitchen, and Twig was gathering strength by the second, Peggy could see it. His head flip-flopped from side to side and his ferocious orbits begun to pop. Then he screamed a slow scream, the eeriest thing she ever did hear, the way he screamed so slow . . . So she jumped up quick and struck him upside the head with the poker, just above the eye—"

"Oh Pete, this is horrible!"

"He was still blinking blood when Ben came running back with a long kitchen knife. Peggy held her dear husband down with the rocker while that man pushed the knife slowly inside him. I remember he poked around with the knife a few times to locate a gap between his ribs where he could shove it into Twig's heart from underneath—sorter like this, with the heel of his hand—she helped too—had to see how it felt—and studied the actual moment which he died, with a slow expiration of stinking breath, kinder like venting the steam from an engine. He was looking at Ben like his nightmares come true . . ."

"*Pete*—" He was trembling. She'd sat up to face him, but his eyes had closed. He looked so pale! After almost a week of captivity, his face was still smooth—not a trace of a beard. Of course, it was cracked and sunburned too. His smallish chin shined like porcelain. His thin smacking lips were split and bleeding, and white sores curdled the corners of his mouth.

Eyes closed, he shook his head. "I shouldn't be telling you this, Josie, I know." Both cheeks were wet. When he opened the eyes, they were begging her, please—please understand . . .

Suddenly she did. All up and down her body, her skin flared up moist. He was blowing away from her, down a long tunnel . . . She reached out to catch him. "I thought you said, Pete—said *you* stopped a man—from beating his wife . . ."

Pete bowed his head. "Well, that's the case of it. I surely did. I got spunk in me, Josie, up to my ears—just like you got . . ."

Josie held his good hand. In that calico dress, blue with brown flowers—dirty and torn—he bowed his pretty head . . . "Shall I finish the story? They dragged Twig's body out to the shed, those two, Ben and Peggy. Ben turned out fine. Nothing like Twig. A mild man for strong. Stayed on a few days. We—I mean they—got along famous. He told Peggy that in Boston, which was antislavery, colored men couldn't go to the theater. Colored men weren't allowed to take their creams and jellies at the same high-class restaurants as whites. The Irish immigrants was taking all the low-pay jobs colored men used to have, and there wasn't any more colored stevedores or mechanics—hardly any colored caulkers. So when Colonel Shaw accompanied by Fred Douglas came through making speeches, Ben joined the army. Colored men could *fight* . . . He watched Colonel Shaw drop with a ball through his heart at the siege of Fort Wagner, where half the colored troops got trapped in a ditch—took a ball in the leg there himself. By the time he got to Georgetown, the war had finished what Boston begun, I mean turned his heart to gall, what with everyone North and South saying what colored men could and couldn't do, so he jumped in the river. Stayed there with Peggy with no one about while the world went more tile loose than ever before. You might say he became her tenderest lover. But Sherman's bummers were coming—they had to leave. So Peggy conceived of a bright idea first, and gave him some of her husband's clothing. Even at that last part of the war, a nigger dressed in Union blues was dead in the South, someone caught him out alone. Then, to fool the rapist soldiers, she dressed in his uniform, which hung like bags at first upon her—so she took it in. Cut her hair short—most scalped herself—and donned that blue Union cap, which fit, as her head was large for a girl. Plenty skinny enough, howsomever, to pass for male, with hardly a bosom. To make a long story short, she made a perfect soldier . . . They burned the place up with Twig Doyle still in that shed, and Ben made his way south, intending to circle back around west, where deserters might get on. She never saw him again. Meanwhile, *she* traveled out to meet Sherman's troops. Blended right in! Made her way north. Most *liked* being masculine. Was in Goldsboro when Lee surrendered, in Raleigh when the word came through that Lincoln was shot, so joined up with a regiment marching back up to Washington. Got demobbed there—"

Josie piped in. "Found work on the horsecars. Changed her name to Pete. Moved to New York—"

"That's the state of the case. Became accustomed to passing for male. Long as it worked, why change back? She made a fine man, just fine and dandy. A Bowery B'hoy! A rare, cleaned-up fellow, up to the scratch. A self-made man! Knew how to keep to the windward of things, knew just where her—his—bread might be buttered. It was one way to never get married again, not to some brute—they's too many brutes in the world, you know, Josie—but also a chance to kiss a few gals, which was something it turned out she took quite a shine to, just like any young man . . ."

"Oh Pete!"

"Peggy."

"Peggy! But you'll always be Pete to me. Dear dear sweet Pete . . ." She leaned forward trembling to kiss poor trembling Pete—kissed him—or her—full on the lips, held tight and kissed hard, causing Patika to rush over shouting and forcibly pry the two lovebirds apart.

Pete! Dear sweet Pete . . .

Chapter

❧ 10 ❧

"And—and—I bite my thumb at your haircut!" Count Léon-Fernand-Léon raised his arm to his mouth to effect this gesture, but couldn't quite complete it, couldn't liberate the vulgar Corsican within him. After all, he was French to the very . . . name. So his left thumb waited cocked before his lips, while the pistol hung straight down from his right hand.

"Bite your bloody dicky for all I care," said Stokes.

That did it, that unearthed the count's scorn with all its greasy nastiness. He hooked the thumb beneath his top incisors, then catapulted the foul thing at Stokes with an aggressive echoing flourish—you mountebank! Oh, if gestures could kill . . .

They faced each other across a mere ten paces marked by stakes Jo had pushed into earth, beneath a cold October sun flat as a pie tin in the sky, surrounded by ridges and benches of land in the middle of nowhere. They'd followed the White River, yes, it still ran beside them, but in five long days of diminishing food they'd come to suspect a vile deception. No Indians had appeared—no captives—nothing. The Agency cattle scattered along the river's length had dwindled that first day, then vanished entirely, while the land went from green and brown to yellow and red in long, high ridges created, it seemed, by gigantic plows, with cliff sides dotted with sage and juniper here and there, but mostly raw dirt.

It made them uneasy. Tempers flared. Stokes followed Bonny around with a stick and beat him silly when he managed to catch him. Meanwhile, the count whined for his haircut in broken English like a spoiled child—bemoaned his split ends and cracked, dusty locks, shoulder-length, dirty, and such a bother!

He held up those scissors he'd purchased from the green-goggled man back in better times—when the world was still young—and insisted that Stokes coupe les messy cheveux. He could do it. Stokes, in fact, had evolved a sixth sense for the human anatomy and how it should look from fabricating puppets, not to mention little men. But he demurred. Haircuts in the desert? He could cut more than hair, he could skin the vain gommy. The count's loveliness had become so tarnished, a mere haircut wouldn't signify. His cutaway velvet coat was a rag. His neck scarf had turned black with dirt, his perfumed hanky smelled of human sweat, his stockings were torn, exposing white legs, his slippers split open . . . Besides, it wasn't *haircuts* his mind should be fixed on, thought Stokes.

But that was all the man spoke of. Each night when they stopped their wagon to camp, the count shaved himself—he could do that. But he couldn't cut his own hair without an extra mirror; a trick of mirrors was required . . . "Mr. Stokes, you will do me the honor, *s'il vous plaît*. A mere snip-snip." The count had the mubblefubbles. Every man jack of them did, except Bonny, who buzzed harshly and talked away stunning flash, saying nothing especial with that swazzle in his mouth—it was there all the time now—but having a good time . . .

Stokes cut the count's hair, at last, to be shut of him. But the count didn't like it. Dreadful spiteful fellow . . . Stokes found himself twixt a rock and a hard place. You egged me on to it, count, now it's done with. It's middlin'. It's an affecting 'aircut. I shouldn't make such a wry face, sir, if I was you. I done it gratis for nothing. It is generally one of the beautifullest coiffures as ever I seed . . .

"*Boucher!* My hair! All my lovely hair!"

It *was* a mite lollygagged. It looked fly-blown for sure. Stokes had got it too short save the parts he'd overlooked, which were therefore too long . . . The count tried repairing it himself, but in his frustration sent the mirror flying, whence it shattered on rocks in a blizzard of glass. Without a reflection, he imagined his topknot to look even worse than it did—and it looked pretty horrible . . . "You have—murdered me," he moaned. "You—crumpet-faced man."

"It's a lost cause, count," said Jo. "Give it up."

Stokes perked up. "If I'm ugly, then tell me, for I've never heard it yet."

The count smoldered on. He sat next to Stokes, who drove. Jo and Bonny lay sprawled in the back, too bruised by the trail to mind such squabbles. It wasn't even a wagon road. Except for the river, all was dry earth and sage, uncongenial to wheels. Every hundred yards or so they had to jump out to push a boulder aside. Gradually, the distant mountains had deflated, giving way to tilted benches of land and flat-topped mesas and winding ravines. Now and then the spur of a hill shot down to the river, making its course loop out, and Stokes had to drive in the water itself, since the hump of the land was too steep to cross.

They should have turned back. Their food supply was low—mostly dried fruit, coffee, and flour from the ravaged Agency supply, mixed with the dirt in which it had spilled. Stokes grew adept at whipping up emergency biscuits of flour and water cooked in tin cans on open fires, which all wolfed down. But how long would the flour last? No one knew how to hunt. They saw plenty of antelopes, and Jo at last took a shot at a herd with one of the dueling pistols, scattering them up slopes and downriver like birds or fish, but no meat dropped in their fry pans from *that* little poof of useless smoke. Nor were there signs that people of any stripe had passed this way, but what were signs, anyway? Products of searching! Their dull trudge forward had a mechanism of its own. Its logic was airtight to sun-parched minds . . .

The count took to endlessly patting the top of his head, to gauge its appearance. "All it required was for taking more care." With that savage hair, his long nose felt more prominent—more bony. He touched it with his fingers—touched his ears, now exposed—his chin, his lips. Then back to the hair with both hands this time, sizing it up with his sensitive palms. Oh, the sheer horror of looking unkempt! He resorted to prayer. Lack of food didn't bother him, having once been enamored of certain ideas expounded by a Monsieur Coëssin in Paris, to the effect that the need for food is a sign of our earthly imperfection, as the shameful results of digestion confirmed—the permanent stain flowing from our First Sin. Still, he could use some mulled wine and fresh pineapple . . . He composed in his mind letters to Eugénie. The eyes of the world are upon us, as we search. France is waiting. He also is waiting. He has waited a long time! In the count's mind, *He* was surely Napoleon—no longer a name, but a flag; not a man, but the image of glory itself . . .

But *He* was also the count's forlorn father, Count Léon *père*, Napoleon's firstborn, in his miserable hovel outside of Paris spending whole days rigid in his armchair before the empty grate for which fuel was wanting, with nary a coin for a bit of tobacco . . .

You are a daughter, Madame, and the generous heart of Your Majesty cannot but tremble at the future prospects of my father, condemned with a species of ostracism by a family grudge. I know something of persecution myself. One's closest allies turn against one. Do not therefore sever

a link in the mighty chain grasped in heaven by the immortal founder
of the French Empire, my illustrious grandfather!

A horntoad clinging to a rock watched them pass with unblinking eyes
round as glass beads, then scrambled for safety in the wake of their
towering shadow.

They stopped for the night. The count's piety persisted. He unfolded
his blankets and knelt to pray, patting the top of his head with his hand.
O mighty Father. He clenched his fist. Call your wrath down upon all
common infidels . . .

Stokes had cooked up a whole passel of biscuits, some on sticks, some
in cans, but the count declined nourishment. "You conceived of this—
defilement," he said on his knees, facing away and raising his voice as
though addressing the hills, "one fine morning. You are proud of yourself? You planned it since two weeks. Harlot! Delilah!"

"It were you egged me on to it," said Stokes from his fire.

They'd camped in a canyon with bulging hills a half mile apart hem-
ming them in. Someone had lowered the clouds since morning like
weighted bags, thus bottling up the colors of things as daylight drained
off—the brown of earth, blue of sagebrush, green of a little grass by the
river . . . Cottonwoods clumped near the river were dead on one side,
alive on the other. Everything here pointed west, the dead side—their
direction of travel.

"You smell like a goat," said the count to Stokes. He'd stood from his
prayers and approached the dumpy man squatting by the fire.

Stokes didn't look up. "And you—like a goat's twat."

"Gentlemen, gentlemen." Jo spoke up with a mouthful of biscuit,
catching precious crumbs with his hands.

"Gentlemen?" said the count. "You insult me by including this creature inside your word."

"It's a greater misfortune to have two nor one," said Stokes.

"Meaning, monsieur?"

"You isn't no more the gentleman than me."

The count removed his hanky from his pocket and hurled it at
Stokes's face.

"You're coming it much too strong, sir. It's gamy." He held the hanky
to his nose and sniffed, then tossed it to Bonny. "Drop it altogether now,
Mr. le count, if you know what's proper."

Count Léon-Fernand-Léon regarded Stokes with an indifferent leer.
He was hunched like a crane, and smiled as he spit, just missing
Stokes's leg.

"Gully-fluff!" said Stokes.

Bonny blew his nose in the count's hanky. The count swung his leg in a vicious kick but came up empty, losing his balance. "You—you—" He was shouting at Stokes. "You practitioner of gush. You gutter of blood. *Foutu couillon!*"

"Translate for me," Stokes said to Jo.

"Vulgar expression," said Jo. "Fucking testicle. Bloody damned cretin."

"Smell-smock!" shouted Stokes.

"*Cascadeur! Putain!*"

"Quim-sticker! Twat-face! Muck-spout!"

"A card, sir. You have a card."

Stokes turned to Jo. "What's he mean by that?"

"He has challenged you to a duel, Mr. Stokes."

"You weasel guts! You can't do that! Tricked up in them pretty rags of yours! The eel pot can't challenge the eel, I say. I'm a firster. I'm topmost. Twiggy-vous?"

The count turned to Jo. "Translate for me."

"I think he means to challenge you first."

"*Impossible!* You cannot challenge myself, a superior. The challenge flows from offended honor. You have no honor."

Stokes slapped the count's face with such force he fell down in the dirt. "I seed it done like that on a packet."

Sprawled there, the count brought his hands to his face. Tears came. He looked up at Jo. From this point on, as a breach had occurred, he would not look at Stokes until he faced him with a weapon. "Jo," he said. "You shall be my second."

Stokes looked about for Bonny. Two camps formed. The world was divided. As the offended party, the count insisted to Jo that they move across the river, but Jo didn't feel absolutely certain that theirs was in fact the offended party. The count after all had questioned Stokes's honor.

"But he slapped my face."

"You threw the handkerchief."

"He made the haircut!"

"The first offense requires the first apology," said Jo. "It is my duty as your second to request an apology."

"I shall not accept it."

"Then he will be the aggrieved."

"Let him choose the weapons!"

"In his country the challenged party chooses weapons."

"In my country, the insulted party chooses weapons."

They had only one pair of weapons regardless, those pistols presented to the Comte de Forzine by Napoleon himself . . .

Jo requested an apology. Stokes laughed in his face. He and Bonny had all the biscuits now, this was hardly pleasant . . . Jo demanded their meager supply of food be apportioned, but Stokes had the right of possession, he said with a pudding-faced smile. After the duel, we'll split *his* share; Stokes nodded toward the count and winked at Jo, as if to say he didn't hold Jo's role in this matter against him. Jo felt it his duty to advise both parties that duels are generally fought at dawn, as tempers might cool during the night, the offender might apologize . . . *Never*, they said. In any case, it was twilight, too dark to fire now. As he and the count forded the river, a coyote howled somewhere to the west. The air had grown cold. The cold river mumbled cold words around their legs. Jo looked up at a mouse-gray sky. Bonny and Stokes had the wagon too—and the pistols—the hot coals. Oh mother, what now?

Jo spent a sleepless night listening for Bonny, who he felt certain would cross that river to slit their dirty throats. He thought of his own duels—the journalist he'd shot long ago now, in another world. Of course, the count slept like a baby.

Something would happen. Someone might get hurt.

Anaxagoras said that snow was black. That significant insight grew in Jo's mind like a mushroom stuffed there, then underwent several cycles of decay, collapse, the scattering of spores, rebirth and growth, all in five minutes' sleep. Sometime in the night the clouds blew out, Jo's eyes flew open, the river slid by on its glistening belly—the stars were just inches over his head! What about snakes, Jo? Snakes might come bite you . . . You might find in your blankets a whole nest of spiders . . .

Neither side cared to apologize at dawn. Jo crossed the river to find a suitable location for the duel, then made the mistake of asking Stokes's approval first. It was a gravelly sandbank deposited by a bend in the river further downstream, fine with Stokes but not with the count. "In my country," he said, "the one who demands satisfaction—myself—is choosing the dueling ground."

"In his country, *Monsieur le comte*, it is the one who *gives* satisfaction."

"In my country, the rules of the insulted party apply."

"In his country, the rules of the challenged party apply."

An impasse . . . Jo spent the first half hour of dawn crossing and recrossing the river to negotiate. He steadied himself in the water with his walking stick. His boots did just fine protecting his feet until the third or fourth crossing, when the toes felt that wet coldness . . . The count's indifference—the hallmark of his breeding—found its limit at these sticking points of etiquette. He grew progressively more nervous and shrill, stamped his foot, pursed his lips. Stokes, on the other hand, appeared to be happy. He smiled opaquely, puffed up his chest, extruded his hindquarters, and resembled for all the world a merchant who'd just concluded a handsome bargain. But he wouldn't give way. "Very well, then," said the count. "Tell him I shall consider myself the one who is giving the satisfaction."

"The aggrieved?"

"The affronted."

"That would make you the challenger. You mean the impugned."

"*Que'est-ce que ça veut dire?*"

"The one whose honor has been questioned."

"Ah! *Parfaitement!*"

That settled it, that worked. Jo felt proud of himself, he should have been a diplomat. Those years of selling specious railroad bonds had perfected his ability to convince folks that what they wanted corresponded perfectly to what he had. This was getting someplace now—it could even be fun! The sandbank it was. And now the count, as the offended party, chose the distance.

Wait a minute—he was the *challenged* party.

"But you see, Jo, in my country the challenged party chooses the distance. I am choosing ten paces."

Ten paces? Oh no . . .

Still, this was perfectly acceptable to Stokes, who appeared to have no real conception of what was happening. He acted like a man preparing for a picnic. Indeed, he and Bonny had cooked up a breakfast of biscuits—and biscuits—but offered none to Jo and the count, despite the ancient rules of hospitality, every bit as sacred as the rules of honor. Very well—let it be ten paces. Five! Besides, Stokes made a better target than the count, who at least seemed to know the Twenty-six Commandments.

Jo inspected and primed the pistols then laid them back in their velvet-lined mahogany case for the count to choose first. Or should it be Stokes? In England, the challenger makes the first choice. Or it might have been the challenged . . . Actually, the challenged chooses the weapons in question, swords or pistols, for example, and the challenger which of the chosen he shall use. On the other hand, these were now French rules . . . And Jo wished to urge the count through eye signals or facial expressions to choose the good pistol, the one with the least disport or throw—the one he'd killed the journalist with so many years back. So he gave him the choice.

But he picked the wrong one! He wasn't paying attention! His hand trembled reaching into the case, Jo could see that, whereas Stokes's meaty fist simply yanked out the other one—hefted it—brought the barrel to his lips in a mocking kiss . . .

This was wrong, all wrong. They stood on the sandbank. Bonny was skipping stones on the water. It was full daylight now, but the hills to the east blocked the rising sun. The river jabbered away beside them. "Gentlemen," said Jo, "I conceive it my duty to tell you that the grounds for this affair are—are insufficient. Trivial, even. A simple handshake could avoid bloodshed. A simple handshake, without imputation of blame. Neither side need apologize if you mutually agree—"

"Nevair!" said the count. Stokes stood there smiling.

"Very well . . ." Jo heaved a big sigh. He felt positively dizzy from lack of breakfast. It could be they both planned to delope. It was all in good fun, they'd laugh about it afterwards . . . But just in case, in pacing the distance, he used as generous a stride as he could manage without losing equilibrium. The show must go on . . . He drove sticks in the ground to mark the two limits. "The handkerchief!" Bonny on his stubby little legs ran to Jo with the count's hanky, the one he'd blown his nose in last night. Jo steadied himself with his walking stick and lifted the hanky high in the air. "Gentlemen—take your positions."

Stokes's backside waddled, while Count Léon's long thin legs picked their way carefully, like a crane's, to their respective stakes. The count assumed a sideways position and folded up strangely, to present a smaller target. He was trembling. His limbs and torso had carefully begun to telescope into themselves, and his skinny buttocks stuck out behind. He looked like a contortionist squeezing into a bottle. His right arm, bent at the elbow to protect his chest, held the pistol at his eye. Since the arm stuck up, not out, his wrist twisted grotesquely forward like a hinge torquing under pressure. Then he thought of something. He dropped the arm gripping the pistol—assumed his full height—faced Stokes straight on—and brought his thumb to his mouth . . .

At that very moment the sun crested the hills to the east, striking Stokes full in the face. "One moment," said Jo.

"You have insulted me gravely," said the count. "And—and—I bite my thumb at your haircut!"

"Bite your bloody dicky for all I care." Stokes faced full front—he was, after all, as thick one way as another. His left hand shielded his eyes from the sun, a breach of the rules.

Jo glanced back quickly at the rising sun, then turned to the duelists. Crouched at Jo's feet, Bonny played in the sand. "One moment," Jo repeated. "When the eyesight of one adversary is blinded by sunlight—"

Suddenly, a flock of birds flew up, sage hens hidden in the bushes across the river—and the count flew backwards, two shots rang out, Stokes dropped to his knees, clouds of gunsmoke blew off . . .

Jo dropped the hanky. A foul stink arose, mixed with the smell of smoke and gunpowder. Jo noticed that Stokes had sat down and Bonny was stumping around in circles of confusion. He ran to the count, sprawled on the sandbank ten or so feet behind his stake, thrown back by the force of the ball, which he'd taken, Jo saw, full in the chest . . .

He'd been shot through the lungs. His neck became red as the blood rushed into it, and blood came out of his mouth in spurts. His eyes fixed on Jo then slowly closed. The eyeballs grew still behind their bulging lids and his face glazed over. Between his mangled hair and dirty neck scarf, now sopping with blood, his face began to harden. All at once it bore a dreadful resemblance—emaciated, to be sure—to Napoleon Bonaparte . . .

At least, thought Jo, he won't marry my mother.

He stood up quickly, caught in a whirlpool. Steadied himself with the gold-headed walking stick. Bonny was darting this way and that, across the sandbank, into the river. Jo approached Stokes. He sat there, still smiling. So—Stokes had won! But the foul smell increased as Jo drew nearer. The man's nose had fallen off. "How is he?" Stokes asked.

"Dead," said Jo.

"Good. I feel swole up . . ."

"Where does it hurt?" Jo touched his chest. "Here?"

"No, down lower."

"Here?"

"No, up higher." All at once, Stokes's fingers, clutching his belly, began oozing brown and red filth. Jo felt sick. "He got me in the trollybags, Jo. It's no way to die. I'm in fizzling pain. It could take hours yet. Finish me off."

It still seemed to Jo he could hear those shots . . .

"Finish me, finish me!" Stokes wasn't smiling anymore. He'd raised his voice, and Bonny, rushing up, began dancing up and down like a fairy-tale dwarf. He picked up the chant: "Finish me, finish me!"

Poor Timothy. Jo's head began to clear. He knew he must do it, but couldn't help pitying the man with the spongy face and half a nose. They'd been through so much together, he and Stokes . . . Jo gagged once, turning aside, then felt his heart nearly loosen its moorings.

To feel *sorry* for someone—what a new sensation!

He stood up. Stokes was gasping for breath. Jo tried not to look at the pudgy hands clutching that leaking belly. He glanced all around, at the half-dead cottonwoods, the bend of the river, the yellow sage hills, the horses and wagon waiting back at Stokes's fire. "Close your eyes, Timothy." Bonny stopped hopping. Stokes closed his eyes. The half-closed wound of his nose flared up red. Jo raised his walking stick with its weighted end of gold high in the air and brought it crashing down on the stubborn skull below him with a sickening crunch. Stokes's breath went with one gasp.

Then the demons broke loose. Bonny looked angry. He was crying or screaming, his face pinched horribly, showing its workings of veins and sinews. He lunged at Jo's ankle with his knife out, shouting, "Finish me! Finish me!" with the buzzing swazzle, but Jo felt alert now and skipped to the side, swinging his walking stick. It caught Bonny square in the ribs—sent him reeling. He ran in a circle like a mad dog, prompted by misfiring signals in his scrambled nerves. An arc of the circle brought him back close to Jo, but he veered off pronto when Jo swung the stick again. The same arc carried him up off the sandbank, back toward the horses. Jo stood there rooted, then thought, No—he wouldn't . . .

One of the horses whinnied with horror and crashed to knees with the little man clinging fast to his mane. Running up desperately, Jo saw the blood pour from the slashed throat. It was nightmare time now, the world seemed to tilt. All fall down, all come to pieces. His stick crashed down splat on Bonny's thick skull just as the knife slashed the other horse's leg, bringing it down. It lay there kicking on top of Bonny, showing its eye whites, too shocked to whinny. Why not? Jo clubbed the horse's head too, clubbed it repeatedly with all his strength, as though somehow the horse was really to blame . . .

Then he stopped, panting. Looked up once at the bright morning sun—sneezed out his brains—fainted away.

You couldn't kill Bonny. Jo should have known that. Sooner or later he'd wake up groggy to worm his way out from beneath that dead horse. Specious life could hardly die, as it hardly lived—just hung on, more or less. It wasn't the first time his head had been cracked, wasn't the first clump of brain cells mashed. With his head full of grapes and watery pulp—that's what it felt like—he pulled on his bicorne, located his knife, and inspected the camp, groping around in a fog of pain—familiar pain—comforting pain . . .

Jo had fled. The horses were dead. A blanket was missing, some flour and dried fruit. Bonny sniffed the air. Threads of trails dangled every-where, caught up and snarled in the scent of blood. He tottered downstream, one leg disjointed. At the site of the duel three crows flapped off. To Bonny, death resembled a word to illiterates. He stared at the count— pulled open his shirt and studied the wound, the white flesh puffed out proud around the hole. He still clung to the pistol in his hand. The world underneath him was sopping wet.

Next, Bonny lurched over to Stokes, who lay on his back, still clutching his belly. Strange spluttering sensations in his chest . . . It was someone else feeling this. Bonny felt confused . . . His cheeks seemed to twitch as he sniffed around Stokes like a dog come upon its fallen master, and touched his cold face—felt the stiffened blood in his hair . . . Stokes's pistol lay beside him on the gravel. Rage or sleep welled up in Bonny. It was sabotage—something in his veins. Little inchworms and swamp things stirring up feelings, popping bubbles underneath. He sat next to Stokes. One tear dropped. Then he viciously beat his own head with his fist, having no Stokes to do that for him anymore. Nothing was fair! He jumped up and, tottering, shot around in increasingly widening circles of fury, trying as he went to kick himself—flailing around with his fists on his person—shouting out, "Finish me! Finish me!" at no one.

He realized he'd somehow swallowed the swazzle.

The sun had dropped down to the afternoon sky. Jo's trail led downstream—he'd caught the scent. As Bonny loped off, he watched for snakes and lizards, anything to practice murder upon. He was slow but steady—didn't have to rest. But every now and then he sat by the river and beat himself about the head and shoulders with rocks in his fists, shouting, "Finish me! Finish me!"

Chapter

❧ II ❧

Peggy Doyle . . . It had a certain ring. When Josie turned it over in her mind, Pete just seemed to blossom into Peggy as easily as a bush into roses. That dress seemed natural—it sort of clung. It outlined the barest of bosoms, Josie—also skinny—realized that now, had even brushed it once with her sensitive fingers . . . She should have known Pete was a gal long ago! The small nose and chin—the little tuck in the curl on the upper lip. The ears! Pete's ears had always looked shy. If you thought he was a boy you could chalk it up to youth—or devilment—but now that Josie knew his real sex her gaze made some minor adjustments, that's all it took, and she stared in wonder . . . They held hands in silence. Vigilance in their small camp went lax with the braves off fighting, and Pete and Josie, in their dresses, clung to each other beneath that aspen tree, surrounded by a world gone strange. Only Pete's short hair spoiled the picture for Josie. They were waiting for Pausone to return, waiting with sharpened sticks concealed in their barest of bosoms . . .

Sometimes they cried, not just for themselves, but for the world's brutality, which required their resistance. Peggy Doyle had stopped her husband from brutalizing her. It takes savage courage to fight savagery, don't it, then? asked Josie. At first Pete agreed, and encouraged Josie. They could certainly do it—that is, stop Pausone . . . They lived in a quiet suspension of rage which half filled the hollowness inside. They sharpened sticks and hid them everywhere, discussed stealing a knife from the squaws. Resistance took on the color of vengeance in a world gone haywire, a world full of gore. And vengeance? It felt just a bit like lust . . . Once the deed was accomplished, they planned to run off and live together far from the world's reach. It gave them some comfort. To conceal their plotting, Josie spent her time sewing together a dress from government annuity blankets, of which they had a surplus. Pete tried to help, having once sewn clothes too. They sat together beneath that tree, two helpless female conspirators stitching and plotting bloody murder. Around them, nature held its breath . . .

Actually, nature didn't seem to care. It stayed more or less the same, despite the world's craziness. Sure, grief was in the clouds, in the grass, in the blue and green mountains, but they all looked so gorgeous! Jack Wilcox was dead. So was Josie's father. Pete and Josie, united by grief, were nonetheless dazed by the generous sun, which shone down equally on those who conspired, those who were miserable, and those for whom things were merely normal. Deer grazed out at the edge of the valley . . .

Men were barbarians, Josie said—that much was clear.

Well, said Pete, some sure are. Might be odd for me, though, to condemn the whole sex, having passed for one these last eight years.

That just proves it's a man's world, said Josie. They can have it, she said, they've bloodied it enough.

Amen, said Pete. And we have to bloody it one more time, just to get quit of it. I've done it before, I know how it feels . . .

Pete looked off at some clouds scudding east.

I know how *men* feel when they kill . . .

Fight fire with fire, *I* say—said Josie.

I'll buy that, sure. Pete nodded with vigor. Nodded and scraped at the dust with a stick, in a squirreling pattern, due to trembling limbs. Poor Pete jumped up and tossed the stick away.

Days passed. Pausone didn't show up. They had all the time in the world for each other, time itself seemed to hesitate, trying to make up its mind. The dome of sky overhead was so blue the valley seemed inside a monstrous eye. Josie sewed away; her dress was becoming a work of art, with its stylish collar folded neatly down, white buttons up the front from the Agency supply—stolen by Susan—and the government stripes along the hem and the cuffs. At last Pete said under the aspen tree: Maybe it ain't such a good idea, Josie.

It ain't? *You* did it. I'll have *my* revenge if you won't help out. You had yours once. Let me taste *mine*.

But what then? Where will you go?

I'll dress up like a man and spit in the world's eye . . .

Josie, this ain't the same as what I faced. I was trapped forever. Twig would've killed me. There's an end to this here, we'll most likely be rescued.

Most likely won't. He said if the troops caught up he'd whisk me off by ourselves to Utah Territory. We'll live out there as husband and wife and eat roots, grubs, and bugs.

What about Patika and Susan?

Oh, he don't care for *them*. He'll leave them behind . . .

Another day passed, and Josie went silent. Pete sensed a growing resistance inside her, a determination hardening like a statue. Only her mother seemed able to soften her. Daily, in that green and blue valley, Arvilla read from *The Pilgrim's Progress*, and Josie wept. Her mother seemed to be growing smaller . . . In her dry, creaking voice with its Midwest twang, she read of how the way to Heaven lies hard by the gates of Hell—and her daughter nodded her beautiful head. Oh yes, hard by . . . *I have laid my hand to the plow*, read Arvilla, alluding to her husband. And the springs that were in their heads sent the waters down their sunburnt cheeks . . .

Pausone's younger squaw, Susan—the one who'd stabbed his horse— pulled Josie aside to say she was sorry for what had happened at the Agency. Everything was changing . . . Together, Josie and Susan wept for Nathan Meeker. Susan sewed Arvilla a new pair of moccasins.

What would happen, Pete asked, to your ma and the other captives if you really killed Pausone?

Hush up, you sissy. It was your idea. We'll all escape!

Escape to where?

To a better life . . .

You don't believe that, Josie. I know. We'll all be killed, more like it. Life is better than death, Pete said, stroking Josie's hair, when you come right down to it. It's a slimy load, sure—but at least you're alive. You might even miss the world if you lost it.

Well, it won't miss me.

Pete embraced her and found her atremble. Her pencil-thin bones felt ready to snap. For almost a week now the camp had clung there in precarious calm, ready to slide, and folks had been walking around inclined, every bit like buildings about to tumble. Of course, they didn't know it. They'd been twisted off level, skywest and crooked—inverted, askewgee, careening, bedeviled . . .

At last, one evening Pausone returned with five other braves on steaming horses ready to drop. Things looked bad. Everything was changing. Floods of soldiers were coming, they'd reached the burnt-out

Agency already. The Utes and their captives broke camp as the sun set and without a lick of sleep traveled in moonlight down that funneling valley in a long, snaking line on tired, hungry horses, with fresh runners catching up every few hours delivering news of more and more soldiers. The valley grew narrow and steep, going down. Hills and mountains fanned down in layers on either side, indistinct in the dark. In the light of a half-moon, Pete caught glimpses of tilted rock wedged between knobby sandstone fingers, eroded hills of red dirt, white exposed cliffs— all the effects of wild western mountains tumbled down helter-skelter around them.

As daylight grayed, the valley broke open. They heard rushing water, a huge river this time, a fast one with sinews—it scooped out this canyon. They traversed a desert of dry mud and sagebrush off to their right to descend to the river and water their horses. The Grand River, said Josie. Sun soon struck the tops of towering yellow cliffs raked from this valley up to the north. To the south, the mountains were greener, more rolling. The river divided the world, slicing west . . .

They stopped, killed the last of their Agency steer, butchered and roasted the meat and ate, then fell asleep in the grass by the river beneath sunlight which had always belonged exclusively to the Colorado Utes. The horses and dogs fell asleep too, the babies, children, lice, flies . . . Pausone had fed Josie first, then his squaws, then eaten himself—then curled up by Josie and slept like the dead out there on the grass. Pete lay twenty or so feet away between the two medicine men with eyes propped open closely watching Josie, who fell asleep first, Pete saw that, or thought so, peering with droopy lids. You couldn't fight sleep, it felt as ancient as the sun, and Pete sank into it through layers of body, through Petes and Peggies shifting as fast as shadows of clouds on a sculpted hillside, finally sinking so far as to slide beneath sex altogether, down the darkened funnel below it where all the umbilicals of sleep led at last . . . Back in Five Points on a summer day beneath the hot tin roof of the shack in Cow Bay, Pete the Great—Peggy Doyle—lay at her/his siesta . . .

He'll always be Pete to me . . .

He sat bolt upright when the camp began to stir. Pausone, still alive, had kneeled to help Josie mount. Stepping on his back, Josie looked kind of funny—tired and either resigned or resolved. Her eyes narrowed either by fright or distant thought, small and black, looked like the eyes of a trapped fox caught sleeping. She seemed softened yet stiff, like the dead come to life. She coughed once or twice, she was coughing more now. She was the only person in the world who knew who Pete really was, but she wouldn't glance in his direction. Well, okay . . . Pete preferred masks and disguises—they provided a watching world to keep ahead of . . .

The sun in the southern sky stood at noon.

They rode through the hottest part of the day down the river canyon. The wind blew a hurricane squeezed by the canyon, and no one could see more than ten feet forward or back for the dust. Pete rode between the two medicine men, the old one and his young assistant dressed like a woman, and wondered what they knew. Often the old man turned to face him, you might think he was *staring* if he weren't blind. Staring as though he'd guessed Pete's secret . . .

The canyon bottom narrowed for the river, so they climbed up to the ridge above it, where the wind was going crazy without anything to strike against, until it felt them . . . Their line snaked back for nearly a mile: fifty or more braves and squaws, captives, spare horses, dogs, a few goats and sheep. Some of the larger dogs had been pressed into service and hitched to travois dragging lashed parfleches of household goods every bit like horses. The horses in fact were being consumed by the constant traffic between here and the soldiers. Pausone and one other brave spent the better part of the afternoon climbing the mountains south of the river to see if they could spot the soldiers through their spyglasses, pilfered from the Agency. They returned in a lather that evening as the tipis were rising in a grassy meadow beside the river. The soldiers had reached their previous camp, that long sloping valley!

Still, they camped for the night. They needed sleep. And Pete did something he hadn't done since he was Peggy—he prayed . . . He listened for Pausone's screams through the long night, sinking into sleep and yanked up again by the slightest noise—a horse chuffing, the river splattering . . . What kind of nightmare was Josie caught in? Pete had been there in Pausone's tipi that first feverish night nearly two weeks ago. In a darkened corner, to the sound of creaking leather, he rolled off her, rolled back . . . Josie gave off weeping after the first hour. Thinking of it now was almost worse than being there. Pete felt far away—excluded—powerless . . . To his horror, he felt stabs of jealousy too. He was jealous of Josie's capacity for suffering, but worse than that, in his darkest moments, jealous of Pausone . . . Maybe Josie *should* just stick him with knives, it tore so much at Pete's choked heart. They probably planned to kill us all anyway. Get it over with, Josie—might as well now . . .

But nothing happened. At dawn, Pausone galloped off with the other braves, and Josie emerged from her tipi to cook up a breakfast for herself and her fellow squaws. Pete cooked some biscuits and deer meat at his fire, thirty or so feet from Josie's. Farther downriver, Arvilla and Flora Ellen Price and the other squaws squatted at fires. They were all squaws now, including Peter Doyle.

Josie still wouldn't glance in his direction. Pete watched her crouched by the fire. Her smudged face tried neither to be seen nor to hide. When she stood, she was beautiful beyond desire. Only Josie could look so handsome wearing, of all things, a dress made from government annuity blankets—and that wide floppy brimmed felt hat, still stylishly cocked. As she cooked, as she walked to the river for water, not a gesture spilled. Suffering ennobled her. She betrayed nothing. She was Josie, poor Josie!

And Pete? Who was Pete?

They lost track of time, moving down that river. For one entire day it rained, but they slogged on. The sky looked like the underside of something. Clouds cut off the tops of the yellow mountains to the north, and rain considerably weakened the light until it was fully overpowered and night came on and they had to camp—then rode on the next day beneath ragged clouds torn open here and there like upholstery, showing blue. At least the wet ground didn't give off dust.

The braves kept on leaving, then coming back. It gradually dawned upon Pete that they were being held as hostages for the moment when the soldiers caught up. They would protect the tribe from being massacred. The Utes' emotions seemed subject to the winds. One night Colorow whipped his squaw, then an hour later danced and sang with her. He induced Flora Ellen Price to sing Negro camp songs with him around the fire. Most of the time the braves seemed glum. Their wives, like Josie, conserved their gestures. The Utes were captives too, with captives in their charge. Gradually their normal patterns returned, and the Ute squaws fetched the water and cooked along with the captives. It seemed they were all in it together . . .

Pete began to think they might actually be rescued, since they hadn't been killed. Maybe Josie did too, maybe that's why she chose to endure her pain instead of sticking it with knives . . . At a place where the canyon narrowed so close they had to ride half the time in the river, they took a side canyon off to their left. Hemmed in by rock, steep and winding, it caused the line of travelers to snake back and forth and ride in review past each other as before. This time Josie returned Pete's glance. She sat high on her horse, proud and straight, though of course she looked tired. She neither smiled nor nodded, but her face flowed out—still, it held back. She was one person—herself—whereas Pete had been two people these past eight years. How would you like to be two people, Josie? It hadn't always worked. There were times you succeeded in forgetting the ruse and thought you really were a Pete, other times it seemed the whole world must know you were actually a Peggy. That time, for example, Pete dropped his pants and squatted to piss beneath a pier near Cherry Street back in Manhattan, and a sailor walking by spotted him, then followed for blocks calling out hoarsely, "Don't I know *you*! Turn around, darling!" Or the time on the horsecars late at night that a well-known congressman grabbed Pete's crotch, and was shocked to find nothing. Walt had come close, but never *that* close.

He'd learned things too. Men had said things to Pete they'd never say to a gal. At the dispatch shed for the horsecars in Washington City, the talk about women sometimes turned so vicious you wondered if men weren't missing a few parts. Pete had sat there nervously grinning. They didn't know his secret—and to make sure they wouldn't he'd joined in the talk . . .

It was one of the hazards of passing for male.

Their deliverance came from an unexpected direction. For the rest of the day they climbed that dry canyon until its high, yellow walls gave up and diminished. Green hills folded around them. They followed the thin rope of a creek up to the right, further north, where a huge, flat, green mass loomed high ahead. Ravines fanned down the mesa's side through pines, cottonwoods, willows, and fields—this was well-watered country. They camped amid lush clumps of trees and meadows, with the wide mesa above them occupying most of the horizon—Thigunawat, the Utes called it. Home of the Departed Spirits. Behind and below, to the south, were the canyons they'd trudged through to get here, yellow and red in a much drier country cracked open by gray, muscular rivers rooted in mountains a hundred miles away . . .

They camped here three days. Goats and ponies grazed in the fields, Ute girls picked berries, and boys hunted snakes. Squaws gathered wood in bundles on their backs. Time seemed to slip—they were back in midsummer. The wide basin below that wider mesa was greener than anywhere Pete had ever been in the great wide West.

Runners came regularly in and out of camp with whispered messages. Pausone hung around all the time now, looking down in the mouth. All the braves moved in slow motion, as though rehearsing defeat. They were playing out as dream an outnumbered future in which nothing was theirs. They slept all the time. They seemed conscious of being watched by the captives. Already, the Utes were becoming statues on courthouse lawns, looking off toward the distance with grim faces etched, and pigeons on their shoulders . . .

One morning a boy searched out Pete and told him in English, "You must go to bed."

"But I just woke up!"

Over by Pausone's tipi a squaw held a blanket to cover the door. But Josie peeked out—then tore the blanket down. She strode out like a skinny Amazon toward five white men approaching their village on horses, not from below, oh no—from above, from the mesa! Some squaws surrounded Josie, then backed off. A mustachioed man in a blue army uniform stepped down from his horse and shook hands with her. She gestured at their camp as though she were in charge. Down by Douglas's tipi the handful of braves still left in the village hung their heads, looking chopfallen. No one raised a rifle, not even Pausone. Was it over at last? Arvilla scurried up on her bad hip with the jerky motion of a wounded crab—hugged her daughter, then kissed the officer's hand. He shook his head, made her straighten up, took off his hat, appeared to deliver an awkward speech. Flora Ellen Price and her children ran squealing. Pete stood poised outside his tipi on the brink of tearing off his dress, and hesitated. A brief spurt of fear shot up and licked his heart. Then he tore it off as though it were a shroud—at least a cocoon—and broke into a jig, Peter Doyle once again, at least to the world, performing a real break-down shuffle so buoyant and lively it began to propel him toward the knot of watching white folk. He reached up to his neck and stopped all at once. His pouch—it was gone! His lucky pouch . . .

After that, everything slid into dream. Turned out General Adams—that was his name—had been delegated by the Secretary of the Interior himself to search out the captives and secure their release. It was in all the newspapers! Nightly prayer vigils were being held right now back in Greeley and Denver. The whole territory—indeed, the whole country—knew of the massacre at the Agency, the death of Father Meeker, the kidnapping of Josie, Flora Ellen, Arvilla—not Pete, though. They didn't know about Pete. One of their rescuers was in fact a reporter, and at first made much, pencil cocked on his pad, of the man named Pete who'd dressed up as a woman to save his own hide. Interviewing Pete, he couldn't squelch a smirk. He wanted to see the dress Pete had worn. Then when he saw it, he began to lose interest. Would it play in Cleveland? He wasn't sure. It was this reporter who began the legend of the powers of Arvilla's edition of *The Pilgrim's Progress*, which had sustained them during three weeks of travail.

The reporter asked Douglas through an interpreter why the Utes had killed Father Meeker.

Because he summoned soldiers to cross the reservation border! They attacked our reservation and killed twenty Utes.

Did you kill Father Meeker yourself?

Douglas looked at the reporter. He spoke slowly in Ute, stressing each high, piping syllable. "I hate all Americans. They are liars and thieves." No one translated.

Douglas and the other braves offered no resistance when the rescuers led their captives away. A thousand soldiers were coming; they had nowhere left to go. While General Adams and an assistant rode down to Grand River to meet the soldiers, their associates—a Count Donhoff, the reporter, and a Captain Cline—escorted the captives on a three-day trek up that huge mesa, across the top, and down the other side to Whitewater Creek, where their buckboard wagons awaited. It took another day to reach the Gunnison River over a washboard wagon road, and two more days after that before they came to Chief Ouray's farm on the Uncompahgre River. There, the handsome chief, who resembled a monument, let them stay in his house with the Brussels carpets on the floor, the lamps on the tables, the curtains on the windows, the spittoons by the stoves, the rocking chairs and mirrors. He was gentle and sweet to the women especially. Folks seemed to ignore Pete on this trip, or regard him from a distance with ill-disguised smiles and half-mumbled whispers. He knew what they said: That's the milksop fellow who dressed up as a girl to save his own skin . . .

A group of about twenty miners were camped in tents in Chief Ouray's village, on their way from Provo, in Utah Territory, where the mines had played out, to the San Juan Mountains, in Colorado Territory, a place where unheard-of fortunes in gold and silver were being unearthed. They knew the story of the captives, everyone did; it had spread across the mountains. One with permanent blackened smudges about his popping eyes pulled Pete aside, and told him those Utes ought to be wiped completely off the face of the earth.

Amen, said another. They're setting on gold mines.

From Ouray's house, they traveled three days before crossing high mountains, as high as any Pete had traversed a month ago with the late Jack Wilcox. For two more days, the whole world was mountains, gray waves of rock capped by white foam in every direction . . . In Saguache, Captain Cline purchased the captives $25.40 worth of gloves, stockings, and shoes for the women, and coats for Mrs. Price's two children— nothing for Pete, though. Here, the gristmills and sawmills chugged away full-time, wagons rushed everywhere, and stores conducted a brisk business selling helmets, picks, boots, and food to wide-eyed miners streaming north to the San Juans. Pete found a doctor to clean and dress his wound and bandage his hand up properly in Saguache. Then the captives traveled south, through the San Luis Valley, through endless wheat farms, passing wagons spilling hordes of fresh immigrant miners, some nearly children, with faces still clean. They waved and cheered and whistled at Josie, Arvilla, Flora Ellen, and the children. They knew who they were!

In Alamosa, they were put up for free at a brick hotel with green blinds on the outside and soft beds inside. Except somehow they didn't have room for Pete. He slept with some miners in a lodging house next door with mattresses thrown on the floors of the rooms and even in the hallways to accommodate the overflow. Of course, all the captives still carried on their persons their White River lice. They deposited some in Saguache, some in Alamosa . . .

Then the Denver and Rio Grande narrow-gauge railroad, spewing cinders and smoke, labored to haul them across one last mountain pass and down to the prairie, to a town called Cuchara, where they stopped for the night—then changed for the main line heading north to Pueblo and Colorado Springs with discreetly applauding crowds awaiting them at every stop. They waved and held up WELCOME HOME signs. When Arvilla showed her *Pilgrim's Progress* at the window, everyone cheered. Bands played, mayors made speeches, reporters asked questions. By the time they arrived in the booming, prosperous city of Denver, another day later, Josie had learned what to say to the newsmen who gathered around her with glittering eyes, seeking to dislodge her ultimate secret. In the lobby of the Alvord House in Denver, where they were honored guests— all except Pete—she spoke to reporters from as far off as New York while wagons, carriages, omnibuses, and pedestrians clattered past outside the plate-glass windows as tall as New York's! Men in top hats looked in the window. Some Indians too, Utes they looked like, also in plug hats, peered in at Josie . . .

"Miss Meeker, did they offer any insult to your person?"

"None whatsoever."

"Did they beat you?"

"No, sir."

"What do you think of them red devils now?"

"They are my friends. They should not all have to suffer for the actions of a few."

"But they killed your father!"

"My father was a stranger to the Utes and was misunderstood by them. Many white men slandered him, but had he managed to live long enough with them and been given the support to carry out his plans, the Indians would have thought differently of him. I believe he would have gradually won them to his goals."

"Do you think they can ever be civilized?"

"They are far more civilized now than the Fourth Ward bummers of New York City."

"You're aware that the governor is calling for their removal?"

"I've read the reports. Where could they go? Surely not to Indian territory."

"To Utah!" someone shouted. "Let them consort with the Mormons."

"They talk of Utah, but it is merely talk. This is their home. It would be unjust to force them to move because of a tragic misunderstanding. I say find the culprits who committed bloody murder and try them by the same laws any white man would be tried by. The rest were merely defending their territory."

At the edge of the crowd, nearly anonymous, Peter Doyle, dressed to the nines once again in a spanking new suit, gazed at Josie with wonder. She commanded that room! Already, arrangements were being made for her lecture tour back in the states. She'd write a book on her experience—so would Arvilla—maybe even Flora Ellen Price. All except Pete, whose story raised titters in young and old. He'd told that reporter to just throw out his dress . . .

But they couldn't keep him off the train to Greeley, he paid his own way, with money he'd carried for six hundred miles all the way from White River—Father Meeker's payment for his mules. And at the train station in Evans, where a stagecoach stood among the welcoming crowds to carry them to Greeley, Josie insisted that Pete climb up with the other captives and ride on top and wave to the people. He sat right beside her! Boys on horseback followed the coach, shot on past it, then circled back. A few people lined the two-mile road—the last two miles!—alongside their sod huts and shanties and fields. The place was getting on. It would soon be a solid town between the train depot and Greeley proper. More ditches, more fields under cultivation, a few farmhouses too with gingerbread trim. Still, it all seemed so precarious and strange, like pieces of paper flying on past. Josie took Pete's arm, kissed him, and winked. They rode up front on the top, so the others didn't see her when she pulled from the bosom of her dress a sharpened stick and dropped it in his lap.

"How come you didn't kill him?" he asked.

"And miss all this?"

Pete wondered what to say. "You're fine then, now?"

"Of course not, Pete. I'll never be fine again. I'm leaning up strong against myself, is what I'm doing."

"Lean up against me. I can take it."

"So you shall."

What did *that* mean? Sometimes you didn't want to test Josie's thinking too soon—it might not be cooked yet . . .

"That was some trick you played on those Indians, Pete."

"Well, I guess it worked."

"Where'd you get that thing?"

"Found it one day. You haven't seen it, have you?"

"Your lucky pouch? No."

Of course, it wasn't the pouch he wanted, but the peter inside it. If Josie didn't take it, who did?

She squeezed his hand and leaned into his ear. "Let's stick together, we girls," she whispered. Approaching Greeley, she felt it only proper to scooch back a little and include her mother. With one arm around Arvilla, and her other hand in Pete's, they rode into Greeley down the middle of Main Street, having completed a circle through Colorado Territory of nearly a thousand miles—rode past new brick buildings with cast-iron shutters, past crowds of people lining the sidewalk, past waving American flags and signs draped on stores—WELCOME HOME, MOTHER— for Arvilla, of course. Thumps and tootles came from the swarm of bodies ahead at the junction of Monroe and Main—a band playing "Yankee Doodle"—and there were Max Clark, Henry West, General Cameron, and Charles Wright, chairman of the Committee of Reception, clutching a speech, and there was Ralph Meeker—all the way from New York!—dressed in a high-buttoned British tweed suit with a scarf and a cap—and, oh my goodness, there was Walt Whitman, dear sweet old Walt! Pete felt the tears rush to his eyes. Walt had come all the way here to greet him! But he looked so different as he tottered toward the coach, leaning to one side on somebody's arm, allowing the inner side of his toe to drag along on the raw Greeley street. He still had that warm open sweet grandma smile, head cocked to one side, but he hadn't quite figured out where to direct it, hadn't spotted Pete yet. Walt! Up here! He looked so frail, so white-haired, so old . . .

"*We proceed to give Miss Meeker's narrative as obtained by a gentleman sympathetic to her sufferings. 'Miss Meeker,' he asked, 'there have been all sorts of wild and differing stories going through the newspapers about the whole affair, and I am sure you would be able to give a true account.'*

"The handsome young woman, who by her indomitable heroism and determination had saved the lives of the whole party, answered: 'I think I can, sir, but I do not think any imagination could conjure up more terrible sufferings and torture than what we endured in reality. Of course they may differ, but, believe me, they cannot exceed the facts.'

"And the tears welled up in her beautiful eyes as she spoke, and for several moments she did not attempt to proceed.

" 'I have no doubt you were all glad when General Adams made his appearance,' was remarked by a friend.

" 'Oh, my! Glad! Don't talk! Glad is but a weak word for our emotions. Just think of our being driven and dragged for a month over mountains in dust and bitter heat and cold alternately; sometimes drenched with rain, fainting under the noonday sun, or pierced to the heart with icy winds at night! When I peeped over the blanket that an old squaw held up so I could not see our rescuers, and beheld General Adams, and knew that we would be taken back, my very soul leaped within me for joy. It was like going directly from perdition to Heaven.'

" 'It is a wonder you were not completely overcome.'

" 'Ah, there was no necessity nor time for any sentimental overcoming,' was the quick reply of the brave girl; 'it was the moment for action, so I just sprang forward, took the squaw by the shoulders and flung her and her blanket away. She went reeling, and I stepped straight to the general and pointed out to him the tent in which I thought Mother and Mrs. Price were kept prisoners. This was immediately visited, but they were not there, for they had been sent down to the stream of water to do some washing.'

" 'Why, it is a wonder your mother survived it at all,' said a friend present.

" 'Yes, it was only through God's kind mercy that she did get through as she did.'

" 'Please tell us the story from the beginning.'

" 'Well, to begin at the commencement, we, at the Agency, never dreamed for a moment of the awful avalanche that was about to fall on us until it came down . . .' "

"Hold it right there, Pete. 'Begin at the commencement'? There's the dead giveaway. I would never in my life utter such a redundancy."

"It's right here in the book."

"Well, I never wrote it—such trash I never heard."

"Wait a minute, there's more." Pete thumbed hastily through the book in question, the size and length of a dime novel—*The Ute Massacre* by Josephine Meeker. He and Walt sat across from Josie and Ralph in the walnut luxury of a Pullman Palace car speeding east through Ne-braska. He'd bought the book from a butcher boy selling newspapers, apples, watch chains, and dime novels about everything from Billy the Kid to Kit Carson and the grizzly bears.

Out the window, the endless prairies flowed by. Was it Pete's imagination or were there more towns now? More red barns, more trees, more water towers, white fences, little green yards, orchards and gardens, wide dusty Main Streets—even some courthouses of cut stone—and not the slightest sign of an Indian.

Walt spoke up slowly. "Miss Meeker, if I had a dime for every instance others have put words in my mouth, I'd be a rich man. I mean by that, *both* enemies and friends. My brother once introduced me to a man who said, 'Say, bubby—are you the one who wrote the dirty novels?'"

Everyone laughed.

"They always think it's *novels* I wrote!"

"Here it is, Josie, listen to this. I don't recall this. *One fellow rushed at me with a huge butcher knife in a frightful passion and threatened to kill me. There were twenty or thirty of his companions nearby. I laughed at him, though my heart was in my mouth with fear, and I exclaimed: 'I'm not afraid of such as you! All the scalps you ever took you got off of women's heads. You never took a scalp from any brave like these warriors here. Go be a squaw!'*"

Josie laughed and winked at Pete, who rolled his smiling eyes. Go be a squaw! Ralph smiled too, relieved that his sister was laughing again, after two glum weeks in Greeley. They were going back east—maybe that did it.

Walt squirmed in his seat, regarding the lovebirds. Hell—Pete didn't even try to hide it. Every now and then she leaned across toward Pete, billed and cooed in his face, and whispered something or other. Pete sat there beaming. He seemed as lively and warm as ever, but Walt had recognized Josie right away—the same girl he'd seen Pete hand into her carriage on Broadway outside Delmonico's, years back. Ah, well. All was lost. Pete had told Walt in strictest confidence that they were planning to settle in Washington City and live together as a married couple . . .

"Josie, I can't find one word about me. I'm not even mentioned in this book."

"Maybe you don't exist at all, Peter. You surely don't stick out."

"How come you didn't mention me?"

"I didn't write that trash."

"Listen to this. It's just a picture of you, but it looks like a girl in a navy suit. Here's what it says underneath it: *On her return from captivity, Josie wore a skirt made of the Indian blanket, a broad leather belt, a bright-colored handkerchief round her neck, and the wide Mexican hat given her by the chief. She looked just lovely.*"

They all looked at Josie.

Chapter

❧ *12* ❧

J oseph Bonaparte Delafolie Benton came to beside a fire on the floor of a cave somewhere on the North American continent. There's a woman over there stirring a pot, maybe she can help . . .

Where on earth was he? The last he remembered was tumbling down an enormous ravine toward endless canyons thousands of feet below. He'd seen rivers—water!—the first in days. To get to that spot hadn't taken effort so much as mindless repetition. He'd constructed a philosophy out of placing one foot in front of another endlessly—forever. The afterlife consisted of walking, the soul was a walker, the gods walked through the universe, demons did also . . . A little monkey caught up and slit your throat, but you continued walking like a stupid mule, you walked and sang the Marseillaise, the bloody flag is raised—*marchons! marchons!*—couldn't shake it from your mind . . . The song gave Jo strength even while it drove him crazy, strength to endure stinging eyes, swollen lips, cracked skin, and itchy privates. Cracks on his feet and hands felt like wires biting deep, and once with horror he'd looked at one foot and thought he detected small white creatures moving around inside the cracks . . .

He still had his walking stick. He took laudanum for nourishment. The rest of his elegance was a ragged corpse held together with twine and winding sheets, an old thing barely clamped on his soul. When he itched all over he knew he was alive. Of course, he'd lost weight, weighed less and less each day, he knew that because the walking grew easier, not harder, despite the bleeding feet, the splendid leather boots splitting at the seams. For food, he had the rest of the flour and some tins of kippered herring he'd found in the count's carpetbag—Count Léon had held out to the last! He'd taken the count's expense money too, nearly four thousand dollars. The food and cash he carried in a blanket slung across his shoulder, and with this bundle on his back—walking stick in hand—the Marseillaise in his mind—he was rich as Croesus and free as a bird, not a care in the world, save Bonny, the little demon . . . He'd murdered the creature, that seemed clear—crushed his head with the walking stick—yet two days later, climbing a ridge to scout the terrain, he'd spotted a little monkey-sized figure tottering along beside the river and stopping now and then to toss stones in the water . . . The slimy crustacean! He was one of those tenacious organisms like certain vermin that kept on living no matter how hard you stomped them with your boot. Cut off their legs and they'll crawl with their hands . . .

So Jo continued walking night and day lest Bonny catch up. Walked beneath a night sky whose massive architecture, exposed, showed every beam and nail, and slept for the hottest part of the day in caves or brush shelters with uprooted sagebrush piled thickly around to warn of anyone or thing approaching. The presence of the river made night walking easier—showed him the way—but at last one day when a faint trail branched off to the northwest and the river curved southwest, he thought, why not . . . The little monster would never suspect! This trail must lead somewhere . . . He walked at first with the lightest of treads so as not to leave a trace, easy enough as he'd lost so much weight . . . If he kept on circling vaguely north, sooner or later—well, later of course—eventually maybe—in a matter of weeks, if his strength held out—he'd intersect the Union Pacific Railroad, that lifeline to civilization which he himself had helped to construct . . .

He hadn't counted on thirst, that wasn't in the plot. Leaving the river had its drawbacks. After a few miles the trail petered out, and he saw clearly why: there was nothing here . . . He'd instinctively marched toward a gap between ridges past wrinkled hills of dirt with explosions of sage all up and down their sides, and higher mesas and long, tilted, mountainous benches in the distance, to the north and south both. Well, it was *something*—it was dirt—the dull earth exposed. In those mazes of walls spread out along the horizon, one might find Cibola, or El Dorado, lost cities of gold! They might have a glass of water to spare . . . The scanty vegetation all around made it clear just how dry this place was, as if he didn't know. Being thirsty wasn't something you could very well ignore. He could try a kippered herring—a spoonful of flour . . . His tongue felt thick and stuffed in his mouth as though in a botched job of upholstery. The protracted rage of thirst was exactly like boredom—you thought it would never end. His only recourse was to take some extra laudanum, to alleviate the thirst and the boredom, both, then fix on a landmark— that one mesa higher than the rest to the north, the only one with trees—and march there one step at a time, biting increments off the gap between it and himself. But it wouldn't come closer. His hands made fists. Wouldn't it be nice, was it too much to ask, if I could just, say, once touch the horizon before it rolled back? If I could *get* someplace? With your kind permission . . .

He squinted up at the sky.

It was flat rolling land with small wrinkled hills and embryonic canyons and ridges, as though the earth were practicing on a small scale with dust what it could accomplish with rivers and great rushing gorges if it so chose. At least back east there were trees and grass; leaves boiled and waved in the summer wind, birds sang, creeks and rivers flowed freely . . . Toward the top of a rise were some large volcanic rocks in the shape of coke ovens tended by faceless men in greatcoats. They stood about mumbling, covered with dust. The slanting sun seemed to be herding them. The hills around turned from ash-gray to yellow. Cheekbones, they looked like. The sun was going down. And where on earth was he? That ridge with the trees now extended across the whole northern horizon, so he must be getting someplace. The setting sun picked out escarpments in its side each the size of a castle. Hooded armies came galloping; the old men shuffled from boulder to boulder . . . The sun stopped setting and rose back up, causing the ridge to flare golden and the sky to unroll its blue from one end of the earth to the other. Jo stopped. He saw someone's shoulders twitching. This meant he was weeping. He missed Stokes and the count. But I hate life, he thought— can't help it, I do. What would God think of that? He possessed in a jar the squeezings and drippings of God's own brain, he could drink a little more . . . The landscape seemed to spread, to overflow, a perpetual landslide, it rolled away from him. Then it rolled back. It did absolutely nothing. Meanwhile, because there was little else to do, he resumed placing one tired foot in front of the other. It didn't help, of course, the ridge came no closer. There was water there too, he could tell just by looking. God, are you listening? Jo pictured his head sliced off at the top and dirt shoveled in by Jehovah himself. Either everything meant something—or nothing meant anything. He chose to cling to the former, as more comforting. Then he decided, yes, I can take it, and accommodated his mind to the more manly view, more amusing too, it was just rocks and dirt. It paid him no mind. Then back to the first view, the world choked with meaning. This went on for several hours, or days, hard to tell which. The earth was a form of destiny or fate. It was nothing but dirt. In truth, it was the very face of God and he walked in its awful wrinkles and crow's feet. Its spiritual meaning had just this minute disappeared like a shadow across the horizon. It was mounting to some enormous revelation! It looked like a string of broken altars vacated overnight by druidic priests who discovered themselves in a mad rush to leave when the walls collapsed and great boulders crashed down in showers of sparks and electric dust . . .

He was there! Enormous red and yellow cliffs loomed above with arroyos and canyons fanning out between them, inside one of which a thin line of green grass signaled, yes, the frayed end of a creek . . . Could he run? He tried it, and came crashing down. What a novel sensation! The earth seemed to shake. He resumed his bundle and, buzzing all over, walked tipping forward, relying upon the gold-headed walking stick, walked with a festinating gait—he saw it himself—like a comic old man. The faintest of trickles came somewhere ahead from the foot of the most enormous of cliffs. Thank you, God, thank you, Mother, thank you, fields of red poppies . . . Cupping his hands, he drank where the water dripped across stones down a dark, curving chasm splitting the ridge, which towered above him. Then the day went black as though slamming its door and Jo fell into mindless oblivion.

He drank more the next morning when his head cleared, shivering, as much as he could hold. Ate some kippered herrings then drank another gallon. The water made him feel giddy with power and cooled his insides for the first time in days. Strange, he hardly needed to piss . . . He liked the way the water sloshed around in his empty stomach, and jiggled a little to feel it there. The chasm itself was a steep, narrow gorge with aspen trees standing and fallen—the first trees he'd seen since the river—and masses of tumbled rock threaded by that life-giving stream. Looking back at the rolling dry folds of earth he'd managed to trudge through to get here, he reasoned the only way forward was up, beside that creek bed. Long sigh. Here goes . . . Over boulders and dead trees, up dry earth and gravel with a tendency to slide. After a while the stream disappeared into a smear of clayish earth. Oh well, *marchons.* Never retreat on a mindless pursuit; the purpose of life is to climb, to mount . . . Climbing, the creaking machinery of his body, freshly oiled, felt nonetheless stiff. Maybe a little more laudanum would help. Just a few drops . . .

He climbed. It went up! Up gulches and folds, across more fallen aspens. Then the aspens gave out, the chasm widened, the morning sun struck his neck as he climbed. Motion blurred into dream, then blurred out. Below, the whole earth had turned into a valley streaked gray and red, from which the heat rose in italics. Mountains galore on the far horizon made more sharply etched horizons, each a different shade of gray below the rising sun. Was that a crow down below, approaching this ridge—or a little man . . . ? Christ almighty, thought Jo. You dragged yourself up out of deadening torpor, sucked reservoirs of strength from your very marrow, all the while of course consuming yourself, and still he keeps coming . . .

Gradually, the gulch inverted itself. Jo walked across a high humpback ridge pushed up into the sky through juniper and piñon. Below, to his left, opened valleys and ridges of bright yellow, red and green, sliced in swirling curves by deep gorges of rock. It looked like a man with his stomach blown open! It became clear to Jo that the ridge he was on was a kind of long, snaking, muscular arm—a series of ridges—with cliffs leading down left and right on either side. No choice but to stay up high and go on. Every now and then a gust of wind brushed past as though something enormous had exhaled. Clouds were blowing down from the north, big gray monsters. Everything swayed when a cloud reached the sun. Did Bonny have the endurance that he did? Of course, Jo had help—his stoppered jar of laudanum . . . Walking forever wasn't so bad with such bully assistance. His body had absorbed like a sponge all that water this morning and gone dry again. The little gray cells felt like empty hives. What did Bonny want with *him*? He didn't have their prize, no one did now. Give it up, wart! Approaching a goal, you draw closer and closer, then forget what it is. Still, you have to act out the slowly diminishing mechanics of approaching it, don't you? Nothing else for it. Whether to stop or go on made all the difference in the world, or made no difference at all.

Which was it, Jo?

His arms and legs buzzed. It occurred to Jo they weren't getting enough blood. Too bad, then—it was out of his hands. His legs were still moving, so he must be alive. It appeared he had chosen to go on. Wait a minute, that wasn't the choice—the choice was whether it made any difference . . .

No more trees up this high, just rabbit brush and sage. This ridge was a desert some force from below had pushed into the sky, breaking it off from the earth all around. At least it was cooler today, with the clouds. He could trade his walking stick in for a horse. Or his last tin of kippered herrings. His tie pin . . . It felt lonely up here! Quite beautiful, though.

Gray clouds overhead . . . He could just sit down and wait for companion-ship. A sigh, a reaching around of hands. A warm embrace, a knife in the windpipe . . . One thing Jo thought he could try was to let himself go, that is, whatever personhood he thought he still had, it was light-weight enough, like an old blanket, that he could just let it slump to the earth and be gone. Turning his head, he watched it recede, abandoned on the ground. He felt sorry for it . . .

That was the skin. Now for the bones. He tossed his walking stick in the air end over end and it crashed down behind him. What was that, Jo? Hell, I don't know. Some crazy old coot. Ran out of water—shrunk to a stick . . .

He missed poor Stokes, and even Count Léon, with all his precious posturing.

It started to mist. A cloud whose bottom had snagged this ridge came barreling at him and closed all around. For a while he couldn't exactly see where he was going, but walked on anyway. Drops of mist seemed to vanish on his open mouth, making him thirstier. All that water in the air, and no way to drink it! Then the cloud blew out and blue sky appeared, with dark clouds behind it on the northern horizon. The earth opened up before him as he walked. A great basin appeared, stretching left and right, with one river snaking down from the north and another from the east, both cutting through rock thousands of feet below. Rivers! Water . . . The rivers met behind an enormous buttress of rock whose flat top looked like a perfect stepping-stone. Canyons broke open the rock shelves bordering both rivers, exposing labyrinths of purple walls swirling like marble and cut in diagonal slabs by tilted benches of land. Above them, a series of dark red tablelands at a slant led directly below Jo's perch to the feet of steep cliffs holding up more tablelands, leading to more cliffs, climbing toward mountains and ridges, of which, scanning south, Jo saw that the ridge he stood on was a spur.

Suppose you had a big hand—God's hand, say—and you reached down and tore a huge chunk off the earth, it might look like this. It looked hugely embarrassed . . . Earth's hidden insides weren't meant to be bared in such a way! It looked like something eroded according to careful plans that had eroded as well. Jo felt quite certain that something down there was about to be revealed, some blind, subhuman, inarticu-late secret on the grandest of scales, some religious impulse, some—or some . . . He walked closer to the edge. Even from here the rivers looked delicious. The way they snaked around was a visible form of temptation. He tried smacking his lips but couldn't unstick his mouth sufficiently. It wasn't funny being thirsty! It could drive you to distraction. Actually, from here he could climb down a bit, it was steep, but not so steep that bushes and piñons didn't grow just below, at least as far as the broken-topped pinnacles of escarpments whose faces he couldn't see from this angle. To the left, a steep gully led down even further. He steadied himself with one hand on the slope, climbing down with care over rocks and loose dirt. A picnic, really. Easy as pie. In fact, you didn't have to move your legs, just more or less slide, leaning back to the side—sort of dragging an elbow—whoa, not so fast! Good gracious, sit down. Get the buttocks involved—drag your ass, Jo! Don't fold those legs under, that's a foolish trick. Soon as you start to tumble it's over. Wait a minute—where's my hat? Where's my stoppered jar of bliss . . . These bones weren't made for such bang-up speed, such hijinks, such a tear-up, such a rampage, such . . .

You'd think that this enormous world so crammed with mountains, its horizon so stretched that it dwarfed the human, let alone the subhu-man, would seem even larger to Bonny than to Jo, but it didn't—it seemed smaller. It conformed to his scale. Actually, he didn't pay it much mind, not being a romantic. Crossing that ridge wasn't too different from crossing the streets of New York. Just the hazards were different, coyotes instead of dogs. One followed Bonny on top of the ridge, circling this way and that, the sneak—disappearing behind rock outcroppings—until precious instinct told him to nix it and he sagged off as coyotes do, chagrined. Not that Bonny even saw him. He didn't notice much, blind-sided as he was by a milky eye, which had turned opaque when Jo bashed his head. That side of his world was searing pain, which pushed all else out. Say a tree grew overnight out of your head and you had to haul it around all the time, say, it might distract you. It made Bonny tip. He'd already bitten off most of his bottom lip. Also, he dripped as he walked, from his head and his mouth.

He would have given it up long ago if he could have remembered in fact what it was. He was following Jo—he'd done that before—that was somewhat comforting—just stick with that. Following Jo had something to do with finishing himself, with Stokes being gone . . . He missed bloody Stokes! It angered Bonny to live in a world in which Stokes wasn't waddling about and coshing him. Stokes raised welts; Jo crushed skulls. The difference was instructive; it showed there had once been kindness in the world. You could slake desire or simply obliterate the thing you desired, or, failing that, obliterate the desire—so he kept on sniffing, past gray rock and sagebrush, through heavy mists. One thing about this place unlike trains and cities was the purity of the trail, which other scents didn't muddle. It was really the last thing to cling to, the last clear path through a scrambled universe.

So coming across that blanket was good. He ate the kippered herrings—not that he was hungry. The money he left where the wind had scattered it—useless paper. The stick he squealed with delight at finding, raised in the air and smashed in two on a rock, keeping the smaller piece for himself. He was getting somewhere, even in the rain! First a gray fog, then daylight, then rain . . . He stepped up his pace; spit out a tooth. Practiced bashing himself with the stick out of sheer anticipation. He sat down, removed his bicorne, and hammered his head on a rock, the good side—the other was blackness. But somehow he lost the scent on that ridge . . .

So he doubled back to the blanket, held it to his nose, and breathed deep. It was fainter this time, the rain was erasing it. As he hobbled in pursuit, the scent trickled off, returned in a rush, drifted and vanished. It was like being met by a hole in the air. He'd been tricked! A wall of nothing . . .

He sat down.

He was being rained on but didn't notice. He didn't even realize he was thirsty. His clothes were wet rags. Let's see, where was I—why am I here . . . He stretched out on the ground, shriveled up, closed his eye. Everything dripped. Blankness surrounded him . . .

Hours later—perhaps it was days—he opened his eye completely immobile and stared at the sun. Mustering all his tiny strength, he contracted himself and gave birth to a shiver. His heart gave a jump like a frog waking up. Something pinching his thigh blossomed into pain, so he knew he was alive. He *saw* it—didn't feel it—by peering out from the skin of his thigh: the gold head of a walking stick . . . Bonny made a fist. He was filling with fluid. His little feet blistered up inside his boots. Sunlight baked him. He sucked at the sleeve of his ragged jacket, but it was dry. New spots of pain appeared, pushing out here and there on the surface of his body, and a mountain of it fanned down from his blank eye. He could smell himself. This wasn't fun! The flood inside carried him out to his fingertips and toes, and the pinching sensation up and down his body turned out to be his skin. He wasn't able to die! He felt rage swelling. *Can't die, can't die* . . .

We'll see about that! He jumped up with fury and ran in a circle. Up the ridge was a humped outcropping of boulders large as a whale's back, with smaller fin-shaped rocks circling it like sharks. He ran up there and smashed his head against a rock. That did it, something cracked . . . With his good eye blurred, he slammed back and forth between boulders, bouncing off one into the other with all the force he could manage. It wasn't enough. He fell down exhausted, still breathing. His single vision couldn't very well double, but it sort of slid off to the side when he looked up. He climbed to his feet, trudged further up the ridge, kicked at boulders as hard as he could. He tried stabbing himself. The leg, the thigh . . . Ran pell-mell up the ridge dripping blood till he came to an edge, and not missing a stride, threw himself off, as boys toss rocks, and arced through the air a spectacular minute kicking his legs, waving his arms, startling birds nesting in that cliff, a meteor of flesh trailing hair and fingers—not making a sound—remembering Stokes whom he missed so badly now, poor Timothy, dead—and landed with a splat, thus breaking both legs and crushing some vertebrae before rolling down a slope head over heels and coming to a halt, still breathing, still conscious. The enormous roar of a river shook the ground. He watched as one of his fingers crawled off. He couldn't stand on his broken legs, so he dragged himself with the stubs of his hands toward the sound of the water, then gave up and blanked out. Came to later on and dragged himself further. This may have lasted days. The roar surrounded him, drowning out thoughts, memory, time—but not pain. It couldn't drown pain . . . The soft earth gave way and he rolled once more down toward the river, rolled off a last cliff into the water with a sudden cold shock that woke him up pronto. It tore at his limbs. His lungs filled with water. He eyeballed some cutthroat trout holding still in silent rows underneath roiling bubbles. The force of the current pushed him and pulled him as though he were inside a rippling muscle. It slammed him on rocks, tossed him in the air, plunged him into holes, and broke every tiny bone in his body, but couldn't extinguish the little spark of life still dragging him on . . .

As for Jo, he woke up by a fire in a cave with a horrible headache and a broken leg. He lay on a deerhide cushioned by boughs. His leg had been placed in a splint and wrapped, and a bowl of cubed meat floating in cooked blood sat by his head. He sat up with the bowl, plunged his face in, wolfed down some meat, felt his stomach fist up . . . Then wolfed down some more. Delicious! Even seasoned . . .

Between him and the fire was the back of a person with long, flowing hair stirring a pot, and he thought for a moment he'd landed in heaven. A competent nurse—exquisite cook—what else could she do? When she turned, he saw the beard. The buzzard-faced man scrambled over to Jo.

Each small black eye seemed to come to a point. In a half-moon circling under his nose, his beard began and didn't stop, racing out everywhere in snarls and explosions. He'd be comical certainly if he weren't so ugly. Boils dotted his dirty face, or round bumps of something. His buckskin shirt and slouch hat were filthy. "You like that? It's my speciality. Son-of-a-bitch stew."

"It's quite good."

The beard opened up and a black hole appeared out of which emerged low thrumming laughter. His eyebrows raised. He wasn't just amused, he was surprised. Jo guessed what the man was thinking—you save someone's life and he says "Quite good"—but felt some pride in his own instinctive presence of mind. This grizzled creature didn't smell very pleasant. Not that Jo smelled much better . . . Were there any others here? Jo's intuition was to give nothing away to this man, not gratitude—not surprise—not his helplessness either. That way, despite being somewhat dependent, his natural superiority would assert itself. You gain ascendancy by assuming it, Jo thought—hardly difficult in this instance. A lift of the eyebrows, a well-placed smile of condescension, put them firmly in their place. "And you are—?"

"Pat Lynch. What's your name?"

"Benton."

"Front name?"

"Joseph."

"I suppose you're wondering where you be?"

Jo smiled. "Well . . ."

"You're hole up in my cave, warmed by my fire, eating my food because I found you in a heap laying wolf's meat outside at the foot of a cliff you won't never clum back up—can't—and I taken you here and trussed up your leg. So don't you think to come it over *me*, you little foofaraw. Fact—you won't never get quit of this place. We're hemmed in by cliffs and a river so sharp it'll slice you to ribbons. Fact—I ain't no respecter of persons. That's why I come here. I come down the river, got spilled by the rapids, and here I am, and so are you. You piroot around here with them fucking airs and you'll wake up deader than piss in a jar. I won't use *this*—" He scrambled back for his rifle and held it up with wide eyes pointed at Jo. "I'll give you the quietus with my ax instead, so's not to waste powder. You savvy that?"

Jo nodded.

Pat swung the gun barrel hard at his cheek, cracking it; blood came. "Say yes ma'am."

"Yes ma'am."

He swung it again, catching Jo's neck. The force of it knocked him over on one arm. "Now say yes sir."

"Yes sir."

"What's your poison? Yes ma'am or yes sir?"

Jo's face hung, spitting blood.

"Speak aloud!"

"Yes sir."

"Good—I'm the brave and that makes you the squaw. Welcome to Pat's Hole." He held out his hand and Jo took it limply. Rougher than granite, bony and cold; one grubby finger scratched Jo's palm. "We're pardners, Joe. Ever been pardners? Ain't near as much of a hell fight as famblies. What's a fambly, you ask? Folks which gives you withering looks if you ever so much as drop a spoon. That's why I come here. Get quit of famblies. Ain't like a *pardnership*, now. That's for *us*. Fellows which *understands* each other." He winked at Jo. "Pardners for life!" He pinched Jo's arm. "Anyways ontil I fatten you up. You'll be gimpy yet. Plenty of time to put *fat* on them bones. This child gets tired of gumming deer meat always . . ."

Jo looked up at the man in perfect horror.

Chapter

❧ 13 ❧

The soldiers said the Utes had to leave Colorado, so that was that, they had to leave.

What about our horses?

You have plenty of horses!

No we don't, the rest are in the mountains. We need time to round them up.

You've had enough time. Leave tomorrow at noon or you'll see what happens.

So they had to leave. That was that. The Americans won. They started the trouble and won anyway. Siwapi saw very clearly why they had to leave: Americans with horses and wagons had gathered across the Uncompahgre River waiting to cut up Chief Ouray's farm and claim his buildings and take all the rest of the land in his village. From there they'd spread out in every direction, including as far as the Smoking Earth River. When the Americans took something from you they removed you from it, instead of the reverse. It was easier that way, they didn't have to see you watching them enjoy what used to be yours. They called it guilt . . . They paid Ouray's widow seven hundred dollars for his farm before she left. Ouray himself had given up and died rather than leave Colorado.

Siwapi's people, the Nupartka, were spread all over. Some had gone back to the Agency, but found soldiers building homes near the ruins. Some had already left the mountains for Utah Territory, where their distant cousins lived—the Nuuci Pakiwunumi. That's where the rest would start for tomorrow. No one wanted to go there. They were poor relations, too poor to own horses, and lived in the desert on seeds, roots, and berries. They didn't live in *carniva* made from hides but in little huts constructed of brush in which you couldn't stand up. Sometimes in the summer the adults went naked. The hunting wasn't good. The few horses they managed to get their hands on they failed to care for properly. Once, the story went, a Uintah family acquired a horse by luck, but it died of neglect, as no one realized it had to be fed and watered. So now a little joke had started up among the braves. It took two to recite it.

Where are you going to live? one asked.

I'll live anywhere, said the other. I'll lie down in one place one night and go on the next day; I'll have no home.

What are you going to be?

I'll be nothing; I'll be like the sunshine.

It wasn't funny. Siwapi remembered laughing with the others not too long ago at the stupid Americans digging through the mountains and laying down tracks for their *panakarpo*. They watched in amusement as the Americans rushed this way and that up in Rawlins at the train station. They did everything frantically. Now the Americans were laughing instead. They'd taken Quinkent away on those tracks to Washington and locked him inside a house made of stone . . .

At the last minute, Colorow's band charged down a ravine toward the soldiers' camp screaming and whooping and waving their rifles. Immediately, from the tops of the mesas on either side, cannons and rifles exploded and hundreds of soldiers thundered into the valley. It was the exact reverse of their ambush of the soldiers months ago now. Confused and surprised, Colorow slackened, reined up, looked around, and parlayed with his men. They turned on their horses and rode back, chagrined. An hour later, their war paint was rubbed off. Instead, each wore a black circle on his forehead, with a black line slashing down across the left eye and cheek toward the heart, for mourning. They rode at the end of the long, winding line of nearly two thousand Utes—braves, squaws, and children—along with their ponies, sheep, goats, and cattle, their travois and *carniva*, dogs, pack trains of food and equipment, everything they owned. It was too hasty, though; blankets fell by the trail. Cooking equipment was left behind, and sheep and ponies ran back toward the hills. Women and children sent up wailing chants. Soldiers on either side of the trail watched as they passed. Because Siwapi was one of the last to pack up and had no one to help him, he left their water jugs behind. Now how could they get water when they needed it? The old man wouldn't help. He refused to make contact with the earth anymore.

When Siwapi wasn't carrying him on his back, or he wasn't on his horse, he lay on a mat of woven willows. He wouldn't touch with his fingers the little food he bothered to eat. Instead, Siwapi fastened pieces of meat on the ends of sticks for him. His bowel movements only came once a week, and resembled deer pellets. He was wasting away. He wore around his neck the pouch he'd taken from that American man-woman, not his necklace of bone pipe. It was some kind of power. It meant the People would have their revenge someday, the Americans would all go away and be bloodclots again. That's what he said. The Utes were like elk who had shed their antlers, but they'd grow back soon, first gristle and velvet, then great heavy racks . . .

For three days they rode through canyons and mountains out toward the desert. The mountains shrank, trees disappeared, and valleys spread out. Things had turned brown with the winter, though sunshine still kept the days warm. Shadows were longer. This country didn't hold half the game their mountains did, mostly antelope and rabbits—no elk or buffalo. Some deer lived here because they didn't know better. Water was usually hard to find.

Nothing exists anymore, said Siwapi. Everything is a dream.

That's not true, said Maasuwini. If everything was a dream, there would be no dreams . . .

But Siwapi wasn't sure. This land seemed more suited to ghosts than flesh. Without meat to eat, they'd have to relearn the skills their tribe had forgotten ages ago, skills of preparing seeds and roots for meals. Already they'd eaten half their dried meat. Everyone now looked tired and confused.

On the fifth day out, approaching a ridge, they spotted some buzzards circling in the air above the far side. Maasuwini wanted to climb up that ridge and see what was happening, which meant Siwapi had to carry him. Crows cawed there too. He told Siwapi he could hear sounds of people having fun, meaning the crows. So when the line of horses stopped, he and Siwapi rode to the base of the ridge, followed closely by a handful of the soldiers assigned to accompany the Utes. The old man reached in his bag and popped the eye-stone in his mouth, then climbed down from his horse onto Siwapi's back. He felt like a sack of bones up there. Despite his *piwán*'s dress, Siwapi was strong, and climbed up the steep ridge—too steep for horses—with Maasuwini clinging to his back at a pace no American could ever match. He had powerful legs.

Dozens of buzzards and crows flew around. Some of the crows had landed on the ridge and were calling to the others. Down the opposite side was the huge rainbow bend of a river they'd all have to cross up ahead. This river marked their new reservation border. The water looked green, with a long streak of reddish brown on the shallow side close to them. Yellow bluffs and cliffs towered over the far side, and a sandy beach fanned out from the bend just below the two men amid cottonwood trees.

Siwapi felt like a man with two heads; the old man's breath warmed his ear. Below them, a mob of buzzards and crows chattering on the ground strutted about with their black wings held partly open like robes. They were having a meeting—a dance—squawking joyfully. One buzzard lunged at another. In their midst, something white lay on the beach. Maasuwini smacked his lips. The white thing looked like an American baby. A buzzard pulled with its beak at the red meat exposed on the white baby's leg, while a crow pecked its eye. Yes, Maasuwini said with a sigh—that's what will happen to all the Americans . . .

All at once it turned its head, and the old man jumped. He seemed to go heavy on Siwapi's back. The American baby shot them a glance with its other eye, which was hideously alive. His mouth opened too; his face was a grown man's . . . Terrified, Siwapi turned and scrambled back toward their horses, slipping on loose rocks, flinging out an arm to steady himself, careful in his haste not to drop the old man . . .

It didn't make any difference. Maasuwini's blood had stopped. When he spread out the mat and lowered the old man, Siwapi saw right away he was dead. The eye-stone dropped out of his mouth. Siwapi picked it up. It had turned a milky gray. The wrinkled lobe of the old man's neck like the wattle of a buzzard hung perfectly still, but his mouth had fallen open, so Siwapi closed it. He looked small and frail. Gently, Siwapi lifted his head, pulled off the leather thong and pouch, and hung it around his own neck.

Then he sent up a wail; others gathered around. They wrapped Maasuwini inside his mat and placed him in a crevice at the base of the ridge, head facing in, then piled on stones, brush and dirt, then larger rocks on top. Siwapi wailed like a *piwán* in mourning. He ran halfway up and down the ridge several times. They shot Maasuwini's horse and left it to bleed to death next to his grave. Siwapi cut off its tail and mane and stuffed them in Maasuwini's parfleche, which was his now. The rest of the old man's things they burned—his clothes, wooden bowls, arrows, feathers, fire drill, pipe, baskets, parching tray. At the fire, Siwapi tore his own clothes to make them rags, cut his long hair, and daubed some pitch on the crown of his head to keep Maasuwini's ghost away. Then he and some of the *piwán* cooked a meal. It was only midday, but they decided to camp there.

Strange things began to happen. It grew bitter cold that afternoon, and one crazy brave who'd been riding around wearing only a breech clout galloped up to the fire, jumped off his horse, and thawing out, burst into blood from a hundred holes in his skin. Siwapi wasn't sure what to do. Should he cure him? Instead, he walked away. Then, out of earshot of the camp, the mice and grass bugs began taunting him, as they'd once taunted Maasuwini: *"Siwapi is a coward!"* they hissed. *"He wears a woman's dress! He'll never be a doctor! His power is weak!"*

He touched his pouch and said, This is my power. They shut up and crawled back into their holes. Good, he thought. Now I know how to get them.

Scratching laughter came from those holes . . .

He walked along the base of the ridge back toward some rocks. Alone, he crouched behind a boulder and unlooped the thong from his neck, but saw that the pouch was tied up tight. He untied the first knot, turned it over and untied another. Keep going, there's more . . . He continued untying knot after knot, all afternoon it seemed. At last he came to the last one, untied it, and everything went dark.

He dropped the pouch. No one else was there. Night had fallen. Back at the camp they'd erected their *carniva* and all gone to bed. Everything was cold. A wet nose pushed against his hand and Siwapi felt one of the camp dogs walking at his side with the pouch in his mouth. He took it from the dog and tried peering into it, but couldn't make out a thing in the darkness. When he probed it with his finger all he could feel was something like old twisted leather inside. It didn't feel dangerous, it felt dead. Above, a thick sheet of stars hung still. Well, what should I do? Something in the rocks made a scratching noise, but it could have been Siwapi himself breathing carefully. Out on the desert, antelopes raced, bit by red-eyed flies on the tender insides of their twitching ears . . .

He retied the pouch and hung it on his neck.

At dawn, he climbed up the ridge again. It seemed higher and steeper this time, it took hours . . . Down the other side at the river's bend a small pile of bones in the shape of a body still twitched with life. Their grease was still warm, he could tell . . . Now, you bones—

He couldn't think of what to say.

Please stay where you are. Don't kill anyone else. Die. Bones should die.

He returned to the camp and decided to fast. Meat sizzled on fires spitting fat and smoke, but he turned away, refusing either to eat or speak. He'd never set up his *carniv* last night, having remained awake until dawn, and with nothing to pack up now, spent his time away from the camp talking to his horse. Today, we'll cross the river. You'll like the new place . . . The horse backed up, showing his eye whites.

Watched by the soldiers, the Utes broke camp, packed up their *car-niva*, and mounted their horses. The line of horses stretched out from the ridge for two miles or more. Waiting for it to move, Siwapi thought of the old man buried nearby in the crevice. Now he was alone. Laughter came from the grass. Alone? He closed his eyes. *"You'll never be a doctor!"* He touched his pouch but the laughter continued. *"Coward! Fool!"*

At last they pulled out. He felt each thud of each hoof in his teeth. Sounds went like slivers into his brain—the creak of saddles, coarse groan of muscles pulling at cartilage. Ahead, the river sounded pretty hysterical, slapping itself. Fish whistled through it. He saw beaded strings of germinating insects slip from their casings piled on the bottom and rise through water, tearing at each other . . . Siwapi's horse wasn't acting right, and shied when a tree limb came shooting down the river. The water was high for this time of the year. In front of him, Patika turned to look back with a puzzled expression. Then he saw that the belly of her mare, just touching the water, was filling with frogs . . . The mare began to swim. The thick and yellow water rose up with holes sucked all across its swirling surface. Further ahead, the line of horses had broken and started drifting downstream. Siwapi's own horse began rolling slug-gishly as though he'd let go, and tossed his head in panic. Wait—let's turn back! The water rose up . . .

He tore off the pouch and threw it in the river. It floated off on the rolling current, soon lost beneath the surface but still pulled along—down the muddy water, past sandbars and cutbanks, spinning and turn-ing . . . Good riddance.

The earth and sky seemed to breathe out a shadow.

Head arching back, eyeballs popping, his horse regained balance and swam the river. The cold water numbed Siwapi's waist and foamed around his dress. When its feet struck bottom, the horse lunged ahead. The Utes had scattered a mile down the river, and regrouped in a flat plain of rabbit bush and brown earth which seemed to harden around them. This wasn't where the new Agency would be—that was miles ahead—but it was their new land. Siwapi looked around. Now that they were here drying out, the lacing made from the skins of dead animals on the leggings and shoes of the braves shriveled up. A few *piwán* wore American shirts with buttons made from the dead bones of animals which clicked against their beads and necklaces. Clothes and hair felt lifeless on their bodies. Everyone looked tired. The dogs that had fol-lowed this far to their new place and swum the river sank exhausted in the dust. It seemed there weren't even horseflies here. Even lizards were hiding.

The voices were right. He'd never be a doctor.

The line started up again. The sun had risen in the sky behind them but hardly struck a thing. A gray ash settled down. They rode into a photograph. Things faced away. Nothing spoke.

Meanwhile, downriver, that pouch rolled along, snagged on a branch, freed itself with a jerk, bounced off boulders through foaming rapids, through canyon walls exposing the centuries . . .

PART
VI

1886

                                    Amherst
                                    May 13, 1886

Mr. Whitman—
               Called back.

                              Emily

                                    Amherst
                                    May 16, 1886

Dear Mr. Whitman,
*I see from my sister's papers that you were one of her frequent
correspondents. She died yesterday. I thought you would want to
know. Her family is much shaken and bereft. You will be interested
in the inclosed notice from the Springfield Republican. Funeral
services to be held on the 19th, at home.*
                              Yours,
                              Lavinia Dickinson

MISS EMILY DICKINSON OF AMHERST

Miss Emily Dickinson, sister of W. A. Dickinson, Esq., daughter of the late Edward Dickinson, died at her brother's home in Amherst on Saturday evening at six. Miss Dickinson had for many years lived a retired life. She was supposed by many of her friends to have been the author of the Saxe Holme stories, though she denied the fact during her life. Very few in the village, except among the older inhabitants, knew Miss Emily personally, although the facts of her seclusion and her intellectual brilliancy were familiar Amherst traditions. There are many houses among all classes into which her treasures of fruit and flowers and ambrosial dishes for the sick and well were constantly sent, that will forever miss those evidences of her unselfish consideration, and mourn afresh that she screened herself from close acquaintance. For those few fortunates admitted to her circle, her talk and writings were like no one's else, and although she never published a line, now and then some enthusiastic literary friend would turn to larceny, and cause a few verses surreptitiously obtained to be printed. Thus, and through other natural ways, many saw and admired her verses, and in consequence frequently notable persons paid her visits, hoping to overcome the protest of her own nature and speak with her. Few succeeded. To her, life was rich and all aglow with God and immortality. With no creed, no formulated faith, hardly knowing the names of dogmas, she walked this life alone with the gentleness and reverence of old saints, and the firm step of martyrs who sing while they suffer. She lived on this earth for fifty-five years.

Propped up by Pete, Walt stared into the coffin. Fifty-five? She hardly looked thirty. Auburn hair without a gray strand, not a wrinkle on her face. Her face looked so *clean*—as though God had just wiped it. It resembled a pebble washed up on shore. Marble brow, wide flaring nose, lips full as any Walt had seen in death. She looked vaguely familiar . . . A little bunch of violets troubled her neck, and one pink lady's slipper lay on her bosom. Someone had placed two hothouse heliotropes in her left hand. Her small body in that small white dress was the size of a boy's, and the coffin around it also was small—and white. Someone had cleaned up the barn, where the coffin sat on a long deal table, but buckets of lysol couldn't chase off that good rich smell of old barns. The beams and planks, having absorbed it, dolloped it out when struck by the sun. The wide barn doors let in sunlight which exposed the least bit of chaff in the air. Outside, birds sang. It was May! Time for funerals . . .

Well, she'd told him she'd show herself . . . He muttered a prayer to the All—or Nothing.

Pete helped ease Walt back into his wheelchair, but couldn't resist a peek himself, then regretted it. Hadn't Walt said an *old* gal? Old friend—woman friend . . . Why, she hardly looked older than Josie when *she* died, just six years back . . . Scrape a fork on your wounds, that's the way, Pete, it hardly mattered if they never had closed. Death might very well single you out, fling its filth like a skunk, but hit someone else—say the one right next to you . . . In Washington City, in the dampest of winters, Pete had caught pneumonia and recovered—then Josie caught it. She died within a week, clutching Pete's hand and dragging his secret underneath with her corpse. Josie's corpse! You don't *never* look into coffins after that. That's a big mistake when your heart is a bomb which some crackbrain like you might toss into a crowd . . .

Pete had kicked around Washington City for a year after that in a sty of grief before pulling out of it. No more silly jigs, though . . . Oh, sure, he laughed once or twice at some folly—the presidency of Chester Arthur, the Star Route scandal. Then he thought of the only person in the world who could cheer him up, and wrote to Walt. Turned out Walt, in Camden, needed a nurse. He lived upstairs in a north-facing room of an old clapboard house with papers, letters, envelopes, and books scattered promiscuously on the floor amid discarded tunafish tins. Autographed volumes of unread poetry hung on the edges of tables and chairs, and Walt somehow negotiated this mess by means of a long cane which pulled toward his wheelchair whatever he required, unless he couldn't find it. Pete moved in downstairs to be close. He aired Walt, cooked for him, washed his flaccid skin . . . When the letter arrived announcing the funeral, it was Pete who checked the timetables and bought the tickets, packed up his and Walt's necessaries, and arranged for a buggy to take them to the station.

Now he leaned down to Walt's ear, pushing his wheelchair back through the crowd in that barn toward a corner, and whispered the same question he'd asked forty times on the train coming here: "Who was she, Walt?"

"I'll tell you the whole story—outside."

Pete couldn't shake off a twinge of jealousy. Walt had secrets too! But their secrets weren't the same. He'd thought of telling Walt the truth about himself some day, but each passing year that seemed less likely . . .

Outside, Walt's head bobbed as he spoke. Pushing the wheelchair, Pete resisted an impulse to stroke—or yank—that flowing white hair, so cornsilky smooth. "She was one of the few persons in the world to excite in me a wholesale respect and love," said Walt. "She was beautiful in bodily shape and gifts of soul."

Good for her, thought Pete. "You said you never saw her."

"Never in the earthly sense, the tangible sight. But *here*, Pete, *here* . . ." Walt thumped his chest. They followed the funeral cortege down a path through sunlight so blinding after the barn that Pete found it troublesome picking his way. Not that he felt like taking special care . . . "God almighty, Pete, steer clear of the rocks!"

"So this gal was your—friend?"

"Friend, lover, soul mate. Call it what you please. She had the voice of an angel and the manners of a codfish. A woman is always heaven or hell to a man, remember that, Pete. They don't spend much time on the borderlines. Women! Can you puzzle them out? Can anyone?"

"Course not, Walt."

"They have more than their share of gushing emotionalists."

"Well, they're just as good as men—ain't they, then?"

"Course they are, Pete. Undeniably. They're just—different. All women snore to beat creation, for one thing. Then they talk too much or they don't talk at all."

Stop smiling, Pete!

"Now, a man you can always count on for jawbation. Look at us with our incessant caterwauling, talking away like dictionaries with legs and mouths on. No wonder some women become silent partners. But not this gal, Pete. The very best of her was her talk. That gal of yours was a talker too, as I recall—though I can't say as she came up to Miss Dickinson. I shall never forget—never forget—her up those stairs out of sight overflowing with screw-point utterance. The steel of strength was there—the heart-point of it. She slurred nothing. No parade in her. Such superb sharp judgment, I only sat and wondered. I remember that day when I left her presence I had to check myself to be fully certain I was still intact. When a gal comes along hungry for your society yet afraid of your society, blowing hot and cold, with praise on her lips that sounds like blame, you're at your wit's end to know what to say. Only gal I ever met who could so outtalk me. She was harmonic, orbic. She hadn't lived much of a real-life, Pete—I mean as far as the business of the world is concerned—what the takers and askers bother us with—the big bugs with their bravura talk—but she was a great woman, a genius! Do not understand me as wishing to deny it. I declare right now, Pete—I've been more than fortunate in the women who have given me their support. My God, son, stay out of the cow pastures!"

"Can't help it, Walt—we're crossing a field."

Actually, they were falling behind, Pete had to heave-ho. The line of mourners up ahead beside a hedge was making a turn through a gate already. Five strong men carried the coffin, five men from Irishtown—her announced wishes. Over fields, along footpaths, past apple blossoms, past trees—past leaves just come out, small and green on the branches, through which sunlight scattered. Pockets of cool-earth smell popped around them, mixing with the perfume of blossoms and flowers. "Smell that, Pete? It's apple blossoms. On a day like this you can smell the earth itself. It's saying to me, come out, Walt Whitman—come out and be born! Can you smell it back there?"

"Sure thing, Walt."

"What a time to die. I shouldn't mind it myself. When I go, Pete, don't have carriages and plug hats. Arrange it like this—in the open air."

"You'll live to be a hundred."

"Don't count on it, Pete. Not very likely. I could go any day. Are you ready?"

"Sure, I'm ready."

"Good. That assures me. I'll come around yet. At my age, Pete, I have to subject my rebellious moods to the necessities of corporeal self. I'm like an addled egg. Have to fish with a short line. I got the trembles *and* the slows."

"Sounds just like you, Walt. What about that gal? Finish the story."

"There's nothing more to say. She declared for me, finally. She stuck to it that Walt Whitman was some pumpkins no matter what the world said. But she kept her distance too. You've no call to be jealous. It was the respect not of camp followers—not of the literary army, so to speak—not the thousand and one gnats and mosquitoes that buzz around my head—rather, the respect of a stranger. There, I've said it. Our closest friends are strangers. Where on earth did they go?"

Pete had no idea. Ahead were hedgerows, fields, and woods, at scrambled angles intersected by footpaths. It was like plowing through a hanging garden. Sun streamed through gaps in the half-leaved branches like a river through nets. The graveyard had to be close by, didn't it? Forging ahead, Pete thumped bumpity-bump over hummocks, rocks, roots, and dead branches—each cursed by Walt—past buttercups and innocents yellow in the fields, past plumes of forsythia just blowing inside out from gold to green, past wild honeysuckle, cinquefoil, veronica, pansies and daisies, lilies of the valley, beardtongue, squawberry, dog violets, ginger—straining to catch up with Emily's coffin.

Afterword

Portions of the letters and the con-
versations between Walt Whitman and Emily Dickinson in this novel are
based upon the letters and poems of the historical Walt Whitman and
Emily Dickinson, as well as upon the conversations of Whitman as
reported by Horace Traubel in his multivolume *With Walt Whitman in
Camden*. Of course, the historical Whitman and Dickinson never met,
let alone wrote to each other; nor did the historical Peter Doyle (a friend
of Whitman) travel west with the historical Meekers. In addition, I
moved the Ute uprising in which Nathan Meeker was murdered from its
actual date of 1879 back to 1873, and moved Walt Whitman's first stroke
from 1873 to 1872—both in the interest of dramatic unity.

In other words, I have shamelessly mixed history and fiction in a
speculative attempt to correct history's minor errors while accurately
describing its major ones.

I would like to thank the administration of the State University of New
York at Binghamton for providing me with released time in order to
begin this novel. The following also assisted me with my research, for
which I am grateful: Dan Lombardo, curator of special collections at the
Jones Library in Amherst, Massachusetts; Carol Birtwistle of the Emily
Dickinson House in Amherst; Peggy Ford of the Municipal Museum in
Greeley, Colorado; the staff of the Colorado State Historical Society, and
E. V. Rader, former mayor of Meeker, Colorado, and guardian of its
past. Finally, thanks, for their help, to Pat and Jack Wilcox, Frank and
Holly Bergon, Bill Snyder, Alex Fischler, and Larry Roberts.

About the Author

JOHN VERNON is the author of six previous books, including a collection of poems, three critical studies, and the novels *La Salle* and *Lindbergh's Son*. He was born in Cambridge, Massachusetts, and now lives in upstate New York, where he teaches at the State University of New York at Binghamton.